RCC

P9-DMH-330

DISTANT THUNDERS

DESTROYERMEN

DISTANT
THUNDERS

TAYLOR ANDERSON

A ROC BOOK

ROC
Published by New American Library, a division of
Penguin Group (USA) Inc., 375 Hudson Street,
New York, New York 10014, USA
Penguin Group (Canada), 90 Eglinton Avenue East, Suite 700, Toronto,
Ontario M4P 2Y3, Canada (a division of Pearson Penguin Canada Inc.)
Penguin Books Ltd., 80 Strand, London WC2R 0RL, England
Penguin Ireland, 25 St. Stephen's Green, Dublin 2,
Ireland (a division of Penguin Books Ltd.)
Penguin Group (Australia), 250 Camberwell Road, Camberwell, Victoria 3124,
Australia (a division of Pearson Australia Group Pty. Ltd.)
Penguin Books India Pvt. Ltd., 11 Community Centre, Panchsheel Park,
New Delhi - 110 017, India
Penguin Group (NZ), 67 Apollo Drive, Rosedale, North Shore 0632,
New Zealand (a division of Pearson New Zealand Ltd.)
Penguin Books (South Africa) (Pty.) Ltd., 24 Sturdee Avenue,
Rosebank, Johannesburg 2196, South Africa

Penguin Books Ltd., Registered Offices:
80 Strand, London WC2R 0RL, England

First published by Roc, an imprint of New American Library,
a division of Penguin Group (USA) Inc.

First Printing, June 2010
10   9   8   7   6   5   4   3   2   1

Copyright © Taylor Anderson, 2010
All rights reserved

Photo of the author taken on the Battleship *Texas* (BB-35) State Historic Site—3527 Battleground Rd., La Porte,
Texas 77571, with the permission of the Texas Parks and Wildlife Dept.

 REGISTERED TRADEMARK—MARCA REGISTRADA

LIBRARY OF CONGRESS CATALOGING-IN-PUBLICATION DATA:

Anderson, Taylor.
Distant thunders / Taylor Anderson.
p. cm. — (Destroyermen ; bk. 4)
ISBN 978-0-451-46333-3
1. Imaginary wars and battles—Fiction. 2. World War, 1939–1945—Fiction. I. Title.
PS3601.N5475D57 2010
813'.6—dc22   2010003854

Set in Minion
Designed by Ginger Legato

Printed in the United States of America

Without limiting the rights under copyright reserved above, no part of this publication may be reproduced, stored
in or introduced into a retrieval system, or transmitted, in any form, or by any means (electronic, mechanical,
photocopying, recording, or otherwise), without the prior written permission of both the copyright owner and the
above publisher of this book.

PUBLISHER'S NOTE
This is a work of fiction. Names, characters, places, and incidents either are the product of the author's imagination
or are used fictitiously, and any resemblance to actual persons, living or dead, business establishments, events, or
locales is entirely coincidental.
    The publisher does not have any control over and does not assume any responsibility for author or third-party
Web sites or their content.

The scanning, uploading, and distribution of this book via the Internet or via any other means without the permission of the publisher is illegal and punishable by law. Please purchase only authorized electronic editions, and do not
participate in or encourage electronic piracy of copyrighted materials. Your support of the author's rights is
appreciated.

FOR: REBECCA—AND MY NIECE, JENNIFER. (I ALWAYS HAVE TO WRITE OR MENTALLY ADD "NIECE" WHEN I THINK OF JENNIFER BECAUSE, IN SO MANY WAYS, SHE WAS ALWAYS THE "DAUGHTER" I NEVER HAD—BEFORE I HAD A DAUGHTER.)

JENNIFER, YOU AND REBECCA COULDN'T BE MORE DIFFERENT, BUT NEVER DOUBT THAT I LOVE YOU BOTH WITH ALL MY HEART

TO: THE MEN AND WOMEN OF THE ARMED FORCES OF THE UNITED STATES—AND THOSE OF ALL NATIONS WHO FIGHT BRAVELY AT THEIR SIDE. PAST, PRESENT, AND FUTURE. GOD BLESS YOU ALL.

ACKNOWLEDGMENTS

As usual, there are some great folks I need to thank: Chief among these are Russell Galen, the best agent in the world, and Ginjer Buchanan, the finest editor anyone could ever hope to have. CPO, (SW-MTS) USN—(Ret.), Bruce Kent ranks near the top as well. He reminded me that I've neglected the EMs and he was right. Granted, there weren't nearly as many things for electrician's mates to *do* on four-stacker destroyers as even I originally thought, but that's because a truly astonishing variety of machinery that would later be electrically powered was either manually or steam operated. That doesn't mean EMs on four-stackers would have been bored. Far from it. They were dealing with the same broken-down, archaic equipment as everyone else; equipment essentially representing the very dawn of the electrical age! Because of that, their contributions would have been particularly difficult and essential. The information Chief Kent kindly supplied, or pointed me toward, was both fun and fascinating. Together we made a number of discoveries that contributed significantly to this story, I believe. If I didn't use the information right, it's my fault, not his.

Dave Leedom, LTC, USAFR, helped, as always, to inspire my aerial high jinks, while keeping my head out of the clouds and my feet on the ground—figuratively speaking. The inimitable (Bad) Dennis Petty continues to provide . . . inspiration . . . and remains a formidable companion during my own unusual adventures. Just so everyone is clear on this, it's *my* turn to shoot *him*—just a little. My parents, Don and Jeanette Anderson, have always inspired me and remain possibly my greatest fans and fiercest critics. My wife, Christine, mostly falls in the general "fierce critic" category, but I guess I'll keep her anyway. James Kirkland and Schuetzen Powder LLC have my deepest appreciation for all their "ballistics testing" support over the years, and all the guys and gals on my gun's crews are still the best in the country. Andy Gillham is the greatest musician alive and I will always fondly—if vaguely—remember the Sasquatch and space alien hunts of our younger years. We never caught any of the boogers, but that never really mattered, did it? Special thanks go to Tom Potter, a fellow historian and "naval thinker" with a brilliant mind. Ha! He'll get it.

Otherwise, the list of usual suspects is long and has been recited before, but I need to add Pete Hodges and Kate Baker to the list. Good friends are hard to find and I treasure all of mine—even Jim. If I forgot to mention anybody or goofed up in any way, it's all Jim's fault. Actually, Jim deserves a lot of credit. He did more in a few brief seconds to disprove the conspiracy theory surrounding the Kennedy assassination than anyone else has done in the last forty-six years. "Magic bullets" do, in fact, exist. We get it, Jim. No need to KEEP proving your point! (Jim is nothing if not thorough, when it comes to science.)

"Weapons more violent, when next we meet."

—*Paradise Lost*

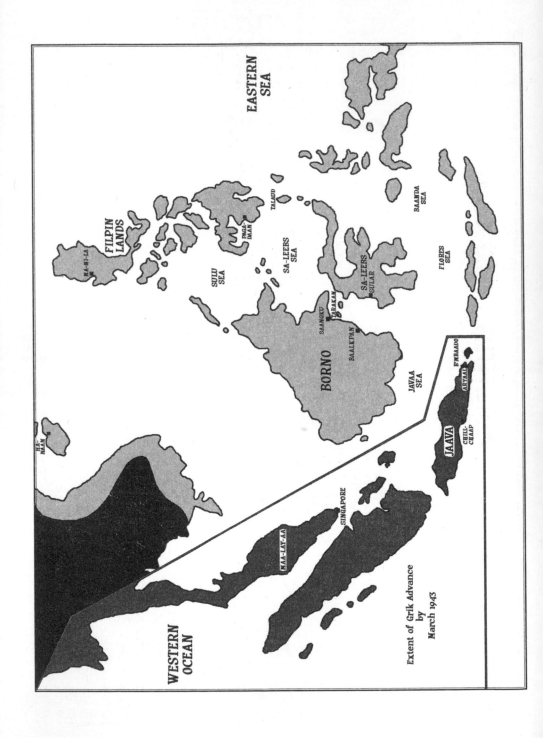

EASTERN SEA

WESTERN OCEAN

FILPIN LANDS

MA-NI-LA

HA-NAAN

SULU SEA

PAGA-DIAN

TALAUD

SA-LEEBS SEA

SA-LEEBS SULAR

BAANDA SEA

FLORES SEA

SAANGKU

TARAKAN

BAALKPAN

BORNO

JAVAA SEA

MA-LAY-AA

SINGAPORE

JAAVA

ARYAAD

B'RAADO

CHIL-CHAAP

Extent of Grik Advance
by March 1943

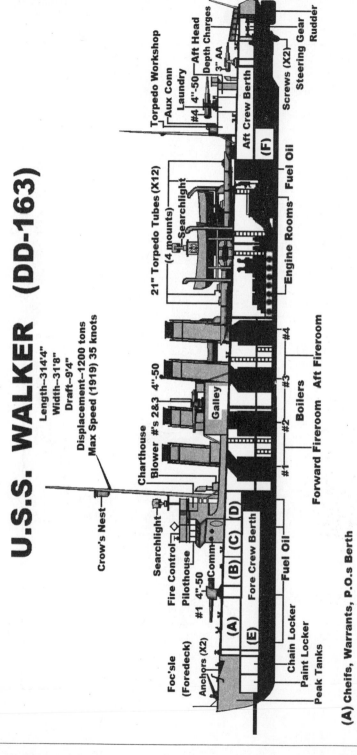

U.S.S. WALKER (DD-163)

Length—314'4"
Width—31'8"
Draft—9'4"
Displacement—1200 tons
Max Speed (1919) 35 knots

Crow's Nest

Torpedo Workshop

Charthouse

Searchlight

Fire Control

Pilothouse

Comm—

Blower #'s 2&3 4"-50

21" Torpedo Tubes (X12)
(4 mounts)

Searchlight

Aux Conn
Laundry
#4 4"-50

Aft Head
Depth Charges
3" AA

Aft Crew Berth

(F)

Fuel Oil

Engine Rooms

Screws (X2)
Steering Gear
Rudder

Galley

#1 4"-50

(A) (B) (C) (D)

(E)

Fore Crew Berth

#1 #2 #3 #4
Boilers
Forward Fireroom   Aft Fireroom

Foc'sle
(Foredeck)
Anchors (X2)
Chain Locker
Paint Locker
Peak Tanks

Fuel Oil

(A) Cheifs, Warrants, P.O.s Berth
(B) Officer's Quarters
(C) Wardroom
(D) Captain's and Passenger's Staterooms
(E) General Storage & Magazines
(F) General Storage & Magazines

///// *March 1, 1942*

his was NAP 1/c Nataka's last chance. Admiral Nagumo, commanding the First Air Fleet, had ordered Nataka's carrier, *Kaga*, home for repairs. She'd scraped her bottom in the Palau Strait and developed an annoying leak. Now she'd have to leave the war right when things were going so well. Nataka was seriously concerned the war might even be over before she—and, by extension, he—managed to get back in the fight.

He'd already seen a lot of "action" and sometimes felt as if he'd been in the cockpit of his beloved *kanbaku* ever since the beginning of this "new" war against the Americans, British, and Dutch. In all that time however, during all the sorties he'd flown, he hadn't managed to hit *anything* with one of his 250kg bombs! He'd missed the glorious attack on Pearl Harbor; he'd been too sick to hide something that gave him a raging fever and they hadn't let him go. He'd flown many missions since, but now heroes, *immortals*, surrounded him. They'd been his comrades, his peers just a few months before, but they'd accomplished the impossible while he lay sweating in his rack. Somehow, he just hadn't been able to catch up.

Many times now, Nataka had dived with the others in his Navy Type 99 against lonely freighters, destroyers, and even a pair of cruisers. He'd tried to do as he'd been taught, fearlessly braving the black clouds of antiaircraft shells and tracers that rose to meet him. He'd bored in relentlessly at exactly sixty-five degrees and released his bomb at exactly the proper instant—and somehow, he always missed. He'd even missed at Port Darwin! Granted, he hadn't gone after a stationary anchored target; he'd attacked a wildly maneuvering, desperately firing destroyer, but his bomb hadn't even come close! Someone must have finally hit the *norou* old American destroyer; he'd seen it afire and dead in the water when his flight regrouped after the attack, but his dive-bomber must have been the only one to return to *Kaga* that hadn't hit *something*! Even NAP 1/c Honjo, his navigator-gunner, seemed to be losing faith. The two were close—they had to be—but something just wasn't working.

Nataka was a good attack pilot; he *knew* he was. He'd always scored among the very best in practice. Of course, practice targets didn't twist, turn, and lunge ahead at flank speed, churning the sea with their deceptive wakes. They didn't make radical, seemingly impossible turns and belch black smoke at the worst possible moment to spoil his aim. He had to remind himself that there were *men* on his targets now: men who controlled their movements with complete unpredictability. Men who didn't want to die. Now, unless this final "hunting trip" he and Lieutenant Usa had been allowed bore fruit, *Kaga* would steam for Japan before Nataka had a chance to prove himself, before he had a chance to break this terrible curse that seemed to hold him in its grasp!

"There is something building in the east!" Honjo said in his earphones.

Nataka glanced left, beyond the gray-green wing, where a squall line was beginning to form. There were always squalls in these strange seas and sometimes they were intense. They didn't usually form this early in the day, however. "Lieutenant Usa has already seen it," he replied, watching Usa's plane bank left, away from the distant coast they'd been approaching so brazenly. Type 99s were slow and fat; easy prey for any good fighter, even if they were surprisingly agile. Regardless, Nataka wasn't concerned. There were no good enemy fighters in the area. As far as he knew, there were no enemy fighters left at all. Without hesitation, Nataka turned his plane to follow his lieutenant's.

"Maybe a big tanker or some poor, lonely freighter is trying to hide in that squall," Honjo speculated predatorily. Nataka nodded. It was certainly possible. The frequent squalls were the only protection left for those desperate ships fleeing Java. "I just hope, if there is, Lieutenant Usa won't report it," Honjo continued. "Those greedy *bakano* in Second Fleet will want us to lead them to it so they can blast it with their battleships, even if it's a rowboat!"

Nataka nodded again. There'd been a lot of that. Slowly, he eased his plane closer to Usa's and they approached the squall together. Was it just his imagination, or did the rain already seem closer than it should? They were flying three hundred and fifty kilometers per hour, but either the thing was growing much more quickly than any squall he'd seen, or it was moving toward them in an unprecedented fashion. It was also growing darker, and wasn't the usual purple-gray that one usually observed, but rather . . . greenish . . . and livid with dull pulses of lightning. Strange.

"Nataka!" came Usa's clipped, terse voice in his ears. "A ship! Two o'clock, low!"

Nataka suppressed an exasperated sigh. Of course it was low if it was a ship! He strained to see over the black-painted cowling of his engine. *Yes!* All alone on the brilliant purple sea, a lone freighter plodded helplessly along. She looked old, medium-size, with a single stack streaming gray smoke. Perhaps she'd seen them, because she was clearly making for the growing squall.

"We will attack together," Usa said over the radio. "It seems to be the easiest way," he added, almost apologetically, it seemed.

Nataka's face heated, but he made no reply.

"I will approach her port bow," Usa continued. "You will attack from the port quarter. Whichever direction she turns, one of us should have her entire length for his bomb to fall upon!"

"It will be done!" Nataka said, and banked left again, directly toward the squall. "Beloved ancestors!" he muttered, and immediately wondered if anyone heard. If they had, they probably thought he was calling his ancestors to aid him in the attack, but what prompted his words was the squall itself. The thing was monstrous! Not only had it swiftly grown to encompass the visible horizon, but it was practically opaque, not like a squall at all, but like a huge wall of water! He shook himself and glanced at his altimeter. Soon he would begin his dive.

The altimeter had gone insane! The needle spun erratically with wild fluctuations! Not only that, but his compass was distressed as well. As he banked back right, to the north, his compass told him he was flying east! Even as he veered around behind the still tiny ship below, his compass steadfastly insisted that west was north.

"Honjo, I . . ."

"Yes? What is it?"

"Nothing. Usa has circled around while we positioned ourselves. He is beginning his dive!"

"Good luck, Nataka! Let us sink this bastard quickly and get away from that wrongful storm!"

So, Honjo was nervous too. Nataka couldn't count on any of his instruments now. Even his horizon and airspeed indicators were malfunctioning. He pushed the stick forward until the ship's fantail appeared in the telescopic sight in front of his canopy. The target was slow. It couldn't be making more than ten knots at best. He doubted it was capable of any escape sprint, like those so many of his targets had employed. Nevertheless, he engaged the dive brakes to slow his descent. He wanted plenty of time to react if the ship took evasive maneuvers to avoid Usa's attack.

Tracers started rising toward him and a single puff of black smoke erupted in his path. *This sheep has a few little teeth*, he thought, concentrating on his angle of descent. Apparently, the target had managed a feeble burst of speed after all, and he pulled back on the stick just a bit. More tracers came and they seemed brighter than before. Brighter? He risked a quick glance away from the sight. No. The world was darker! The squall was in the west, he *knew* it was in the west, but outriding clouds above must have blocked the morning sun. *No time.* Usa was nearly upon the target, the gray-green of his plane and the bright red circles on its wings still clearly contrasted against the darker sea. *Excellent!* The ship was turning toward Usa, just as the lieutenant predicted! *Usa might still hit. . . . No!* A massive, dirty plume erupted just off the ship's port bow! Tracers followed Usa's plane as it pulled up, up. . . . But wait! The plane was smoking!

Nataka focused once more on the target. Later there would be time to discover the lieutenant's fate. Hopefully, Usa and his gunner would be all right, but they'd certainly left the ship at Nataka's mercy! Tracers still reached for him and he felt the plane shiver as a few bullets found their mark. He fired his own 7.7-millimeter guns to disperse the defenders. Another black puff materialized to his right and fragments of steel sleeted into his wing. He heard Honjo yell.

Soon, he crooned to himself. His angle was perfect; the target couldn't possibly escape. He had the entire length of the ship from stern to bow for his bomb to strike . . . !

That was the thought NAP 1/c Nataka took to his watery grave. Just as his hand caressed the knobbed lever to release the five-hundred-pound bomb, another pathetic, miraculous black puff appeared less than four feet to his left. Hot steel shredded his canopy and tore away most of his head. More sparkling fragments from the three-inch shell slashed the left wing root and ignited the fuel. The wing fluttered away and the remaining, still dutiful wing sent the flaming wreck into a tight roll that edged it, just slightly, toward the port side of the ship.

With a mighty roar and a blinding flash of flame made even brighter by the dark, eerie squall, the plane and its powerful bomb combined the force of their detonation alongside the old freighter. Technically, Nataka had missed again, but as far as the crew of the SS *Santa Catalina* was concerned, a torpedo couldn't have done much worse.

Santa Catalina's captain quickly assessed the situation. His ship was badly damaged. The near miss forward had opened some seams, but that last stroke left the aft hold quickly flooding. Still, they might just make it. Australia was out of the question, but unlike every other remaining Allied ship in the area, his wasn't bent on escape. The South

6 Java port of Tjilatjap was his destination. Grimly, he ordered as much speed as his old, battered ship could muster; then he stepped out on the bridge wing and stared at the bizarre . . . malignant . . . squall crawling up her wake.

///// *Late March, 1943*

An oppressive smoky haze from the epic battle and resultant, seemingly endless funeral pyres clung to the savaged city and the wide expanse of Baalkpan Bay. Almost three weeks after the Grik invaders churned themselves to offal against Baalkpan's defenses, the smoke and sodden smell of wet, burnt wood still lingered like a sad, ethereal shroud. Captain Matthew Reddy, High Chief of the "Amer-i-caan" Clan, and Supreme Commander of all the combined Allied forces, surveyed the somber scene from *Donaghey*'s hastily repaired quarterdeck as the battered frigate tacked on light, humid, northerly airs toward the mouth of the bay. The water remained choked with the shattered remains of the Grik fleet, causing a real menace to navigation. Occasionally, *Donaghey* thumped and shivered when she struck some piece of floating wreckage and it clunked and shuddered down her side as she passed. It was the first time Matt had returned to the water since that terrible night when the Battle of Baalkpan achieved its cataclysmic peak. Much of the flashing intensity and grief he'd felt had slowly begun to ebb, but the brief interval and the dreary day conspired to reinforce his gloomy mood.

By any objective measure, the battle had resulted in a momentous victory for the Allies, but it came at a terrible cost. The mighty Japanese battle cruiser *Amagi* had accompanied the Grik host, and her shells had shredded the remaining Lemurian ships in the bay and pounded the carefully prepared fortifications to matchsticks and heaps of earth. Lemurian losses had been horrifying, and both precious, aged American destroyers—survivors of the U.S. Asiatic Fleet that had been swept by a mysterious squall from one war (and world) smack into the middle of another—had ultimately been sunk in the battle. *Mahan* (DD-102) was a total loss, having virtually disintegrated herself by ramming the Japanese ship with a load of depth charges set to explode. That blow to *Amagi* had probably been mortal, in retrospect, but she'd still been under way and apparently on the verge of escape. She was finally destroyed by the combination of a lucky, forgotten mine, and the dogged determination of battered *Walker* (DD-163) and her crew, who fought to their final shell despite their own damage and casualties.

USS *Walker* was more fortunate than her sister. She'd managed to crawl back to the shipyard before succumbing to her grievous wounds, and even now, an effort was under way to refloat her. *Amagi* lay on the bottom of Baalkpan Bay, broken and gutted by flames, her warped and dreary superstructure protruding from the water as a constant, grim reminder of that terrible day and night.

Matt himself commanded *Donaghey* for this brief sortie, and it was a slightly awkward situation. He was familiar with *Donaghey*'s historical design, but knew little about actually operating a square-rigged ship. Her assigned captain, Greg Garrett—Matt's former gunnery officer—had become quite a sailor, but he was still recovering from serious wounds. Russ Chapelle, a former *Mahan* torpedoman, had learned quite a bit, however. He'd been the ship's master gunner and was elevated to "salig maa-stir" (sailing master), or executive officer, after *Donaghey*'s own Lemurian exec was killed. Garrett would get his old ship back, or a newer one, when he recovered, but for now, Russ was creditably taking up the slack.

Matt knew Garrett chafed at his inactivity, but his wounds were severe, and Nurse Lieutenant Sandra Tucker insisted he heal completely before exerting himself. All Sandra's patients were important to her, but Greg was human, and humans were an increasingly rare species. The titanic struggle—seemingly destined to encompass the entire locally known world—had already claimed many of the mere handful of humans actively engaged in aiding what was clearly the side of right. No one knew how many Japanese sailors the Grik had saved from *Amagi*, but even if the Grik hadn't eaten them they were, of course, not friends.

According to the charts they'd captured showing the extent of the enemy holdings, the Grik could replace their losses in a shockingly short time. They bred like rabbits and Courtney Bradford theorized that their young reached mature lethality within three to five years. If the remaining Americans and their allies were to have any chance of survival—not to mention victory—they needed all the skills and experience of every last destroyerman. Their window of opportunity would be fleeting and there weren't nearly enough hands and minds for all the work that lay ahead. Matt found it ironic that the ragtag remnants of the Asiatic Fleet who'd wound up here—men once considered the dregs of the Navy by some—were now the indispensable core of innovators: the trainers of the native force they'd need to see them through.

Great work had already been accomplished. They'd begun an industrial revolution of sorts, transforming the nomadic, insular, isolationist Lemurians—people who still reminded many destroyermen of a cross between cats and monkeys—into seasoned professional soldiers and sailors—but those ranks of professionals had been cruelly thinned. Recruitment was constant and Captain Reddy had secured important alliances that would supply the raw material to rebuild their forces, but it would take time to train and equip them, and in spite of their great victory, the war had just begun. The combined human survivors of *Walker, Mahan,* and S-19 now numbered just over a hundred souls—constituting the known (friendly) human population of this new world—unless somehow, they could befriend the "visitors" who'd appeared that morning beyond the mouth of the bay.

Matt didn't know if their visitors could or would help them, but as much as they needed more friends, they certainly didn't want more enemies. According to Chief Gray, the last meeting between Allied forces and the ships lingering in the strait had been . . . strained. That was one reason Matt wanted *Donaghey* for this meeting. She was the only "home-built" U.S. Navy ship yet made seaworthy again and, scarred as she was, she was the only ship available that should be a match for one of the visitors' powerful steam frigates. Of *Donaghey*'s two sisters, they'd try to salvage *Kas-Ra-Ar*'s guns, but the ship was gone forever. *Tolson* had also very nearly sunk. She'd require much more yard time before she was ready for sea. Several of the massive aircraft carrier–size, seagoing Lemurian Homes had returned after the battle, but impressive as they were, they were too slow to join the delegation. That didn't mean *Donaghey* was approaching the mouth of the bay alone.

Nearly two dozen "prize" ships were taken in serviceable condition after the battle. It would have seemed a great accomplishment, and it was—that they'd been alive to take them. Nevertheless, they'd been the only repairable ships of almost three hundred similar ones—virtual copies of the venerable British East Indiamen their lines were stolen from two centuries before—that had attacked Baalkpan packed with as many as one hundred and fifty thousand Grik warriors. No one would ever know for certain how many there'd actually been. Some of the terrifying, semireptilian Grik had escaped at the end, and many thousands died in the sprawling land battle that had surrounded the city. Far more met their fate in the sea, and the water of the bay had churned for days as the voracious flasher fish fed upon the dead.

Four of those ships now sailed with *Donaghey*, quickly armed with a few cannons each, their once red hulls repainted black with a white stripe between their gunports, according to Matt's new Navy regulations. They'd been cleaned as well as possible and their crews were glad to have them, but they'd never forget who made them. The barbaric nature and practices of their previous owners would taint the ships forever, regardless of how well they were scrubbed.

Matt leaned on the windward taffrail, still gouged and splintered from battle, and focused his intense green eyes on the squadron of strange ships anchored outside the bay—just beyond the reach of the grim-faced gunners serving the heavy cannon of Fort Atkinson. They did look formidable. All were warships, with three masts and sleek-looking hulls. Large half-moon boxes for their paddle wheels and tall, smoke-streaming funnels marred their pleasing lines, but lent a determined, businesslike aspect to their appearance. Matt was impressed by their sophistication. The Empire hadn't quite caught up with the "modern world" the destroyermen had lost, but, in some ways at least, it had advanced to within a generation or two.

The banners streaming above Fort Atkinson caught his attention momentarily: the Stainless Banner of the Trees, Rolak's Aryaalan flag, the gold pennant the Sularans had adopted for their own—and the Stars and Stripes, of course, fluttered from separate poles above the re-inforced fortification. The sight of that last flag, and the fact that it still flew after all they'd been through, couldn't help but stir his soul.

Among the sea folk, each of their huge, island-size ships or "Homes" were like nations unto themselves, and their leaders enjoyed co-equal status as "High Chiefs" among their peers. Before the war, those Homes often had clan devices or representative colors, but they hadn't used flags. As "chief" of *Walker*, regardless of her comparative tiny size, Captain Reddy had been afforded the same status as High Chief of the American Clan. With the coming of the war and the Grik Grand Swarm, changes to this age-old system began to evolve. An alliance started to take shape that included not only sea folk, but land folk as well, and a collective, coordinating leadership was required. Nakja-Mur, High Chief of Baalkpan, had been the first leader by default, since his "nation" hosted the other chiefs and, for a time, was the seat of all industry. The city on the southern coast of Borno was also where the first truly decisive engagement had been fought. With Nakja-Mur's death, the leadership of Baalkpan fell to Adar, High Sky Priest of *Salissa*, or *Big Sal*, as the Americans called her. She'd been the first seagoing Home of the Lemurian People to make contact with the Americans.

Amazingly, considering the disparate cultures, a true alliance began to form. Not one merely of expedience, but one designed to unite all willing Lemurians. Keje-Fris-Ar, *Salissa*'s High Chief, had been the first Lemurian to understand the significance and unifying power of flags. He'd directed the creation of the Banner of the Trees, and an infant political union began to take shape.

The stainless Banner of the Trees was composed of a circle of golden tree symbols, one for each Allied Home, surrounding a simple blue star representing the Americans. The star was in the center not to show dominance, but to symbolize that the Americans had been the organizing force, the glue holding everything together during those early, terrible times. Also, unlike the trees surrounding it, the star now represented more than a city-state, personified by a single ship or place. The precedent for that had been set when it became apparent that Captain Reddy was High Chief over both *Walker* and *Mahan*, something difficult for the 'Cats to understand at first, but clearly true. Matt was also acclaimed commander of the first Allied Expeditionary Force and later, all Allied forces. Thus it didn't seem wrong that even though *Mahan* was on the bottom of the sea and *Walker* might never fight again, the single star originally representing two ships, then tiny Tarakan Island, should remain prominent on the flag.

Besides, the United States Navy wasn't dead.

Just as Matt once gave Nakja-Mur a ship he'd captured early in the war so Baalkpan might be represented at sea, so had the bulk of the prizes taken after the Battle of Baalkpan been given, without reservation, to the United States Navy—a navy represented only by Lieutenant Commander Matthew Reddy and his surviving crews. Every Lemurian who joined that crew became a member of the United States Navy and swore to defend a vaguely understood "constitution" against all enemies. Captain Reddy had insisted on that. Therefore, wherever they came from, any Lemurian who swore the oath became a Navy man and a member of the Amer-i-caan Clan for as long as they kept that oath and followed the Americans' strict rules.

Nothing like those rules, or "regulations" as they were called, had ever occurred to any Lemurian, anywhere. The People did as their leaders specifically instructed them, but otherwise, they did as they pleased. No Lemurian leader ever imagined many of their people would willingly submit to the level of discipline demanded by the Americans. The thing was, though the rules were strict, the protections against abuse of power inherent in those rules were equally strict. To their surprise, far more volunteered for the "Amer-i-caan Naa-vee" than for the planned Combined Navy of the Alliance, to be composed of the rest of the prizes and new construction.

Certainly, prestige was a factor, but results were convincing as well. The American Navy had become a tight, close-knit clan of elite professionals who watched out for their own, no matter what they looked like, and it soon became clear the Combined Navy was a nonstarter. For better or worse, the entire Navy—minus the Homes, of course— became Matt's clan, and above every United States ship flew the Stars and Stripes.

That morning, nosing through the last of the debris in the mouth of the bay, everyone crewing *Donaghey* and her prize consorts, human or Lemurian, male or female, was American. Matt was awed by the responsibility, but humbled—and proud—as well.

Raising his binoculars, he focused them on the strange ships they'd sortied to meet. Their guns weren't run out and they were at a distinct disadvantage while anchored, but the men he saw upon their decks appeared tensely vigilant.

"It will be Captain Jenks, I shouldn't wonder," came a small voice. It sounded almost embarrassed.

Captain Reddy glanced at the tiny form beside him. Large jade eyes regarded him with something akin to trepidation, and long, carefully groomed golden locks framed her elflike face. Gone was the tattered waif they'd rescued from Talaud Island, south of Mindanao, with a handful of other civilians and a few S-boat submariners. In her place was this well-dressed, almost regal . . . child . . . possessed of a near adult maturity and resolve. Despite her size and age, her bearing—and presence—made it easy to believe Rebecca Anne McDonald was, well, a princess of sorts. As it turned out, she was the daughter of the governor-emperor of the Empire of the New Britain Isles, and that explained quite a lot that had mystified them before: such as why an entire squadron of warships would search so long and hard for her in a region they hadn't visited in over two hundred years.

"I shouldn't wonder," Matt echoed as amiably as possible, despite his mood and the uncertain situation. The girl had been convinced that Jenks and his squadron would come to their aid. For them to arrive now, so soon after the battle they *had* to have known was brewing, and behave so . . . distantly was irreconcilable with her worldview. Matt motioned to the Bosun, an imposing older man standing nearby with a battered, almost shapeless hat on his head. "Boats is certain of it. He says those are the same ships he . . . met . . . at Tarakan."

"Yep," Chief Bosun's Mate Fitzhugh Gray replied neutrally. "Biggest one's *Achilles*. If Jenks ever named the others, I don't remember. There *were* four of 'em, though."

Gray was a gruff, powerful man, close to sixty, who'd gone a little to seed on the China Station but had since trimmed down and muscled back up considerably. He, at least, had thrived on the activity and adventures they'd experienced since the Squall. He'd also appointed himself Matt's senior armsman and commanded a detail of enlisted humans and Lemurians who'd volunteered for the duty—knowing the man they'd sworn to protect didn't always make it easy. Like Juan Marcos, the little Filipino who'd appointed himself captain's steward, their job had just . . . evolved. Unlike Juan's rank, the Captain's Guard had become an official posting at the urging of Keje and Adar. Keje had even proposed that they make their oath to Adar, who, as chairman or prime minister or whatever he was of the Alliance, was technically the only chief to whom Matt answered. Maybe by his command, they could use the Captain's Guard to keep their Supreme Commander out of harm's way.

Gray refused. He said he'd keep the job he'd already given himself, but he'd sworn an oath when he entered the Navy. That was good enough. Now that his job was official though, he could choose the very best from two battle-hardened and increasingly elite forces: the 1st and 2nd Marines. With the exception of four human destroyermen, the rest of the Captain's Guard were Lemurian Marines.

"What type of signals do your people use?" Matt asked Sean O'Casey who'd joined them by the rail. The powerful, one-armed, dark-skinned man with flowing mustaches had been the girl's companion and protector when the equally lost crew of the U.S. submarine

S-19 had taken them from an open boat. The old S-boat had been dragged to this world the same way *Walker* was: through the mysterious Squall. Out of fuel and with nowhere to go, the sub ultimately wound up on a Talaud Island beach. All the sub's passengers were safe—twenty children of diplomats and industrialists, evacuated from Surabaya with four nannies and a nun to care for them—but half its crew had perished in the year before their rescue.

He, and ultimately the girl, had become fonts of information about the Empire, represented by the visiting ships, although both still hedged when asked its exact location. It had been ingrained in them that only secrecy kept their homeland safe, and a lifetime of indoctrination to that effect was hard to overcome. The destroyermen and their allies had learned much about the political situation there, however, and what they knew might prove problematic. O'Casey had actually been evading its authorities because of his participation in a rebellion of sorts, not against the legitimate rulers, but against the Company—the Honorable New Britain Company—that increasingly subverted them.

"Flags, guns, lights, rockets . . . much as ye, it seems, but the meanings are doubtless different."

"What signal for a truce, a parlay?"

"A white flag."

"Some things never change, I suppose. Very well." Matt addressed Chapelle. "Have a white flag run up. The crew will remain at General Quarters."

The ships slowly approached the intruder's squadron until they were close enough to lower one of the surviving motor launches. Matt recognized it as the *Scott*—named for his lost coxswain—as he climbed down into it. Scott had been a true hero, but after the Squall, he'd become terrified of the water—understandable, considering the horrible creatures that dwelt in it here—but he'd been killed on land, by a "super lizard." It had been a terrible, ironic loss.

"Captain Reddy," O'Casey called from the ship. For obvious reasons, he wouldn't be making the crossing. Only later, after the character of their visitors was determined, might he be revealed. "Beware Jenks. As Her Highness has said, he may be a man o' honor, but he has a temper." He grinned beneath his mustaches. "As do ye, I've learned." Matt replied with a curt nod.

Keje-Fris-Ar, High Chief of *Big Sal*, awkwardly found a place beside the captain, favoring his wounded leg. He looked something like a cat-faced bear, and his short, brownish red fur had become increasingly sprinkled with silver. Today it was groomed immaculately. He was dressed in his best embroidered blue smock and highly polished copper scale armor. His battered "scota," or working sword, was at his side—unbound—and on his head was a copper helmet adorned with the tail plumage of a Grik. He grinned, though as usual with his species, the expression didn't touch his red-brown eyes. "That one-armed man has learned you well, my brother. Perhaps it might be best, just this once, to watch that temper of yours. I don't know about you, but I believe we have a sufficient war at present to keep us occupied."

Matt snorted. "I don't know what you're talking about. Sure, I have a temper. So do you. But I don't lose it very often."

"Perhaps," Keje hedged, "but when you do, well . . . you do." He left it at that.

Courtney Bradford descended next, puffing with exertion and trying not to lose the ridiculous, oversize hat that protected his balding pate. Bradford, an Australian, had been a petroleum-engineering consultant for Royal Dutch Shell. He was also a self-proclaimed "naturalist," and despite an absentminded, eccentric personality, he was an extremely valuable man. It was he who showed them where to drill for the oil that had fueled their war effort so far. Of all *Walker*'s company who'd arrived on this "other earth," he'd probably changed the least—personality wise—and still tended to greet each day as a blooming opportunity for discovery and adventure.

"Larry the Lizard," as the men had taken to calling Lawrence, Rebecca's Grik-like pet/companion, scampered down to join them and found a place to perch near the front of the launch. He wasn't as large as their Grik enemies, and his orangeish and brown tiger-striped, feathery fur easily distinguished him from the washed-out dun and brown of the Grik. Otherwise, the physical similarity was striking. He was a kind of "island Grik," a "Tagranesi" he claimed, from somewhere in the Eastern Sea. Apparently a different race from their enemies, he'd become Rebecca's friend and protector. So striking was his similarity to the enemy, Matt had kept him hidden aboard *Walker* until after the great battle out of real concern for his safety. It may have been just as well at the time. Despite their previous, almost pacifistic nature, the Lemurians *hated* the Grik, and he sure looked like one. After the battle however, he'd emerged as something of a hero, and to Matt's honest amazement, the Lemurians had once again displayed their capacity for tolerant adaptability. Somehow, despite his appearance, the 'Cats were able to accept—on Matt's and Adar's word alone—that Larry was on their side. *Walker's* crew had grown accustomed to him by the time they brought him back to Baalkpan on the eve of battle, but Matt *knew* that under similar circumstances, no equally large group of humans would have embraced Larry as quickly.

The mighty chief gunner's mate Dennis Silva clambered down the rungs last, with Her Highness Rebecca Anne McDonald clinging to his back. Silva winced occasionally, pained by his many wounds, and Matt wished again he'd insisted the big man remain behind. But Silva took his role of protecting the princess seriously and Matt couldn't bring himself to discourage anything the irreverent, depraved pain in the ass actually *wanted* to do—as far as his duty was concerned. Of all of them, Silva might have changed the most—maybe even more than Matt himself. He didn't *seem* much different to the casual observer, despite the patch that covered his ruined left eye. He was still huge, powerful, and still kept his blond hair burred close—even as he let the sun-bleached brownish beard grow longer than everyone knew the captain approved. He remained coarse, profane, and fearlessly reckless, and there was still the more or less unresolved question of what, exactly, constituted the relationship between him, Nurse Pam Cross, and the 'Cat female Risa-Sab-At. Risa's brother, Chack, probably knew, but no one else did . . . for sure. Other than that, however, Silva caused few real problems anymore.

Maybe his wounds slowed him down, but Matt had seen him shoulder more and more responsibility—sometimes of his own accord—even before he was injured. It was as if he'd taken his role as *Walker's* Hercules to heart, and saw it as his personal duty to protect her survivors as best he could—with the possible exception of his primary rival,

Chief Machinist's Mate Dean Laney. His protectiveness was particularly focused on the little girl clinging to his back. She had . . . done something . . . to Dennis Silva, and Matt believed the big man would somehow contrive, with his bare hands, to destroy the ship they were about to visit if it threatened the girl in any way.

When all the passengers were aboard, Gunner's Mate Paul Stites advanced the throttle and the launch burbled across the choppy sea to *Achilles'* side. The closer they drew to the "British" ships, the more impressed Matt became. Each Imperial frigate seemed quite well made, and mounted twelve to twenty guns that looked somewhat larger than the American frigates' improved eighteen pounders. Maybe twenty-fours? But the ships simply couldn't be as imaginatively and redundantly reinforced as his own Lemurian-built frigates, and their steam power would be an advantage only until their vulnerable paddle wheels were damaged. Then they'd become a terrible liability. They were more than a match for his "prizes," though, and he had only one frigate to oppose them if it came to that. Of course, there was no way they could enter the bay past the guns of Fort Atkinson and the other big guns they'd quickly emplaced on the southeast entrance. For a melancholy moment, he considered that *Walker* could have taken all of them by herself, but he shook that off. He didn't want to fight them, and despite Gray's assessment, he doubted he'd have to. Most likely, they just wanted to take the girl and go, but it was always wise to consider possibilities—particularly when they weren't necessarily going to get what they wanted.

The barge bumped alongside and Captain Reddy hopped across to an extensive ladder arrangement, complete with manropes that had been rigged while they crossed. Climbing to the top, he saluted the curiously familiar ensign, with the red and white stripes and Union Jack in the field at the ship's stern, then saluted a man he suspected was Captain Jenks, by the description Gray had given him.

"Captain Matthew Reddy, United States Navy. Supreme Commander, by acclamation, of the Combined Allied Forces united under the Banner of the Trees. I request permission to come aboard, sir."

A side party was present, with drums and a pair of trumpets, but they made no sound. The man in the elaborately laced white coat with braided mustaches frowned, then returned the salute with a curious rigidity. "Of course," he said gruffly, apparently somewhat taken aback, "do come aboard." He gestured at the side party. "And please forgive our incivility," he added when he recognized a much cleaned-up Chief Gray reaching the top of the ladder. "We were under the impression your people preferred informal greetings."

"An impression you got when you were rude to us right after a fight," Gray growled over his shoulder. He took the girl from Silva, who'd passed her up from below. Turning, he set her on the deck and glared at Jenks. He pointedly didn't salute the flag or the Imperial officer. Jenks stiffened, but then beamed at the girl before him. At the signal of another officer, the drums rolled loudly and the trumpets blasted a rapid and again tantalizingly familiar fanfare.

"Your Highness!" Jenks exclaimed, going to a knee and sweeping off his hat when the trumpets subsided. Everyone in the vicinity did the same, leaving the Americans standing awkwardly beside the girl.

At that instant, Silva stuck his head over the rail and gawked around, festooned with the evidence of his wounds. His hands were bandaged and blood seeped through the cloth of his white tunic. The garish black patch covering his eye, and the gap-toothed grin that split his bearded face gave him a decidedly piratical air. Faced with an opportunity, he proceeded to prove that nothing could temper his customary irreverent exuberance. "Goddamn," he muttered in the silence, "the skipper just hops aboard and a whole shipload o' limeys surrenders to him!" Jenks's face flushed.

"Silva!" Matt hissed.

"Rise!" Rebecca Anne McDonald said loudly, forcing down a giggle. Behind her, the rest of the occupants of the launch continued to arrive on deck—all of them, even the Lemurians, saluting the flag.

Jenks's face turned even redder, if possible, perhaps with shame over his pettiness. He stood, followed by his officers, and took a step forward. "I'm so glad!" he said to Rebecca, ignoring the other visitors. "Surely it's a miracle. We've found you at last! We'd nearly lost hope, searching much farther and longer than most believed you could possibly survive. Thank God I decided to search among the Ape Folk, thinking they may have taken you in. Only chance brought us to their huge ship, which told us strangers were also searching for others of their kind in waters you may have reached! I believed it possible they may have found you and hurried here, but I honestly cherished little remaining hope!"

"You have found me," the girl agreed, "and I give thanks for your diligence. Sadly, of all those who accompanied me on that ill-fated voyage, only one remained to aid me. Injured though he was, I could not have survived without him. Alas, even he was denied this happy reunion." Rebecca spoke of O'Casey, who'd begged her not to mention him, since he was, after all, a wanted man. But she was determined that he receive his due and, ultimately, a pardon. What she'd said would suffice, however. For now, she'd let him remain anonymous.

"A noble man, surely," Jenks commiserated, "but at least the Empire has you safely back! Their Majesties will be so relieved!"

"How are my parents?" Rebecca asked anxiously.

"Well enough when we left, five months ago, though desolate with worry and grief. Your father blamed himself, you see, for sending you to stay with your uncle, the governor of the Western Isles."

"He sent me to protect me!" the girl insisted.

Jenks glanced at his other visitors again, perhaps wondering how much they'd learned about his nation. "Of course, but . . ."

Matt cleared his throat. "Excuse me, please. This is all very touching and even fascinating, but"—he pointed toward land—"we've recently fought a great battle against a rather large fleet of Grik. I understand you know about them?"

Jenks seemed annoyed by the interruption, but nodded. "From legends, the old logs of the founders." His eyes went wide when Lawrence scrambled aboard. Wide with surprise, but not shock or horror, Matt noticed.

"The young lady . . . Her Highness . . . said you know about his people," Matt said, pointing at the tiger-striped creature gazing about with open curiosity. "I even gather you've been on expeditions to some of their lands. What do you think of them?"

Jenks waved his hand. "Formidable predators, but relatively peaceful. Slow breeders—there aren't many of them on their rocky, jungle isles—mildly intelligent and capable of limited cooperative behavior, but incapable of speech."

Lawrence bowed low and said, "How do you do?"

Jenks's mouth clamped shut and he goggled at the creature before him.

"I must present my particular friend Lawrence," Rebecca added quickly. "He contributed as much to my survival as any other. He speaks very well indeed, as long as he needn't use Ms or Bs or other such words that require . . . lips like ours, I suppose. I haven't learned much of his language, I'm afraid."

"Shows what you know, Jenks," Gray jabbed.

Matt sent him a stern look before turning back to Jenks. "The creatures we fight are a different version of Lawrence: bigger, stronger, just as formidably . . . armed, but who breed like rabbits—you know rabbits?" Jenks nodded. "They breed like rabbits and have mastered ships like the one they stole from your ancient squadron. Now they have cannons, and their only purpose seems to be eradicating all other life they encounter. With me so far?" When Jenks nodded again, Matt continued. "We killed a hundred, maybe a hundred fifty thousand of 'em here a few weeks ago and we lost a lot of people doing it. We have a lot of work to do and not much time to do it. We have to take the fight to them, or someday they'll be back."

"My heartiest congratulations for your victory," Jenks said. "And, of course, you have my country's most profound gratitude for rescuing and protecting Her Highness."

"Thank you, Captain . . ."

"It's 'Commodore,' actually," interrupted one of Jenks's officers. Like the others, he'd remained silent so far, wearing a variety of expressions. There'd been no real introductions on either side and Matt suspected Jenks's officers were as surprised by this breach of protocol as he was. But things were moving fast.

Matt frowned. "Look," he said, "my point is, if they roll us up, they'll keep going. Eventually they'll find you too."

"I'm confident you'll make short work of them, Captain," Jenks said, somewhat condescendingly, "if the carnage I saw on the little island where I met Mr. Gray is any indication."

"That fight was against three ships, Jenks," Gray growled. "*Hundreds* of 'em came here."

"Hundreds of their ships," Matt confirmed, "each filled with hundreds of their warriors. Creatures that look like Lawrence here, but who fight with swords and spears, and now cannons too."

"I'm afraid that can be none of my concern, Captain."

"Maybe not yet, but if we lose, it will be someday. Guaranteed."

"Perhaps. What are you suggesting?" Jenks paused, his mustaches twitching over a smirk. "Surely not an alliance?"

"Essentially, yes."

Jenks shook his head. "I *am* sorry, Captain Reddy, but that's simply impossible. Our duty was to find the princess and we've done so. Her safety is thanks in large part to you, I confess, but our duty now is to return her where she belongs. I'm sensible to the possibility that your arguments may even have . . . merit, but I don't have the authority to get involved. You must understand, my squadron has been engaged in this search for quite some time; time it has been unavailable for . . . other pressing duties. We have even suffered the loss of one of our number, to a leviathan"—he glanced curiously at Gray, as if wondering whether the Bosun had deliberately misled them when they met—"so I seriously don't know what difference my three poor ships might make to your cause." His face betrayed the belief that his "poor" ships would probably make quite a difference indeed. "In any event, even if I had the authority I'd be obliged to refuse. As I've clearly stated, my duty is to return Her Highness to the bosom of her family and no other consideration can prevail."

Rebecca had listened with growing astonishment. Suddenly, she spoke and all eyes fell on her diminutive form. "Then *I* will give you something to consider, *Commodore* Jenks: I refuse to abandon my friends, my *saviors*, while it is in my power to aid them. They are not proposing an alliance only with *you*, you silly man. You already refused Mr. Gray's request for aid when your small squadron might have made a difference. I have proposed they seek an alliance with our country!"

"Ridiculous!" erupted the other officer who'd spoken before, and Matt looked at him again. He wore a mustache much like Jenks's, but so did many others. It seemed to be the style. Unlike the others, he seemed stuffed into his uniform and wore little braid. The braid was unique, though, the gold laced with red. It still struck Matt odd that an apparently comparatively junior member of Jenks's staff would be allowed to speak so freely.

"Perhaps . . ." Rebecca sighed, regarding the man as well. "Perhaps honor *has* become so devalued in my absence. Nevertheless, I will seek an alliance on their behalf and ours. Not only is it the right thing to do after all they've done for me, but it's the sensible course as well. They have dealt the Grik a terrible blow, but the Grik will recover. There will be no better chance to break them forever—before they eventually menace *us*. If we wait and my friends are lost, we will face them all alone and we cannot succeed in that."

"But, Highness!" said Jenks. "Perhaps what you say is true, but I have no choice! I must get you safely home!"

"You do have a choice, Commodore. I have a choice." She glared at the outspoken officer. "The Company may have stripped my family of most of its power, but the governor-emperor is still commander in chief. As the highest-ranking member of his household present, I can order you to help. You might refuse, but I tell you now, if you do, I . . . I will not accompany you home."

"But, Your Highness!" Matt and Jenks both protested at once, but only Matt continued. "We appreciate it, but Jenks is right: we have to keep you safe. Sure, we could use his ships now while we're . . . a little short . . . but his squadron will make little difference, in the end."

Jenks bristled. "I assure you, sir . . ."

"Oh, knock it off! I know exactly what your ships can do, and as I said, we can always use the help. But you really don't know what you're up against." Matt paused, struck by the irony of his argument. A moment ago, he'd been trying to convince Jenks to help. Now he was encouraging him to run away. He sighed. "Look, we want friendship between your people and ours . . . for a lot of reasons, not just this war. And no matter what you think, your three ships can't make much difference in the campaign we're preparing. How likely are we to remain friends with your people if you and the young lady are destroyed defending us?"

"It remains to be seen whether we are indeed destined to be friends," Jenks replied, again glancing at Gray. "That is not my decision to make. For now . . . if—*if*—we join you, it will be solely because it is in the best interests of the Empire."

"Of course we shall be friends!" Rebecca insisted. "We already are. Mr. Flynn and his submersible-boat sailors rescued us from the sea and shared all they had."

Jenks looked at her, even more incredulous. What had she said? Clearly, there was still far more to the princess's story.

Rebecca turned to Matt. "And our ships might make more difference than you think, Captain Reddy," she protested. "There are several hundred armed Marines between them as well."

"Armed with muskets, and with no experience fighting the Grik," Matt mused aloud. He knew the girl had seen their own weapons, but wondered if she truly appreciated the qualitative difference. As an historian, he wasn't sure muskets were much of an advantage over Grik arrows, either. They were probably more lethal and there might be a psychological effect, but arrows reloaded faster.

"Perhaps I might offer a compromise," Courtney Bradford said, speaking for the first time.

"Excuse me," Matt interrupted, risking embarrassing Jenks still further, but it was also possible they needed a brief pause to defuse the mounting tension. "May I present . . . the honorable Courtney Bradford, esquire." Silva barely contained a snort. "He's Minister of Science for the Allied powers. He also has broad diplomatic experience and influence." He shrugged. "And I may as well present the others here. Chief Gray I think you know?" Jenks nodded and worked his jaw. Matt continued. "I understand Mr. Gray's status may have been unclear during your previous meeting. We apparently share some of the same rank designations, and 'chief bosun's mate' doesn't reflect the extent of his responsibilities. He's also my chief, personal armsman, and commands the Captain's Guard. He's not a commissioned officer, but he's the highest-ranking noncommissioned officer in the Alliance. He has commanded detachments including commissioned officers, and in those situations he acts as my direct personal representative."

He waited with some satisfaction while Jenks digested that. "Beside me is Keje-Fris-Ar. *Admiral* Keje-Fris-Ar. In addition to being High Chief of *Salissa* Home and a head of state in his own right, he's assistant chief of naval operations and answers only to me in military matters. His people are not 'Ape Folk.' They call themselves Mi-Anaaka, but our term, 'Lemurians,' doesn't offend them. They were once peaceful, unwarlike people. That's probably how your histories remember them. They've since become some of the best warriors in the world. I wouldn't call them Ape Folk if I were you, because that *does* offend them. I honestly don't know why, since they've never seen an ape, but there it is." Matt suddenly wondered if *Jenks* had ever seen an ape. *Later.* He started to introduce the other members of his party, but they weren't officers. Besides, then he'd have to name Silva, and how would he describe him? The most depraved, dangerous human on the planet? He stifled a chuckle.

Jenks—somewhat reluctantly, it seemed—introduced his officers then. None smiled or offered his hand and most appeared to regard the entire party, the Lemurians in particular, with disdain. Matt dismissed them all as junior copies of Jenks—except the one who'd spoken up. His name was Billingsly, and judging from Rebecca's distasteful glance, he decided to remember him.

"Now, Mr. Bradford, I apologize for the interruption. Please continue."

"My dear," Bradford continued, addressing Rebecca, "you once said when the time came for you to return home, you wanted us, Captain Reddy in particular, to take you. Do you still mean that?"

"Of course."

"Very well. Then I propose that Captain Reddy and other dignitaries escort you home as soon as either *Walker* is . . . repaired . . . or other suitable ships are ready to take you." Bradford realized Jenks knew about *Walker*, their "iron ship," but doubted Captain Reddy was ready to admit that, right now, she was underwater. "That may take some months, but what is that compared to the time you have been gone, after all? The mission will be a diplomatic one with the goal of securing a true alliance. In the meantime, Jenks might dispatch one or two of his ships to bear the happy news of your rescue, but he and *Achilles*, at least, could remain here to augment our fleet until you are ready to leave." He smiled. "That should certainly not interfere with his imperative of protecting you. He should then, of course, accompany you home. Hopefully to return here with reinforcements." He glanced around owlishly. "What do you think?"

"I think this is all a waste of time," Keje growled unexpectedly. He'd learned a lot about the curious face moving of humans and didn't much care for what he saw. He looked at Matt. "They do not want to help us, and now that we have slaughtered the cream of the Grik horde, we have sufficient allies who do. Saan-Kakja has promised many thousands more of her warriors and artisans. Many who fled are now returning, eager to fight. Our fleet is rebuilding and we have more than sufficient iron for our needs, at least for now." He turned back to Jenks. "You have apparently formed the mistaken assumption that we came to you today as supplicants. Not so. Now we have met, it matters little to me if you stay or go, but Adar, High Chief of Baalkpan, chairman and High Sky Priest of the Alliance, would meet with you. He desires friendship, true, but his primary interest in you is . . . historical. He is not naive. We will always welcome friends, but we will not suffer vipers in our midst."

Matt was surprised by Keje's outburst. Who had been warning whom about tempers?

Jenks was also taken aback, as much by Keje's attitude as by his near-perfect command of English. And by what he said, of course. He scrutinized Keje. He'd met other Lemurians on the massive ship coming out from the Philippines. They'd all seemed glad to see him and treated his people with something akin to reverential awe. Just what he would have expected of the simple wogs he thought they were. Wogs extremely talented at building fantastic ships, but wogs. Now he wasn't so sure. He didn't think there was much chance of a real alliance—he glanced at Billingsly—particularly if the Company had anything to say about it. The very word "ally" was too closely associated with "equal partner," and that was out of the question. However, perhaps an arrangement might be made. Besides, speaking of vipers, it might be a very good idea, in the interests of the Empire, for him to learn as much about this Alliance as he could. The Empire had enemies of its own, and though they were preoccupied for now, he suspected these Lemurians and their American friends might someday become formidable enemies indeed, if given reason enough—or allowed.

"Mr. Bradford has made an interesting proposal," he said at last, carefully. "And it might provide the basis for negotiations. I would be . . . honored to meet with your chairman." He glanced at Matt. "I have your word of safe conduct, of course?"

"Of course. We'll escort you under the guns of the fort and provide you with an anchorage. Your people may even have liberty if you give your word they'll behave themselves—and some parts of the city are off-limits. That's not subject to discussion or debate at this point. Perhaps later. In the meantime, any of your people found screwing around in restricted areas will be shot. Understood?"

Jenks bristled again, but calmed himself. "Understood." He turned to Billingsly. "I assume you will want to remain? Very well. Choose someone from your . . . department. He and Ensign Parr will transfer to *Agamemnon* and proceed home with the happy news about the princess. *Ajax* will remain here for now, with *Achilles*. I will draft orders and a brief dispatch." He turned to Matt. "Is that acceptable?"

For some reason, Matt was hesitant. But that had been part of Bradford's proposal, after all. "Sure."

"We should have just sent him away with the promise we would bring the girl," growled Keje quietly as the launch burbled back to *Donaghey*. "The girl" was still with them, having refused to part with her friends. She was distressed and confused by Jenks's attitude, not to mention Billingsly's presence. She didn't know Billingsly, but she knew *what* he was. For now, she much preferred to remain among people she trusted unreservedly. That was what she'd whispered to Matt, and he wondered if Keje overheard or just picked up on it too. That might explain his sudden animosity. *Agamemnon* was already piling on sail and beginning to slant eastward. With the freshening breeze, her paddle wheels were free-spinning. "With Jenks hanging around here, he'll see too much," Keje added.

"Possibly." Matt nodded at the Bosun. "Gray's always been a pretty good judge of character and he said Jenks is an asshole." He sighed

resignedly. "Having met him, I'm inclined to agree. But Adar's probably an even better judge. He won't let his fascination with the 'ones
who came before' cloud his judgment."

Keje huffed noncommittally. Before ascending to his current lofty
title, Adar had been Keje's own High Sky Priest, and the two had been
like brothers their entire lives. Keje knew Matt was right, but his own
impression of Jenks had been very similar to Gray's. He'd actually been
surprised by that. According to Matt, his Amer-i-caans and Jenks's
people were related in some way. He supposed he'd expected them to
behave more alike. Jenks's reaction to Keje's people's situation couldn't
have been more different from that of Matt and his destroyermen.

"Besides," said Gray, "he never would've gone for that—just leaving, I mean."

"Right," Matt agreed. "And over time, maybe we can loosen him
up. *If* we can make friends with the Brits, and *if* we can trust them,
we'll have to bring them up to speed on our programs anyway."

Gray snorted and shook his head. "You know, it sure is weird—not
trusting Brits, I mean. Sure, in *our* history we weren't friends all the
time, but we were on the same side in the last war, and we were best
friends in the war we left behind—both of us fightin' the Japs. Those
guys on *Exeter* and *Encounter* and all the others, they were the same as
us. They were our guys. We might've gotten in fights in bars, made
fun of other, and called other names, but we'd watch out for each
other too. This Jenks guy drives it home in no uncertain terms that we
ain't on the same side here. Some of the fellas are liable to get . . .
confused."

Matt was thoughtful. "Good point, Boats. Make sure everybody
knows these aren't the same Brits we knew back home. No fights, no
trouble—we *do* want to be their friends—but right now, we're not.
We'll have talks, and I'll use the fact that we had a special relationship
with the descendants of Jenks's ancestors. Maybe that'll help. But once
our visitors know that, we don't want them to take advantage of it either, buddy up to our guys and pump them for information. That sort
of thing."

"Aye-aye, Skipper."

A dar, High Chief of Baalkpan, Chairman (by acclamation) and High Sky Priest of the Grand
Alliance, paced restlessly in the large conference
chamber. He felt uncomfortable in his new role,
and truthfully, he would have done almost anything to avoid it. Almost. The problem was, uncomfortable as he felt, there were very few people
he personally trusted with the responsibility at this critical and confusing time. Those he did trust already had crucial and possibly even
more important roles to play.

Keje could have done it, even though he'd probably never spent six
consecutive months on dry land in his life. He was a hero and he'd
nearly sacrificed his Home and his life to defend the "land folk" of
Baalkpan. Keje had actually been the first acclaimed as High Chief, but
he'd flatly refused. He had a Home. Battered and wounded beyond
imagination, *Salissa* Home was still his responsibility and he was her
High Chief.

Adar understood that. Being Sky Priest of *Salissa* was all he'd ever aspired to himself. Over the last year however, old Naga, High Sky Priest of Baalkpan, had grown increasingly disassociated and Adar had assumed more and more of his duties. Land folk needed a Sky Priest to help chart their course through perilous times, just as sea folk looked to their priests in perilous seas. With Naga's death, and that of the great Nakja-Mur, Adar had been Baalkpan's second choice and he found himself practically drafted to fill the void caused by the loss of both leaders. He really hadn't had a choice. He'd become a prominent, well-known figure to all the diverse elements of the Alliance and he was one of the few people everyone seemed to trust. Ultimately, he'd concluded, the one thing he couldn't do to avoid the job was let someone less committed than him or Keje take it.

He honestly believed Matt could have won the necessary support, even though he wasn't "of the People," but there would have been *some* dissent. They needed unity now above all things, and Matt was far more useful at the point of the spear. They'd never even discussed it, but Adar knew Matt would have agreed. He probably would have been astonished and horrified even to be considered. That left only Adar with the popularity, strength of will, and determination not only to continue the fight, but to carry it to the enemy once more.

He still wore the priestly robes of his former office, but his responsibilities had expanded dramatically. Though all Homes on land or sea were considered equal by tradition, Baalkpan had taken the lead in the war and its leader had gained at least the perception of being a little more equal than other members of the Alliance. Adar agreed with the arrangement in principle; somebody had to be in charge, but he wasn't convinced he was up to the task. Becoming a High Chief was difficult enough, but leading the entire Alliance was something else again. Chairman was the loftiest title he would accept.

He knew he was a better choice than some, since his dedication to "the cause" was unwavering. He spent most of his time convincing less enthusiastic allies that the war wasn't over and all they'd won at Baalkpan was a single battle. Final victory would be achieved only when the Grik were utterly eradicated. That was an argument he could put his heart and soul into, one he'd advocated ever since they'd discovered the true nature of their enemy. He wasn't as confident he was the best choice to *implement* the policy, however. He allowed himself a small grin. Of course, that was what he had Captain Reddy for.

The conference would soon begin and the chamber was filled to overflowing. It wasn't as large as Nakja-Mur's Great Hall had been, but it would be months before that edifice was completely rebuilt. At least the great Galla tree the hall once encompassed had survived the fire. When the first new leaves began to unfold on its charred branches, the People took it as an omen of healing and heavenly favor. It had given them even greater confidence in their choice of Adar to lead them. Adar only wished he were as confident as they. He was beginning to understand the profound difference between strongly advocating a course of action, and ordering that action carried out.

He continued to pace while the expectant chatter grew ever louder. Nakja-Mur would have lounged on a cushion, outwardly calm. Even when inwardly terrified—as Adar had known he often was—he'd always managed an air of confidence, if not always in himself, then in the people he'd chosen to advise him. Adar had many of the same advisors, those who'd survived, and he'd even acquired a curious new one since the return of the evacuated seagoing Homes: a human holy woman, a nun who'd been with the Amer-i-caans Captain Reddy rescued from the amazing diving ship. Matt called its crew "sub-maa-ri-ners," and apparently, their wondrous vessel still lay on the beach of Talaud Island.

The nun, Sister Audry, was an . . . interesting creature. She spoke the Amer-i-caans' tongue with a different sound and Adar had learned she sprang from yet another human clan, the Dutch. He understood she was attractive too, by human standards, yet she had no mate and cited an oath to her God to take none. Adar couldn't imagine why any God—and he was beginning to suspect his Maker of All Things and the human God were one and the same—would require such an oath. Nevertheless, an oath was an oath, whether demanded or freely given. He didn't understand it—yet—but he did respect it. With the scarcity of human females in the vicinity, however, he would have thought she'd face resentment. Not so. All the Amer-i-caans appeared to respect her abstinence as a matter of course, and many sought her out just to talk. Adar did too. On the few occasions they'd had leisure to visit, he'd been charmed by her conviction, personality, and philosophy—even as he'd been troubled by the implications of much of what she'd said.

There was no more devoted servant of the heavens than he, but he was fully aware there were . . . gaps . . . in the dogma of the Sky Priests. He'd once theorized the Amer-i-caans didn't believe that differently than he did. He'd been wrong, but as Matt would say, the devil was in the details. He'd finally concluded that they simply sailed a different path to the same destination. He was learning from Sister Audry that it was a *much* different path . . . and yet . . .

He shook away those thoughts and tried to concentrate on the business at hand. This was a staff meeting, planned days before the strangers from the east arrived. They had much to discuss before Commodore Jenks and his officers entered for their first official audience. Adar had actually already met them. Instead of waiting for the strangers to come to him, as was traditional among the People when visitors called, he'd greeted them on the dock with the full courtesy and fanfare Matt told him they'd expect. Adar was nervous at first in the presence of those he had no doubt were descendants of the "ones who came before," since so much Lemurian liturgy was founded on that ancient visit. But he'd been struck by how different they'd been from what he'd expected. Jenks, in particular, had been formal and polite, but also . . . condescending. Adar quickly shed his initial awe when he realized these representatives of the Empire of the New Britain Isles were mere men, after all: other humans like those he'd come to know. Certainly not holy messengers. They no longer made him nervous, except for whatever . . . worldly significance their presence might imply. That added yet another dimension to his religious ponderings.

Adar was anxious to speak to their leader again, but this meeting was for high-level staff only. Even those residents of Baalkpan who'd begun returning after the battle were not allowed. They'd run before; they might again—this time carrying sensitive information. There *were* foreigners present, but only ones who'd proven themselves steadfast allies.

Saan-Kakja, High Chief of the Fil-pin Lands, was perched rigidly on an ornately embroidered cushion, attended by several of her closest advisors. She and her personal guard had arrived at the height of the land battle for Baalkpan and had helped turn the tide. Since then, more of her troops, artisans, laborers, and beasts of burden—not to mention precious materials—continued to arrive in an uninterrupted stream. Saan-Kakja herself was a spirited, darling creature. She was quite young for her office, but Adar had discovered she had a will of iron. She'd once been led astray by self-serving advisors and seemed determined that it never happen again. She had the most mesmerizing eyes Adar had ever seen: warm and inquisitive like yellow-gold stars, but woe was he they fell upon when they were touched with fire. Adar thanked the Heavens continuously for the alliance Captain Reddy had forged between them.

Safir Maraan, Queen Protector of B'mbaado, was striking as always, her jet-black fur and polished silver breastplate complementing her penetrating eyes. She was older than Saan-Kakja, more experienced, and far more self-assured, but she too was an "orphan queen," and despite the utterly different societies they'd sprung from, she and Saan-Kakja had become fast friends.

Her betrothed, Chack-Sab-At, accompanied Safir. Once a simple, pacifistic wing runner on *Salissa* Home, the amber-eyed, brindled Chack was now a scarred and hardened veteran. Somehow, he'd managed to retain a measure of his irrepressible humor, but it had been tempered by a sharp, worldly wit. He'd seen so much of war already that his innocent youngling's soul was gone forever. He was now a respected warrior, bosun's mate for sunken *Walker*, and a captain of Marines.

General Muln-Rolak, onetime High Protector of Aryaal, also attended Safir. He was old and scarred from many battles—almost to the point of disfigurement. Many of the scars dated from a time when he'd battled Safir's own father. He stood with her now as a trusted friend and colleague. Their lands had once been bitter enemies, but in this war, they fought together as inseparable allies and their relationship had become almost one of father and daughter. Together, at least until Saan-Kakja's regiments were up to strength, they commanded the second-largest army in the Alliance. It was composed of warriors and refugees from both their enemy-occupied homelands on Java.

People of lesser rank stood for the steadfast Sularan regiments who'd remained to fight after the bulk of their own people, across the Makaassar Strait on Sa-leebs, fled in the face of the Grik horde.

Then there were the Amer-i-caans, of course.

Beside Captain Reddy, as always, stood Nurse Lieutenant Sandra Tucker, petite, sandy haired, and much shorter than the towering (by Lemurian standards) man she so clearly loved. Despite her size, she was a dynamo, and through her skill at administration and trauma surgery, a truly astonishing number of People literally owed her their lives. Adar had appointed her Minister of Medicine. With the other surviving nurses who'd come through the Squall—Karen Theimer (Letts), Pam Cross, and Kathy McCoy—she'd created, from scratch, a highly efficient and professional Hospital Corps.

Commander Alan Letts (Karen's new husband) was still chief of staff, and due to his administrative abilities—he'd been *Walker*'s supply officer—Adar had named him Minister of Industry. He'd undergone a transformation from his old Asiatic Fleet days, and Karen was probably responsible for changing the easygoing, arguably lazy, fair-skinned kid from a place called Idaho into one of the most industrious and indispensible logisticians in the Alliance.

Bradford, who emphatically claimed *not* to be an Amer-i-caan, was Minister of Science, and served as plenipotentiary at large.

Commander Perry Brister, *Mahan*'s former engineering officer, was Minister of Defensive and Industrial Works. Lieutenant Commander Bernard Sandison, *Walker*'s torpedo officer, was Minister of Ordnance. The big Marine, Pete Alden, was General of the Army and Marines, and Tamatsu Shinya was his second in command. Lieutenant Steve Riggs was Minister of Communications and Electrical Contrivances, and Brevet Major Ben Mallory was minister for their still nonexistent Air Corps. Ben, like Bernie, was still recovering from serious wounds they'd suffered in the battle.

Adar recognized that he'd bestowed lofty-sounding titles upon them, despite the fact they each had other jobs. It was also clear that, except for "Aahd-mah-raal" Keje-Fris-Ar being Assistant Chief of Naval Operations, and a few other People in charge of agriculture, labor, etc., most of the titles belonged to destroyermen. It didn't matter. After the battle, they were so popular they could all have become kings, but they'd insisted he take the lead. No one would object. Besides, they knew best what they were doing. That being said, everyone except Matt, Sandra, and Pete were new to their "jobs," including Adar, and though he'd never had any difficulty with public speaking before, he decided to let them go first, to set the tone.

He began to call on Matt, but briefly wondered *what* to call him. "Supreme Commander of All Combined Allied Forces" seemed much too stiff and unwieldy for everyday use. Matt had refused the rank of aahd-mah-raal for reasons of his own, but even though there were other aahd-mah-raals now, and many captains, there was no question who was in charge. Adar supposed it didn't matter. There was only one Captain Matthew Reddy. That was how Adar addressed him now, summoning him to speak: "Cap-i-taan Reddy, if you please. Before we begin this discussion in earnest, what was your impression of our visitors?"

Matt appeared thoughtful for a moment. "My initial impression," he began, "was much like Chief Gray's. I thought they were a pack of arrogant jerks. In fact, the more we talked with them—with Jenks, anyway—the stronger that impression became. If I'd had time to think about it, I'm not sure I'd have let them send off a ship."

"What would you have had us do?" Bradford retorted, sensing a reprimand for his compromise. "Hold them hostage? We were not in much of a position to do that. Or were you thinking of holding the girl against her will?"

"Don't be ridiculous, Courtney. Of course not. But the girl doesn't want to go with them; she wants us to take her home. We might have used that as leverage to keep all their ships here. As it stands, they'll know about us, and where we are, long before we're ready to send an expedition to meet them."

"Do you consider them a threat?" Adar asked.

"Sure. Why not?" Matt sighed. "Mr. Chairman, I consider everyone not in this room a threat, because only these people, and those they represent, have *proven* they're not. Do I think these 'new' Brits'll swoop down like the Grik and attack as soon as they know where we are? No. Jenks acted like they had other problems besides us, although neither

Rebecca nor O'Casey seems to know what they are. Something that's sprouted up since the two of them have been gone? Maybe." Matt shrugged. "And I don't think they're a threat like the Grik, either. They certainly don't eat people, and I don't think they're much interested in our real estate. They may see us as a rival, though, which we might be soon enough." He looked down at Sandra. "To be honest, based on the technology we've seen, in the months it'll take them to get back to wherever they came from and return here with a sizable force—if that's their intent—we'll have enough of the new weapons we've planned that we'd paste them good. The thing is, they're a threat in the sense that they're a distraction. Just the possibility that they'll send a fleet is enough to pin some of our resources here and in the Philippines when we should be chasing the Grik before they catch their breath."

"No one wants to destroy the Grik more than I, but is haste truly so important?" Adar asked.

"Yes, Mr. Chairman. It's essential."

"But you won't be ready to pursue them for months. These weapons you speak of, this 'technology,' won't be ready for some time."

"True, but we can, *must*, mount *some* operations fairly quickly. And when the new stuff's online, I'd rather use it against the Grik."

Adar nodded. "It seems, then, that we have several imperatives: First, keep the pressure on the Grik; keep them off balance, as you've said. Perhaps we might accelerate the departure of our new Expeditionary Force. Second, we must treat with this Jenks and keep him satisfied that we truly are preparing an expedition to return his lost princess. Try to befriend him and avoid alienating him. Finally, once we do return the girl to her people, we must do everything we can to make friends with them, not only for the benefit of our war effort, but—and I notice you did not mention this—to alleviate the 'dame famine' that afflicts your human destroyermen." The lack of female companionship for Matt's men after an entire year had created what Silva had coined a "dame famine." In the pre-war Asiatic Fleet, it would have been considered extraordinary for the men to "do without" for a couple of weeks.

Matt shifted uncomfortably. "What you say is true, Mr. Chairman. All of it. To accomplish everything you described would be ideal. Lifting the dame famine would sure be a help, too, but I didn't want to mention it, to seem selfish. . . ."

"Nonsense. To . . . abstain as long as most of your people have is unnatural, and cannot be good for them. Rest assured, that imperative is as essential as any other, as far as I am concerned."

"Thank you, Mr. Chairman."

"Now, let us continue with how to accomplish the goals laid before us. Aahd-mah-raal Keje; what of the Navy?"

Keje rose with some difficulty. His leg was stiffening up. He should have been using a cane or something, but he'd refused. "The Navy, Mr. Chairman, doesn't exist, for all practical purposes. *Donaghey* is fit for sea, as are some of the prizes, but it will be weeks before *Tolson* can sail. The shipyards survived major damage in the fighting—I believe the enemy meant to take them intact—so the new construction is proceeding almost uninterrupted. We have abundant hardwood laid up from when we cleared the killing fields around the city. It has remained covered and is drying well. Perhaps we will complete this 'kiln' thing Mr. Brister has begun. The yards are already working around the clock"—he grinned quizzically at Matt as if wondering if he'd used the phrase appropriately—"and the keels for six more modern warships have already been laid." His grin became eager. "This technique of 'mass production,' where all the parts for each ship are made to a particular plan and any one of them will fit each ship, is truly a wonder. It speeds production amazingly."

Letts nodded. "I'm glad you approve and I'm glad it's working. We'll use the same technique for just about everything, eventually. As soon as we've settled on the various plans"—he winced—"and overcome the . . . reluctance of some of our craftsmen." He looked at Matt and explained. "We've always been amazed by Lemurian ingenuity, and their structural design techniques are beyond anything any wooden human navy ever launched, but they aren't used to blueprints. They just make 'em the way they've always made them. The quality of their craftsmanship is beyond debate, but master shipwrights dominate the shipbuilding industry and they're jealous of their status. They don't much approve of just anybody being able to look at drawings and knock something up."

"Understandable, I suppose," said Matt, "but they're going to have to get used to it." He nodded at Saan-Kakja. "The finalized plans for our first steam frigates have already been sent to Manila, but you'll probably run into some of the same problems."

Saan-Kakja bowed and replied in her almost little-girl voice, "The plans were accompanied by my personal command that they be followed to the letter. I have allowed some innovation within the design parameters, as you suggested, but there will be little variation."

"Fine," said Matt. "Don't want to stifle new ideas, but we need a lot of good ships more than we need a few perfect ones." He turned to Keje and his expression softened. "What about *Big Sal?*"

Keje frowned. "She is refloated," he grumbled. "A simple matter of pumping her out. However, the damage to her upper works was . . . extreme. Your . . . bizarre . . . idea might not only be the best means of returning her to the fight, but the single realistic one as well." He sighed. "I mourn my Home and yearn for her to be as she was, but I might as well yearn for the Grik to leave us alone of their own accord. I fear, with her conversion, our way of life will be altered forever. Will other Homes be changed as well? Will they even *be* Homes anymore, or forever become dedicated weapons of war? What of the wing clans? There is already resistance. How will I sort that out? I also confess that I find it exceedingly strange to rebuild her as a . . . conveyance for weapons that do not yet exist."

"They'll exist," Ben Mallory assured him. "It's going to take time, but there's no question we can do it. Also, knowing the way you 'Cats like gizmos, I bet there'll be less resistance than you expect."

"You've settled on a design, then?" Matt asked.

Adar watched as the conference increasingly shifted from his grasp. He didn't mind. In fact, it was as he'd hoped. Captain Reddy had been somewhat withdrawn since the loss of his ship, but the man was made for command. The situation required that someone step up and take it, and he was the best one for the job. Adar had set the policies, the goals they'd work toward; it was up to his Supreme Commander and the rest of his staff to decide how to implement those policies.

"Sir," Mallory replied, "we've come at this from every angle and run into problems with just about every design." He grinned. "I'd love to have P-40s, but that's just not going to happen. Right now, I'm leaning toward a variation of the old Navy-Curtiss, or NC, flying boats."

"Flying boats?" Matt asked, eyebrows raised. "I thought we'd decided to raze *Big Sal* to a steam-powered flattop. Use her as an aircraft carrier."

"She'll still need to be flat to carry and maybe even launch the planes—like the old *Langley*—but we'll fit her with cranes to lift the planes out of the water. See, the problem is wheels. That, and it would be nice if the aircrews could set the planes down if they're damaged. If they don't float, we're going to lose a lot of guys. Sure not going to fish many out of the drink."

"I see what you mean, but why not floats *and* wheels?"

Mallory scratched a scar under his bearded chin. "Well, believe it or not, Skipper, there's no rubber. I know, it would be all over the place around here back home, but Courtney says even then it wasn't indigenous. Whether anything like it exists somewhere else, who knows." He paused and glanced at the blank faces around him. Of course, Lemurian faces were always blank, but none of them spoke up. "Anyway, there's nothing like it here. Given enough time, we'll probably come up with a synthetic, but our refining capability just isn't that far along yet, and frankly, I don't know how." He looked at Bradford, who shook his head.

"'Fraid not. As Mr. Mallory has suggested, I know there has been some success making a synthetic rubber from petroleum, but I haven't the faintest idea how it's done."

"So in the short term," Mallory continued, "we'd be better off using rigid wheels and some sort of shock-absorbing arrangement. I still think floats are the way to go, though. At least for now." He shook his head. "Believe me, Skipper, I wish that wasn't so. Floatplanes add a lot of problems. They'll likely be bigger, heavier and slower. Payload will be less and they'll have greater power-to-weight requirements. More complicated, too. Basically, like I said, NC flying boats . . . Nancys."

Matt grimaced. "I was proud when I heard we flew those things across the Atlantic—little before my time—and *Walker* was even one of the picket ships before she joined the Asiatic Fleet. But if I recall, only one of 'em made it all the way."

"We'll make 'em better. We have stronger, lighter materials to work with. Hell, most of a British Hurricane is made of wood, and they're pretty good fighters. The toughest thing in the air might be those British medium bombers—what are they . . . or were they? Hell, I can't remember."

"Wellingtons," Bradford supplied, rolling his eyes at the young pilot.

"Right. They may be slow, but they can take punishment. They use the same kind of diagonal bracing the 'Cats use on their big ships. We can do that too. Even the engines shouldn't be too hard. We off-loaded all the machine tools from *Walker* and *Mahan* before the battle and we've been building new machines hand over fist. Maybe we can even get the lathes and stuff off *Amagi*. Then there's the submarine, with all her tools and steel—if we can salvage it. We'll make the engines of iron, but flute the cylinders to save weight. Water cooled, if we can cast the crankcases as well as I think we can . . ."

"Very well," said Matt, almost laughing. "I see you've given this some thought. Have you considered, however, that if the planes have floats and fly off a Navy ship, they can't possibly be part of the Air Corps? All the crews you train to fly them will have to be naval aviators!"

"Hey! Wait a minute!" Mallory shouted good-naturedly, but he was laughed down. They needed the humor but after a moment, Matt sobered.

"Madam Minister of Medicine?" he asked stiffly. Sandra looked up at him with a small smile for the title, but realized Matt had already begun to retreat into his funk.

"Better," she said. "We still have a lot of wounded, but I think the vast majority have turned the corner. A lot have already returned to duty"—she glared at Ben and Bernie—"although some shouldn't have. The Lemurian's polta paste continues to work miracles." She referred to an antiseptic, analgesic, viscous paste made from the still somewhat mysteriously prepared by-products of seep fermentation. Seep was a less refined version of the substance made from polta fruit and was a popular spirit and strong intoxicant. The analgesic properties were fairly straightforward, but Sandra still didn't know why it fought most infections so well. Neither did the Lemurians. They'd had no concept of germ theory when the destroyermen arrived, but they'd had the paste since before recorded history and knew it worked. Before the Squall that transported them here, Sandra had heard of experiments with a type of mold being used to fight infection. She wondered if the same principle was at work here. She didn't know and couldn't even begin to guess without a microscope, but the stuff was a lifesaver that beat sulfonamide all hollow.

"How's Mr. Garrett? And did Silva report to you like I told him?" Matt asked.

"Mr. Garrett's wounds are healing nicely; he just had so many. It's a miracle he survived. Same with Silva, but even though Mr. Garrett's unhappy just sitting around, he does behave. Silva, as you know, is less reasonable. He swooped in for a moment and let Pam Cross patch him up again, but she was going off duty and he took off with her. Frankly, I think she and Risa can make him take it easy better than I ever could." She sniffed, and while others laughed, she noticed a ghost of a smile reappear on Matt's face.

Silva's antics were as legendary as they were infamous. He'd carried on what sometimes appeared a genuine affair with Chack's own sister, Risa-Sab-At. Risa had been captain of *Salissa*'s forewing guard, but now they'd amalgamated all the various guards into fewer unified commands. She was now captain of what would become *Salissa*'s entire Marine contingent—after they'd undergone the more rigorous training required of Marines. In many ways, Risa was clearly Silva's soul mate, just as reckless and fearless and with the same warped sense of humor. The Lemurians hadn't cared about the rumors surrounding them, rumors Silva and Risa did their best to encourage—only initially—to get Chack's goat. Now, either they seemed determined to get *everyone's* goat—or the rumors weren't really rumors.

The addition of Nurse Pam Cross from Brooklyn to the ménage added a measure of disgust, as well as a grudging respect for the gunner's mate among the human destroyermen. They'd come to accept that Silva might have taken up with a "local gal," whether anything physical was involved or not. They just assumed, naturally (or unnaturally), that there was. For him to then snatch one of the only available dames did breed resentment, but it was more of a wistful "how does he do it" sort. Lurid speculation regarding how the threesome might . . . interact . . . was probably actually good for morale in a roundabout way, and none of them—Silva, Risa, or Pam—would confirm or deny anything.

Three soul mates, Matt chuckled to himself, *two of whom had to come to another world to find each other.* Well, there was nothing he could do about it. He'd once ordered Silva to quit carrying on with Risa, thereby breaking one of his own fundamental rules: Never give an order you *know* won't be obeyed. But in almost every other way, Silva had really straightened up. "Silva's been helping you with ordnance development?" Matt asked Bernard Sandison.

Bernie grimaced. "Yes, sir. When it suits him. He's hurting, I know, so I haven't pushed him yet, but some of his best work has been on 'toys' for himself."

"Do his 'toys' have practical applications?"

"Oh, yeah, but they're not exactly priority items. The man's a diabolical genius when it comes to figuring out new and better ways to kill things, and he does *love* to try them out. It's just . . . his priorities are generally more . . . tactical than strategic."

Matt allowed a genuine laugh then, at Bernie's tact. "You mean he concentrates on 'up close and personal.' Well, we need that too. Give him his head, but try to run him off for a while. He needs to heal up."

"Aye-aye, sir."

"Speaking of that, what have you come up with?"

Sandison shifted on the cushion his wounds made him use. Matt knew the young, dark-haired torpedo officer was highly motivated to please; he still blamed himself for not recognizing the—perfectly good—Mk 10 torpedo among the condemned fish they'd scrounged in Surabaya so long ago. That extra torpedo might have made a lot of difference if they'd known they had it and used it at a different time.

"Right now we're rebuilding to some degree. One of the shops took a hit from *Amagi* and it's a real mess. None of the machinery was badly damaged, thank God, but we're still getting a roof back over it. That said, we've begun to refine some of the projects we were already working on. I think I can give you guncotton, or gun . . . whatever they use for cotton around here, pretty soon. That'll give us a high explosive capability for the four-inch guns. We've already started making exploding shells with a black powder bursting charge, like the ones they used in the last war. Not as good, but . . ." He paused when he saw the captain's grim expression. The only four-inch guns they had were on *Walker*—underwater. They'd salvage the guns, certainly, and maybe the one on the submarine, but they wouldn't know if they could salvage the ship until she was dry. "Anyway," he continued softly, "I wouldn't recommend using it for a propellant charge until we've had a lot more practice with the stuff. Better stick with ordinary gunpowder for now. Same goes for small arms. We just about shot ourselves dry, I'm afraid, and black powder won't work worth a hoot in the automatic weapons. At least not the BARs, thirties and fifties. They gum up too fast.

"That brings up another problem: brass. I've got brass pickers combing everywhere looking for spent shell casings. We're okay on the four-inch guns, and the shells for those are big enough to turn more on a lathe, but we'll have to extrude small-arms brass and . . . I really just don't know how. We can reload what we've got; make it work pretty well, in fact. Before we lost power, we made molds and swages for thirty-, forty-five-, and fifty-cal with grease grooves. We can make bullets out of solid copper, tin, or lead with a gas check of some kind, so they'll work with the fast-twist rifling. Lubed copper bullets work fine in the Springfields and Krags with a slow rate of fire. You can use 'em in the Thompsons and the 1911s too, but they get really filthy. And like I said, when the brass is gone, it's gone—unless we can figure out how to make more."

"I knew about all that stuff," Matt said, "and we'll see what we can do about power. Mr. Riggs, I'll get to you directly. But what about other stuff, Bernie? The 'new' weapons you mentioned?"

"Yes, sir. Personally, I'd love to have torpedoes, but that's going to take a while longer. We've still got the propulsion body of the condemned torp with the crumpled warhead and we're reverse-engineering that, but the precision required . . ." He sighed. "We're just not there yet."

"What can you give me?"

"Exploding four-inch shells and bombs, sir. Lots and lots of bombs. Pretty powerful ones too, eventually—if the guncotton works like I expect." He glanced at Mallory. "I know the bigger ones might not do us a lot of good until we have something to drop them from, but when we do—"

"Don't build them before I find out how much weight the planes'll carry!" interrupted Ben.

"Don't worry." Bernie grinned. "We're working on little ones first, like mortar bombs. In fact, that's what they are." He nodded at Alden. "Pete— the General—and Campeti came up with the idea. Real mortars—the 'drop and pop' kind. Way safer, lighter, deadlier, and with a lot longer range than the ones we've been using. No reason you couldn't drop 'em from an airplane, though."

"Very good," Matt complimented him, "but that still leaves us, in the short term, with a dwindling number of small arms when what I want is more."

"Yes, sir. I'm afraid our best short-term option is still a musket of some kind, like you said. That's one of the things Silva's been fiddling with, although his idea of a musket—"

Matt interrupted. "But I've also said I'm not sure muskets really give us much advantage."

Pete Alden spoke up. "Skipper, I think they will. You're worried about arrows reloading faster and being about as accurate. Normally, that would be true. You're also thinking they're not much advantage over what we've got, but what about the enemy? They don't use longbows. I don't think they can. They're just not built for them, so they're stuck with crossbows, which take about as long to load as a musket and they're not as deadly. Besides, they'll be an improvement in another respect: right now, all our spearmen have to carry a longbow as well. Once they have muskets, with socket bayonets, they can shoot and stick with the same weapon. There might also be a psychological effect on the enemy. Maybe they'll flip and go into one of Bradford's 'Grik rout' fits after a single volley. I'm not counting on it, but they *will* be better than what we've got. As to the accuracy issue, as lame as our industry is right now, that's going to improve. We can already make the barrels much better than they did in the seventeen hundreds, and eventually, smoothbores can be rifled. . . ."

Matt was nodding. "I see what you mean, Mr. Alden. Very well. You're the infantryman and I'll defer to your judgment. I guess we have to be prepared to backtrack a bit before we can leap ahead. At least see what you can do about preparing for simple breechloaders, if you can." He took a breath and looked at Bernie, decision made. "For now, if muskets are what we can do, that's what we'll do." He paused for a moment and glanced uncomfortably around the chamber. "What about . . . that other thing we talked about?"

Sandra gave him a stormy look, but remained silent. She'd clearly already stated her opinion.

Bernie's eyebrows knitted. "You mean . . . the gas?" Matt nodded and Sandison frowned, glancing at Tamatsu Shinya. He sighed. "Making the stuff isn't that big a deal. Mustard or chlorine is dangerous, but not hard. The problem is dispersal—and dispersing it far enough away from *us*, but close enough to the enemy. Wind would always be a factor." He hesitated. "Some may not be all that concerned about ethical issues, as far as the Grik—"

"*I* am concerned about the ethics of such weapons," Shinya interrupted sharply.

Matt looked at him and shook his head. When he spoke, his voice was quiet. "Believe it or not, Colonel Shinya, so am I. So is everyone here. Maybe not for the sake of the Grik, really; I wish God would stomp them all like bugs, but gas is just *wrong*. Using the stuff would take us and our friends to a level almost as bad as the Grik—a level I don't want to be on and I don't want our Lemurian allies to ever see." He took a breath before continuing, now directing his words primarily at Adar, who'd shown an interest in the "wonder weapon." "Gas kills everything. Indiscriminately . . . horribly. It'll kill animals, Grik, 'Cat prisoners—and any of Shinya's people who might be working for the Grik under duress. I *will not* gas 'Cats or men—even Japs who *aren't* working for the enemy against their will."

Matt rubbed his eyebrows. "I know it may be hard for you to understand, Mr. Chairman, but I grew up around guys who somehow survived gas attacks in the Great War and . . . well, 'survived' isn't the best way to put it; 'lingered in misery' is probably better, and they only got a little of the stuff. Honest to God, much as I hate them, it would turn my stomach to gas even the Grik. I'd rather burn them alive. We're going to have to think about this a lot more."

The chamber grew quiet for a moment and Adar was genuinely taken aback by the intensity of Matt's evident revulsion toward what seemed, by description, such an effective and efficient weapon.

"Moral issues aside," Matt continued soberly, "even if we made gas and solved all the problems with delivering it, how do we protect our troops? Unfortunately, we *do* have to think about it and we *do* have to solve that problem, at least. Does anyone honestly think this Kurokawa wouldn't give gas to the Grik if he thought it would benefit him? He's helped them in every other way. Like Ben said, we don't have any rubber, and even if we did, how do you make a gas mask for a Lemurian?" Matt shook his head. "There's no Geneva Convention on this world, governing this war, but we have to decide right now that if we *ever* make gas, it won't be used willy-nilly. Won't be used *at all* unless we're in a jam so tight we don't have any choice." He shrugged and Sandra grasped his hand. He looked at Adar. "That's how I feel, and that's the deal."

Adar said nothing. He had no choice but to agree, but he was perplexed. Clearly, Captain Reddy was extremely sensitive about the subject; all the humans seemed to be. Gas must be a terrible weapon indeed if one was willing to sacrifice the lives of one's own troops to avoid using it.

"We don't even know if Kurokawa and any other Japs are left," said Captain Ellis, speaking for the first time. He'd been Matt's exec on *Walker* before the Squall and had commanded *Mahan* on her suicidal dash. He was currently without a ship, but he was one of Matt's best friends, and Matt was always interested in what he had to say. "We know the Grik 'rescued' a lot of survivors off *Amagi*," he continued, "but they might have eaten them, for all we know."

"Perhaps they did," Shinya grudgingly admitted, saddened by the possibility, but glad they'd changed the subject. "Our prisoner thinks otherwise however." He referred to Commander Sato Okada, the lone survivor the Allies had taken into custody. Matt still hadn't talked to the new Jap directly; he'd been too busy. It was probably time he did, but he honestly wasn't sure how to approach the interview. Shinya had spoken with the prisoner at length and the man was a font of information about Captain Hisashi Kurokawa and the Grik—he hated them passionately and yearned for their destruction—yet unlike Shinya, Okada hadn't put the "old war" behind him. He'd been willing to cooperate with the Americans against the Grik, and if he'd been able to arrange such cooperation before *Amagi* was destroyed, he would have. That didn't mean he was willing to *ally* himself with the enemies of his emperor. Wounded by Kurokawa in the battle, he'd hidden from the Grik "rescuers" and allowed himself to be taken by the Americans and their allies for the sole purpose of supplying information about their common enemies: the Grik—and Kurokawa. Beyond that, as a Japanese officer and a prisoner of war, he had no other reason to live.

Shinya continued. "Okada says this Regent-Consort Tsalka, and their General Esshk are different from other Grik. They may have taken the lesson of their defeat to heart. He believes if they themselves are not killed for their failure, they will try to preserve as many Japanese as they can to help prepare for . . . well, what we are preparing for: our next meeting." He looked at Matt somewhat accusingly. "As Captain Reddy knows, there was a minority faction aboard *Amagi* already . . . frustrated with Kurokawa's command in general, and his association with the Grik in particular."

Matt nodded at Shinya, accepting blame for not telling him he knew some of *Amagi*'s crew were unwilling to aid the Grik. But it hadn't made any difference in the end, as he'd known it wouldn't. With *Amagi* coming for them, they couldn't pick and choose those aboard her they might kill. Shinya knew that, and he also knew that, by not telling him, the captain had been sparing Shinya's own conscience. Nevertheless, his point was sound and heartfelt.

Matt cleared his throat and turned to Riggs. "Now, Mr. Riggs, all these grandiose schemes depend on power. What have you got for us?"

"Simple reciprocating steam engines, Skipper, just like we're planning for the ships, but dedicated to powering generators. Nothing very difficult about building the generators; we still have plenty of copper and there's more coming in. People here already knew how to make wire, even if it wasn't for carrying current. It was mostly for structural reinforcement or ornamentation. We're standardizing most things on one-twenty DC, just like the ship. Nearly everything we have runs off that. We're also going to have to at least wash out *Walker*'s generators when we get them up so we should make new ones as much like hers as we can. We have all the specs, and it's always nice to have spares! The ship's generators are little guys, though, twenty-five kilowatts, about the size of a car engine and transmission. We might need bigger stuff eventually. We'll need some steel, too."

Matt grimaced. "Plenty of steel in the bay," he said, referring to *Amagi*. As soon as *Humfra-Dar* and *Aracca* had returned, they'd moored beside the sunken battle cruiser and begun stripping her exposed upper works. *Amagi* rested in about sixty feet of water, and the eventual plan was to flood down four of the mammoth Homes to build a cofferdam around her. Then they could retrieve the entire ship, piece by piece. Matt didn't even want to contemplate the stresses involved in holding back sixty feet of water, but the Lemurians assured him their ships could take it. Commander Brad "Spanky" McFarlane, *Walker*'s engineering officer, and now chief naval engineer for the Alliance, was convinced they could do it. A lot depended on where *Amagi*'s bow had come to rest after breaking away, however. They were fairly certain it was "inside the box," but there was probably other heavy wreckage scattered on the bottom. If one of the Lemurian Homes flooded down on top of any of it, it might cause serious damage.

"Okay," resumed Matt, "but that brings up another issue. Acetylene. We removed all the oxygen and acetylene bottles from *Walker* and *Mahan* before the . . . last battle, but with all the repairs we'd made, we're just about dry. We need more, lots more, to break *Amagi*, not to mention repairing *Walker* . . . if she can be salvaged."

"Never fear, Captain," proclaimed Bradford cheerfully. "I may know little about synthetic rubber, but acetylene has been around for a hundred years! Quite simple, really."

Matt inwardly groaned. What was "quite simple" to Bradford in theory was rarely as easy in practice as he made it sound. "How do we make it?" he asked guardedly.

"Well, acetylene gas is the natural result of combining water with calcium carbide! It can be safely stored in acetone."

"Okay, where do we get the calcium carbide and acetone?"

"Calcium carbide is made by baking limestone with other easily obtainable ores at extremely high temperatures—I understand an electrical arc furnace is best."

"An electrical arc furnace?" Matt repeated. He looked at Riggs. "*Big* generators."

"Indeed," agreed Bradford. "But the result will be abundant calcium carbide, which we can use for other projects as well—desulfurization of iron, for example, once we get around to making our own. Acetone can be made by distilling wood. We have quite a lot of that, but it is a wasteful process. During the last war, it was made with corn to produce vast quantities. Perhaps we can find some local flora with similar properties. We still need ethyl alcohol anyway, to improve the quality of our gasoline, since tetraethyl lead is certainly out of the question for the foreseeable future!"

"Why do we need 'vast quantities'?" Riggs asked, and Bradford looked at him with astonished eyes.

"Why, if we are ever to make genuine cordite propellants, we must have acetone!"

Matt sighed. "Okay. Letts? Get with Mr. Bradford and Labor and decide what you're going to need." He looked back at Riggs. "That leaves communications, and if we're going to have to cross the whole damn Pacific, or Eastern Sea, to take the young princess home, we'll need sonar, or some other acoustic mountain fish discourager."

They'd found active sonar was the best way to deter the gigantic ship-destroying monsters, or mountain fish, that dwelt exclusively in deep water.

"I don't have anything to tell you on the sonar yet, Skipper, but communications is looking up. We still have all of *Walker*'s radio equipment, and, as you know, I'd already built a decent transmitter here after the Japs bombed our other one. We just didn't have the power to run it. We've begun mass production of even better crystal receivers too. Right now, I'm drawing up plans for a simple, powerful, portable spark-gap transmitter based on a surplus Army Air Corps set I picked up when I was a kid. It was a BC-15A, made in 1918 for airplanes, believe it or not. No tubes or anything really complicated. The only problem with it was that it was pretty . . . broadband . . . as in, all-band. My folks used to get mad as hell when I'd play with it when they were trying to listen to the radio."

Matt laughed. "That's not going to be a problem here. Even if the Japs still have a receiver, we'll be transmitting everything in code. Good work. I guess that still just leaves us with power—power to make the things that make power, I mean."

"Yes, sir. No fast-moving water or anything so, at first, I guess we keep using the method the Mice cooked up. The 'brontosaurus merry-go-round.'"

"Right." Matt glanced at the precious watch on his wrist, then looked at Adar—almost apologetically, it seemed—as if he regretted taking over the meeting. "I guess that's it then. Mr. Chairman, do you have anything to add before our guests are shown in?"

"Nothing for now. I do so enjoy having a plan. Let us speak with these Brits, as you call them, and discover whether anything we learn from them conflicts with our own priorities. I may have something to offer then."

As always, Matt was happy to be back on the water. He sat comfortably in the stern sheets of Scott's launch with Sandra Tucker snuggled tight against him, companionably quiet, ostensibly shielding herself from the occasional packets of spray with his larger form. Her mere proximity seemed sufficient to infuse him with a sense of well-being and optimism that was sometimes so elusive when he was alone with his thoughts. The launch moved through the light chop and the engine burbled contentedly while Matt gazed about the bay, memories of the battle still fresh in his mind. For once, the company and the quality of the day eased the pain those memories brought. His eyes lingered a moment on the two Imperial frigates moored near the fishing wharfs and he felt a twinge.

The Imperial liberty parties had generally behaved themselves, but there had been some incidents. Matt often met with Commodore Jenks, but their discussions were always short and to the point and Jenks invariably asked the same questions: "How much longer must we wait?" and "What progress have you made toward outfitting an expedition to return the princess to her home?" Matt's answers were always the same as well: "Not much longer," and "Quite a bit." The answers were lame and he knew Jenks knew it too. Sometimes Matt got the impression Jenks didn't *expect* a different answer and he asked only so they'd have something to argue about. He was a weird duck and Matt couldn't figure him out. He chased Jenks out of his thoughts and concentrated on enjoying himself.

Sandra was pleased on a variety of levels. She was glad she and Matt no longer had to hide their feelings. She remained convinced it had been the right thing to do, but their ultimately futile attempt to conceal their attraction had added even more stress to their situation. Now, even though their public courtship remained strictly correct, the feel of his large hand unobtrusively enfolding hers seemed comforting and natural. It was amazing how restorative such simple, innocent pleasures could be. The day had a lot to do with her mood as well—their situation always seemed less grim when the sky didn't brood—but she was also pleased with the progress one of her patients was making.

Norman Kutas, quartermaster's mate, was the coxswain today. After the battle, she wouldn't have given odds he'd ever even see again, much less handle a boat. He'd taken a faceful of glass fragments on *Walker*'s bridge, and though she'd worked extra hard to get them all out, the damage had frightened her. But Norm was tough and his eyes were were still intact. Norman would be scarred for life, and those scars were still pink and angry, but he could see. It bothered her that she hadn't been able to save Silva's eye, but in his case there hadn't been anything left to save. At least his empty socket was healing well. Once again she'd been amazed by the healing powers of the Lemurian polta paste.

Courtney Bradford, Jim Ellis, Spanky, and the Bosun were in the boat as well, but they seemed equally charmed by the pleasant day. Either they just weren't inclined to speak, or they were allowing Sandra to treat her most important patient for a while in the best way she could at present. By mutual consent, apparently, all the men knew that a day on the water with his girl was a dose their skipper needed.

Inevitably, however, someone had to break the silence. They were in the boat for another reason too, after all. Just as inevitably, that person was Courtney Bradford.

"I say!" he practically shouted over the noise of the engine, "the military equipment is all well and good, but have they managed to salvage anything *interesting* at all?" he asked. He'd turned to face Matt and had to hold his ridiculous hat on his head with both hands.

Matt shrugged. "Not sure what you mean by 'interesting,' Courtney, but they haven't gotten far into the hull yet. No telling what's in there. We'll see." Bradford turned back to face their destination. Not far away now, the huge pagodalike structures of four Homes protruded from the sea, as if the massive vessels had sunk there in a square. The tripod masts were bare, and massive booms lifted objects seemingly from beneath the sea between them. Matt knew the Homes *were* sunk—in a sense—having flooded themselves down to within thirty or forty feet of their bulwarks. As they drew closer, they saw there was still more freeboard than Matt's old destroyer ever had when fully buoyant. Courtney's question had ruined the moment, but not in an entirely adverse way. They were all anxious to see what had been revealed within the cofferdam formed by the Homes. At last, they'd see what was left of *Amagi*.

Kutas throttled back and the launch gently bumped *Aracca*'s side. Cargo netting of a sort hung down from above and they carefully exited the boat and climbed to the deck. Tassana, High Chief of *Aracca* Home, greeted them with a formal side party and full honors as they'd evolved among the Lemurians that were technically independent of Navy regulations. Her short, silken, gray-black fur glowed with the luster of healthy youth, and around her neck hung the green-tinted copper torque of her office. Her father had been High Chief of *Nerracca*, and when that Home was brutally destroyed by *Amagi*, she became a ward of her grandfather, the High Chief of *Aracca*. She was also his only remaining heir. When he died in the Battle of Baalkpan, she was elevated—at the tender age of twelve—to take his place. Lemurians matured more quickly than humans, but she was still considered a youngling even by her own people. She'd been through an awful lot and was clearly aware she had much to live up to, but Matt suspected she'd do all right. Her father's blood ran in her veins and she had a spine of steel. She also had a lot of help. Keje had practically adopted her, and a better tutor in seamanship and command didn't exist. Already, Keje loved the tragic child as his own, and Tassana adored him as well. In fact, she had quite a serious case of hero worship for just about everyone present, since they'd all been instrumental in avenging the death of her kin.

As always when he stepped aboard one of the enormous seagoing cities of the Lemurians, an awesome sight greeted Matt. The main deck, with the polta fruit gardens lining the bulwark, was normally a hundred feet above the sea, and three huge pagodalike "apartments" towered above it like skyscrapers. The massive tripods that supported the great sails or "wings" soared another two hundred and fifty feet above the deck. Larger than the new *Essex*-class aircraft carriers Matt had glimpsed under construction so long ago, *Aracca* was double-ended, flat-bottomed, and built of diagonally plank-laminated wood that was six feet thick in places. He was always impressed by the incredibly tough, sophisticated design that ensured that she and others like her would last for centuries upon this world's more hostile seas. Looking at *Aracca*, he couldn't imagine any natural force overcoming her. He vividly remembered how vulnerable her daughter Home, *Nerracca*, had been to ten-inch naval rifles, however.

After the ceremonial greeting, the youngling High Chief embraced Matt. He knew she felt great affection for him and he certainly returned it, but hers always made him feel a little awkward. He couldn't convince himself he deserved it. Tassana hugged Sandra next, then Spanky and Courtney. Kutas had stayed with the boat.

"Good morning, my dear!" Courtney said, pecking the High Chief's furry cheek. "We have come to view your progress firsthand! Judging by the increasing quantities of scrap arriving at the shipyard, you must be proceeding beyond our dreams!"

"It goes well," Tassana admitted with a touch of pride. She had the support and assistance of the vastly more experienced High Chiefs of the other Homes, but she was essentially in charge of the project.

"Anybody hurt today?" Sandra asked solicitously.

"A few, not serious. Torch burns, most. The new 'a . . . aa-set-aaleen' does not, ah, reg . . . reg-ulate the same as old, and of course we no have gay-ges for new torches either."

"It takes a little trial and error, I'm afraid," Courtney commiserated. Raw materials had been their very first priority, so fulfilling their need for more acetylene had dominated all other concerns for a while. The first large steam-powered generator was devoted entirely to the new furnace for cooking limestone, and the stuff was coming in from everywhere. Great, billowing white clouds arose from the crushing grounds near the shipyard, and workers emerged from a day's labor resembling long-tailed spooks. A still for the acetone was much easier to manage, but just as hard to feed. The volatile liquid resulting from the process also tended to evaporate as quickly as it was made, negating tremendous labor, so the quality control required for the combination and compression of the gas was a little haphazard. Courtney had taken personal charge of the project, with Letts's logistical assistance, so he felt a little responsible for each injury sustained.

"The burns not serious," Tassana thoughtfully assured him.

"I'm glad to hear it," Matt said, a little impatient to see the work. "Mind if we take a look?"

"'Course not." Tassana led them up a long stair from the catwalk above the polta garden to the amidships battlement platform above. They strode across it to starboard and peered down over the rail. The view they beheld was amazing and terrible, like something from Dante's *Inferno*. The water level within the cofferdam was considerably lower than that outside, and pumps heaved great geysers into the bay. The main portion of *Amagi* had actually settled atop her own ampu-tated bow, and the scene of tangled, twisted wreckage and destruction was horrifying in a visceral way. The once mighty ship lay exposed down below her main deck and was still quite recognizable, but great arcs of molten steel jetted away from dozens of torches, spewing into the sea and causing a haze of steam to linger in the basin. Heavy booms lifted rusty, unrecognizable chunks, and even small structures. They heaved them across the expansive decks of the Homes and placed them on barges alongside.

"Goddamn," muttered Spanky around his perpetual wad of yel-lowish Lemurian tobacco leaves. "'Scuse me ladies, but . . . goddamn. Looks like Mare Island down there. Upside down or inside out—whatever—but damned impressive." He looked at Tassana, the usual fond expression he bestowed upon her mingled with respect. "I'm impressed," he repeated. "Keje said you could do it, that I should worry 'bout other stuff, but you know, I admit I was a little skeptical. I had a chief when I was a kid who helped cofferdam the *Maine*, to refloat her, and he told me about it. That was a hell of a job—but this!" He gestured around. "The *Maine* was a rowboat compared to *Amagi*."

"You proud?" Tassana asked eagerly.

"You betcha. You're going to get a lot of leakage, and I'm not sure how you'll manage to get her bottom up, but it looks great so far."

"There already leakage," Tassana admitted, "but pumps stay ahead. Also, when we get to bottom, we sink holes to pump with you hoses. We get bottom."

Spanky shook his head. "I bet you will."

Gray was watching the workers. Now that they weren't on a moving boat, the day had turned hot, and with all the steam . . . "Poor devils down there must be boilin'," he said.

"It . . . uncomfortable," Tassana agreed, "but I go down much . . . The workers . . . cheerful, yes? They cheerful knowing steel they bring up will kill Grik." She grinned. "Some would like to bring up whole ship."

"That might make salvage more convenient," Matt said, "having her closer to the shipyard. But it would take years to fix her. She's torn in half, and that doesn't even count all the damage she took before she got here. And everything on her is just so damn big! We still don't even have cranes remotely big enough to lift her guns."

"Prob'ly have to cut 'em up," Spanky lamented.

Matt shook his head. "I'd rather have her steel now than maybe have *her* a few years from now." He didn't add that they'd need some of that steel to restore his own ship—if it could be done—but Sandra heard it in his voice.

They lapsed into silence for a while, just staring at the monumental undertaking below. There must have been five hundred 'Cat workers on the wreck, cutting, unbolting, swinging heavy sledges, and dragging loose objects to convenient locations for the booms to reach. Their old nemesis resembled nothing as much as a murdered beetle on an ant mound being dismantled, ever so slowly, by the proud but remorseless mandibles of its killers.

Matt shook the thought away. Any sailor hated the breaking yard, but he would *not* attach any sentimentality to that . . . monstrosity that had tormented his dreams and threatened the existence of everything he loved on this world for over a year. He knew *Amagi* herself was not to blame; Captain Kurokawa and the Grik had wielded the weapon she'd been. Still, she'd embodied the threat they posed, and he enjoyed the irony that he and his people would now use her against her former masters. She'd been a scourge, but now she was a precious gift. She wasn't given willingly or received without great cost, but her corpse would provide the bones to which they could attach the sinews of modern war. She'd been the ultimate weapon of the Grik and the Japanese on this world. Now she would help destroy them.

Sandra had noticed the range of expressions that crossed Matt's face. Some she recognized and her heart went out to him. A few confused her. The strange smile that replaced them all left a chill in her bones.

Dean Laney, former chief machinist's mate aboard USS *Walker*, winced and shifted uncomfortably on his stool. Damn, his ass hurt! It had started bugging him a lot lately, and now he had an intermittent case of the screamers, which only aggravated the problem. He sipped his coffee, or "monkey joe," and gazed around. Large, crude machinery hummed, rattled, and roared loudly all around him. The chassis and casings were mostly copper or brass, but some were even made of wood. Only bearings, shafts, chucks, and tool heads were made of real, precious steel, although more and more iron parts and castings were coming from the foundries. Over his head, high in the ceiling beams, leather belts whooped and whirled and spun in all directions around a precarious clockwork of rattling wooden pulleys of various sizes. Having all that motion right over his head sometimes gave him the creeps, but usually he was able to ignore it.

He didn't know what his rank was anymore. Everybody had been getting fancy-sounding promotions, but if he had a new title, word hadn't leaked down to him yet. It didn't really matter, he supposed. It wasn't like he'd get a raise in pay. Besides, his domain had certainly been enlarged. Instead of *Walker*'s cramped engineering spaces and modest machine shop, he now oversaw a sprawling, impressive industrial complex. Three long buildings and hundreds of workers were under his direct supervision, and he was responsible for turning out the machines that would make other machines that would ultimately go to the various project directors.

It wasn't as much fun as what Bernie, Ben, and Spanky were doing—making all sorts of swell stuff to use directly against the lizards—but they couldn't do their thing unless he did his. Besides, he never really was a "tight tolerance" guy, he admitted, and the majority of the machines that made machines could be relatively crude.

His wandering eyes fell on a 'Cat machinist almost in front of him. "Hey, you," he grumbled loudly, "watch what the hell you're doing!"

The 'Cat stopped turning the traverse handle, and the coils of brass that had been crawling away from the shaft she was turning abruptly sprang away to join the growing pile around her feet. "What I doing?" she demanded.

Caught off guard, Laney was stumped. Usually, his gruff comments went unanswered. He felt it was his duty to make them periodically to keep the workers on their toes. His face turned red and he stood up—making his ass hurt even more. "You mean you don't *know* what you're doing?" he demanded hotly, questing with his eyes for some fault.

"I know what I doing," came a shockingly abrasive retort. "Do you?"

"Why you . . . ! Just look! Look at all that shit coiled around your feet! It looks like a goddamn tumbleweed! What if that chuck snatches it up? It'll yank you in by the tail and all there'll be is a cloud of fuzz! Who the hell taught you to be a machinist's mate?!"

"Dennis Si-vaa! He teach me good! He make weapons to kill Grik, not stand around all day making big pole less big!"

Laney's eyes bulged. "Silva?! Why, that big malingering ape couldn't machine a proper turd with his ass!" Inwardly, Laney blanched at his own comment. Lately, he literally couldn't do that himself. He forged ahead. "I want you to slip the belt on that machine this goddamn minute, find your chief, and tell him you want to learn how to be a *real* machinist!"

Dean was so intent on his harangue that he didn't hear the sudden *snap-hack!* or the shrill, warning cries of alarm. He *kind* of heard the dull, buzzing *whoosh!* of the broken belt that slapped him on the back of the head.

He was still mad when he woke up in an aid station sometime later, but couldn't remember why. He felt like he'd jumped off a roof head-first, though.

"Whadami doin' here?" he mumbled. When no answer was immediately forthcoming, he closed his eyes and raised his voice. "Hey, goddamn it! Why am I here?"

"Shut up!" came a harsh, heavenly, female voice. "You want to wake everybody up? Besides, you might burst a vessel!"

Laney opened his eyes and saw Nurse Ensign Kathy McCoy hovering over him.

"It's an angel!" he said wonderingly.

"Nope." Kathy laughed. "Just me."

"You're an angel, all right," muttered Laney, "and there's damn few of you. Scarcer than the kind with wings, I bet. You danced with me a couple o' times at the Busted Screw."

Kathy grimaced. "Yeah. I try to dance with all the fellas. I'd never forget you, though." Laney's eyes went wide and he beamed. "You stomped all over my feet," Kathy explained. "I haven't walked right since."

Destroyed, Laney uttered a groan.

"Head hurt?"

"Yeah. Who hit me? One of those chickenshit monkeys I have to put up with?"

Kathy frowned. "Not who, what. One of those leather belts that runs your machines broke. Conked you pretty good. Didn't break the skin, but you'll have a goose egg the size of a baseball. You guys ought to be wearing helmets in there."

"Mmm. Ought to be doing lots of stuff. We do what we can."

"Yeah. Hey, you hurt anywhere else? You've been squirming around like a worm on a hook, even in your sleep. By the way, now that you're awake, you need to stay that way for a while in case of concussion."

Laney nodded—painfully—but hesitated.

"What? You *are* hurting somewhere else. Where?" Kathy demanded.

"I'd, uh, rather not say. I'm fine."

Kathy nodded. She easily recognized the code words for "I'm not telling a broad about my private agonies." "Okay, without telling me *what* hurts, tell me what it *feels* like."

"Like I'm shitting busted glass!" Laney blurted, then caught himself. "Hey! You tricked me!"

"It's my job," Kathy said. "And it was easy. I won't even ask to do an exam, and I don't really want to. But judging by your physique, your complaint, and your job, I bet you spend a lot of time sitting, right?" Reluctantly, and somewhat indignantly, Laney nodded. "Just as I thought. Hemorrhoids. Piles. You know."

Laney shook his head. "Piles! That can't be it. Sometimes I think I'm gonna die! You can't die from piles . . . can you?"

Kathy almost laughed, but shook her head. "No, and I'll give you something that ought to help, at least a little . . . on one condition."

Laney's eyes narrowed. "Doctors ain't supposed to put conditions on helping folks, are they?"

Kathy shrugged. "Maybe I'm a doctor here, but I'm just a nurse back home. I can do what I want."

"What's the scam?"

"Tell you what. I get a lot of guys—'Cats—in here who work for you. Just like you, they get hurt now and then. Anyway, they're doing important work and they're proud of that. Some would rather be doing something else, and I understand, but your division, or whatever it is, is just as critical as any other—maybe more so—and they know it. They don't mind the work or the hours or even getting hurt, but nearly everyone I see—though anxious to get back to work—is *not* anxious to get back to work for *you*. You're a jerk, Dean. Right now you're a hurt jerk, so I'm trying to be nice. What it boils down to, the 'scam,' I guess, is this: promise to *try* to quit being such a pain in the ass, or I'll let your 'pain in the ass' keep reminding you how you make everybody around you feel. Deal?"

*   *   *

Chief Electrician's Mate "Ronson" Rodriguez heard the exchange between Ensign McCoy and Laney through the thin reed screen that separated them. He'd come in to get his hand fixed after he'd cut it on some of the sharp Lemurian copper wire. Now stitched, disinfected, and bandaged up, he'd been taking his ease for a few moments away from the "powerhouse," the factory he'd been put in charge of where they built, refurbished, and experimented on the various electrical contrivances Riggs was in charge of. The problem was, that stupid ox Laney was always cruising through his shop looking for deserters. Rodriguez knew Laney resented him as a jumped-up electricians' mate third class, and thought he could toss him around with his size and personality. He was wrong.

Ronson might have let him get away with it once, but a lot of things had changed besides relative ratings. Rodriguez had been wounded in action far more often than Laney, and besides Laney's genuinely impressive underwater adventures, Rodriguez had seen a lot bigger "elephants" than the chief machinist's mate. His most recent escapade was the one that finally earned him a nickname. His first name was Rolando, and his shipmates had tried to tag him with "Rolo," "Rodent," and even "Rhonda," but none ever stuck. When *Walker* took that Jap shell in her auxiliary fuel tank in the forward fireroom, somehow Rolando's sweatband and longish hair had caught fire. Silva put him out, but the mental image of him running around on the amidships gun platform like a lit match had left him with "Ronson" Rodriguez, and this time it took.

Since then, he kept his head shaved to his slightly scarred scalp and the only hair he cultivated was a Pancho Villa mustache. The men were allowed trimmed beards and razors were scarce, but the chiefs were allowed a little more leeway by everybody, captain to Lemurian cadet, because in most cases, they'd earned their stripes the hard way. All of *Walker*'s and *Mahan*'s chiefs who hadn't gone to other ships had filled dead men's shoes except Campeti—and the Bosun, of course—but Rodriguez didn't think Laney filled Harvey Donaghey's very well. If Laney felt the same way about him, he could eat turds and chew slow.

The arguments they had over Laney's "defectors" always escalated to bellows of rage and interfered with work in the powerhouse. Laney did know better than to take a swing, and the contention between them always had to be taken to Riggs or Spanky—more lost work in both departments. Riggs and Spanky tried to be fair, but if Laney really needed the deserter in question, the poor bastard got sent back. Rodriguez suspected the two officers were getting as tired of the situation as Rodriguez was, and Laney was probably out on a cracking plank. He wondered whether Kathy McCoy's comments would do any good.

Well, with that bump on his head, Laney would probably leave him alone for the rest of the day, anyway. Time to quit malingering. He stood up from the chair he'd been sitting on, cradling his wounded hand. The throbbing had nearly passed. Neat stuff, that pasty goo, he reflected. Not waiting to be released by the nurse, he ducked out of the aid station and headed back for the powerhouse.

He trudged through the muck of the recent rain and avoided the heavy carts pulled by bawling brontosarries until he saw the smoke rising from "his" boiler. Several 'Cats tended the beast, and it shimmered with heat and suppressed energy. The engine it powered was one of the first they'd built, and it wheezed and blew steam from its eroded and imperfectly packed pistons. He hated the engine and wanted another one, but he had to respect it as well. It had been a prototype, crudely built and not expected to last, but here it was, still chugging away after, well, *thousands* of hours. The generator it turned was also one of their first and he was proud of it. He'd designed it himself, and it was doing fine. Laney's shop had actually made the transmission gears that boosted the RPMs of the slow-turning engine to spin the generator fast enough to provide the calculated voltage, but Laney probably didn't do it himself.

"Silly, useless bastard," he muttered, and opened the fabric flap that covered the entrance to his domain.

"How you hand?" asked one of his new strikers solicitously. Rodriguez didn't remember the 'Cat's name. It was unpronounceable and he hadn't earned a nickname yet, but he'd been one of the deserters he'd succeeded in keeping. The kid was working on one of their simplest products: thermocouples for the vast variety of temperature gauges everybody was screaming for. Essentially all he had to do was join a piece of copper to a piece of iron. When heat was applied to the joint, current was produced. The higher the heat, the more current. The reason he got to keep *this* 'Cat was that when he was trying to explain intangible, invisible free electrons, the little guy actually seemed to understand. He had high hopes for him.

Lemurians in general were almost naturally mechanically inclined and great with practical geometry. They were accomplished jokesters and pranksters and could conceptualize common hypothetical outcomes. They loved gizmos, and if they could *see* something, they could understand it without much trouble. They were very literal-minded, though. When it came to things they couldn't see—like electricity—or even hypothetical outcomes they had no experience with, they had more trouble. He'd been forced to set up a few grade-school demonstrations to let them *see* electricity before he could convince them it was real. He also let them *feel* a little now and then, but had to caution them very carefully about feeling too much of it! He still wasn't sure how much most of his 'Cat electrician's mates and strikers really grasped, but they knew they had to make gizmos to create and harness the semimythical electricity, and they were good about scrupulously following safety regulations. The fact that he'd threatened to give them to Laney if they goofed around with the juice probably helped in that regard.

He waved his bandaged hand at the 'Cat with the unpronounceable name and moved along. He wanted to check on the progress of the portable DC generators they'd been working on when he hurt himself. He was surprised to find Steve Riggs waiting for him at the benches they'd set aside to assemble the things.

"Mr. Riggs! Good to see you, sir."

Steve laughed. "You mean it's good to see me without Laney for a change. Otherwise, you're probably wondering what I'm doing here, getting in the way."

"Well, yes, sir."

"How's the hand?"

Rodriguez raised his hand and flexed the fingers in the bandage. "Fine."

"Good. Look, I really don't mean to pester you, but these transmitters we're putting together are pretty simple affairs. They don't have tubes and their voltage requirements are somewhat critical. I just wanted to see for myself how you're coming along."

"Fair enough." Rodriguez motioned him to a bench where several 'Cats were cleaning up a stack of short, pipe-shaped objects. "Those are the frames. They came out of Laney's shop and they're rough as hell. I have to have the guys file the burrs —with shitty files out of Laney's shop. . . ."

"I get the picture. Laney's a piece of work. Skip it."

"Aye-aye, sir. Anyway, those are the frames. These guys over here are wrapping the field coils." He stopped, self-consciously. "That's how I cut myself. It's great the 'Cats can make wire; I just wish it was a little more, you know, round."

"We'll get to that someday," Riggs said patiently. "For now, just be thankful. We're starting to get a lot of wire out of *Amagi*, but we need it for other stuff."

"Yes, sir. Anyway, there's the pole shoes. We screw 'em to the frame on the inside and it holds the coils in place."

Riggs gestured at a bin with a number of internal assemblies. "Those armatures look like they came out of the Delco factory."

"Thank you, sir. They're a bitch. First we have to turn the shafts on the one little lathe we have. . . ."

"It *is* one of the ship's lathes."

"Yes, sir, thank you, sir. It would be nice if we could get the guys in the ordnance shop to make those, though. Them and the core. We can't make those like they do at Delco. We have to mill the slots on the rotary table. It's still not a huge job, but we're going to need more capacity. We have to make the big generators one at a time, mostly using crap from Laney, and we can't work on those at all while we're doing this."

"The guys at ordnance have their hands full. I'll see if I can get you one of the new, bigger lathes, and maybe a bigger mill. You'll have to make motors for them, though. This isn't a belt-drive shop, and it isn't going to be."

"I understand. Motors we can do."

"So, what are you insulating the coils with?"

"Fiber. Just like the real thing, only we mulch up some of Mr. Letts's gasket material and mix it with some other stuff. Mikey's in charge of that."

"How does it hold up? What about heat?"

"So far, so good. We haven't had the glue-up issues Ben has, for example, and it does insulate well. It's kind of like putty. We cram some in on top of the coils in the core slot too. Anyway, the coils are soldered to the commutator bar."

Riggs inspected one of the brush end frames that a 'Cat was finishing up. "You wave-wound the core, but you're only using two brushes?"

"Yes, sir. We've still got a hell of a spring shortage. We're actually using the same gear springs Ordnance is making for their musket locks! Wave-wound generators will work with two brushes or four. We might want to put four in later."

Riggs pulled the short whiskers on his chin. "Musket springs!" He snorted. "How do the brushes hold up?"

"The springs are fairly stout and they don't have much range of motion. The brushes'll have to be replaced every hundred hours or so, I'm afraid. Since we have to use brass bushings, they'll have to be kept lubed and replaced pretty often too."

Riggs nodded. "Okay, I want a dozen extra brushes, two extra musket springs, and half a dozen bushing sets for each completed generator. What are you doing to regulate the voltage?"

"Well, sir, since you want these things to be wind powered, we've calculated a low cut-in speed and a high charging rate at those lower speeds. If a serious blow hits, it'll need to be disconnected. If they spin up too fast, centrifugal force will throw the windings out of their slots and thrash the whole thing. To cap the voltage, well, we've got to use a voltage regulator." Rodriguez pointed at yet another group of 'Cats working at a separate bench. "They're making vibrating regulators. I don't think they have a clue what they're doing, but I calculated all the values and gave them the plans. They could all be watchmakers after the war. They won't screw 'em up. Of course, I've got my ammeter to double-check each one. Managed to save *that*."

Riggs smiled. "Very good. Very, very good. If you weren't already in charge, I'd put you there."

"Uh, thanks."

"Now, one more thing; just a little matter, really. How do you plan to refurbish the generators, motors, and other essential equipment on *Walker* after we raise the ship?"

"And this, dear boy, if I'm not much mistaken, is the spleen!" Courtney Bradford leaned back and fanned himself with his sombrerolike hat, as much to clear the vapors of the quickly putrefying creature as to cool himself. It was hot, even in the shade of the trees surrounding the parade ground where the lesson was under way. Abel Cook, his most avid student, leaned forward to view the structure. Abel was thirteen, and he'd long since grown out of the clothes he'd been wearing during his evacuation from Surabaya aboard S-19. Most of the other boys who'd been similarly saved had applied to become midshipmen in the American Navy. Abel had too, but of all of them, he was the only one who'd shown an interest in the natural sciences. Bradford couldn't— and wouldn't—try to prevent the boy from serving, but he saw in the blond-haired, fair-skinned, somewhat gangly teen a much younger version of himself. "We need more of me around here," Courtney had argued with Captain Reddy, and to his surprise, Matt had agreed. Abel was still a midshipman, and naval dungarecs had replaced his battered clothes, but Courtney would have him as an apprentice. For a while, at least.

"I believe you're right," the boy replied, his voice cracking slightly. "And that must be the gallbladder," he said, pointing. "It *is* quite large!"

"The better to digest the dreadful things they eat, I shouldn't wonder!" Bradford beamed.

Other students attended the dissection as well, 'Cat corpsmen trainees, and they shuffled forward to look. The cadaver was that of a local variety of skuggik, a much smaller but clearly related species to the Grik. Skuggiks were vicious little scavengers, mostly, and their arms had evolved away, so their external physiology bore marked differences to that of their enemy. Internally however, they were virtually identical smaller versions. Courtney had attempted to save actual Grik for the demonstrations, but there was no means of cooling them. His modest hoard of postbattle corpses had been revealed by their stench and he'd been forced to surrender them. For now, his little open-air class on comparative biology would have to make do with skuggiks.

"And what is that lobed structure it is attached to?" Bradford asked. "Be silent, Abel," he admonished. "Let someone else answer for a change."

"Lungs!" proclaimed one of the young Lemurians triumphantly. Most of the others snickered.

Bradford sighed. "Would you like another try?"

The 'Cat looked more intently and wrinkled her nose. "You say that other st'ucture is a spleeng? I thought you say spleeng is on lungs?" There was chittering laughter this time.

"Perhaps, my dear, you might consider applying for another posting?"

"It is liver!" burst out another voice. "Big, ugly Grik-like liver!"

"Precisely!" exclaimed Bradford, his gentle chastisement instantly forgotten. His eyes narrowed and he looked at the organ in question. "A rather dry, reeking liver, in fact. Perhaps it's time we called it a day. Our specimen is withering before our very eyes . . . and noses!" He nodded at his assistants. "Please do dispose of this chap with all proper ceremony. We'll continue the lecture tomorrow with a fresh, um, subject. Weather permitting, we may start before the heat of the day!" With that, all but Abel scampered away, glad to escape the stench.

"Well!" said Bradford, still fanning himself and gauging the height of the sun. "Still some hours before dinner, I fear. Most barbarous, this local custom of eating only twice a day! Most barbarous. I'll never grow accustomed to it, and I may not survive." Secretly, he was glad Abel hadn't scurried off with the others. He didn't know why, exactly. He'd always generally loathed children: silly, mindless little creatures. His own son had been different, of course. A rare, exceptional specimen, most likely. He doubted he'd ever see the boy again, or even know if he was alive. He'd gone to fly Hurricanes for the RAF back in '39, and Courtney was slowly growing to accept that pining over his son's fate was pointless. In his heart, the boy would live forever. His ex-wife never entered his thoughts. That left Abel. Maybe that was it? Perhaps the

boy was becoming something of a surrogate son? He was clearly unusually bright: unlike the other children who'd been aboard the submarine, he had the sense to seek Courtney's company and he had an
insatiable curiosity.

Abel seemed to commiserate with him for a moment about the
local customs, but then brightened. "Well, sir, if you're hungry, I'm
sure we could find something at the Castaway Cook."

Bradford arched an eyebrow and looked at the boy. The Castaway
Cook was a ramshackle, abandoned warehouse a short distance from
the shipyard. It had suffered serious damage in the fighting and was
really little more than a standing roof when *Walker*'s cook, Earl Lanier,
appropriated it as a kind of enlisted men's club. It currently had little
value as a warehouse, since there was no pier. In fact, it sported one of
the few actual beaches on the Baalkpan waterfront. Earl was a ship's
cook, and that was all he was. With his galley underwater, he'd decided
he better get back to doing what he knew before somebody made him
do something he didn't. Besides, "the fellas is always hungry," he'd explained. He was right. The American destroyermen and submariners
he fed were still accustomed to three meals a day, and with all the work
there was for everyone, the Lemurian destroyermen and other naval
personnel were often hungry too. It was good for morale. The various
army regiments were beginning to establish haunts of their own, and
with Captain Reddy and Adar's approval had come the stern warning
that Marines would also be welcome at Lanier's establishment. Or
else.

Earl did a booming business. Besides Pepper, he had five more
cooks and half a dozen waitresses. There were also several bartenders
and that was what made Bradford's eyebrow rise. The Castaway Cook
had another, possibly more common name: the Busted Screw. The en-
tendres of that name were too numerous to count, but the accepted
reference was to the party they'd held after replacing *Walker*'s damaged propeller with *Mahan*'s at Aryaal.

Bradford studied the boy's innocent expression. "Well, I suppose,"
he relented. Together, they dodged the 'Cats and marching troops,
stopping now and then to admire various sea creatures on display in
the bazaar. Coastal artillery crews drilled on their guns behind rein-

forced embrasures with augmented overhead protection. Abel watched it all, fascinated, and Courtney felt a growing benevolent affection for the lad.

"Do you ever miss the other children, the ones you were stranded among so long?" Bradford probed.

Abel cocked his head to the side. "I see them now and then," he said thoughtfully, "but we never had much in common, you know. The girls were all—mostly all—ridiculous, squalling crybabies. Miss, uh, Princess Rebecca was the exception, of course."

"Indeed she was. And is. Most extraordinary." Even though Rebecca was also clearly a child, Bradford actually admired her. She had a quick mind and was utterly fearless. With a flash, he suddenly realized that Abel Cook obviously "admired" her as well. "Indeed," he repeated. He motioned toward the martial exercises under way. "Do you wish you had more of that to do? Your, ah, other comrades, the ones old enough, are quite involved in it, you know. Of course you do."

"I do miss it some," Abel confessed. "I'd like to be a soldier or a naval officer." He paused. "I think my father would expect it. Did you know, of all the children aboard S-19, I am the only one whose father was a military man? He was a naval attaché and interpreter for Admiral Palliser." He paused again, and continued more softly. "He was liaison aboard *DeRuyter* when she went down. I don't . . . I'll never know what happened to him." The boy's lip quivered ever so slightly, but his voice didn't. Bradford knew then that he had far more in common with this lad than he would ever have imagined. "All the other children—the boys, at least—were the sons of important men, but I think Admiral Palliser got me on the submarine himself. Mum was supposed to come, but there wasn't enough room there at the end. Sister Audry offered to leave the boat, but Mum wouldn't have it. The captain, Ensign Laumer, even Mr. Flynn wanted to take her anyway, but that Dutch cow," he said, referring to a somewhat dumpy Dutch nanny in charge of most of the girls, "said it just 'wouldn't do.' Things were 'quite cramped enough as it was.'" Abel's tone turned bitter. "There would have been room for several more people if they'd have just set that one ridiculous woman ashore. I'm sure she weighs as much as a torpedo and occupies three times the space!"

"Now, now," admonished Courtney gently, "I can certainly see your point. But one mustn't be unkind."

Besides Sandra and Karen Theimer Letts, only two other Navy nurses had survived: Pam Cross and Kathy McCoy. Pam was engaged in a torrid part-time affair with Dennis Silva, and for a time that had left only one known, and . . . wholesomely unattached female in the entire world: Kathy McCoy. This intolerable situation had resulted in the increasingly desperate "dame famine." That famine still existed to a degree. The only practical means of truly breaking it seemed to lie in establishing good relations with the Empire, but there were a *few* more women in Baalkpan now. There'd been four nannies, not counting Sister Audry, on S-19 to care for the twenty children of diplomats and industrialists aboard the sub. Two of them, one British and the "ridiculous" Dutchwoman, dropped all pretense of nannyhood and had taken it upon themselves to "thank" as many of their destroyermen rescuers as they could in the best way they knew how, as soon as they returned to Baalkpan after the battle. Both women were rather plain and had probably landed right in the middle of their version of heaven. Perhaps the dame *famine* was broken, but in spite of terrible losses, the male-to-female ratio was very considerably out of whack. They were only two women, after all, and their energy and gratitude had limits. For now, the dame *drought* still smoldered.

"Besides," Courtney continued, "your mother surely found a far safer transport, in retrospect."

"Possibly," Abel allowed, but his tone sounded unconvinced. For a while, the pair walked in silence.

Beyond the breastworks, they entered what was left of the old warehouse district and followed the strains of music that gradually emerged from the general noise of the nearby industrial productivity. The music came from Marvaney's portable phonograph—a larger, tin resonance chamber had been attached to increase the volume. Bradford didn't recognize the tune, but he rarely recognized any of the music recorded on the depleted, but still large collection of 78s the dead gunner's mate had owned. The surviving records were almost all upbeat American tunes: jazzy, or something the destroyermen called swing. There were a few whimsical Western songs, and some stuff the men called country that sounded more like Celtic chanteys than anything else. Bradford was a classicist, and to his horror he'd learned the late Marvaney had been too, but most of his collection of that sort of music had been used as an object of weight to carry his corpse to the deep. Regardless, all the records were priceless relics now and were carefully maintained. It was rare that two songs were played in a row without a pause to sharpen the needle.

Bradford knew that sometimes, at night, they had live music at the Busted Screw. A small percentage of the Americans had been musicians, of a sort, and like virtually every item nonessential to the two destroyers' final sortie, their instruments had been off-loaded. There were several guitars, a pair of ukuleles, a trombone, and a saxophone from *Walker*. A concertina, a trumpet, and a violin came from *Mahan*. Oddly, a pump organ, of all things, had been aboard S-19. Bradford knew space had been extremely limited on the old submarine and he again wondered vaguely where it had been kept and how they'd managed to get it through a hatch to salvage it. It wasn't much larger than a console Victrola, but still . . . at least there'd been a considerable collection of classical sheet music tucked inside. The original owner was dead, but a lot of the fellows could play a piano. Bradford couldn't, really, but he could read music. He'd attended a concert at the Busted Screw and had to say the sound created by the unlikely orchestra had been . . . unusual. Throw in a variety of Lemurian instruments, and he couldn't quite describe the result. He wasn't without hope that the bizarre ensemble might eventually be arranged into something less cacophonous.

Outside the Screw, on a makeshift hammock slung between two trees on the beach, Earl Lanier lounged in bloated repose. He wore shorts, "go-forwards," and had eyeshades on. There was a large, faded, bluish tattoo of a fouled anchor on his chest, pointing almost directly at a bright pink, puckered scar above his distended belly button. He wore no shirt, and other than a thick mat of dark, curly hair, they were the only things upon his otherwise tanned, ample belly. Beside the hammock stood the battered, precious Coke machine, powered by a doubtlessly clandestine heavy-gauge wire. As Courtney and Abel watched, a black-furred 'Cat with specks of white appeared, complete with a towel over his arm, and took a chilled mug of something from inside the machine and handed it to Lanier. Before Bradford could form an indignant comment, Pepper retrieved another pair of mugs and brought them over.

"One is, ah, you call it beer," he said, knowing Bradford's preference for the exceptional Lemurian brew. He looked at the boy before handing him a mug. "The other is a most benevolent and benign nectar."

"Thank you, dear fellow," Courtney said. "I was just about to ask why you put up with such treatment from that ludicrous creature."

Pepper grinned. "I like cool drinks," he said, and gestured toward the shade of the club, "and so do guys." He shrugged. "No happy Earl, no Coke machine. Also, I like being assistant cook. I like to cook. You wanna eat?"

"Well, now that you mention it . . ." Courtney and Abel followed Pepper under the shade and plopped themselves on bar stools before a planked countertop.

"What'll it be?" Pepper asked as their eyes became accustomed to the shade. "I know you not like fish, but I got fresh pleezy-sore steaks."

"Plesiosaur," Bradford corrected, almost resignedly. "That will be fine. At least they aren't technically fish."

"It is quite good, actually," came a small voice nearby. Bradford squinted and realized that Princess Rebecca sat almost beside him.

"Goodness gracious, my dear!" Courtney exclaimed. "What on earth are *you* doing here?" He glanced quickly around. Abel had suddenly become very still and Bradford suspected, if he could see it, he'd discover a deep blush covering the boy's face. Apparently, sometime during their seclusion on Talaud Island, the young midshipman became smitten with the princess. He wondered if he'd known she'd be here. "And where is that abominable Dennis Silva, your supposed protector?"

Silva popped up from behind the bar like a jack-in-the-box. He teetered slightly. "Right here, Mr. Bradford, and I'm ambulatin' fairly well. Thanks for askin'."

Courtney was taken aback by Silva's sudden, towering presence. He was also just about certain he'd quite understood the word "abominable." Silva had always traded shamelessly in being much more than he appeared to be, and that was doubly true now. Bradford liked the big gunner's mate—chief gunner's mate now—and honestly owed him multiple lives, but if Silva had been frightening before, the eye patch and spray of scars across his bearded face made him positively terrifying. Particularly since Bradford knew Silva's capacity for violence was exponentially greater than his appearance implied as well—and his appearance implied quite a lot. Nevertheless, he stood and faced the apparition with a stern glare.

"Mr. Silva, I find it difficult to believe even you would bring Her Highness to such an iniquitous place. Filthy, sweaty men and Lemurians often gather here and exchange ribald, obscene tales. There is foul speech, and on several occasions one of the Dutch . . . *nannies* . . . we rescued from Talaud has actually performed a striptease! There have been fights, and contrary to regulations, there's often drunkenness. I won't go into your personal life and speculate upon what a poor example you set as a man, but bringing that child with you here is an act of irresponsible depravity!"

Silva leered at him across the counter, and in his best Charles Laughton impression—which wasn't very good—he uttered a single word: "Flatterer!"

Bradford took a breath, preparing to launch another salvo.

"Then what does that say about you, Mr. Bradford, and your bringing Midshipman Cook," Princess Rebecca said, glancing at Abel and offering a small smile. Now that his eyes had adjusted, Bradford clearly saw the blush coloring the boy's face.

"Well," Courtney sputtered defensively, "but that is different, of course! He is young, but he's a warrior and needs male example. Perhaps not as . . . sharply defined an example as Mr. Silva, but . . ."

"Mr. Bradford," Rebecca continued, "I know Mr. Cook and consider him something of a friend." The boy's blush deepened, if that were possible. "You should remember we spent the better part of a year as castaways together. I also know he is barely older than I, and through no fault of his, I expect I have seen considerably more combat. Lawrence and I were aboard *Walker* during the final fight with *Amagi*, if you will recall."

Speechless, Bradford glanced about. Only then did he see Lawrence himself, coiled in the sand like a cat where the sun could still reach him, staring back with what could only have been an amused expression. He was panting lightly, and immediately Bradford's mind shifted gears, wondering why Lawrence would lie in the sun . . . and pant . . . so close to shade. He shook his head.

"Besides," Rebecca said, ending the argument with her tone, "Mr. Silva did not bring me here; I brought him. He is still in some considerable pain from his wounds, you know, and a measured amount of seep helps alleviate that."

"Right," Silva said, resuming his search behind the counter as if he'd lost something. "I'm here for a medical treatment prescribed by medical treaters! I'm on limited, excyooged—excused duty." He vanished again entirely, groping on the floor.

"He's also quite incredibly bored," whispered Rebecca. "Captain Reddy said he must remain here when the expedition to Aryaal departs. He was not pleased. He *understands*, with Mr. O'Casey forced to remain in hiding and Billingsly's spies on the loose, that someone suitably menacing must watch out for me. But . . . he was not pleased."

"Where the devil did it *go*?" came Silva's muted mumble.

"Say, what *is* he looking for down there?" Bradford asked quietly.

Rebecca shrugged sadly. "It could be anything, but usually it's his eye." She shook her head at Bradford's expression. "He has not lost his mind, but he *is* in danger of losing direction." She spoke louder. "And he has clearly had quite enough seep!"

They needed a break from the daily rains, Gilbert Yeager thought. The sun rode overhead, but it wouldn't do much about the humidity. Make it worse, maybe. Didn't matter. The pyres had long since ceased, but black smoke piled into the hazy sky, and the industrial smoke they were making now, combined with the humidity, made every breath an effort. He coughed. Damn, he wished he had a cigarette.

He sighed and took a pouch out of his pocket, stuffing some of the yellow leaves within into his mouth. Chewing vigorously, he tried to get through the waxy, resinlike coating to the genuine tobacco flavor within as quickly as he could. "Gotta be a way to clean this stuff off," he muttered. So far, everything they'd tried to remove the coating so the leaves could be smoked had failed. The native tobacco could be chewed, but it was practically toxic when lit.

The nearest sources of the choking smoke were a pair of crude, but functional locally made boilers. They'd been leveled atop layer upon layer of good firebrick on the once damp shore, but they'd long since cooked all the moisture from the ground around them. They roared and trembled with power in the red light of their own fires that seemed to diffuse upward around them. Dozens of 'Cat tenders tightened or adjusted valves, checked gauges, or scampered off on errands at the monosyllabic commands of another scrawny human, Isak Rueben.

The boilers powered several contraptions—none exactly alike, since each was virtually a handmade prototype—that chuffed along amiably enough, their twin pistons moving methodically up and down. Gouts of steam added even more humidity to the air with every revolution, but at least it was honest steam—not the useless, invisible kind the sun cooked out of the ground. The end use of each machine was a series of shafts, or in one case, a piston-pitman combination. One was a small, prototype ship's engine they were testing for durability. The others spun large generators in crudely cast casings that supplied ship-standard 120 DC electricity to various points.

More engines were under construction that would eventually supply electrical or mechanical power to the pumps that would drain the nearby basin. The mechanical pumps were of a remarkably sophisticated Lemurian design. The electric ones were, like everything else electrical, experimental models Riggs, Letts, Rodriguez, and Brister had conjured up. If Gilbert had any money and if anyone would accept it, he'd lay every dime that the electric pumps would croak the first time they tried them.

Tabby, the gray-furred 'Cat apprentice to the two original Mice, ran lightly up behind him and playfully tagged him on the shoulder, then scampered to where Isak was standing. Hands in his pockets, Gilbert sauntered over to join them. "How they doin'?" he asked, when he was near enough to be heard over the noise.

"Fair," Isak replied skeptically. "Fair to middlin'. They ain't turbines," he accused no one in particular, "but they're engines. Least we got a real job again."

Gilbert nodded. They'd finally trained enough 'Cat roughnecks to take their places in the oilfields, both near Baalkpan and on Tarakan Island. The relief was palpable to them both. They hated the oilfields. Their time in the oilfields back home was what drove them into the Navy in the first place. They'd become firemen, and that was all they really wanted to do. Everyone called them the White Mice, because before the event that brought them here, they never went anywhere but the fireroom and they'd developed an unhealthy pallor as a result. They actually resembled rodents, too, with their narrow faces and thin, questing noses. Nobody ever liked them before, but now everyone treated them like heroes—which they were—Tabby included. First, they'd designed the rig that found oil when the ship was completely out. Then they'd managed to maintain enough steam pressure to get *Walker* to the shipyard after the fight. They were remarkably valuable men, but all their popularity hadn't changed them much. Everyone liked them now, but they still didn't like anybody, it seemed. Except for Tabby.

They'd originally treated the 'Cat like a pet, even though she'd proven herself in the fireroom. She'd even saved both of their lives at the end, by pulling them out of the escape trunk as the ship settled beneath them. Now she was one of them, another Mouse, even if she didn't look anything like one.

"I think they swell," Tabby said, referring to the engines in a passable copy of their lazy drawl.

"Yah, sure . . . for a myoo-zeeum. They're a hunnerd years outta date."

"Buildin' a pair of 'em with three cylinders, triple-expansion jobs—ten times as big—for *Big Sal*, I hear," Isak said.

Tabby's eyes blinked amazement. "Be somethin', to be chief of that."

"You expectin' a promotion?" Gilbert asked accusingly. "Hell, they've made gen'rals an' ad'mrals outta ever'body else, why not you?"

"I never be aahd-mah-raal," she retorted, angry enough to let her language and accent slip. She looked at the engine. "But chief be nice." She turned on Gilbert. "But only if you two be chief-chiefs."

The two men remained apologetically silent for a moment. It was their version of abject contrition. Finally, Isak spoke: "Bosun been to talk to you two?" he asked. Gilbert and Tabby both nodded. "One of us gots to go on the mission they're cookin' up, he says, since they're takin' the first new steam frigates." He pointed at the engine. "They've got one like that, only bigger. That's why we been testin' it to failure." He grunted. "Least this time they're lettin' *us* decide." He looked at Tabby. "An' this time she's in the pool as deep as us. Metallurgy aside, Tabby prob'ly knows these jug jumpers *better* than us. Bosun'd have to find a three-sided coin to make up his mind."

"You just said it," Gilbert accused. "It don't matter what we decide. They'll keep her here just because o' that!"

"Maybe we oughta go ahead an' tell 'em we're sorta related after all," Isak murmured. "Tell 'em we can't bear to be apart." He snickered at his own remark. He and Gilbert had never let on that they were half brothers. There was a certain resemblance often remarked upon, but usually in a mocking fashion. Besides, their last names were different. They'd never told anyone, because not only did they have different fathers, but their mother never married either man. In a sense, they figured that made them each kind of a bastard and a half. Things like that didn't seem to matter as much to them as they once had, but they still saw no need to brand it on their foreheads. "Hell, if it comes to it, I'll go," Isak said. "Kinda got the wanderlust flung on me the last time they busted us up."

"You didn't do any wanderin'," Gilbert accused. "You just stayed on that damn island while me and Tabby went a-wanderin'."

Isak nodded. "Yep. That's what I mean."

"Well," said Gilbert, clearly relieved, "just don't get ate."

With a look around the noisy ordnance shop to make sure no one was paying any particular attention, Dennis Silva clamped the brand-new musket barrel in the mill vise. The barrel was made of relatively mild steel plate, about three-eighths of an inch thick, taken from *Amagi*'s superstructure. Dennis figured they could ultimately salvage enough of the stuff from *Amagi* alone to make millions of barrels, if they wanted. The plate had been cut and forged around a mandrel, reamed to its final interior diameter, and turned to its finished contour. Finally, it was threaded and breeched. It was a simple process really, with the equipment they had, but it had just been perfected, and only a few of the barrels were complete. Dennis figured the odds were about even that Bernie would have a spasm when he noticed one missing.

So far, the Captain and "Sonny" Campeti hadn't insisted that Dennis return to his duties full-time—they must have understood he had issues to sort out: some physical, a few domestic. He doubted their forbearance would last much longer. He was malingering, in a sense, and even he was beginning to feel bad about that. There was a lot he could be doing, after all. Should be doing. But he was a blowtorch. He'd go full-blast while there was fuel in the tanks, but when they were empty, they were empty. He'd needed this time to refuel, not only physically, but mentally—to put the "old" Dennis Silva back together. The time was just about right, and if the truth were known, he was actually starting to get a little antsy to return to duty. Besides, he had some ideas.

Carefully focusing his one good eye on the neatly scribed lines he'd drawn on the breech end, he cranked the table up and powered the mill. The cutter spun up and he turned a valve that started misting it with the oily coolant Spanky had devised. Slowly, he turned the crank in front of him. The cutter went through the breech like butter and he turned the other crank on the right side of the table and pulled the cutter back through the breech, widening the gap. Half a dozen more passes gave him the rectangular opening he wanted in the top of the barrel's breech.

"Oops," he mumbled happily, "I guess this barrel's ruined!"

He brushed the chips away and replaced the cutter with another that would leave a rounded, dovetail shape. He measured the depth, traversed the table, and made a single pass at the front of his rectangular cut. Changing the cutter again, to one with a slight taper, he made a final cut at the breech. Looking closely to make sure he'd hit all his lines, he switched off the machine and removed the barrel from the vise.

"God damn you, Silva, what the hell are you up to now?" came an incredulous bellow. A lesser mortal might have at least flinched just a bit despite the almost plaintive note to the shout.

"Goofin' off," Dennis replied mildly. "Cool your breech, Mr. Sandison. Ol' Silva's just keepin' hisself 'occupied,' like you said."

For an instant, Bernie was speechless. "Cool *my* breech? You just hacked a hole in the breech of one of my new musket barrels and you tell me that?" He looked almost wildly around. "Where's Campeti? If you won't listen to me, maybe he can control you! In fact, I want him to *hang* you!"

"Why's ever'body always want to hang me?" Silva asked, as if genuinely curious. "Calm down, Bernie, you'll hurt yourself. You 'cumulated a extra hole or two in the big fight yourself, if I recall. If you start leakin', Lieutenant Tucker's gonna get sore, and she'll have the skipper down on you. He'll make you take a rest, and you'll be countin' waves in the bay at the Screw while Campeti runs this joint. Besides, just 'cause I'm goofin' off don't mean I'd dee-stroy a perfectly good musket barrel without a pretty good reason."

Bernie paused and took a breath. Silva was right. He was a maniac, but when it came to implements of destruction, if he wasn't actually a genius, he was at least a prodigy of some monstrous sort. He still had his "personal" BAR, and was one of the few people allowed to run around with such a profligate weapon and a full battle pack of precious ammunition. His new favorite weapon however, that he carried just about everywhere he went, was of an entirely different sort. Bernie glanced at the thing where it leaned near Silva's workstation with the bag of necessary equipment it required.

It had begun life as an antiaircraft gun aboard shattered *Amagi*, a Type 96, twenty-five millimeter. The breech had been damaged in the battle and the flash hider shot away, so Silva "appropriated" it during one of their early trips to the wreck to salvage anything that remained above water. He told Sandison what he was doing, and the still painfully wounded (like nearly everyone) torpedo officer and Minister of Ordnance gave his blessing to the project. For most of his life, before joining the Navy, Silva had just been on the loose. For a time however, he'd worked for an old-school gunsmith near Athens, Tennessee. In that part of the country, even in the mid-thirties, many guns they worked on were old-fashioned muzzle loaders, even flintlocks. His time there was probably what made him strike for the ordnance division in the Navy. In any event, he'd learned a lot about "old-timey" guns, so Sandison gave him the flintlock from the shortened musket O'Casey had when they rescued him.

Silva turned the Type 96 barrel down as light as he thought was wise on one of the lathes, breeched it, and fitted it to a crude stock. Then he made a hollow-base .100-caliber bullet mold like a Civil War Minié ball, so the bullet would expand and take the gain-twist rifling. He still worked on it now and then, dolling it up, but what he had was a massive weapon, weighing almost thirty pounds, with a five-foot barrel. It was amazingly accurate with its quarter-pound bullet, but the recoil was so horrifyingly abusive, nobody but Silva had ever even fired it. Probably no human but Silva *could* fire it more than once without serious injury. He called it his Super Lizard Gun, and was anxious to test it on one of the allosaurus-like brutes. He never wanted to go up against one of those incredibly tough monsters with a .30-06 again.

"So," Bernie said resignedly, "show me why you shouldn't hang. And this had better be something useful!"

"Sure." Silva held up the barrel he'd altered. "Alden wants muskets, and that's fine. That's what we can do right now, so that's how we go. What you're making—*we're* making—is basically an old muzzle-loading Springfield. You settled on cap instead of flint because they're simpler and we can make the caps. Good call. Might want to make a few flintlocks for scouts, explorers, or such in case they wind up out of touch for a while—they can find flint if they run out of caps—but that's beside the point. You're also startin' out with smoothbores because we haven't built a rifling machine yet, and with the way Griks fight, a good dose of buck 'n' ball is just the ticket. Again, fine. The main thing right now is to get guns with bayonets in the hands o' the troops. Eventually, we can take the same guns and rifle 'em, use Minié balls just like ol' Doom Whomper over there. Everything's great, and we move the 'Cats from fightin' like they did in Roman times to the 1860s.

"But the skipper wants breechloaders, and that got me thinking. Everybody seems to figure that means, all of a sudden, we hafta jump from the *old* Springfields to the kind of Springfields we brought with us, our 'oh-threes. That'd be swell, but it's a lot bigger jump than folks would think, and it's bigger than we hafta make."

"It is?"

"Yeah. The Army—our old Army—had the same problem once. After the . . . War Between the States, they had millions of muzzle-loadin' Springfields, see? Thing is, everybody was startin' to go to center-fire breechloaders. Even f . . . likkin' *Spain*. Whaddaya do? This fella named Ersky Allin—er somethin' like that—had sorta the same job as you. Anyway, he figured a way to make center-fire breechloaders outta all them muskets, and it was a cinch!" Silva brandished the barrel again, then fished around on a bench covered with strange-looking objects he'd been working on. He picked something up. "He, this Allin fella, cut the top outta the breech, like I just done, and screwed and soldered this here hinge-lookin' thing to the front of the gap." Silva held the object in place. "The thing on the other side of the hinge is the breechblock—we can cast 'em a lot easier than I milled this one out!— and the firin' pin angles from the rear side to the front center!" He held the pieces together and the breechblock dropped into place with a *clack!*

"I ain't pulled the breech plug out and milled the slot that locks the thing closed, but again, it's a simple alteration. You cut a barrel, put this on, then grind the hammer to where it hits the firin' pin square. All else you gotta add is a easy little extractor!"

Bernie's eyes were huge. "Silva, you *are* a freak-show genius!"

"Nah. Maybe Ersky Allin was, though."

Bernard Sandison looked at Dennis. "How did you do this? I mean, how did you *know* about this?"

Silva shrugged. "I had a couple over the years. First rifles I ever owned. Sometimes huntin' was the only way a fella could stay fed, what with the Depression, and you could buy one surplus at just about any hardware store, or order one from Monkey Wards or Bannerman's for a few bucks."

Bernie shook his head. His childhood and Silva's had been . . . different. "What did they shoot? And how . . . ?"

"That's another neat thing. You're forgin' these barrels on a five-eighths mandrel. Once you ream 'em out smooth, they're about sixty-two-caliber or so. You go ahead and build yer riflin' machine and rifle forty-five- or fifty-caliber *liners* to solder in the old barrels and then chamber 'em! Simple as pie. The first Allin guns they put liners in were fifty-seven. When they started building rifles like this from the ground up instead of convertin' 'em, they made receivers for 'em an' did 'em in forty-five-seventy. That's a forty-five- or fifty-caliber bullet on seventy grains of powder. Black powder, just like we have now. Both had a pretty high trajectory, but they'd stomp a buffalo to the ground. Probably a lot better for critters around here than a thirty-aught-six. Big and slow gives you big holes and deep penetration. Small and fast gives you small holes, and maybe not so deep penetration. If you're too close, light bullets, even copper jacketed, just blow up on impact and never hit anything vital."

Oddly, Bernie noticed that when Silva was talking ballistics, he didn't sound as much like a hick, but he'd already begun tuning him out. Silva had just solved one of the biggest problems he'd expected to face over the next year or so. It had bothered him for a number of reasons. He'd felt a little like everything they did before they came up with "real" weapons was sort of a wasted effort. Silva's scheme might not give them truly modern weapons, but they were leaps and bounds beyond anything they were likely to face. But what about cartridges?

"These fifty-seventies and forty-five-seventies, what were they shaped like? The shells?"

"Straight, rimmed case," said Silva, grinning. He knew what Bernie was thinking. One of the problems they faced with making new shells for the Springfields and Krags they already had, not to mention the machine guns, was the semi-rimless bottleneck shape. "Even if you haven't solved the problem of drawing cases—which I figure you will—you can turn these shells on a lathe if you have to."

Bernie beamed. "I swear, Silva! Why didn't you just *tell* me you wanted a musket barrel? I'm going to see you get a raise out of this . . . or a promotion, or something! Take the rest of the day off. You're still technically on leave anyway. Go hunting or have a beer! Kill something; you'll feel better!"

"Raise won't do me any good, an' I don't want no promotion. All I answer to is you, Campeti, and the skipper anyway. You can call 'em 'Allin-Silva' conversions, if you want, though."

"You bet! Do whatever you want! I have to talk to the skipper!"

With that, Bernie rushed away with the still-dripping barrel and trapdoor arrangement in his hand. Silva watched him go. "Whatever I want, huh?" Silva said, eyebrow raised.

Lieutenant Tamatsu Shinya, formerly of the Japanese Imperial Navy, and currently brevet colonel and second in command of all Allied infantry forces, unbuckled the belt that held his modified Navy cutlass and pistol. Handing it to the 'Cat Marine sentry at the base of the comfortable dwelling, he climbed the rope ladder to the "ground" floor—roughly twenty feet above his head. It was inconvenient, but virtually all Baalkpan dwellings were built on pilings like this so their inhabitants could sleep secure from possible predators. He reflected that the practice was as much tradition now as anything else, since the city never really slept—even before the war—and over the centuries, dangerous animals had slowly learned to avoid the city carved out of the dense wilderness around it. Now there were fortified berms and breastworks, constant lookouts, and vigilant warriors as well. He wondered as he climbed the ladder if the inconvenient tradition would long survive. At the top, he struck the hatch, or trapdoor, above his head and, raising it, entered.

Once inside, Shinya removed his shoes and stood. A curtain separated the entry chamber from the rest of the dwelling and he passed through it. Finding the occupant seated cross-legged on the floor, facing a small window overlooking the bay, Shinya bowed at the waist.

"Commander Okada," he said in Japanese. "My apologies for disturbing you."

Okada turned then. His uniform had been wrecked and he wore a robe not unlike the ones the Lemurian Sky Priests used. He was older than Tamatsu, but had the same black hair, untinged with gray. He regarded Tamatsu for a moment before dipping his own head in a perfunctory bow. "At least you still remember how to *behave* somewhat Japanese," Okada observed.

Shinya felt his face heat. He straightened. "And you, sir, it would seem, have learned to behave somewhat like your Captain Kurokawa."

Okada shot to his feet, anger twisting his face. "Still you will compare me to that *kyoujin*?"

"You have called me a traitor on several occasions now. If I am, what are you? I did not surrender when my ship sank; I was captured while unconscious. I had no idea any of my countrymen even existed in this world. I made an honorable accommodation with a former enemy to help confront an evil I am quite certain our emperor would despise. Our primary differences with the Americans are political, and not . . . on anything approaching the levels of our differences with the Grik! You condemn me, yet you supported the actions of a man you know the emperor would have never condoned!" Shinya fumed. He couldn't help it: Okada's attitude infuriated him and he didn't understand it. "Perhaps *General Tojo* would have, but the emperor wouldn't; nor would Admiral Mitsumasa!"

Okada seemed to deflate. "I *tried* to oppose him," he offered quietly. "I helped Kaufman send a warning."

Shinya's voice also lost some of its heat. "Yes, you did. Moreover, you should be proud you did. I too oppose Captain Kurokawa—and the Grik. I do not and will not fight others who do, nor have I done so. I gave Captain Reddy my parole and had no difficulty fighting the Grik. When I learned of your ship, I faced a choice—a choice I was *allowed*, by the way—to abdicate my duty to the troops I command, or risk the possibility I might face you and others like you. I was spared that agony, but I would have done it if forced, because those troops would have been aiding Kurokawa and, by extension, the Grik."

"You make it sound as though I am guilty of aiding that madman simply because I did not rise openly against him sooner! Believe me, I wanted to! But all that would have accomplished is my death before I had any real chance to make a difference." Okada looked down. "In the end, it made no difference anyway."

"It did," Shinya assured him. "You gave us warning. Without that, we would not have been prepared."

"Prepared to kill our countrymen!" Okada almost moaned. "Do you not see? Perhaps you are not a traitor for what you have done, but I can't stop *feeling* like you are, even as I *feel* like one for doing even less. They were *my* men!"

"Yes," Shinya agreed. "But do not think the decision was less difficult for me. Now, to do nothing further, while those same men are in the grasp of such evil, is impossible for me. Don't *you* see?" Shinya waited for a response. When there wasn't one, he sank to the floor across from Okada, who finally joined him there.

"What do you want to do?" Shinya quietly asked.

"I want to go home."

Shinya took a breath. "Unless you have knowledge beyond mine of the mystery that brought us to this world, I fear that is impossible."

Okada looked at Shinya a long moment, weighing the words. Finally, he sighed. "That is not what I meant. Of course I want to go 'home,' but I have no more idea how to do that than you profess to have. No, what I want is to go to that place that *should* be home. The place your allies at least still call Japan."

"Jaapaan," Shinya corrected. "But why? The Lemurians have two land colonies there—a small one on Okinawa and another, larger one on southern Honshu. They have never, by all accounts, encountered any of our people. On this world, Jaapaan is not Japan. Besides, your knowledge of Kurokawa and the Grik is invaluable to those who oppose them."

That was true enough. Thanks to Commander Okada, the humans and Lemurians finally knew more about their enemy now. They still didn't know what drove the Grik to such extremes of barbarity, but they'd learned a little about their social structure. For example, they now knew that the average Grik warrior came from a class referred to as the Uul, which possessed primary characteristics strikingly similar to ants or bees. Some were bigger than others, some more skilled at fighting; some even seemed to have some basic concept of self. All, however, were slavishly devoted to a ruling class called the Hij, who manipulated them and channeled and controlled their instinctual and apparently mindless ferocity. There seemed to be different strata of Hij as well. Some were rulers and officers; others were artisans and bureaucrats. Regardless of their positions, they constituted what was, essentially, an elite aristocracy collectively subject to an obscure godlike emperor figure. Nothing more about their society was known beyond that. The Hij were physically identical to their subjects, but were clearly intelligent and self-aware to a degree frighteningly similar to humans and their allies. They didn't seem terribly imaginative, though, and so far that had proved their greatest weakness.

Shinya persisted. "Don't you want revenge for what Kurokawa has done to the people under his command? *Our* people? Can't you set your hatred of the Americans aside even for that?"

"I do not hate the Americans," Okada stated with heavy irony. "But they are the enemy of our people, our emperor. I cannot set *that* aside. How can you?" Okada shook his head. He didn't really want an answer to his question. "It is true I had hoped, with *Amagi*, to work in concert with the Americans against the Grik, because, like you, I recognize them as evil—perhaps the greatest evil mankind has ever known. I never intended an *alliance* with the Americans, merely a cessation of hostilities. An armistice perhaps. It is not my place to declare peace and friendship with my emperor's enemies"—he glanced with lingering accusation at Shinya—"and no, I would not have broken the armistice. However, with *Amagi*, I could have felt secure that the Americans wouldn't either. In any event, together or independently, we could have carried the fight to the Grik and then inherited this world in the end." He shrugged. "It is a big world. Whether it was big enough for us and the Americans, in the long run, would have been a test for much later—and at least one of us would have survived the Grik." He sighed and looked at Shinya. "An imperfect scheme, perhaps, but a less radical . . . departure from my sense of duty than the choice you made."

"An impossible scheme," Shinya stated derisively. "Without the Grik, where would you have been victualed, supplied, repaired? A simple armistice would not have gotten you those things from the Americans and their allies. You would have been at their mercy!"

"No! With *Amagi*, I could have *demanded*! As I am now, a prisoner, I have nothing! Not even honor! I can demand nothing as an equal and I have nothing to even bargain with but what is in my head!"

Shinya stood, talking down to Okada. "No. Impossible," he repeated. "I respect what you did, what you tried to do. You could—*should* be a hero for it instead of a prisoner. But the old world is *gone*! If you had succeeded in the rest of your plan, if you had tried to dictate terms, to conquer support from the Allies, even I would have opposed you."

"Even if it meant killing your own countrymen?"

"Even if it meant killing every man on *Amagi*," Shinya answered quietly. "You say you understand, that you hate the Grik and everything about them. You move your mouth and the right words come out, but you really don't understand, do you? Even now. The Grik are the enemy of everything alive in this world! They . . . You haven't . . ." He paused, shaking his head. He could see he was wasting his breath. He did respect Okada, but the man was just . . . *too* Japanese. He wondered what that said about him?

"I will see what I can do," Shinya said at last. "If you agree to work with the Allies and continue to tell them what you know of Kurokawa and the Grik, I will try to convince them to let you go 'home.' Perhaps there you will find the honor you think you have lost. If so, I hope you can live with it. I doubt it, though. I fear for you, Commander Okada. I fear that someday your misjudgment will fade and the honor I still see in you will rise within your heart and demand a reckoning. Because of the blood we spill on behalf of you and uncountable others, you will die a tortured old man, who missed his opportunity to *be* honorable by mistakenly trying to do the honorable thing."

*   *   *

"What would you have me do?" Matt asked the mustachioed man sitting across the table. The table was split bamboo, with a rough, uneven top, and it served Matt as a desk of sorts in the semi-finished chamber known as the War Room. The chamber was one of many in the "new" Great Hall, still undergoing noisy reconstruction. The irregular surface of the desk didn't really matter much; paperwork was kept to a minimum and consisted of sun-dried skins, like parchment, only not as fine. Usually, the rawhide parchment supported itself well enough to write on.

"What would you have *me* do?" Jenks replied. He was dressed in his best, as always now, for these biweekly meetings. He sat stiffly on a stool in his no longer perfectly white uniform, with its ever so slightly tarnished braid. Under his arm was the black shako with braid that matched his sleeves and collar. It was raining outside and sheets pounded against the hastily covered ceiling and the chamber was humid and damp. Jenks's coat smelled of musty cotton and the half-soaked hat would have added a wet wool and leather odor if the similar wet-'Cat smell hadn't overpowered it. Between them on the desk was a large decanter of purplish amber liquid and two small mugs. Neither mug had been touched.

"I know we haven't often seen eye-to-eye," Jenks understated, "but I do have my duty. I must return the princess to her family—something you promised to help me do—but I don't see any measurable degree of preparation under way to accomplish that task."

Matt cocked an eyebrow at him. "No? We captured two more of your men spying on the shipyard from a boat they'd hired last night. Don't tell me we've caught them all. Surely you have some idea what we've been up to?"

Jenks sat even straighter and his face went hard. "Do you mean to execute those men, like the one you caught a few weeks ago?"

"I *should* hang them," Matt answered darkly. "I told you what the penalty would be if we caught your men snooping around where they don't belong. The entire city has been open to them and they've been treated well, by all accounts. Better than well. Still, you can't resist fooling around where you've got no business."

"If I perceive a threat to the Empire, it is my duty to evaluate it. We have cooperated with every one of your ridiculous requests, languishing here in this place quite long enough for you to prepare an envoy to my people." Jenks's eyes widened slightly in genuine surprise. "Somehow, you have convinced the princess to support you in that. In the meantime, all I get from you are delays, accusations, and, I believe, sir, distortions of truth. You have done nothing to alleviate my concerns about your Alliance. If anything, those concerns have grown more acute. And my question remains: will you murder these men like you did the last one?"

Matt stood, angry. "We didn't 'murder' anyone! The last man we caught had murdered a sentry to get where he was. He was captured and executed as a murderer and a spy! Would you have done otherwise? Please don't insult my intelligence by telling me you would."

Jenks only sighed.

"Very well," Matt continued, seating himself again. "The men we caught last night did no such thing, and I doubt they saw much either. I'll return them to you, but you'd best restrict them to your ship. If I catch them ashore again, they *will* be hanged!"

Jenks cleared his throat, calming himself. For some time he sat still, staring at Matt as if appraising him anew. "Just so," he said at last, with a hint of resignation. "And you have my appreciation and . . . my apology. You won't see *them* again. I cannot assure you that there will be no more spies, however."

Matt looked closely at the man. He'd spoken the word "spies" with distaste. Did he mean he wouldn't make that assurance, or couldn't? This wasn't the first time Matt got the impression that some things happened on and off Jenks's ship over which he had little, if any, control. He wondered if the vague admission was a crack in Jenks's facade, or if he was merely tiring of the aggrieved role he seemed to think was expected of him. By somebody. Matt merely nodded. He doubted he'd get an admission if he continued to press, and he wanted to use Jenks's comparative openness while he had the chance.

"I do assure you we're doing all we can to prepare the expedition as quickly as possible. As I've said, a reconnaissance of Aryaal is part of that, and a reconnaissance in force is essential—thus the delay. That has to be our first priority. We need to know what's going on there before we dare weaken our defenses here. Our estimates of the Grik may be entirely wrong—they have been before," he added bitterly. "Besides, you've been here only a little more than two months. Bradford said it might take a few. My definition of 'a few' is three or more. Isn't it the same with you?" Matt thought he detected the most subtle of smiles flash across Jenks's face.

"Indeed. But one can always hope for the best, and 'a few' is a somewhat vague expression." Jenks's tone hardened slightly. "Just as your notion of what these Grik are capable of seems vague as well. Come, you defeated them badly when last they came. Surely you cannot be as . . . concerned . . . about them as you claim?"

Matt leaned against the backrest he'd had installed on his stool and regarded Jenks for a moment, rubbing his chin. "Tell you what. I'm about to have an interview with a man who probably knows more about them than anyone alive. Why don't you join us? You may find it . . . enlightening." Matt took Jenks's silence as agreement and rang a little bell. Instantly, the War Room door opened, revealing a small, dark Filipino who eyed Jenks doubtfully. "Juan, please have General Alden and Colonel Shinya escort the prisoner inside."

Juan stood straighter, as if at attention. He'd been *Walker's* officer's steward before the war, and he'd since evolved into Matt's personal steward and secretary. No appointment to that effect had ever been made; Juan just took it upon himself. By sheer force of will, he'd made it stick.

"Of course, Cap-i-tan," he said. "Should I bring coffee?"

Matt hid a grimace at the prospect of Juan's coffee, or at least the stuff that passed for coffee here. Back when he'd had the real stuff to ruin, Juan's coffee had been ghastly. With the ersatz beans he now had, it had improved to the point that it was only vile. Still . . . "No, that's not necessary, but thanks."

With a somber bow, Juan closed the door. A moment later it opened again, revealing three other men whom Juan ushered to seats across the desk. All had recently arrived and were soaked to varying degrees. Once they sat, Juan left the chamber, discreetly closing the door behind him.

"Commodore Jenks, I understand you've met General Alden and

Colonel Shinya?" There were nods. "Then may I present Commander Sato Okada, formerly of the Japanese battle cruiser we're stripping in the bay?" Jenks nodded, but Okada continued staring straight ahead.

"Yes, well. I've now spoken with Commander Okada on several occasions and I've discovered he prefers to remain aloof from civilities. You must understand that before we . . . came to this world, his people and ours were at war." Matt's expression darkened. "Quite bitterly at war, as a matter of fact, and that war almost certainly still rages. Since we rescued him from his sunken ship, we've come to an . . . understanding regarding our association. By his choice he remains a prisoner of war. In recognition of the threat posed by the Grik, however, and in exchange for transportation to that region that *would* have been Japan, he's willing to answer any questions about the enemy to the best of his ability. He was *Amagi's* first officer, and as such had frequent direct, personal contact with the Grik. More than anyone else from his ship, in fact, since his former commander, Captain Kurokawa, forced him to perform most of their correspondence. Okada believes this was mainly a form of punishment, since Kurokawa knew how much he loathed their 'allies.' Ask him whatever you want. If you don't believe me about the menace we all face—your precious Empire as well—you must believe him. He's as objective a source as you'll find. You see, he doesn't like us much either."

"Who's to say the information he gives you is genuine, then?" Jenks demanded. "Perhaps he inflates the threat to discourage you from attacking while his own people are still in their hands."

Okada spoke through clenched teeth. His enunciation was careful, if heavily accented. "If this . . . British man doubts my word, I will say nothing to him. I do not even understand why I am here. Surely you have already told him everything I have said. Americans and British are the same. Both are enemies of my emperor. You act in concert and remain as one people, despite your supposed split."

"Hmm," said Matt, "I'm sorry, Commander. Clearly, you *don't* understand. Commodore Jenks is no more British than you are." For an instant, Okada's facade dropped to reveal an expression of confusion while Jenks sputtered. Matt plowed on. "His *ancestors* were British, mostly, from what the princess says, but they came to this world the same way we did before the United States even existed. I've tried to persuade him to accept the historical bond that's existed between our two countries for the last few decades, but he professes not to believe it. If he does, he doesn't care. So don't think of him or his people as enemies of your emperor; they're not. Remember your history. When his people last came through here, Japan was closed to them. They knew it was there, of course, but they knew little of the people who inhabited it. They were too busy in China and India."

"I *am* British, sir. I am a subject of the Empire of the New Britain Isles," Jenks retorted hotly. He glanced at Okada. "But I am no enemy of yours. I apologize for forming my question so tactlessly. Please tell me, in your opinion, how serious is this supposed Grik threat?"

Okada regarded Jenks for a moment, evaluating the sincerity of the question. Finally, he relaxed slightly, and as he spoke, it was clear that evil, shrouded memories marched across his thoughts. "They are a threat beyond imagination. You are familiar with the shape of the world, from your ancient charts?" Jenks nodded. "Besides their recent conquests in Malaysia, they control all of India, the Arab coast, and at least eastern Africa almost to the cape. I believe their imperial capital, where their 'Celestial Mother' resides, is on Madagascar, one of their earlier conquests. They have no sense of honor as even an Englishman might recognize it. Their individual warriors have no sense of honor at all. They are voracious predators who exterminate all in their path, feasting not only on the bodies of their victims, but on their very own dead. They eat their *young*—a practice I have seen with my own eyes— and they have eaten . . . members of my own crew when we failed to conquer Baalkpan on our first attempt. All failure is considered a failure of spirit, and those who fail are considered prey to be devoured. That is why we aided them, why Kurokawa aided them: through fear of being preyed upon if we refused. Kurokawa may have had other reasons of his own, but for the vast majority"—his eyes drooped—"for me, it was fear."

"But what of the battle here?" Jenks demanded. "Surely such a defeat must have hurt them."

Okada looked wistful. "I certainly hope it did. Nevertheless, I have *seen*. I have been to Ceylon, where their teeming hordes are beyond number. I have seen how they so readily replaced the ships and war-riors destroyed in their first offensive against Aryaal and this place. A grace period may have been won, but it will be short. They breed rap-idly, and if they do *not* eat their young, within five years they may re-turn with three times what they lost—and still maintain control of their frontiers."

"My God," Jenks muttered.

"Nothing we haven't told you before," Alden growled.

"True, perhaps, but . . ."

"Tell you what," Matt said, making a decision he'd been pondering for days. "Now that you have a fresh perspective on why we're in such a hurry and why our expedition to return your princess has received a lesser priority, I'll take you to the shipyard myself. Just you. I don't know what other agenda your spies may have, but I'll let you see what we're working on and let you decide whether we're doing it to fight the Grik, or threaten your Empire. All I ask is that, on your *honor*, you don't divulge what you see, but I'll leave the evaluation up to you."

Jenks seemed flustered at first, but quickly regained his composure. "That is . . . generous of you, Captain Reddy, particularly considering the previous prohibitions. But I cannot possibly swear not to report what I see if, in my estimation, it poses a threat to my Empire."

Matt sighed. "I thought that was understood. Look, I don't really like you very much and I know you don't like me. But I'd have thought, by now, you'd have accepted the fact that we really do want to be friends with your people. If we become friends—real friends—we'll share all the technology we show you. In spite of what you may believe, it's con-siderable. I wouldn't let you see it at all if I thought you'd still doubt our preparations are devoted to defeating the Grik." He paused, decid-ing to go for broke. "But face it: we're aware there are . . . elements of your own crew—officers—over whom you seem to have little control. Elements much more interested in their own political agenda than they are the safety of this Alliance, definitely. Maybe even the safety of your own precious Empire—as that safety is envisioned by the prin-cess. I think given the choice, your vision of your Empire more closely reflects hers than you might be at liberty to admit. All I'm asking is, if you don't get the impression that our preparations are geared toward striking your country, don't immediately spill what you see to those other 'elements' I spoke about. Keep an open mind."

Jenks considered. Here was a chance he'd craved—to see what the Americans and their furry allies were up to beyond their guarded barricades. He wouldn't admit it, but he already knew a little. A few spies had gotten through. But he hadn't been told everything they'd discovered either. There was much truth in what Captain Reddy said about those "other elements," just as there was truth in the man's observation that Commodore Jenks was less than pleased about how those elements operated, or about their influence over his government. He would have to step carefully, but he sensed an opportunity.

"Very well," he said, "I can give my word to that." He smiled sardonically, his sun-bleached mustaches quirking upward. "So long as it is not generally known I have done so."

Matt almost mirrored his expression. "Oh, I don't think it'll hurt for folks to know I've given you a tour. No way to hide it anyway, so we might as well give them a show. But we won't tell anyone you promised not to blab if you don't feel like it. All I ask is, once we enter the secure area, give us the benefit of the doubt."

"On that you have my word, Captain Reddy."

Matt nodded and glanced at his watch. "Very well. I have another interview to attend to. If you'll excuse me for an hour, maybe we can put some of your suspicions to rest." Matt's gaze rested on Okada. "Thanks for your cooperation, Commander." He rang the bell again and Juan reappeared.

"Cap-i-tan?"

"Juan, ask the Marine sentries to escort Commander Okada back to his quarters, if you please; then send in Ensign Laumer." He stood and extended his hand to Jenks. For the first time, the Imperial took it without any apparent hesitation. "I don't believe this will take all that long, actually. Juan will see that you're comfortable and provide any refreshments you might ask for."

"Thank you, Captain. I look forward to our outing."

When Juan closed the door behind the three, Matt resumed his seat and took a deep breath.

"You're sure this is a good idea, Skipper?" Alden asked.

"You got me. I don't know what else we can do. We can only stall the man so long—and his beef is valid. We've been playing him for time and he knows it. If we don't show him *why*, the 'incidents' will only increase—understandably—and sooner or later, any chance we might've ever had for an alliance with his Empire will go over the side." Matt shook his head. "No, it's time we put our cards on the table. Besides, Her Highness, Becky"—he grinned—"knows everything we're up to. It's not fair to ask her to continue keeping secrets from her own people."

"Except these political officers, these Company wardens," Shinya reminded him.

"Of course." Rebecca and O'Casey had told them about the Company watchdogs aboard Jenks's ship, and had described their function in a way that brought the Nazi SS or Gestapo to Matt's mind. Or maybe the Soviet naval political officers Shinya referred to was a better analogy. Either way, they were sinister and apparently powerful figures, and, given the opinions of O'Casey and the princess, dangerous and subversive as well. Matt had been waiting for some sign that Jenks didn't necessarily work with them hand in glove before he made his earlier invitation. Rebecca was certain he didn't, and even O'Casey—who had his own reasons to be wary of Jenks—agreed, but Matt had to be sure. After Jenks's veiled admission, he thought he was. Of course, Jenks could have suspected their concerns and put on an act. . . . Matt shook his head. He couldn't believe it. He didn't like Jenks, but he grudgingly respected him. The few times he'd actually spoken to Commander Billingsly, he'd decided there couldn't have been more difference between his and Jenks's *character*, at least.

Jenks might be an asshole, but somehow Matt sensed he was an honorable, even gentlemanly asshole. Billingsly was just an asshole, with no class at all. He remained as arrogant and condescending as Jenks had been when they first met, and his open, blatant, almost hostile bigotry toward the Lemurians was offensive and unsettling. If all the Honorable New Britain Company was like Billingsly, Matt's destroyermen and their allies might have as much to fear from them as they did from the Grik. But Jenks was pure Navy, according to O'Casey, and Matt was very glad that seemed to make a difference. For a number of reasons.

"Yeah," Matt resumed, "we'll have to convince Jenks to keep them in the dark. I think we can, once we show him what we're up to—and then offer to let him see some of the stuff in action! If he accepts, and I bet he will, maybe we'll have some time to work on him." There was a knock at the door.

"Enter."

Juan swept the door open and Ensign Irvin Laumer stepped inside, hat under his arm, and stood at attention. He was towheaded and lanky, but not particularly tall, and he didn't look quite old enough for the uniform he wore. The seriousness of his expression meant he did have some idea why he was there, however, and Matt felt a tug of uncertainty. From what he'd heard of Laumer, he had high hopes for the boy. The kid had good sense, clearly. He'd been the highest-ranking survivor of S-19's complement, but he'd allowed the more experienced chief of the boat take de facto command. The decision must have been a tough one, because Laumer didn't *seem* the type to defer responsibility. Hopefully that meant, like any good officer, he knew when to take responsibility and when to delegate it. Matt's main concern now was that maybe Laumer felt he had something to prove.

Actually, he did, in a way. All of Matt's senior officers, human and Lemurian, were veterans of fierce fighting now. All but Laumer. If the ensign was ever going to be followed where he led, he *did* have to prove himself, Matt reflected. He only wished Laumer's baptism didn't have to be on such a difficult and potentially important mission. He'd love to send Spanky or Brister, or any of half a dozen others, but he couldn't. They were just too necessary where they were. The simple, hard fact of the matter was that Laumer was the only one he could spare with the experience and technical expertise.

"Sir, Ensign Laumer, reporting as ordered!"

"At ease, Ensign," Matt replied mildly, and gestured at the stool Jenks had just vacated across the desk. "Please have a seat." Irvin sat, still rigid, upon the creaky stool. "Coffee?"

"Uh, no, thank you, sir."

Matt waited a moment, staring at the ensign. He decided to get straight to the point. "I want that submarine," he said simply.

Irvin Laumer nodded. He'd obviously expected as much. "I'll get it for you, sir, if it's the last thing I do."

Alden grunted. "Son, that's the point. We want it, sure, but we don't want it to be the last thing you do. You or the people you'll command."

Matt glanced at the Marine and nodded. "Exactly. We've discussed this at some length and decided your mission will have a hierarchy of agendas. First, of course, you must determine whether she can be salvaged at all. She might not even *be* there anymore. Remember too, given the nature of some of the creatures on this world—and under its seas—it's not imperative that we get the submarine back *as* a submarine, if you get my meaning."

Laumer looked troubled, but nodded. "Yes, sir, I think I do."

"You must *know* you do, because that's the deal. If she's still there, it'll be up to you to decide if you can get her off the beach. Don't fool around too long trying if it's not practical. If you can, swell. You'll have fuel, and Spanky, Gilbert, and Flynn all say at least one of her diesels ought to come to life. If you can get her under way, hopefully Saan-Kakja can provide an escort to get you to Manila. After that, bring her here if you can, but that's not essential either. What is essential is the stuff she's made of. Decide quickly if you can get her off, because if you can't, you've got to strip her—and I mean *strip* her! I want her engines, batteries, wiring, screws, gun, bearings, instruments, sonar—hell, I want every *bolt* you can get out of her; is that understood? Even if you get her all the way back here we might strip her anyway, so that's the absolute top priority. Like I said—and I can't stress this enough—we need what she's made of more than we need her. Her whole, intact carcass would be nice—she's got as much steel as *Walker*—but this is strictly a 'bird in the hand' operation. Get what you *know* you can get."

Irvin gulped. "I understand, Captain."

"Very well. Now." Matt leaned back in his chair. "We can't afford to send much with you, but you'll get what we can spare. You can have five of your submariners if you can get them to volunteer. Concentrate on those with critical engineering and operating skills."

"Flynn?" Irvin asked.

Matt shook his head. "No. Two reasons. First, we need him here. Second, and don't take this wrong; he assured me he has the utmost respect for you, but . . . to be honest, he's had enough of subs in these waters." Matt shrugged. "I already asked him, but . . . well, let's just say we've had a little experience with people who've been through too much and pushed too far." Matt was thinking of his old coxswain Tony Scott. "Sometimes they lose focus and make mistakes," he added in a quiet tone. "We'll use Flynn in the shipyard for now, but he's asked for an infantry regiment, if you can believe that." To Matt's surprise, Laumer actually smiled.

"Yes, sir, I can believe it."

Instead of asking the ensign to elaborate, Matt pushed on: "You'll have two of the prize ships to transport equipment and personnel, and bring back what you can salvage. You won't command the ships, obviously, but you'll be in overall command of the expedition."

"Thank you, sir," Laumer said. "Thanks for the opportunity."

Matt grimaced. "There may be plenty of 'opportunity' to get yourself killed, and I'm ordering you to avoid that. Period. Otherwise, besides those previously mentioned, your orders are to depart Baalkpan aboard the prize USS *Simms* in company with another prize sloop. . . ." He shook his head. "We're really going to have to sort that out."

The destroyermen, 'Cat and human, found it difficult and confusing to use the old terms for sailing warships. A small faction insisted "sloops" ought to be destroyers and "frigates" should be cruisers. This caused contention among the frigate sailors, who thought *they* ought to be destroyers and sloops were mere gunboats. God only knew how weird it would get when they had even bigger ships—and seaplane tender/carriers like *Big Sal*. The fact was, no one of either race wanted to give up the title "destroyerman," no matter what they served on.

"Anyway," Matt continued, "you'll escort *Placca-Mar*." He hoped he said it right. His 'Cat was finally improving, as was his pronunciation. "She's the Home Saan-Kakja's returning to the Filpin Lands aboard, along with plans and some of the large machinery we've completed. Colonel Shinya and the prisoner will also be aboard. The colonel will be escorting Commander Okada, but his primary mission is to take charge of training Saan-Kakja's troops in Manila. While you're with *Placca-Mar*, you'll be under Colonel Shinya's direct command, and if you run into any marauding lizards, his orders will supersede any I've given you today. In other words, feel free to disobey the one about avoiding opportunities to get yourself killed, because you *will* defend Saan-Kakja to the last. Understood?"

Irvin gulped, but nodded. "Aye-aye, sir."

"Barring incident, you'll depart company with *Placca-Mar* in the Sibutu Passage, hug the Sulu Archipelago to Mindanao, and proceed to your destination."

"What about mountain fish, if we run across any?" Irvin asked hesitantly, and Matt looked at him, scratching the back of his neck.

"Sparks—I mean Lieutenant Commander Riggs—is working on stuff. So's Ordnance. I also hope to squeeze some advice out of Jenks, if I can. We'll do everything possible to make sure you have solid communications as well, but"—he shrugged—"who knows? You might wind up on your own."

Irvin knew the entire mission was a test of sorts, as much for the captain to evaluate him as for him to evaluate himself. He'd missed all the fighting and really had little reason to expect such an opportunity— and an opportunity was how he viewed it. Somehow he'd prevail. He had to.

"I've been on my own before, Captain," he said at last. "Sort of. Before you took us off Talaud in the first place, we didn't even know what had happened. Even if we lose communications, I'm confident we'll manage."

Matt looked at him for a long moment, then glanced at the others in the chamber. "I sincerely hope so. I implied earlier that you're the only man we can spare for this, but remember, the war's just begun. We can't spare anyone in the long run."

"No, sir."

As was customary by midafternoon, the rain had stopped by the time Captain Reddy, General Alden, and Commodore Jenks gathered at the base of the great, scorched Galla tree. As was also customary, the re- mainder of the day would be humid and oppressive and the clothes worn by the little group had barely begun to dry before perspiration replaced the moisture. Sandra, Keje, and Alan Letts had joined them. Shinya had departed to prepare the troops for "inspection," and Matt had asked the Bosun not to attend. Chief Gray uncomfortably agreed. His and Jenks's antagonism toward each other was well-known, and Matt wanted the commodore as comfortable about the tour as possible.

A two-wheeled cart appeared out of the bustling activity of the city, the driver reining his animal just short of the overhead that protected them from the incessant dripping. The cart itself looked like an over-size rickshaw, complete with gaudy decorations. The beast pulling it had never been seen in Baalkpan before it and a large herd of its cous-ins arrived from Manila a few weeks before. It looked a little like one of the stunted brontosarries from a distance, although it was smaller and covered with fur. It also had a shorter neck and tail, even if both were proportionately beefier and more muscular. The head was larger too, with short, palmated antlers.

The Fil-pin 'Cats called them paalkas, although Silva's insidious influence had reached Baalkpan before them and here they were al-most universally called pack-mooses, even by the local 'Cats. They were herbivorous marsupials, of all things, and Matt was glad to have them. He wondered why no one had ever imported them to Baalkpan before; they were obviously more sensible draft animals than the ubiq-uitous brontosaurus. They were much more biddable and, from what he'd seen, at least as smart as a horse. They could even be ridden, al-though no kind of conventional saddle would serve. They were half again as big as a Belgian draft horse, and any rider would have been perpetually doing the splits. Matt primarily wanted them to pull his light artillery pieces and they should be great for that. Shinya and Bris-ter were working on ways the gun's crews could ride them.

Other creatures that *could* be ridden like a horse had arrived from Manila. They were me-naaks, and nobody objected when their name was changed to "meanies." They looked like long-legged crocodiles that ran on all fours, as they should, but their legs were shaped more like a dog's. They ran like dogs too, fast and focused. Their skin was like a rhino-pig's, thick and covered with long, bristly hair, and they had a heavy, plywood-thick case that protected their vitals. Matt was dubious about them, and admitted they were scary. When he'd first seen them in Manila, they'd borne troops in Saan-Kakja's livery, apparently on errands. The crowds gave them a wide berth and Matt had noticed their jaws were always strapped tightly shut. They seemed to obey well enough, and Saan-Kakja had since assured him that they'd make fine cavalry mounts—once he'd explained the concept to her—as long as a rider didn't mind the fact that his mount's fondest wish was to eat him.

Cavalry, and the mobility it provided, was something Matt had been wanting for a long time. It wasn't something 'Cats had given a great deal of thought to, since, as little as most of them ever envisioned fighting, they'd *never* envisioned fighting an open-field battle. The terrain just didn't suit. For the campaign taking shape in Matt's mind however, cavalry of some sort—or at least mounted infantry or dragoons—would come as a nasty surprise for the Grik indeed.

"How . . . interesting," observed Jenks, staring at the conveyance.

Matt shook off his reverie and smiled. "More practical than walking." He gestured around at the aftermath of the squall. "Especially in this muck." Sandra smiled at him and gravitated to his side.

Jenks looked at her briefly, then shook his head. Apparently, what he'd been about to say or ask wasn't something he wanted to discuss just then. He peered into the cart. "Is there space for all of us?" he asked doubtfully.

The paalka dragged the cart through the bustling city. There was so much activity that, except for the remaining damage, it was difficult for Matt to tell a massive battle had raged around and through Baalkpan not so very long before. It was easy to remember they were at war however, since much of the seemingly chaotic commotion was geared toward military preparation. Squads of troops squelched by in cadence, either toward or from the expanded drill field. Quite a few of these wore the distinctive black-and-yellow livery of Saan-Kakja.

Matt, Alden, and Letts returned the salute of a platoon of Marines that marched by on the left, heading for the parade ground. Matt had finally allowed the reconstitution of the Marines as an independent force. They'd be needed as such and the 'Cats' various guard (or, increasingly, army) regiments had sufficient veteran NCOs and officers now to lead them. The Marine uniform was also strikingly regular, now that it had become official. It consisted of a dark blue kilt with red piping along the hem for veterans. NCOs sported red stripes encircling their kilts, from the bottom up, to designate their rank. All wore thick white articulated rhino-pig leather armor over their chests as well. Stamped bronze helmets like those the destroyermen wore (except for the ear holes) completed the basic uniform. Baldrics, straps, belts, and backpacks were all black leather, and had become universal among Allied forces.

The "Army" had begun a similar attempt to provide uniforms for its troops, but the colors varied, since its forces represented different members of the Alliance. In the case of Baalkpan, which fielded numerous regiments, the leather armor was a natural dark brown and the kilts were bright green. This was the color of Nakja-Mur's livery and Adar hadn't changed it. The various regiments had gold numbers embroidered on their kilts.

Matt, and everyone else, had been surprised and gratified to learn that the Aryaalan and B'mbaadan regiments (formerly bitter foes) had been integrated by Lord Rolak and Queen Maraan and had chosen red-and-black kilts, also with regimental numbers, and gray leather breastplates.

As much as Baalkpan's industry had recovered, and even leaped ahead after the battle, none of this would have been possible without Saan-Kakja's support. She'd ordered as much material and supplies, and as many troops and artisans, be brought forward as her nation could realistically afford. Until the frontier could be pushed back, Baalkpan remained the front line of the war, and without her aid, another battle like the last would have finished it. Of course, *Amagi* was no longer a threat, but as things had stood, she wouldn't have been needed.

A lot of Baalkpan's runaway population had returned as well. Perhaps goaded by shame that they'd left in the first place instead of defending their home, they set to work with a will. Matt believed that, with the returns and additions, Baalkpan's population was now greater than it had been when his old, battered destroyer first steamed into the bay.

Smoking pitch assaulted their sinuses as the paalka drew them past the expanded ropewalk, and sparks flew from forges as swordsmiths shaped their blades. Iron had been known to the People, but had been little used except for weapons. Now, an abundance of good steel wreckage was available, as well as a new steady supply of iron ore from the interior, and the Lemurians were drawing out of the Bronze Age at last. Matt watched Sandra's face as the sparks fell and sizzled on the damp ground. He knew what she was thinking. The various Lemurian cultures had been very fine, and with some exceptions, almost idyllic before they came here. Now all was in a state of flux, changing forever to meet the necessities of a nightmarish war. For a bittersweet instant, Matt wondered what changes the war back home would bring to America.

They eased through the congested area surrounding the new sawmill. The big, circular blades sprayed chips and sawdust in great arcs, while brontosarries plodded through a slurry of muck, turning a massive windlass that transferred its rotation through a series of gears that spun the great blades. The quaint display of ingenuity had come from the quirky minds of the Mice. They had certainly risen to the challenge of this new world, Matt thought proudly, as had all his destroyermen.

As they neared the waterfront, the buildings were no longer elevated. Instead, all the shops and warehouses stood right at ground level. A great berm lay beyond them with but a single gated opening, and swarms of workers thronged in and out of the bottleneck. A squad of Marine sentries watched keenly for unknown or suspicious faces. Fortunately, the only faces they had to examine closely were human, and the hundred-odd remaining Amer-i-caans were well-known to them. When the paalka brought them to the gate, the crowd parted and the sentries waved them through.

If anything, the chaos beyond the gate seemed more apparent than in the heart of the bustling city, but only at a glance. Here, the warehouses, workshops, and open-air industry that sprawled around the basin teemed with what only appeared to be disconnected activity. The racket of tools, shouted commands, and roaring furnaces was over-whelming, and smoke and dank steam hung like fog. In the distance, across the yard, the skeletal frames of numerous ships rose above the activity and haze. Matt and his companions quickly perceived the un-derlying order—they'd all spent considerable time there, after all—and Matt suspected Jenks saw it as well.

"Here we are, Commodore," Sandra said brightly as Matt helped her down from the rickshaw. Jenks hopped lightly down with the un-expected grace of an athlete and stared around with all the indications of amazement. Alden, Keje, and Letts joined them, and while the oth-ers stared about with expressions of proud accomplishment, Keje con-tinued glaring at Jenks. He hadn't been in favor of letting this stranger view their greatest secrets and he still didn't trust the man. His initial dislike had only been intensified by the frequent attempts at espionage, and now they were going to give him a guided tour! He trusted Matt's judgment, and intellectually he knew they had little choice, but he still didn't like it.

"Most impressive, my dear," Jenks replied, somewhat awkwardly. He glanced at his escort. "Gentlemen. Most impressive indeed. You have accomplished all this in the three months since your battle?"

"No, sir," said Letts. "The basics were here when we first arrived. We added a lot while we were preparing for the enemy, and not much was damaged in the fighting. Evidently, they wanted these facilities preserved. Baalkpan would've made them a good base from which to go after our other friends—as well as your people, eventually."

"Indeed," came Jenks's noncommittal reply.

Letts looked at Captain Reddy and saw the nod. This was his show now. "If you would all follow me, I'll point out some of the more inter-esting things we've been working on."

They trudged past furnace rooms from which an endless relay of naked, panting 'Cats pushed wheelbarrows loaded with copper round shot. These they brought to waiting carts, where others stood with heavy leather gloves to transfer the still-hot spheres. There were hisses of steam and scorched wood when the shot dropped on the cart's wet timbers. Most of the party smiled and returned the waves of the work-ers. Jenks said nothing, but clearly took note.

Moving along, they reached one of the several foundries that now dotted the basin. Great bronze gun tubes, each with carts of their own, waited in patient rows for their journey to the boring and reaming loft. These new guns had rough, sand-cast bores and would still be smooth-bores after reaming, but even as their interior diameters had increased, the quality and sophistication of their shape had improved and the weight of metal they required was much reduced. Most of the original guns that had defended Baalkpan had already been recast, and generally, they could get five or six guns from four of the earlier, much cruder weapons. The next foundry they passed was pouring molten iron under an open-sided shed and gouts of sparks and fiery meteors arced out and sizzled on a damp beam decking roped off for safety.

Jenks saw all this and was much impressed. Matt and Sandra talked excitedly of what they'd accomplished and Letts seemed almost jubilant. Even Keje had lost some of his earlier overt unfriendliness. As often as he must have seen it now, he still seemed to have an air of wonder. A long, high shed stood nearer the water, covering an assortment of bizarre shapes in various stages of evident completion. Before they headed in that direction, the group was distracted by a series of shouts followed by what sounded like a rough volley of musket fire. The noise quickly settled into a sustained roar.

Brevet Major Benjamin Mallory twisted his arm to stretch the aching muscles. His T-shirt and Lemurian-made dungarees were sweat blotched and stained, and a dark rag dangled and swayed from his belt as he grabbed the wrench and strained against the final bolt.

"There," he said to no one in particular, "my built-in torque wrench says that's about right." He stepped back from the odd-looking machine and dragged the filthy rag across his forehead before he plopped the hat back on his head. It was the only item remaining to him that had once been Army brown. The OD pistol belt and leather holster were his, but they were essentially the same as everyone else's. The machine was an engine—he hoped. It was a vague copy of an upright, four-cylinder Wright Gypsy that would serve as a prototype power plant for the airframe design they'd—tentatively—settled on. It was inherently more difficult to balance a four-cylinder engine than one with six cylinders, but they were trying to keep things as simple as possible for now. The cylinders themselves were air-cooled legacies of the crashed PBY, and they'd dredged up as much of the old plane as they could hook from its scattered resting place on the bottom of Baalkpan Bay. They'd recovered only one of the engines, but fortunately, it wasn't the one they'd already removed a couple of damaged cylinders from. It *had* been damaged beyond repair by a couple of holes through the crankcase and a warped crankshaft sustained when the spinning prop hit the water, but twelve cylinders, fifteen pushrods, eleven piston rods, eighteen valves, and nine pistons were still up to spec. They'd serve his purpose of testing the *rest* of the new engine they'd built from scratch.

Seaman (maybe Ensign now, if his transfer came through) Fred Reynolds stood nearby poring over a black-bound book with red writing on it. It was a copy of Brimm and Boggess's *Aircraft Engine Maintenance* they'd found in the tool kit of the PBY's doubtless long-dead flight mechanic. It was exactly like a similar copy Ben had done his best to memorize in pilot training. He liked to think he *had* memorized enough to build something like the simple engine before him on the stand, but when they inevitably went on to build bigger and better things, the wealth of formulas, diagrams, and general tidbits of information including things as mundane as hand file designs would prove invaluable. Even when one considered the relatively large, eclectic library of *Walker*'s dead surgeon, "Doc" Stevens, and the many technical manuals they'd off-loaded from the two destroyers before their final sortie, it was, in many ways, the single most precious book they possessed. Some of Adar's Sky Priest acolytes had already made a handwritten copy, and others were being copied from it.

The book was already invaluable to poor Reynolds, who stared at the pages like they were written in ancient Greek. Ben stifled a chuckle. Apparently, Reynolds had finally decided what to strike for; he wanted to fly. He'd said he wanted excitement, but he was a little guy, and that would have made Ordnance hell—or so he believed. Ben suspected that in reality, the kid was scared to death of Dennis Silva—completely understandable—and since Silva was the most . . . visible representative of that division and had as yet untested limitations on his authority . . . the fledgling Air Corps, or Naval Air Arm, or whatever it would be called, probably seemed like a comparatively safer billet. Ben chuckled aloud at that, unheard over the machine noises emanating from the rest of the shop.

He glanced at the only other human in sight: Commander Perry Brister. Formerly *Mahan*'s engineering officer and now general engineering minister of the entire Alliance, the dark-haired young man was making a final inspection of the fuel line leading to the simple, crude carburetor. Ben knew Perry had other things to do that day, but he'd always liked fooling with small engines, he'd said, and he wanted to be there when they cranked it up.

"Looks good here," Perry rasped. His once soft voice had never recovered from all the yelling he did during the great battle. Ben looked at the two Lemurians poised near the propeller. One, a sable-furred 'Cat with a polished 7.7-millimeter cartridge case stuck through a hole in his ear, grinned.

"You boys ready?" Ben asked.

"You bet," answered the 'Cat Ben called Tikker. Mallory shook his head and grinned. It was Captain Tikker now. Stepping to a small console, he flipped a switch.

"Contact!" he shouted.

"Contact!" chorused the 'Cats, and, heaving the propeller blade up as high as they could reach, they brought it down with all their might. For a moment, the motor coughed, sputtered, and gasped while the 'Cats jumped back. With a jerk, the wooden propeller came to a stop.

"Switch off!" announced Mallory, and the two 'Cats approached the propeller again. They hadn't thoroughly tested the remote throttle adjustment, and Brister stepped forward and squirted a little fuel in the carburetor. Nodding, he joined Ben.

"Contact!"

This time, the propeller spun with an erratic, explosive, *phut, phut, phut!* sound, backfired, burped, then became a popping, vibrating blur. Brister hurried forward, careful of the spinning blades, and tinkered with the throttle linkage. Slowly, the vibration diminished and the smooth roar overwhelmed their cheers.

*   *   *

"This way!" Letts shouted over the din, and they hurried toward the noise. Another shed, smaller than the first and enclosed on all sides, was nearby. Letts moved a curtain aside and the racket flooded out. In he went, and Jenks was swept along with the rest. Oil lamps dimly lit the interior of the shed, but there were small, brightly glowing objects placed near large, complicated-looking machines. Lemurians and a few men toiled at those machines with singular concentration in spite of the noise emanating from another brightly lit area toward the back of the shed. As he passed them, Jenks saw the machines were turning and spinning, throwing coiled pieces of metal aside. They were also noisy—or would have been—without the cacophonous roar. Most were fairly straightforward. He'd seen their like in Imperial factories: lathes, mills, etc. Great leather belts whirled around pulleys attached to the high ceiling and transferred their rotation to the machines. A very few of the machines had no belts whatsoever, but seemed to run off insulated copper cables terminated at the same source as the brilliant white lights. The mystery fascinated him as much as the roar that grew even louder as they approached.

A haze of smoky fumes was gathering in the light, swirling in a strange, artificial wind. In it stood three men and a couple of Lemurians staring intently at a relatively small machine vibrating on a stand. A big paddle of some kind whirled to a blur at one end of it.

"Mr. Mallory!" Matt shouted at one of the men who stood, hands on hips. He turned.

"Captain Reddy!" There was a huge smile on the man's bearded face. "Good afternoon, sir." He motioned at the machine and eyed a set of gauges on his console. "Temps are a little variable on the cylinders, but that's to be expected with an air-cooled in-line. The production models'll be liquid-cooled and heavier, but the horsepower ought to be similar. The main thing is that it looks like we've solved the crankcase and oil pump issues—at least for straight and level." For the first time Mallory noticed Jenks and his smile faded a little.

"It's okay," Matt shouted. "It's time."

Mallory shrugged as if to say, *You're the skipper*, and motioned to one of the 'Cats stationed near another panel. "Bring her up, Tikker!"

The sable-furred 'Cat with a shiny brass tube in his ear nodded and advanced a small lever. Immediately, the noise increased and the paddlelike object whirred even faster, redoubling the gale of wind and noxious fumes. Jenks began to feel a little ill. Sandra coughed violently and patted Captain Reddy on the arm. Matt looked at her and nodded, noting Jenks's expression as well. He patted Mallory, and when he got his attention, he made a "cut it" gesture.

Tikker noticed and backed the throttle down until the engine finally wheezed and died. The sudden, relative silence was overwhelming.

"Mr. Mallory, you're going to choke all your workers," Matt said with a grin. Ben looked around. If anything but excitement made him feel light-headed, it didn't show.

"Well, yes, sir," he said, beaming, "but it works! The damn thing works! Uh, begging your pardon." He glanced at Jenks and his euphoria slipped a notch. "Yeah, it stinks, I guess, but we've been trying to keep things under wraps."

"I know. That's over now." Matt clapped Ben on his good shoulder and nodded congratulations to the others. "Besides, it looks like we'll be ready for flight testing soon and there's no way to keep *that* a secret. I think it's time Commodore Jenks, at least, sees what we're up to."

Jenks finally surrendered to a coughing fit of his own, but when he composed himself, he pointed at the engine. "What is that thing?" he asked. "Some sort of weapon?"

"Not by itself," hedged one of the other workers who'd joined the group. He was a former *Mahan* machinist's mate named "Miami" Tindal.

Tikker stepped closer. "We put it on a plane, and it'll be a weapon," he said excitedly. A lot of Lemurians acted uncomfortable around the Imperials and were hesitant to speak to them. Tikker never seemed uncomfortable talking to anyone.

"What's a 'plane'?" Jenks asked.

Matt looked at Ben. "If you and . . . Captain Tikker would accompany us?" He paused, his amused, understanding eyes on Perry. "You as well, Commander Brister."

Workers raised awnings to vent the exhaust while together, the growing entourage returned to the larger, open shed. There they showed Jenks an array of ungainly contraptions. Some were mere skeletons, made from laminated bamboo strips, cannibalized even before they were complete. A couple had a kind of taut fabric stretched across their bones to which some kind of sealant or glue had been applied. One, the nearest to the shop, rested on a cart or truck much like the earlier gun tubes. This one not only appeared almost finished, but was painted a medium dark blue. There were darker blue roundels—significant devices of some kind, Jenks was sure—in several places, with large white stars and small red dots painted within them.

"So this is it?" Matt asked appreciatively. It didn't look much like the NC craft he remembered seeing pictures of. If anything, it looked like a miniature PBY. The fuselage/hull form was virtually identical, except there was a single open-air cockpit behind a slip of salvaged Plexiglas where the flight deck would have been. Another open cockpit was positioned halfway to the tail, where the PBY had possessed a pair of observation blisters. The large single wing was supported by an arrangement of struts instead of being attached to the fuselage by a faired compartment. It was easy to see the motor would go in the empty space between the wing and fuselage—with the prop spinning mere feet behind the pilot's head.

"What about wing floats?" Matt asked. By the tone of his voice, he was reviving an old argument.

"They'll be cranked down mechanically by the observer/mechanic in the aft cockpit." Ben looked a little sheepish. "I know you wanted to keep it simple, Skipper, but this is a lot simpler than putting fixed floats on a lower wing. Not to mention we don't have to *make* those lower wings." He gestured at one of the incomplete skeletons. "This way she'll be lighter, faster, more maneuverable, and honestly, we should be able to put her down on rougher seas. With that bottom wing so close to the water, I was really worried about that."

"That's fine, Ben. I told you, when it comes to flying you're the boss, and your arguments do have merit. I just want to make sure the things aren't overly complicated. Like the ships, I want a lot of good ones, not a few of the best."

"I agree, sir. But with this design, I think we get a little of both."

Jenks interrupted. "Flying . . . you mean to say that thing will . . . *fly*?"

"Hopefully." Matt nodded toward a large heap of twisted wreckage piled in the space between the two buildings. It was all that remained of the crashed PBY. "That one did."

"Not very well," Jenks observed skeptically, "if its present condition is any indication. And that one is metal. Why not these new ones?"

"You'd be amazed how well it flew," Matt answered wistfully, "and for how long. But our enemy managed to knock it down. Do you think you could shoot down a flying target?"

Jenks didn't answer.

"Anyway, the metal it was made of is called aluminum. It came from our old world, and I don't know when or if we'll ever be able to make it here. We're having enough trouble with iron. When we get that sorted out, we'll try steel—besides what we're salvaging from the enemy ship. I'm afraid the lizards are probably ahead of us there. . . . Anyway, once we get real steel, and plenty of it, you'll be amazed at what we can do."

Sandra pulled him down to whisper in his ear and Matt's face became grim, but he nodded. He straightened and looked Jenks in the eye.

"Now we're going to show you something else," he said. "So far, you probably haven't seen anything that would assure you we aren't a threat to your empire."

"Quite the contrary, Captain," Jenks answered honestly. "I could even argue that what I have seen here today proves you are a threat that should be quashed before you reach your stride, as it were." There was no hostility in Jenks's tone, only a dispassionate statement of fact.

"Very well. I'll prove it to you. I'll show you something that, up until now, we've been willing to kill your spies, if necessary, to keep them from seeing. I guess you could call it an industrial achievement of sorts"—he waved around—"but not like these others. Mainly, it's an admission of vulnerability, I guess, more than anything." His green eyes turned cold. "Something I damn sure wouldn't show you if I was trying to intimidate you with our power. That alone should convince you we mean you no harm."

"Does this have to do with your mysterious iron-hulled steamer you've been hiding from us since we arrived?" Jenks asked quietly.

"Follow me," was all Matt said.

The group gathered on the dock overlooking the old shipyard basin. Oily brown water coiled with tendrils of iridescent purple and blue lapped gently against the old fitting-out pier. It was quiet where they stood, although considerable activity bustled nearby. Four of the great Homes had been flooded down across the mouth of the inlet in two ranks. Work was under way to seal the gaps between them, fore and aft, so there would ultimately be a pair of continuous walls from land to land.

A single "wall" was the customary dry-dock technique Lemurians had always used to build their great ships in the first place. Inspired by that, and realizing the need for a permanent dry dock, Spanky and Perry had designed one. It was a hard sell at first, since the effort required *Walker* to remain on the bottom even longer. Also, even though he helped design the dry dock, Brister had made a reluctant but strong argument against taking labor and resources away from construction of the new Allied fleet. It was actually easier, he'd reasoned, to build entirely new ships than it would be to fix *Walker*. He'd been in favor of using the Lemurian method to refloat the ship—and then only so they could stabilize her and prevent further deterioration. Perhaps someday they could attempt repairs. In the meantime, they should concentrate all their efforts on the new construction. As for the dry dock, it would certainly be a useful convenience, but one they could postpone.

Spanky argued that a permanent dry dock was essential, not only to refloat *Walker*—and do it right—but because the new construction Brister referred to would be much more prone to require repairs below the waterline than other ships the Lemurians built. He vividly remembered how difficult it had been to remove one of *Mahan*'s propellers and install it on *Walker*. With the ravenous nature of the aquatic life on this different Earth, no underwater work could be performed without elaborate preparation. Besides, once they got her up, Spanky wasn't ready to write *Walker* off. No one had any illusions that repairing the badly mauled destroyer would be an easy task; it might even be impossible. But they had to try. They owed her that much.

As commander of all Allied forces, Captain Reddy had to make the decision, and he'd agonized over it, wondering if he was being entirely objective. He wanted his ship back, and everyone (particularly the Lemurians) wanted him to have her. She'd been instrumental in achieving every success they'd enjoyed, and the dilapidated old four stacker had become a powerful symbol to everyone involved in opposing the scourge of the Grik. The problem was, until they could get at her, there was no way to know if she could even be repaired, and Matt was realistic enough to know Brister was right: they *had* to have those new ships.

Spanky, Jim Ellis, and Sandra had been anxious too, but for a different reason. They knew they couldn't influence his decision, but they also knew how important it was not only to the future of the man who had to make it, but to all of their futures as well. Matthew Reddy had lost . . . a piece of his soul . . . when his ship went down. Only when he knew she was safe and afloat and alive did they think he'd gain it back. And he had to gain it back. Spanky's insistent argument that they needed a real dry dock—one way or the other—was finally sufficient to gain Matt's support.

It was still necessary to flood down the Homes—twice as many as would have been required to simply refloat the ship—since they had to create a dry lane in which to work. It would take longer, but the wait would be worth it. The Lemurian city of Baalkpan would have a real, dedicated, honest-to-goodness dry dock, and the implications of that went far beyond simply pumping out and patching up a single battered, overage destroyer.

What Jenks saw was a lot of heavy, new-looking machinery being erected, and he recognized much of it in principle, as well as the strange variety of crude, open air, steam engines. Tarred canvas hoses were coiled in heaps and a pair of large cranes were under construction. Then his eyes rested on the unfamiliar, scarred, and dreary structures protruding from the water. He gasped.

"It has sunk!" he exclaimed. "Your iron-hulled steamer, your *Walker*, was sunk!"

"She was badly damaged in the battle," Matt confirmed woodenly, "and barely managed to make it here. We'll try to refloat her, but we've got no idea if it's even possible. She might be damaged beyond re-pair."

Jenks turned a sympathetic glance to Matt. He fully understood the trauma of losing a ship and wondered if that might explain a lot of Captain Reddy's distance. Of course, he chided himself, not having known of the loss, he'd possibly been less than sensitive himself. "I didn't know," he managed. "Nobody knew."

"That was our intention. You keep wondering if we're a threat to you, but how are we to know you're not a threat to us?" Matt shook his head. "I don't think you could *conquer* us. No offense, but based on what we've learned from the princess and . . . Well, we're pretty secure here now. We've stood against a more massive assault than I think you could ever mount. Our concern is, we already *have* an enemy and we have to strike as quickly as we can. As much as we'd like to be friends with your Empire, we can't afford to be distracted right now. We have to go after the Grik with everything we have, and that *would* leave us vulnerable here. We're not really even asking for a true military alliance, much as we'd like one. We just want you to leave us alone!"

"Releasing the princess into our care would go a long way toward assuring that," Jenks said with a trace of sarcasm.

"Possibly, but she doesn't *want* to be released, does she?" Sandra suddenly interjected with a passion that disconcerted Jenks. He'd been surprised she was even present. Different people had different customs, but he'd never met any culture that encouraged women to speak so boldly, or even allowed their presence in situations such as this. The rules were different for nobility of course, but the Americans didn't have a nobility. . . . Did they? Perhaps they'd been influenced by the Lemurians. Lemurian females clearly enjoyed a status here the likes of which he'd never seen. Maybe the scarcity of American women gave them more power? No, he rejected that. He knew Miss Tucker held the rank of lieutenant and was their Minister of Medicine. She clearly had real status and felt no constraints in demonstrating it. Odd.

"I think she has more reason to fear for her safety aboard your ship than she does here," Sandra continued. "You may not have noticed, but she's something of a heroine to the people of this city. If they ever found out something happened to her while she was in your care, there probably *would* be war, and there wouldn't be anything I or Matt or anyone else could do about it—even if we wanted to."

She sighed, and Jenks saw the pain on her face. "None of us wants or needs such a stupid, wasteful war. There would be terrible losses on both sides, and no matter who eventually 'won,' both of us would ultimately lose in the end," she said with certainty. "We don't have *time* to let the Grik catch their breath, and we need every warrior we have to face them—just as I think you need all your troops and ships to avert threats of your own. To *your* east, perhaps?"

Her last punch was a good one, judging by Jenks's expression, even if it was just a guess. Rebecca and O'Casey had described other humans east of the empire who had been a growing threat. They hadn't known of any recent, open confrontations, but they'd been gone a long time and Jenks had certainly been jumpy about something from the start. Their revelations had practically pinpointed the location of the heart of the Empire as well.

"Perhaps you are right," Jenks temporized, still overcoming his surprise. "Perhaps we both have more pressing concerns than fighting one another. But even if you are right about that, surely you can see why I personally chafe at this interminable delay? Honestly, how long must my squadron languish here while it might be needed elsewhere?"

Matt pointed to a small forest of masts clustered beyond the point, where the new fitting-out pier was. These were not just more captured Grik ships under repair. They were new ships, built and fitting out along the same lines as the first human/Lemurian frigates that had performed so well in the previous battles. This construction was different however. Structurally as stout and almost identical to their predecessors, these were steam powered with a central screw propeller. Matt disliked what he considered the Imperial's dangerously exposed paddle wheels, and now that they knew the Grik had cannons, he'd insisted they not take any chances that a single lucky hit might put a ship out of action.

"Over there is one of the main reasons I invited you here today. The *main* reason." He paused. "Why don't you see for yourself?" he asked. "In just a few weeks, we'll mount an expedition to assess the situation in Aryaal, and possibly a few other places. Come with me. By the time we return, we'll know whether or not we can push the Grik on our own terms, or if we'll have to continue preparations for a more costly campaign. Either way, with that knowledge, I hope to be free to escort Her Highness home."

Commander Walter Billingsly was writing furiously in his journal, quill scritching violently on the coarse paper and spattering little drips and blobs among the words. The writing style was a reflection of his personality: get to the point, regardless of the mess, and do it at a furious pace. Today, he was most furious to learn Commodore Jenks had been given a tour of the "apes" industrial center and he had not been officially informed, nor had he been allowed to send any "escorts" along. Jenks's growing independent-mindedness regarding this entire fiasco was becoming increasingly tiresome. His hand stilled when he heard the sounds of the commodore being piped back aboard. Quickly, he capped the inkwell, wiped his quill on a stained handkerchief, and sanded his most recent passage. Closing the leather-bound book, he stood and straightened his overtight tunic and rounded the desk on his way to the door and the companionway beyond.

On deck, he moved to intercept the commodore as soon as the side party was dismissed.

"What is the meaning of this, Jenks?" he demanded quietly, but with an edge. One must always observe the proprieties of the fiction that the Navy actually controlled its ships.

"The meaning of what, *Commander*?" Jenks replied through clenched teeth. He was clearly angered by Billingsly's tone, but also somewhat . . . distracted.

Billingsly straightened, glancing about. He had a lot of men on this ship, some known, others secret, but the vast majority were loyal Navy men. The charade must be maintained.

"Might I have a word with you, sir? In private?"

Jenks seemed to focus. "I suppose," he muttered resignedly. Raising his voice, he addressed Lieutenant Grimsley. "Lieutenant, there will be an unscheduled boat alongside shortly, I shouldn't wonder. They'll request our coaling and victualing requirements for an extended period. Say, two months. Have a list ready when they arrive, if you please."

"Of course, Commodore," Grimsley replied, eyebrows arched in surprise.

Billingsly was equally surprised, but said nothing as he followed the commodore down the companionway to his quarters. Inside, Jenks tossed his still-damp hat on his desk, undid the top buttons of his tunic, and loosened his cravat. Pouring a single small glass of amber liquid, he relaxed into his chair with a sigh. The stern gallery windows were open for ventilation, but it was still oppressively hot. Without waiting for an invitation, Billingsly took a seat in front of the desk.

"I take it the Americans and their Apes have finally agreed to return the princess to us?" he ventured. "Even so, two months would seem . . . uncharacteristically parsimonious. They have not stinted our supplies before, and such a quantity might not see us home."

"Her Highness still insists on returning home with her 'friends,'" Jenks announced. "I spoke with her myself just prior to returning to the ship. You will be glad to know she is well, happy, and thriving," he added with a barb.

"But . . ."

For once, Jenks saw Billingsly's perpetual scowl dissolve into an expression of complete confusion. He had to stifle a sense of amusement and satisfaction over the bloated bastard's discomfiture. "In slightly under three weeks' time, *Achilles* will accompany an Allied squadron to the place they call Aryaal and perhaps points west and north, in an attempt to discover the current dispositions of these Grik of theirs. Captain Reddy made the offer, and after consulting with the princess, I accepted. I consider it an invaluable opportunity to assess the strategic threat posed by the Grik, as well as our hosts. We will be going as observers only and will not engage in hostilities if any do, in fact, occur. If they do, at the very least I will have the opportunity of seeing the Grik for myself and I'll learn quite a bit about the military capability of this Alliance of theirs as well."

Billingsly's scowl returned and deepened while Jenks spoke. "You should not . . . *must* not make a decision like that without consulting me!" he said menacingly.

"I must and I did make the decision, Commander," Jenks replied. "The offer was phrased in a 'take it or leave it, now or never' fashion," Jenks lied smoothly, "and I saw no choice but to accept."

"Of course you had a choice!" Billingsly countered hotly. "They will never send the princess on this 'expedition' of theirs! With the cream of their naval force otherwise engaged, we could easily take her and be gone!"

"Past those bloody great guns in the fort?" Jenks replied, his own voice rising. "You must be mad."

"Plans could be made. They already have been," he hinted. "With a judicious use of force, a few diversions, and a bit of mischief here and there, we could be gone before they could possibly respond."

Jenks paused, considering his next words carefully. He knew they could condemn him of treason in any Company court. A naval inquiry might see things differently, but who was to say how things now stood after their long absence? He had no choice. "You are forgetting their iron-hulled steamer. I have seen it now, and I tell you it could easily catch us even if we proceeded under full steam for the entire trip— which we certainly cannot do. They intend to leave it here to ensure against any such scheme as you suggest."

Billingsly's expression suddenly became blank, unreadable. He took a breath. "A point," he said. Then an incomprehensible thing occurred; Billingsly smiled. The expression was so foreign to his face that it almost seemed to crack under the strain. "You make a valid point," he continued more earnestly. "And I apologize for my earlier rashness. You have clearly scored a coup! A major intelligence-gathering opportunity! I congratulate you."

Taken aback, Jenks stared at the man. Billingsly's mood had changed so abruptly and uncharacteristically, Jenks couldn't avoid a creeping suspicion. But if Billingsly somehow knew he'd lied about *Walker's* condition, he would have arrested and usurped him on the spot. Wouldn't he? Moreover, the opportunity was just as significant as Jenks had argued, after all. Perhaps the inscrutable Company man had simply recognized that in an apparent flash of insight, just as it seemed.

"Well, then . . ." Jenks said. "Very well."

"I will, of course, remain here aboard *Ajax* in your absence, to continue to advance our interests and ensure the Apes understand we have not forgotten our princess," Billingsly said.

Jenks was actually relieved. He'd expected Billingsly to demand to come along and he really didn't want him breathing down his neck. Captain Rajendra of *Ajax* was a good officer and would keep him in check. Still a little disconcerted by his good fortune, Jenks spoke a little hesitantly: "Of course. Um, I don't expect you to curtail your . . . surreptitious activities, but please do try harder to avoid being caught. A temporary cessation, at least, might actually be in order. Perhaps they'll drop their guard."

"An excellent suggestion, Commodore. Perhaps they will think, with you and *Achilles* away, they have less reason to fear. I will encourage that perception for a time." Billingsly stood. "Perhaps, at long last, we will see some movement here!" he said cheerfully. "By your leave?"

"Indeed."

Commander Billingsly created what he considered a reassuring smile and left the commodore's quarters. In the passageway beyond, his more comfortable scowl returned. "Damn him!" he muttered to himself, a kaleidoscope of thoughts whirling in his mind. He passed a midshipman—he didn't know his name—in the passageway.

"You there. Boy," he snarled.

The youth forced himself to pause, an expression of controlled terror on his face. Billingsly's proclivities were well-known—as was his power to indefinitely delay a midshipman's appointment to lieutenant. "Sir."

"Run along to Lieutenant Truelove, with my compliments, and ask him to join me in my quarters!"

Visibly relieved, the midshipman raced off.

Captain Hisashi Kurokawa, formerly of His Imperial Japanese Majesty's Ship *Amagi*, followed obediently behind his "masters" as they were escorted through the dark, dank, labyrinthine passageways of what was roughly translated as "the Palace of Creation," toward the Holy Chamber of the Celestial Mother herself. He remained fully erect as he strode, carefully groomed and outwardly confident in his meticulously restored uniform complete with all his medals and many other meaningless, gaudy decorations he'd added for effect. Inwardly, he was terrified, and he'd learned enough about Grik body language—particularly that of the Hij—to know his masters weren't quite as collected as they tried to appear. That Tsalka, General Esshk, and Kurokawa had actually achieved this audience and not merely been killed out of hand seemed a good sign. At least the Celestial Mother wanted to hear what they had to say. Chances were, worst case, they'd be allowed to destroy themselves and not simply be torn to shreds. Regardless, he knew his masters had some fast—convincing—talking to do if any of them were to have any hope of survival.

Tsalka, still dressed in the fine robes of his office as Imperial Regent-Consort of Ceylon and "Sire" of all India, had cautioned Kurokawa to say nothing unless directly addressed, and for once, for his very life, he'd better prostrate himself before the Celestial Mother. A formal bow simply wouldn't do. Tsalka seemed the most concerned, and he nervously fiddled with his robes as they drew closer to the chamber. General Esshk was at least as outwardly calm as Kurokawa. Resplendent in his crimson cape, bronze armor, and polished, crested helmet, he still reminded Kurokawa of a fuzzy, reptilian caricature of a Roman tribune. He alone seemed oblivious to the heavily armed escort that accompanied them and only the occasional nervous twitch of his stumpy, dark-plumed tail beneath the cape betrayed any concern at all.

Of course, to his credit—Kurokawa supposed—Esshk's concern was more for the survival of his species than for himself. He knew how critical were the observations and ideas the three of them brought to this interview. If the Celestial Mother disregarded their arguments—that to defeat the ancient "Prey That Got Away," all the Grik must make profound, fundamental changes to their precious culture that had thrived in its present form for thousands of years— the ultimate foundation of that culture was doomed. Worse, from Esshk's perspective, failure to adapt could mean the extermination of his very species. Somehow, the Celestial Mother, the keeper and protector of that culture, must be convinced that change was essential—at least temporarily—and he, Tsalka, and the Japanese "hunter" named Kurokawa were indispensible as the only possible agents of that change.

Finally, the Holy Chamber opened before them and Kurokawa got his first glimpse of it, and the Celestial Mother herself. The chamber wasn't much different from Tsalka's he'd seen in Ceylon, except in size. Flowering ivies carpeted the floor and crept up the walls, the farthest of which was lost in the distant gloom. They constituted the only real decoration besides the throne itself, situated in the center of the chamber and bathed in sunlight that entered through an opening high above. A complex system of ingenious mirrors made sure that whatever time of day it was, sunlight always reflected downward upon the intricately carved and gilded throne, bathing it with its warming rays.

Absently, Kurokawa wondered where the monster sprawled whenever it rained.

The Celestial Mother was immense. He'd been told roughly what to expect by Esshk, but he was still taken aback. She was at least three times as big as Esshk, who was big for a Grik, and she was incredibly, grossly, shockingly obese to such a remarkable degree as to defy imagination. He was instantly reminded of the mythical, flightless Chinese dragons, except the Celestial Mother had none of their sinewy grace. More like a monstrous grub, he thought. Rolls of fat bulged beneath her skin and drooped from the saddlelike throne like half-empty sacks of grain. Jowls hung just as alarmingly around her polished, bleached-white teeth, and her carefully manicured and painted claws extended, unused, much farther than normal beyond fat, stumpy fingers. Her fur was unlike any Grik's he'd seen before, either. Instead of the rather downy, striated, earth-tone covering he was used to, the Celestial Mother was adorned with actual plumage of a reddish gold hue, almost like new copper. It was beautiful. The contrast between the sparkling glory of her coat and the flabby obscenity it covered was striking. He had to remind himself that this ridiculous, virtually helpless creature before him might well be the most powerful being on this earth.

Together, Tsalka, Esshk, and Kurokawa mounted the first step of the triangular stone dais surrounding the throne and the two Grik instantly prostrated themselves. Kurokawa, with a surge of terror, took the gamble he'd been steeling himself for over the months-long journey to this place, ever since the three of them decided what they must do right after the defeat at Baalkpan: still standing, but making an elaborate flourish with his hands, he bowed very low. Tsalka couldn't see him, but he must have known what he'd done because he emitted a barely audible hiss. The Celestial Mother shifted slightly, causing rolls of gelatinous fat to ripple, and regarded him with her relatively small, bloodred eyes.

"So," she hissed, in a surprisingly high-pitched voice, "in addition to treason, incompetence, and a murderous waste of my precious Uul, I must add criminal impertinence to the charges against you." Tsalka practically moaned. Saying nothing, Kurokawa held his pose. "Well, creature, *formerly* of the "Iron Ship Folk," what have you to say for yourself?" The question was the opening Kurokawa had been hoping for.

"My most abject apologies, Your Majesty," he humbly intoned in English—a language he knew she understood, even if she couldn't speak it. "Among my people, this posture conveys the same meaning as that of Regent-Consort Tsalka and General Esshk. If anything, it signifies even greater respect. True warriors do not crawl on their bellies before any . . . being . . . in victory or defeat, and this posture is reserved only for those we consider worthy of our greatest respect and esteem. Forgive me if I have erred in presenting you with the most sincere honor and unreserved respect I am capable of."

The Celestial Mother leaned back, considering, as surprised by the creature's ability to speak so fluently in the "Scientific Tongue" as she was by his . . . interesting excuse. "Arise, Regent Tsalka, General Esshk," she said, almost as an afterthought. She turned her full attention to the general as he rose and her voice became harder. "The Invincible Swarm is defeated," she stated simply. "As you were once considered the greatest living general of our people, and particularly since you chose not to gently destroy yourself, but to come before me with an explanation— knowing your destruction here will *not* be 'gentle'—I will allow you to speak." She glanced at Tsalka. "You are blameless for the actual defeat. You are no general, after all, but I understand you were deeply involved in the planning that led to this disaster, so either you meddled inexcusably or Esshk displayed even greater incompetence by heeding your untrained counsel. Regardless, you have attached yourself to his failure and will share his fate . . . unless you can convince me, as you claim, that you and Esshk, as well as this unwholesome creature you bring before me, deserve to exist." She paused. "No, in fact you must convince me beyond any doubt that your continued existence is essential not only to our ultimate success, but to our very survival as a species."

She allowed them a moment to contemplate that and, with some effort, contorted herself enough so that she could reach the basket of struggling hatchlings beside her throne. Seizing one, she popped it in her mouth and began to chew. Selected by the Chooser, they were the rejects from her own nest, and her favorite snack.

Tsalka cleared his throat and began to speak. The Celestial Mother had succinctly laid it out, and as tall an order as it was, the opportunity was greater than he'd secretly suspected.

"I thank you, Giver of Life. It is true that General Esshk and I took a great risk by coming before you, but not merely for our meager selves. Against the knowledge we bear, our fates are insignificant. We risk your wrath because we *do* believe the existence of our very race is at stake. We have some few advantages, technological miracles our . . . partner in the Hunt has brought us." He gestured with lingering annoyance at Kurokawa. "Those miracles have already been used to some good effect and we have many more at our disposal, not yet implemented. But truly our only hope for survival, I fear, is that some very fundamental changes be made."

"Such as?" the Celestial Mother demanded, still chewing.

Tsalka paused, measuring his next words very carefully. Finally, almost resignedly, he pointed at the basket beside the throne and, by implication, the morsels within. "Well, for example, we must stop eating those. The Choosers cull them because they are not fiercely aggressive. They defend themselves fanatically against their nestmates that attack them, but are not attackers themselves. Thus they are not considered fit for the Hunt. Distasteful as the concept might be, General Esshk has convinced me that defense is something we must learn to do."

"Defense!" shrieked the Celestial Mother indignantly. "Defense is for prey! We are the predators all other creatures must defend *against*! It has ever been thus! You would rend thousands of years of culture, tradition, based on a single defeat by an incompetently underestimated opponent? If that is the counsel you bring, prepare yourselves for the Traitor's Death!"

Tsalka prostrated himself again, but to his credit, Esshk remained standing beside Kurokawa. Inwardly, Kurokawa trembled with dread, but he knew that if he showed any doubt or fear now, all was lost.

"Giver of Life," Esshk said quietly, "with respect, and my most fervent worshipfulness, my life is, of course, yours to do with as you please, but I beg you to hear us. The Invincible Swarm was destroyed not only because we underestimated our foe—true enough—but because we were culturally unable to recognize the fact that the simple Tree Prey we met so long ago might have progressed into Worthy Prey. They have become other hunters who, in their fashion, have matched our capacity for the hunt. They had assistance, others like him"—he gestured at Kurokawa—"who taught them new miracles of war, but they adapted to those miracles more readily than we and used them more effectively. If we do not adapt as well, they will sweep us from the world."

"Prey?"

"*Worthy* Prey, Celestial Mother. And like other Worthy Prey, they have become hunters as well. Given time, they will pursue us."

"Then we must mount another Swarm, greater than the one you wasted, and destroy them forever! Surely they suffered greatly as well. Now is the time to exterminate them!"

"I would agree . . . but where will we get the Uul, the warriors, for such a Swarm? Our frontiers are vast, and are we not now in contact with other Worthy Prey in the south? And in the west as well? I have heard rumors. . . ."

The Celestial Mother waved a hand. "It is true. We always meet new prey as we expand, and sometimes the great storms deliver others unto us . . . like your pet, perhaps? This new "Worthy Prey" in the south and west is weak in numbers, and infests a small, chill, and undesirable land. We are in no rush to hunt them, and they are no threat to us. We will manage. We always have."

"I propose that this time, you won't," Kurokawa interjected. He recognized the quaver in his voice and hoped the others didn't. "Not without us," he added more firmly.

"And what makes you so indispensable?" The Celestial Mother's tone was suddenly low, threatening.

Kurokawa forged ahead, counting his points on his fingers. "First, you could probably destroy the Tree Folk—prey—as you said, with one more major campaign, but the losses would be staggering. Where will you get the troops . . . the Uul warriors? Second, they know your weakness now." Even Esshk bristled at "weakness," but Kurokawa continued. "No doubt they have seen and understand your inability to defend. As soon as they are able, they will attack. They *must*. Most likely, they will do so before you can adequately reinforce your forward outposts, like Aryaal." He paused and took a deep, tense breath. "Without proper *defensive* tactics and preparations, those outposts cannot hold. To avoid even further pointless loss of . . . Uul"—he pronounced it "Ool"—"I most respectfully recommend that you evacuate them. The *strategy* of trading land for time is no disgrace if part of that strategy is to eventually recover what has been lost. Third, if we gain that time, we can use it to prepare. While the enemy—the prey—flounders along impotently behind us, extending their lines of supply while ours contract, we can build the cannon-armed armored ships I have proposed. We can make the flying machines, the artillery, and train your . . . *our* troops, our Uul, in tactics that will succeed." Kurokawa shrugged imperceptibly, going for broke. "And yes, those tactics must be defensive at first." He held up a fourth finger. "Finally, when we have built these weapons, trained . . . our troops, swelled their ranks with an entirely fresh generation that has not known defeat, we wait until the prey is overextended and has stretched his lines of supply to the breaking point. . . ."

"Then attack?" asked the Celestial Mother, suddenly thoughtful.

"Then attack," confirmed Kurokawa. "The enemy does not breed or reach maturity as quickly as you. Break their Army and Navy and they will have no defense. You can then roll them up with ease and conquer every land from here to the Eastern Sea."

The Celestial Mother scratched her jowls. "Interesting," she hissed thoughtfully.

Esshk was staring at Kurokawa. They'd discussed all this before, but it was supposed to be he who presented their argument to the Giver of Life. "Indeed," he said, equally thoughtful.

Alan Letts stood from his place at the long table in the now almost fully restored Great Hall. The formal reception was intended to commemorate that, as well as the other grand undertakings that would soon commence. In spite of a general mood of joviality and goodwill, there was also a bittersweet understanding that they stood, once again, at a crossroads. The tightly knit members of the Grand Alliance that had hurled back the Grik would scatter again. Some would resume operations against the enemy at long last, while others like Shinya and Saan-Kakja would depart for the Fil-pin Lands, to oversee the development of an even greater arsenal of freedom than Baalkpan could ever be. Laumer's little squadron would accompany Saan-Kakja on his way to perform the perhaps impossible task Matt had set him. Regardless of their missions, the possibility always existed that they would never all be gathered like this again. They'd lost too many friends in this terrible war to take such things for granted. Letts tapped his mug with a knife to gain everyone's attention, and raised it high.

"Ladies and gentlemen, may I propose a toast?"

Matt smiled as he released Sandra's hand under the table and stood with everyone else. He was proud of Letts. Like all of them, he'd come a long way. He'd earned his post as chief of staff and had developed the confidence that went with it. The main reason for that rose to stand beside him. Nurse Lieutenant Karen Theimer Letts, now Sandra's medical chief of staff, had once been rendered almost catatonic by their situation. Her recovery had inspired Letts to apply himself, and they made a good team. Karen's pregnancy was also beginning to show, and that had gained her an almost reverent consideration by the same rough men who might once have resented the depletion of the "dame" supply in the middle of the famine her marriage to Letts had made even more extreme.

"Ladies and gentlemen," Letts repeated, "I give you Saan-Kakja, U-Amaki ay Maa-ni-la!"

The diminutive High Chief of Manila and patriarch of all the Fil-pin Lands regarded those at the table and the rest of the assembly in the hall. She was even more striking than usual with her fiery, golden eyes and polished, chased-golden breastplate. Her yellow and black clan colors decorated her cape and kilt, and a short, ornately hilted dirk hung from an elaborate belt in a golden sheath. The martial ensemble clashed with her tiny stature and evident youth.

"They're all so *young*," Sandra whispered in Matt's ear, and he squeezed her hand. It was true. He reflected that the veterans of every war probably thought much the same of all the recruits who joined them in battle—even while they themselves seemed young to the veterans of earlier wars. Rarely were the *leaders* quite so young, however. It suddenly struck him that most of the positions of high authority in the Alliance were held by young, comparatively inexperienced . . . amateurs. Saan-Kakja was by any definition, human or Lemurian, little more than a child. The strikingly competent and just as exotic Safir Maraan wasn't much older. Neither was Chack, who'd probably command a Marine battalion before long. Tassana-Ay-Arracca, whose father had perished with *Nerracca*, had risen to High Chief of *Aracca* Home after her grandfather fell in battle. The commander of the growing Sularan Brigade couldn't be much over twenty. General Muln-Rolak was practically ancient, but he wasn't technically a head of state—although Matt suspected that would change when they retook Aryaal. That meant, as representatives of the Alliance, Keje and Adar were the "geezers," since they were in their early forties.

On the human side, Matt knew how young everyone was. The Bosun was around sixty and was the oldest human in the Alliance, but at the august age of thirty-two, Matt was the oldest officer, just after Spanky. If the newly minted Ensign Reynolds was eighteen yet, he'd eat his hat. Of all the Allied commanders, Matt had the most combat experience by far—all of about fifteen months—and here he was, Supreme Commander of all Allied forces. Again, he wondered what Tommy Hart would have thought of that.

Conventional wisdom would imply they were *all* too young for their jobs. The thought was a little intimidating, but Matt wondered if it was true. The old guys back home, commanding their rectangular dreadnoughts, hadn't been doing so hot. It was their stupidity and shortsightedness, to a large degree, that had made Pearl Harbor such a disaster—and even possible in the first place. Matt didn't want to think about the hoary old men in Congress who'd virtually invited the attack by allowing the Navy to wither to a point that it couldn't credibly enforce their threats and policies. Maybe conventional wisdom wasn't always wisdom at all.

He decided, experience aside, it was probably a blessing they were all so young. Particularly the Lemurians. There'd been numerous times when he'd had trouble dealing with older, more entrenched 'Cats. Saan-Kakja's own sky priest, Meksnaak, was a prime example.

Nakja-Mur had been exceptional in many ways, but even he'd been a little difficult until his own Home was at stake. Matt knew it had been difficult for the old 'Cat. It was hard for the young ones, watching their whole world change with the exigencies of war, but they could at least *comprehend* change and feel confident they could absorb it, accommodate it, *use* it. It occurred to him then that if all the Lemurian leaders had been a bunch of stick-in-the-mud, geezer bureaucrats—like those back home—they'd all be dead by now.

"It's a good thing they're so young," he whispered back to Sandra. "I think it's made things a lot easier. And besides, it could be a very long war." He saw her nod, and believed she understood more than he'd said.

"Please do sit," Saan-Kakja said when the cheers and stamping feet subsided. Obediently, the crowd returned to their stools or cushions. The request was more than a courtesy. With everyone standing, no one could see her. "Tomorrow I must leave you," she resumed, "and return to my own land. Colonel Shinya and I must oversee a replication, even an enlargement of what you have accomplished here; this 'in-dus-tree.'" She smiled. "Some may not like it. Maa-ni-la has been a refuge for many of the runaways, as you call them, from various lands, and there will be dissent among those who prefer the old ways." Her eyes flashed and her chin rose slightly. "Their obstructionism will not be tolerated. Fear not."

There was more cheering, and Matt realized he needed to talk to her again about her own security. They'd already learned that even Lemurians were capable of appalling treachery.

"Even when I depart, do not think Maa-ni-la has left you. Half my personal guard will go with me, to become officers and form training cadres in the new, changing ways of war, but many more of my people have arrived here since the Great Battle and I shall leave you over five thousands." She looked directly at Matt. "Lead them as you will. My troops are your troops, and I have no doubt you will cherish them as your own."

Touched, Matt bowed his head, acknowledging the compliment. And the responsibility.

"Soon I will return with even more troops, ships, and many new weapons. I look forward to 'raa-di-o' reports from your upcoming expedition, when we will know the enemy's stance. Regardless, I am confident that if we seize this time that has been granted us by your valor and the Heavens above, when we bring our full, combined might against the scourge, we will stamp it out forever!"

Further cheers filled the hall, and, unnoticed at the far end of the table, Billingsly leaned toward Jenks. It was the first time he'd been ashore for an official function and he'd been haughty and uncommunicative throughout. "And still you do not consider them a threat to the Empire?" he hissed. "The force they are planning will be almost as large, and considerably more advanced than that of the vile Dominion that even now menaces our people back home."

Jenks looked at him and blinked. "Don't be ridiculous, Mr. Billingsly. Of course I consider them a threat, but not at present. Look about you! These . . . creatures"—he'd almost said "people," and what would Billingsly think then?—"are clearly preparing to renew their war with an enemy of potentially greater menace even than the Dominion. These Grik are possibly even more savage, if not as depraved."

"They have a Roman priestess among them," Billingsly reminded him darkly.

Jenks frowned. "I have heard that too, though I haven't seen her. From what I understand, there is a difference. The Roman 'faith' as practiced by the Dominion is an abomination, and as much as our ancestors may have disagreed with the old version, they wrote that it became something entirely different on this world. If she is a priestess of the old version who got displaced here as did the others, her fundamental beliefs are not much different from our own." Jenks smiled. "Besides, I have seen no temples or altars or any of the other trappings of the perverted faith. If she serves the Roman Church, as we know it, she certainly hasn't gained many converts."

"I implore you," Billingsly said, with a hint of what might have been true sincerity, "with the child queen gone, the Americans and the bulk of their Army and Navy away, and much of their new construction incomplete, we would have our absolute best opportunity to rescue the princess and be on our way."

Jenks's expression hardened. "And then we *would* be at war with them, fool! Do you think we could take her without bloodshed? Do you think they would ever trust us then? I have given my *word* to accompany their expedition. I could not change that now, nor would I. You think them a threat? Very well. What better way to gauge that threat than by watching how they fight? I would much rather make those observations while they fight someone else than while trading broadsides with them!"

Billingsly's face hardened as well, and he sat back in his chair. Around them, the festive atmosphere resumed after the speeches were done and the smells of unusual dishes reached them as servers came to the table.

"So be it," he muttered to himself, unheard.

///// *July 1943*

*T*wo weeks after Saan-Kakja and Tamatsu Shinya took their leave of Baalkpan in company with (now Lieutenant) Laumer's small squadron, another, considerably larger force prepared to sail. Saan-Kakja departed amid sincere, exuberant fanfare, but though the turnout of well-wishers was even bigger this time, the mood was more somber. The Second Allied Expeditionary Force was not encumbered by any lumbering Homes—those would come later, when they were fully prepared and sent for—but the fleet was still impressive. *Donaghey* was Matt's flagship, back under the command of a much recovered Commander Garrett. *Tolson*'s refit was considered sufficient to allow her participation as well. The first two new steam frigates, with their fewer but more powerful thirty-two-pounder smoothbores, were fresh from the new fitting-out docks. A lot depended on them even though this was essentially their maiden voyage and shakedown cruise combined. Jarrik-Fas commanded USS *Nakja-*

Mur, and Captain Jim Ellis commanded USS *Dowden.* Ellis would serve as second in command and commodore of the steam element of the fleet if it was detached for independent operations. Additionally, there were now seven former Grik Indiamen that had been razed and rerigged into single-deck corvettes. Observers found it difficult to believe that the far lighter, sleeker-looking ships, glistening with fresh black and white paint, had been reworked from ships originally belonging to their hated foe. The final consensus concerning designations—regardless how they were rated—was that since none of the ships were big enough to be considered "cruisers," all were still destroyers, in a sense. The only difference it made was to morale.

It was an impressive force, considering all were heavily armed, crowded with Marines, and covered with stacked landing craft. Four relatively unaltered Grik ships (except for color) carried Lord Rolak's 2nd Aryaal, Safir Maraan's "Six Hundred" as well as extra field artillery, draft beasts, and other baggage. Ten large feluccas would serve as the eyes of the fleet and dispatch vessels. *Achilles* was also making final preparations for getting under way, her black coal smoke coiling lazily into the light morning air contrasting with the gray smoke of the Allied steamer's oil-fired boilers. The reason for the more somber mood was that this force, at some point, would certainly make contact with the enemy for the first time since the Battle of Baalkpan. There was a sense of confidence that the fleet could handle itself, but no one knew what they would find. Had the enemy withdrawn, or been reinforced? Had the Grik also made unforeseen improvements? They already had crude cannon when they attacked the city. What other surprises might they have introduced since their last meeting? No one knew, and it was frustrating.

They'd grown accustomed to having reports of enemy dispositions from the flying boat, but they were still a week or more away from discovering whether their "new" aircraft would even fly. They were moving forward with the conviction that it would; many more airframes and engines based on the prototype were already being built, but it would take time before *Big Sal*'s conversion was complete, and they still had to train a lot of pilots. Flight training was already under way, in an ingenious simulator that mimicked flight controls, but it remained firmly on the ground when students climbed aboard. What would happen when/if they actually flew?

In many ways, perhaps the greatest test of the Alliance would be faced in the coming days and weeks, and the thought no one was willing to voice was that, for the first time, Captain Matthew Reddy didn't have *Walker* beneath his feet. He wouldn't even be here when they learned, once and for all, whether he ever would again. That simple fact was the source of tremendous unease. In the past, the mere existence of the old destroyer had been a source of considerable comfort and security. They'd fought without her before, but she'd always *been* there, *somewhere*, somehow always ready to come to their aid just in the nick of time. This was the first time the Alliance had engaged in any major military undertaking without *Walker* to back them up.

Nakja-Mur and *Dowden* were tied to the dock, but *Donaghey* was moored beyond them. Scott's launch was waiting to take Matt over after he said his good-byes. Adar, Keje, Spanky, Sandison, Brister, and Letts were all there, but the only one Matt really had eyes for was Sandra Tucker. She and Princess Rebecca had joined them mere moments before, almost out of breath. Sandra had obviously come straight from the hospital, where she'd been working either quite late or very early. Even after all these months, many of those wounded in the battle to save the city required ongoing operations. Her long, sandy brown hair was swept back in a girlish ponytail that accented her pretty face and slender neck.

Everyone knew Captain Reddy and Sandra Tucker were nuts about each other, even though they'd once tried to hide their feelings out of respect for *Walker*'s crew. Of course, the crew probably knew how they felt before they did, and their poignant sacrifice was the source of much sympathy—and respect. Only after the Battle of Baalkpan, when it was clear that *everyone* knew and further denial was pointless, did Captain Reddy and Lieutenant Tucker show any open affection. Even then, public displays were limited to holding hands, an occasional embrace . . . and spending as much time together as they possibly could. It was obvious their love continued to grow and each was a reservoir for the other's strength, but still they didn't marry or "shack up," as Silva and Cross had apparently done. They did nothing, in fact, that all the surviving destroyermen from *Walker* and *Mahan* couldn't do. The men rolled their eyes in exasperation, called them dopes . . . and loved them for it.

Alan Letts liked and admired Sandra, as did everyone, but she always made him feel a little guilty. He loved Karen very much, but they'd convinced the captain to marry them when they'd all fully expected to die. Now things had changed, sort of, but his happiness was undiminished. He was guardedly ecstatic that he'd soon be a father. But his very happiness inspired much of his guilt. He couldn't help thinking it wasn't fair for him to be happy when so many of the men were still miserable. And not all those who were miserable were men.

Alan was amazed by Matt and Sandra's self-sacrificing willpower. Again, he compared their situation to two star-crossed lovers from a John Ford western trapped in a Cecil B. DeMille epic, complete with a cast of thousands, monsters, and freak weather events. He noticed, with a surge of relief—for both of them—that as soon as Sandra arrived, she'd unobtrusively inserted her hand into the captain's, and he'd reached to caress her face.

"Do you guys realize yesterday was the sixteen-month anniversary? A year and a third to the very day since we arrived . . . wherever we are?" Letts interjected into the awkward silence that ensued.

Matt nodded. "Sixteen months since the Squall. Since we escaped the Japs—and watched them sink *Exeter* and *Electra* and *Pope* . . . since we nearly got sunk ourselves." He shook his head. "We lost a lot of good destroyermen that day. I didn't forget."

"Well . . . maybe you ought not go just yet. The dry dock's finished and we'll be pulling the plug in a few days. Ben's going to fly. . . ."

"It's time to go," Matt said simply. "You and the fellas can handle all that stuff."

Letts nodded reluctantly.

Princess Rebecca stepped forward. "Mr. O'Casey is safe aboard your ship?"

"Stowed away, and no one the wiser." Matt smiled at her concern for the one-armed man.

"I suppose it is best," she reflected. "With Billingsly here and his spies on the loose, I fear they would have discovered him sooner or later. He grows weary of hiding. I do worry about him, though."

"He'll be fine," Matt assured her. "And he *wanted* to go. Like you said, he's tired of staying out of sight. Aboard ship he can *do* something, and the only time he has to be scarce is if Jenks comes aboard." Matt grinned. "Besides, he has full confidence Silva could protect you from a super lizard with his bare hands." He raised an eyebrow. "Where *is* Silva, by the way?"

"Sulking," Sandra said, wryly. "He wanted to go too. Talk about bored! God knows what mischief he'll cause! Until I let Mr. Sandison have him full-time, he was always either trying out his 'toys,' or down at the Busted . . . I mean, the Castaway Cook." She tousled the princess's hair. "Right now, I have 'the duty.'"

Suddenly, Rebecca lunged forward and embraced the captain. He was so surprised that he stood there a moment, hands away from her. Slowly, he lowered them to encompass her and returned the hug. "Do be careful, Captain Reddy," the girl said blearily. "I know your cause is just and I shall miss you, miss you all, terribly. But you must take care! I cannot help but feel you are protecting my people as well as your own, and somehow, all our fates are tied to you in the end!"

A lump had mysteriously formed in Matt's throat. "I'll take care, Your Highness," he muttered self-consciously, "and I'll watch out for your Mr. O'Casey."

He shook hands with the other men and embraced Keje and Adar. That was their way, like Russians, he supposed, but it was like hugging a . . . well, he didn't know what. "We'll see you soon," he said to Keje. "I'll look forward to seeing the first flattop this world has ever known come steaming over the horizon!" He stepped back, but before he could compose himself, Sandra was in his arms. Wolf whistles and howls of delight came from *Nakja-Mur*, tied nearby.

After a reluctantly chaste kiss, Sandra looked up at him, her eyes swimming. "Do be careful, Captain Reddy," she said, repeating Rebecca's words.

I love you, he mouthed, then turned for the launch.

Walker had always gotten under way with an almost spastic energy, as if straining at her moorings like a dog on a leash. The 2nd AEF proceeded more ponderously. The steamers in particular seemed almost reluctant to get under way. *Donaghey* was much quicker. As soon as her cable was up and down, she snatched her anchor from the bottom and surged ahead with the quickening breeze, flag streaming to leeward. She piled on more sail, and soon she was slanting down toward the mouth of the bay. *Tolson* and the corvettes followed in her wake and it was clear the corvettes would be fast, handy ships. Then came the swift feluccas and slower transports. Finally, the steamers began to move. *Nakja-Mur* and *Dowden* slashed at the water with their single, center-mounted screws and began to gain headway with a lot of activity, shouted commands, and considerable noise from their engines and boilers. Steam jetted. It was clear their crews were learning as they went. *Achilles* gained far more efficiently, with her paddle wheels helping her maneuver, but didn't pick up speed as fast. Soon, the entire fleet was steering for the Makassar Strait—and whatever awaited them beyond.

*T*hey came for him as he stepped away from the morning feeding trough. Somehow, on some level, he'd been expecting it. Feeding sounds continued unabated, punctuated by frequent snarls as Uul contended over a particularly choice boiled, meaty bone. He watched as the four specially armored warriors of the Chooser worked their way in his direction through the hissing horde that jostled to and from the trough, and for the slightest instant, he contemplated resistance.

That alone was enough to stun him into immobility. That, and the fact that he realized—*realized*—his sated torpor would allow the warriors to make short work of him. He was armed with only the weapons the Mother had given him. Alone, they would be no match for the armor. There was no mistake. Harshly, they called his name and their eyes were fixed on his. He was the only Uul within the stone feeding chamber who *had* a name, and, resignedly, he moved to meet them.

It was time. He'd had a good life, but now he was old—he knew it was so—and his joints ached and he'd lost several teeth. He'd been just slightly slower in the arena of late and if he noticed it, certainly the Chooser had. He'd still been victorious, and his surge of exultation had been affirmed by the hissing approbation of the Hij spectators, but he knew each of his victories over the last few cycles had been more difficult than the last. It was time for *his* boiled flesh to fill the feeding trough of the Sport Fighters. At least many were his own get, and the tradition would be unbroken. Better to feed his own here than strangers on some distant battlefield, he decided, in an uncharacteristic burst of insight. Still, it would have been better to die fighting.

He'd been a fighter all his life and he'd tasted the chaos and mad joy of major battles often, usually against his own kind. First, he'd merely been one of ten. Through skill he'd eventually become first of ten, then second of twenty—all Grik could count that high; they had two arms, two legs, and sixteen fingers and toes, after all. Time and many battles passed and he was elevated to first of twenty, first of two twenties, and ultimately first of *five* twenties, as high as any Uul could aspire. That was when he'd been taken to the arena for the pleasure of the Hij and given a *name*. He had little sense of the passage of time or how many victories he'd won. Tens of twenties, certainly. All he knew was that he'd been in the arena a long, long time. He'd enjoyed it. But all good things, like life, must end.

"Greetings, Halik-Uul," spoke one of the armored warriors, less harshly than before.

"In the name of the Mother, I greet you," Halik replied easily. Less certainly, he continued, "The Chooser time, now?"

"Indeed," stated another of the warriors. "Your time has come. Your destiny awaits."

Halik didn't know what a "destiny" was. It was probably elevated speech for "cook pot."

"Come," commanded the one who seemed first of four.

Obediently, Halik followed as the warriors led him through the now quieter, staring horde. They passed through the locked gate to the underground chamber and up into the light. Halik blinked as they strode across the arena he'd fought in so many times. He couldn't help but gaze around. He'd never seen it empty before. They reached another gate, and through it, they ascended a gradually spiraling stair. Halik grew slightly confused. He didn't know where the cook pots were, but the smells never reached them when the wind was from this direction. His heart quickened. Maybe they were taking him to a female! Sometimes warriors who'd shown greater strength and skill were allowed that honor before they faced the butchers. If that were the case, it would make his death slightly less unpleasant, at least.

He'd been paired with a female only twice before, and the result had been dozens of squabbling young he'd never seen, for the most part. Some of the survivors, a fair percentage actually, had eventually appeared in the warrior dens destined for the arena. He'd been ordered to train them himself and he'd complied, though at the time, he'd felt no real connection to them. Two he'd ultimately killed in the arena himself. Recently, however, he'd begun to feel a subtle attachment to those of *his* that remained. Perhaps it was pride of a sort that he'd sired such well-developed and cunning warriors. He didn't think much about it; it was just something he felt.

"This way," ordered the first of four when they reached the top of the stair and a passageway forked away from it. They took the passage to the left. It was dimly lit and there was no sound but the clack of claws and footpads on the stones. The passageway continued for a considerable distance and his excitement grew. He could *smell* females! Oddly, he didn't think any were present now, but they had passed there recently. Perhaps one awaited him in a chamber nearby? Suddenly, the guards halted him at a chamber entrance that had strange scents, but not those of females, and he was confused, disappointed. Regardless, he entered at their command and stood where they placed him.

His eyes had grown accustomed to the dark passage, and the torches that drew his eyes blinded him to the rest of the chamber. He sensed there were others in the room, and one that smelled . . . wrong. Suddenly, one of the guards grabbed him from behind, holding his arms at his sides. Another grasped his feet. Without warning, yet another guard draped a cloth over his eyes and quickly wrapped it around them and over his snout, tying his jaws securely shut. An instant later, he was released.

Rising terror threatened to overcome him. He'd never expected it to be like this. That they would destroy him he had no doubt, but he'd never expected them to make sport of him when they did. He could see nothing, but oddly, they'd left his hands and feet unrestrained. He waited, gaining control of his fear.

A terrible blow struck him across the belly. It burned like the strike of a sword or a claw and he expected his insides to fall to the floor. Reflexively, he grasped at the terrible wound . . . and felt nothing. Another sharp blow slashed at the back of his leg, and he should have fallen with his leg ropes cut . . . but he didn't. Repeatedly the blows fell upon him, and he stood there and took it despite an almost uncontrollable urge to run, to flee, to try to escape toward where he thought the passageway should be. Reaching up, he tore the blindfold and gag from his face, but now his eyes were even more dazzled by the torches.

"Kill me," he gasped, controlling his voice, "but no play at me as hatchlings with food pets! I fight for The Mother all my life. I honor Her, submit to Her! Kill me!"

"Sounds almost like *pride*, does it not?" came an urbane, well-spoken voice. Something answered in a tongue Halik had never heard. He felt fear again, but not the visceral, dangerous kind of fear, the kind that would make him prey. This was different. Another blow fell across his back, and finally, a mounting rage drove all fear from him and he lashed back. By some fluke, he managed to grasp the weapon and realized it was a whip. He jerked it toward him and then lashed up against the extended arm of his tormentor with his forearm. The whip was his! He reversed the handle and flailed it about himself with practiced ease, creating a wall of lashing leather while his eyes began to adjust. Another blow fell across his back, and with lightning speed, he spun and directed a reply. The whip cracked against the only target he could see—a pair of glowing eyes. He was rewarded with a shriek, and the glowing orbs were extinguished. Every instinct drove him to fall upon his wounded tormentor, but he forced himself to remain in a protective stance, backing toward the wall. He could see the shape of his attackers now, and saw there were others in the chamber as well. The others were gathered to one side and posed no threat, but the three remaining guards were approaching him, in the classic style, and now they had swords.

"A dilemma, Halik-Uul!" said the urbane voice—so calm! "Whatever will you *do*? You are not in the arena now!"

Halik forced his own passion to subside. The voice seemed . . . familiar . . . and on some level, he somehow knew the words were meant
as guidance. What *would* he do? He must think! Suddenly, a wild insight took him. This was not a slaughter, a preparation for the cook
pots. It was a test! A test to see if the strange thoughts and awareness
he'd experienced of late had some greater meaning. What would he
do? In the arena, a match like this would be hopeless. One could use
only the weapons one brought to the fight. Sometimes things were deliberately staged that way, to see what would happen, but a single whip
against three swords was a losing proposition. But he wasn't in the
arena! The voice had said so!

His back was almost to the wall; he could feel it with his tail. A quick
glance behind revealed one of the torches—although it wasn't a torch.
Not like he'd seen before. An iron bracket supported a small glass globe
with a burning wick protruding from a funnel shape on top. He didn't
know what the liquid in the globe was, but he knew it would burn. He'd
used small bombs in the arena before. Just as the guards rushed him, he
snatched the globe from the bracket and hurled it at the one on the far
left. It shattered and spread burning fluid across the guard's face and
torso. He lunged past the conflagration and leaped upon the blinded,
moaning guard. He didn't kill him, but instead, snatched his sword
from its hand. Sprinting to the opposite side of the chamber, he took a
position with his whip in one hand and the sword in the other. The
burning guard had flopped on the floor, flailing and rolling, trying to
extinguish the flames. That left two. Confidence soared within him. A
moment ago, he'd been doomed. He didn't know exactly what the
meaning of all this was, but he did know that with a sword and a whip,
he could defeat any two warriors with swords he'd ever faced.

"Enough," came the voice. At a gesture from the darkened figure,
the guards obediently slew their wounded comrade and dragged him
from the chamber. Halik had no doubt they'd have killed him just as
thoughtlessly as they had the others, but now was forgotten.

"In the name of the Celestial Mother," came the voice, as placid as
it had been from the start, "you may lay down your weapons and no
harm will come to you. I even promise they'll be returned. The sword,
in particular, you may wish to keep."

Only then did Halik glance at the weapon. He'd also begun to notice things recently, in ways he never had before. Just as a visit with a female might bring pleasure, he'd discovered other things sometimes did. Success in the arena brought intense pleasure, but suddenly, so did the memory of an unusual sunset he'd once seen. Looking at the sword, he realized that the sight of it gave him pleasure as well! It was the most . . . beautiful thing he'd ever beheld. The blade was a type of layered iron he'd seen carried only by generals, and the hilt was elaborately decorated. Gently, he laid it on the floor.

"Come here."

Obediently, Halik did so. When he drew closer, he could finally discern four robed Hij—and some other creature standing with them. He was still too invigorated to take much notice, and his eyes quickly sought the source of the voice.

One of the Hij drew back his robes and revealed himself as a first general, the highest of the high, and a member of the Celestial Mother's very house. Halik flung himself onto the cold stones of the floor.

"He did well," murmured another voice grudgingly. "The fire was a nice touch, and he is the first to have used it. Clever."

Halik certainly recognized *that* voice. It belonged to the Chooser himself! He'd heard it many times over the years during the Sports.

"Arise, Halik-Uul," came the first voice again. "The Mother's Chooser will take you from this place and his assistants will prepare you for the usual Holy Rites of Elevation. You and I will talk again, and I look forward to conversing with you as one Hij to another."

After Halik was led, dazed, from the chamber, General Esshk looked at Kurokawa. "An interesting recruiting method you have devised. It tests their wits as well as their discipline, ability, and resistance to the Urge. Ultimately, it tests their obedience as well. Most interesting." He glanced at the bloodstains. "Perhaps a trifle wasteful."

"Perhaps," Kurokawa agreed, "but for the war we must prepare for, one Halik is worth a hundred of those others. Maybe a thousand."

Esshk hissed a sigh. "I believe you speak truth, or this activity would not be allowed. There is resistance, however. The Celestial Mother remains unconvinced, but she is willing, at least, to experiment." He glanced in the direction Halik had been taken. "That Uul is not unique, but he is rare and we will need many, many more like him."

"The Chooser opposes us?"

"The Chooser opposes all change. Nevertheless, the hatchling proposal progresses. We will see."

LOGBOOK
OF THE
U.S.S WALKER (DD-163)
DD Rate, COMMANDED BY:
M. P. REDDY, LIEUTENANT COMMANDER, USNR
DESTROYER SQUADRON 29
Attached to: **ABDAFLOAT**

Commencing: 0000, **July 1, 1943,**
at: Baalkpan—formerly Balikpapan
and ending: 1943

LIST OF OFFICERS

Attached to and on board of the USS WALKER (DD-163), commanded by M.P. REDDY, Captain, USNR, during the period covered by this Logbook, with date of reporting for duty, detachment, transfer, or death, from 1 July 1943, to 31 July 1943

NAME	RANK	DATE OF DUTY	DETACHED
M.P. REDDY	Lt. Cmdr/Capt.	5 Sept. 1941	Commanding*
*TDY Commanding 2nd Allied Expeditionary Force.			
J.G. ELLIS	Lt./Capt.	6 Sept. 1941	XO*
*TDY Commanding USS *Mahan* 1 Mar. 1942. Commanding USS *Dowden* 23 June 1943			
B. McFARLANE	Lt./Cmdr.	18 Oct. 1938	Engineering*
*TDY Minister of Naval Engineering, Baalkpan. Commanding salvage/refit operation USS *Walker*.			
B.L. SANDISON	Lt./Cmdr.	1 Nov. 1941	Torpedo*
*TDY Minister of Ordnance, Baalkpan.			
G.C. GARRETT	Lt./Cmdr.	8 Oct. 1941	Gunnery*
*TDY Commanding USS *Dona*ghey.			
S.B. CAMPETI	2CPO/Lt.Cmdr.	9 May 1940	Ordnance*
*TDY B.L. SANDISON			
P.J. BRISTER	Lt./Cmdr.	6 Sept. 1942	Asst. Engineering*
*TDY Minister of Defensive and Industrial Works, Baalkpan.			
S.H. RIGGS	1CPO/Cmdr.	12 Aug. 1940	Comm & Navigation*
*TDY "Minister of Communications and Electrical Contrivances," Baalkpan.			
A.G. LETTS	Lt./Cmdr.	15 May 1941	Commisary & Supply*
*TDY "Minister of Industry and Chief of Staff 'President' of Baalkpan."			
S.M. TUCKER	Lt.	28 Feb. 1942	Medical Officer*
*TDY Minister of Medicine, Baalkpan.			
J.R. MILLER	Lt.	22 June 1941	Medical Officer*
*TDY 2nd Allied Expeditionary Force.			

(This page to be sent to Bureau of Navigation monthly with Log sheets)

UNITED STATES SHIP WALKER (DD-163) Tuesday, Sept. 2, 1943

00-04 As before. No problems to report. Woke up pumping detail and inspection party so they could begin final preparations.
Sonny Campeti, Lt. Cmdr. USN

04-08 As before. Pump boilers at full steam pressure despite leaks. Detail reports all in readiness. Inspection party discovered and repaired a faulty joint in the #4 main pipe. Split ends were the cause—like we have seen before. Inspection parties will continue to observe all joints throughout the operation.
Bernard L. Sandison, Lt Cmdr, USNR

08-12 As before. Weather clear. Water smooth on the bay. Slight easterly wind. Conditions optimum. 0800 mustered all hands and fed them at their stations. No absentees. Final visual inspection of all lines and seals. Heard reports from divisions. Lemurian Homes Humfra-Dar and Woor-Naa standing by to assist with ship-board pumps. Engaged primary pumps 0920. Observed first streams of water being expelled from dry dock basin. Engaged in brief verbal celebration.
Brad McFarlane, Cmdr, USN

12-16 *Not* as before. 1350 observed slight reduction of water level around exposed superstructure of ship. Having difficulty controlling exuberance of all divisions. Self included. Large numbers of civilians have come down to the dock to observe. Detached Marines from other duties to make sure they did not interfere. No question of deliberate interference, just do not want them underfoot and causing distractions. Water flow is difficult to estimate but best guess is 6000 gpm.
Brad McFarlane, Cmdr, USN

16-20 Pumps steaming as before. (Great relief to use that phrase again.) Two minor casualties in the water pipes repaired. Pump engine running well and within Mr. McFarlane's expectations. *Humfra-Dar* has added her pumps to the operation. Water level dropping slowly still, but noticeably. His Excellency, Adar, High Chief of Baalkpan, appeared briefly at the dock to inspect the proceedings. Informed Cmdr. McFarlane that a celebration of thanksgiving and appreciation would commence at 1900. Celebration seems general already at 1700. Chief Laney took a banca boat out to the protruding aft mast of the ship and ran a new ensign up. Tattered remnants of the old ensign (there since the Battle of Baalkpan) were removed and carefully brought ashore. Letts took them in his charge.
PERRY BRISTER, CMDR, USN

20-24 Lights rigged. Water flow uninterrupted. No stoppages. Cmdr. McFarlane has allowed the hands to join the celebration by divisions. Inspection details to remain in place by rotation. A damn good day.
Steven P. Riggs, Cmdr., USN

Approved: Examined:

* * *

Riggs held a lighted Zippo so he could see, and Spanky signed his name by "Approved" at the bottom of the page. Then he handed the log to Letts, who signed beside "Examined." Before he closed the log on the previous day, Letts glanced up at the date and shook his head.

"Five days late for the 'year and a third,' but close enough, I guess."

"That's one of the reasons I pushed so hard to pull the plug yesterday. Give the guys something to celebrate so they wouldn't dwell on what we left behind. What we lost," Spanky replied.

Letts returned the log to Spanky, who handed it to Campeti, who had the watch again. They were all tired, but *nobody* was going to oversee this operation but *Walker.* Sandra Tucker had arrived, looking disheveled, but as anxious as they were for her first glimpse of the ship. Now she stood beside them, peering intently into the predawn gloom of the dry-dock basin at the still only vaguely defined shape.

They stood on what had once been the old fitting-out pier, but was now merely a walkway between massive wooden cranes and equipment sheds. The skeletons of still more new warships rose on the other side of the basin, silhouetted against the new dawn. Until recently, when the dry dock neared completion, the new ships had remained the priority projects. Now, for just a few days, work on them would slow while a large percentage of the laborers concentrated on another task. Steam and smoke jetted from crude, noisy engines while 'Cat "snipes in training" crawled all over them, oiling every conceivable point of friction. Some spun the huge, amazingly efficient Lemurian-designed pumps, and others powered generators that ran electric pumps of human design. The jury was still out on which were better, but Spanky was pretty sure the 'Cat machines would last longer. Hoses pulsed and brown water coursed into the sea beyond the dry-dock wall.

Together, Sandra, Spanky, Alan, Campeti, and Bernie, a growing crowd of human and Lemurian sailors and Marines, sleepy civilian revelers, and finally, to no one's real surprise, Adar himself, watched the dawn gradually reveal what the ravages of seawater and battle had done to USS *Walker.* Throughout the night, while most of her crew and the people of the city celebrated her raising, the water level in the dry dock had steadily dropped. Now she lay, with a slight list to port, where she'd settled after her fight with *Amagi*. Almost half of her upper hull was now exposed and every heart sank as they looked upon her.

A clear demarcation showed how much of the ship had remained above the surface when she sank. It was plain to see, about three-fourths of the way up her four slender funnels and about halfway up her aft mast. The forward mast was gone. Automatic weapons had riddled her bridge, but the line glared dark and glistening below her empty pilothouse windows like an angry, oily slash. Above it, the paint was blackened by fire and dark with rust. Below the line she looked . . . even worse.

An entirely new color had been created. Dark brown mixed with tan, with malignant yellow streaks for contrast. A fair amount of blackened green dangled here and there, where rotting vegetation festooned her. Angry red globs and smears were everywhere and of every different hue, as the rust that caused them dried. Slimy gray-black tar pooled and oozed, and covering all was a translucent rainbow slick of oil that had leaked from her ruptured bunkers. Hatches stood agape, revealing dank interiors. Tangled cables drooped down her side, and brackish water gushed from countless holes as the water level in the basin receded below that still inside the ship. Eel-like chopper fish squirmed like maggots on her deck, their vicious jaws gaping and snapping as their gills labored in the morning air. As primitive as they were, it might take them hours to die.

Walker was a corpse, Sandra thought, and they'd been nothing more than ghoulish grave robbers to expose her to the sun. Hot tears ran down her cheeks. Thank God Matthew wasn't there to see it.

"Lord," Sandison murmured, "what are we going to do?"

Spanky patted his arm and sighed. "We're gonna fix her, Bernie."

The way *Walker* rested looked almost normal by the time the first boats went across: listing slightly and a little low by the stern, but the water wasn't much higher than the greasy black boot topping. She was still full of water, however, and jets of varying intensity coursed from her many wounds. As a result, the volume of water the pumps displaced was reduced as the day wore on. If they emptied the basin more quickly than the ship could drain, they ran the risk of causing even more damage. But her crew was restless to get to work, and by early that afternoon, the first repair parties clamored up her slippery side and stood once more on her leaning deck.

Spanky McFarlane put his hands on his skinny hips and stared hard in all directions, his lips grimly set. A short while before, he'd been Minister of Naval Engineering for an infant nation. Right now, for a time, he was *Walker*'s engineering officer again and nothing else. "All right, ladies," he said at last, as men and Lemurians squelched through the ooze, "we got work to do. Mr. Riggs? Take your party to the bridge. Charts, manuals, anything like that we might've missed before are the first priority. Easy does it. If there's anything left of that stuff, it'll go to pieces if you're not careful." He looked quickly around. "Campeti! Where's Mr. Sandison?"

Campeti gestured over his shoulder. "Went tearing ass up to the bridge. We removed the gun director a long time ago 'cause we could get to the platform, but he wanted to see the torpedo directors. He was like a cat havin' kittens!" Campeti caught himself and looked quickly around. Some of the Lemurians were looking at him strangely. "Uh, no offense. Different kinda cats . . . Little buggers . . ." He held his hands close together, but then his face clouded with embarrassment. "Oh, just get to work, damn it."

Spanky shook his head. "Well, until he gets back, or sends for you to help him, I want you to check the four-inch fifties and see if there's anything left of the machine guns on the amidships deckhouse. When you get through with that, put together a detail to salvage as many fire hoses as you can. We'll start rinsing the old girl off." He couldn't stop a grin. "Just think what the Bosun would say if he saw his decks in such a state."

Campeti almost giggled. In spite of the herculean task ahead of them, the spirits of those who'd come aboard were rising. Finally, after the long months of anticipation and helplessness, of toil and labor on other projects, they could get to work on what mattered most to *them*. It almost seemed as if they could sense something within the ship itself begin to stir as well. A renewed sense of purpose. A new lease on life.

"We wanna go down," grouched a reedy voice behind Spanky, and he turned to look at the pair standing there. It was Gilbert Yeager and the silken, gray-furred 'Cat named Tabby. He had to concentrate for an instant, because without Isak Rueben, the scene just didn't add up. Then he remembered Isak was the one they'd decided would accompany the AEF. Understanding complete, Spanky glared at Tabby when he saw she'd stripped almost completely, in the Lemurian way, to the point that all she wore was what looked like a skimpy little skirt. Despite her fine fur, her breasts appeared very human. It was distracting and annoying and she knew it. Sometimes Spanky harbored a secret, superstitious sense that the presence of women (the nurses' first) aboard his ship was what had caused all their problems to start with. He'd finally allowed Tabby to stay in the firerooms at the captain's orders and because she was a damn fine snipe. He'd broken one of his own cardinal rules, however: if something someone is doing bugs you, either make them stop, or pretend it doesn't bug you. In Tabby's case, he'd failed miserably in both respects. He couldn't—wouldn't now— make her go away, and there was no way he could pretend she didn't bug him.

"You're out of uniform, sailor!" he said harshly, almost plaintively. "Again!"

"Dirty work ahead, Chief," she replied with a creditable drawl. "We ain't got enough new uniforms yet to get 'em all scruffed up."

She even sounds like them now, Spanky thought uncomfortably. She was also the only creature alive that the Mice were actually nice to, in their way. As a result of their association, she'd begun to take on many of their less agreeable attributes. But she *looked* like a pinup in a catsuit.

"I don't give a good goddamn! You *will* put on some clothes or I'll have you on report!" he bellowed. "We'll see if you can remember to . . ." He stopped and watched her slowly unroll a T-shirt she'd been holding behind her back.

"Aye-aye, *Mr. McFaar-lane*. I'll throw somethin' on if it make you happy."

"You . . . !" He stopped. She'd done it to him *again*! He whirled and pointed at the very deck access she'd pulled her companions

from months before. "Down there. Let me know if the water's drain-
ing out of the aft fireroom! I want you to describe every single piece
of equipment as it becomes visible!" He ignored them then, and
began delegating other tasks to different details. The Mice shuffled
away and ducked down the hatch. Once inside, out of earshot, Gilbert began to chuckle.

"I swear, Tabby, you keep waggin' yer boobs at Spanky like that, one
o' these days he's gonna bust a vessel—or grab hold of 'em! You know
it drives him nuts. Just havin' wimmin aboard ship is enough to cause
him fits—then you keep doin' that!"

"He still needs to laugh," Tabby replied. "I like to make him laugh
and he will, later. He always does." Her eyes grew unfocused and she
continued softly: "And maybe someday he *will* grab 'em." She looked
away, but Gilbert could tell she was blinking embarrassment.

Jeez! Gilbert thought, stunned. *Tabby's sweet on Spanky!* "Yeah,
well," he said, his chuckle now gone as he peered into the darkness
below. The stench was unbearable and the water was still over the top
of his beloved boilers. "Ain't much to laugh about right now. Look at
this mess!"

The oily water receded slowly, and purplish brown foam swirled
and clung to everything as its support drained away. At some point,
one of *Walker*'s own hoses snaked down through the trunk with a bellowed, "Slide it in!" and moments later, it began to pulse and throb.
The drainage picked up. Another hose, new made, joined the first and
was soon jolting and juddering alongside it. Gilbert no longer noticed
the smell, and as the water went down, he carefully descended to the
upper catwalk, creeping slowly so he wouldn't slip in the oily slurry.
His beloved fireroom was a dreary sight in the gloom. He didn't dare
make a light.

He suddenly remembered finding a dead, bloated cow out in a pas-
ture when he was a kid. It was one of his ma's, and he'd been curious
why it died. While he stood there staring at it, its hind legs started to
move. At first, he thought he'd met a ghost cow, because there was no
question it was dead. He started to run, but something stopped him.
He'd never been scared of a live cow. What could a dead one do to him?
With that certain mixture of horror and fascination only kids could

conjure, he'd watched a medium-size possum come crawling out of the cow's ass!

He'd pondered that occasionally over the years, that possum squirming around up in there. No matter how hungry he got after that, and there'd been some starving times during the Depression, he'd never eaten possum again. Now, looking at his fireroom, he suddenly imagined he knew what the inside of that old cow had looked like to that possum so long ago.

"Go get another hose, Tabby. A water hose!" he shouted. "Might as well rinse some of this shit down while they're suckin' it out!"

The water came from the basin and wasn't by any means clean, but at least the pressure let him blow the worst of the goo away. Also, it didn't hurt that he'd exposed a little of the lighter paint and it grew brighter in the compartment as the sun hung overhead. Soon, he and Tabby were standing on the slimy deck plates. While he aimed the hose, she held it for him. A couple of times, they raised a plate and stuffed one of the drain hoses in the bilge.

"Gonna need some kind of detergent!" he shouted.

"We use wood ashes, make lye soap?"

"I dunno. Lye does goofy stuff. Not much aluminum down here, but there's zinc in brass and galvanize. Shoot lye on that and we get hydrogen gas! I doubt wood ashes'd be pure enough, but it might corrode the hell out of stuff." Gilbert paused and wiped his face with his shirt. It was stiflingly hot. "I wish somebody'd raise those goddamn vents!" he roared. Almost as if they'd heard him—and maybe someone had—the grungy, nearly opaque skylight vents started going up. Soon, the fireroom was relatively bathed in light and at least a little air was getting in. A few more 'Cats soon came to join them. Gilbert felt mildly guilty. He knew everyone was busy, but hell. He and Tabby turned the hose over to their relief and started to go topside for a much-needed drink. He paused.

"You know," he shouted over the gushing water, "speakin' of corrosion, there ain't much here. Not new, anyway. Maybe all this oily, slimy shit did us a favor." He moved to one of the big Yarrow boilers, kicked the latch, and opened the door. A flood of black water gushed out all over him, knocking him down. Tabby picked him up, and together they peered inside.

"Ook," Gilbert said. He couldn't see much, but the firebricks were gone. Probably disintegrated when the cool water hit them. The lines looked okay, though, and even if a few had popped, he could fix that. New firebrick had been stockpiled long ago during their previous refits. He gently patted the old boiler. "Hey! We can hose her out! No need to get all black and sooty cleanin' her!"

Tabby looked at him. He was covered from head to foot with black, slimy ooze. She laughed aloud. Gilbert grinned too, realizing how ridiculous the statement was under the circumstances.

"Well, we can," he defended. "Mainly, though"—he patted the boiler again—"we can fix this."

It was nearly dusk and it had been a long, eventful, and mostly happy day in spite of their early misgivings. Faces grew somber a few times when the occasional bone was discovered and reverently removed. There weren't many, and those they found were deeply gnawed. There was no way to identify whose they were and it didn't really matter anyway. Courtney Bradford might have told them whether the bones were human or Lemurian, but it ultimately made no difference. Lemurians traditionally preferred to be burned, so their spirits might rise with the smoke and join those in the Heavens who'd gone before, but regardless how distasteful most Lemurians considered the human practice of burying their remains, many Lemurian "destroyermen" had requested burial like—and beside—their shipmates. Their clan.

All the bones were sent to join those of destroyermen already buried in the little cemetery at the Parade Ground in the center of the city, that lay in the returning shade of the Great Tree of Baalkpan. The tree, and the new leaves sprouting from it, was a symbol of hope that all might be made right in the end—not least because of the graves it sheltered with its mighty boughs.

After the grisly chore of removing the dead was complete, spirits rose again. Not because anyone had discovered that the task before them would be easier than they thought; if anything they were beginning to cope with the fact that it would be much harder. Absolutely everything would have to be painstakingly repaired, including all the little things they hadn't even thought of. But now at least the wondering was over. They knew what they had to do. It would be hard, but they could do it. *Walker* would live again.

Alan leaned across a table erected under a colorful awning on the pier. A tired but upbeat Spanky was using a blueprint he'd hand-drawn from memory to describe some of the below-deck damage he'd seen.

"I was really surprised by how little silt there was in the turbines and boilers. The lube oil in the port reduction gear looks like peanut butter, though. Worn-out seals must have leaked." He shrugged. "Everything'll have to be taken apart piece by piece and cleaned, and the seals and gaskets will all have to be replaced—thank God we have plenty of gasket material! You really came through with that weird corklike stuff!"

Alan nodded self-consciously. "Yeah, well, like I said, Bradford discovered it. Some sort of tree in the northwestern marshes—where all those tar pits are. The trees draw the stuff up in their roots and deposit it in the lower outer layers of their trunks. Bradford says it protects them from insects."

"Whatever. It's good stuff. Mallory swears by it. He ran his little airplane motor for twenty hours straight the other day and never got a leak. He says it's kind of hard to take stuff *apart* after it's been heated up, though. It sort of glues things together. He's calling it the 'Letts Gasket' and says you ought to take out a patent, since you're the one who figured out the application."

"I'll be sure to share my wealth with Courtney."

Adar had joined them, and when the laughter subsided, he addressed Alan. "What is a 'patent'?"

Alan looked at him and his expression turned serious. "Well, it's sort of a reward, I guess. It's a way people are rewarded for coming up with good ideas. Where we come from, laws protect those ideas from being used by other people. For example, if I invented a new gizmo— say the 'Letts gasket'—and got a patent on it, nobody else could swipe my idea and make the same thing without my permission. Usually, people would pay . . . or, ah, trade for permission."

Adar blinked concern. "Among our people there are clans or guilds that possess secret skills only they may pass on. That has caused many of my problems with the shipwrights. Is that much the same? Are you telling me you want permission to use your 'gaas-kets'?"

"No, Adar. It was a joke. 'My' gasket material is at everyone's disposal! I'm afraid we do need to have a long talk about that sort of thing when we get a chance, though."

Alan knew he was going to have to sit down with Adar one of these days and figure out some sort of financial system. Right now, everyone was highly motivated by the war effort and there was little grumbling about long hours, depletion of resources, and a somewhat lopsided distribution of labor and wealth. Before the war, Lemurian finance was based on an age-old, carefully refined, and fairly sophisticated barter system. Everything was worth exactly so much of something else. Even labor was valued in such a way. Some types of labor were worth more than others, but "wages" were still calculated by time-honored equivalent values. So much time in the shipyard, for example, was worth so many measures of gri-kakka oil, or grain, or seep. One length of fabric was worth so many weights of copper or fish, and so on. Obviously, people didn't carry their "wealth" around with them, or always even have possession of it, but everyone kept careful tabulations of who owed what to whom. To Alan, it was all profoundly confusing and inefficient, but he could see how it had worked for so long and, admittedly, well.

The problem was, right now there was an awful lot of activity and production under way and nobody was being "paid" anything. The situation struck a lot of the destroyermen as downright Stalinist, or at least mildly Red. With so much time ashore to think about such things, there'd been increased grumbling over how many barrels of gri-kakka oil a month being in the U.S. Navy was worth. The guys were fed and their booze at the Busted Screw was free, but the time was approaching when they might want to *buy* something. Going back to the old barter system was almost impossible too, since no one had been keeping tabs for a long time now. They'd have to start all over from scratch, and Alan knew from experience how hard it was to clear the books when it came to trades and favors.

He'd been reluctant to approach Adar about the problem because the guy already had so much on his plate. There was the war, of course, and the question of what to do about Jenks. Sister Audry and the presence of the descendants of the "ancient tail-less ones" had him all stirred up about religious matters, and he was walking a tightrope while he tried to figure that out. All were serious matters, but the financial cloud beginning to loom had the potential to eclipse all those other concerns. Somehow, Alan and Adar had to make time for this talk. Soon.

Adar sighed. "Very well. I think I know what you mean and you are right. If we had been keeping track, the people's surplus—guarded by Nakja-Mur and now myself—would have been gone long ago. With everything else . . . I do not look forward to that talk, but I welcome your suggestions." He motioned to the ship in the deepening gloom. "What have you discovered . . . besides bones?" His tone was suddenly urgent. "Can you fix her? You do understand she has become something of a . . . talisman to my People. Younglings carve images—icons of her, almost like Sister Audry's saints. The good sister speaks of your Lux Mundi, ah, Jesu Christo, and I must give that issue much thought." He paused. "Perhaps very much was lost in translation long ago. In any event, right now *Walker* is seen as the savior of my People—the People of Baalkpan and many others. Can you comprehend how important she has become to all of us?"

"Yeah," said Spanky, uncharacteristically quiet. "I wouldn't go runnin' around calling her a 'savior' or anything if I was you"—he glanced at Letts—"but we can damn sure comprehend how important she is. Trust me."

CHAPTER

9

*T*he sky was perfect. There were just enough puffy clouds to provide an occasional respite from the overhead sun, and the blue was so pure and fresh from horizon to horizon that the contrast with the clouds was as sharp as a knife. Matt had spent a great deal of time staring at the sky over the last few days, since he now knew from experience that they were entering the stormy time of year. Currently, the sky meant them no harm and the sea retained that glorious, possibly unique purplish hue he found so difficult to describe. The steady cooling breeze blew up just enough chop to give it character. Gentle whitecaps magically appeared, sparkling under the sun, then vanished like unique little lives. Ahead lay the northeast coast of

B'mbaado and the broad bay beyond. B'mbaado was not as thickly forested as Java, but from his perspective now, all Matt could see was a brilliant bluish green, turning golden at the top. If he lived to be a hundred, he'd never be able to reconcile the sheer, exotic, primordial beauty he beheld all around him with the savage lethality that lurked behind the mask.

Donaghey was an absolute joy, and he understood why Garrett loved her so. She and the other "first construction" frigates were built at the same time, but by the old methods. Unlike the new construction, there were subtle differences from one to the next. *Tolson* was a proud, stout ship and had a proud record too, but no matter what her crew did, she just didn't have *Donaghey*'s speed and grace. Her bow was blunter, her beam a bit wider, her shear not as sharp. She was formed a little more like her Grik counterparts. *Donaghey*'s builders had made everything just a bit more extreme. The result was that the flagship of the 2nd Allied Expeditionary Force was also its fastest element, besides the feluccas, and she could outrun them with the wind abaft the beam.

Tolson cruised not far behind, but the steam frigates were in the distance, laboring to keep up. They were screened by the altered corvettes whose characteristics, as expected, were respectable, and Matt grinned to think how frustrated their skippers must be. The problem wasn't that the steamers were terribly slow; they weren't. They were faster than anything they'd seen of the Grik under any circumstances. They were much faster even than *Donaghey* when the wind was still.

With a good wind, the steamers were faster—and far more economical—under sail, but their paddles and screws caused drag and there was nothing they could do about that. On one of the new ships, *Nakja-Mur*, they'd tried a solution attempted in the previous century. Her screw was designed to be raised and lowered by means of a complex system that had slowed her construction considerably. The scheme worked, after a fashion—and at least it hadn't failed catastrophically— but it didn't really do much for her speed. Even with the screw retracted, there was still the large, blunt sternpost to consider. She did steer better however. Jim Ellis complained that *Dowden*'s steering was "mushy" unless she was under power.

The new engines hadn't really had a test yet. They'd gotten the ships under way and out in the Makassar Strait without anything flying apart, but since the discovery that they only slowed the ships while under sail, they'd been secured. Matt wished he'd been able to test them further while they were close to home, but what if he needed them later and they'd already failed? It was a balancing act of necessities. Eventually he *would* need them. He just wished he knew whether he could count on them.

As usual, Matt and Greg Garrett were standing companionably silent on the quarterdeck. It was a custom they'd observed many times. Sometimes there just didn't need to be words. Matt knew Jim understood it too. The three of them had been through so much together, small talk was often not only superfluous, but distracting Safir Maraan and Lord Rolak ascended to the quarterdeck and caught their eyes. Matt smiled at them and waved them over. The B'mbaadan and Aryaalan troops were mostly on other ships, but Chack was aboard with most of his 2nd Marines. Rolak went where Matt went; he was still insistent on that, but Matt suspected Safir was aboard because of Chack. They weren't "officially" mated yet, but it was just a matter of time. Matt expected a formal announcement and ceremony to cap the liberation of B'mbaado.

"Cap-i-taan," Safir greeted him.

"My lord," said Rolak.

"Queen Protector, Lord Rolak," Matt replied. He looked at Rolak. "Feeling better?" The old warrior grimaced and blinked irritation.

"A glorious day and a beautiful ship!" said Safir. She'd grown almost giddy with excitement the closer they came to her home. With luck, it would be hers again. Hers and her people's.

"Indeed they are," Matt agreed. "And as for the ship, I think I love her!" he admitted.

"You can't have her, Skipper," Garrett said with a grin. "I just got her back!"

Matt chuckled. "Don't worry, Greg. I think peeling her paint with tweezers would be easier than getting you off this ship." He nodded past the masts and taut canvas forward. "There's your coastline, Your Majesty, and not a Grik ship in sight. You'd think they'd at least have a few pickets out, but we haven't seen a thing." He shook his head. "Silly to expect them to think like us, but we *know* they've picked up a *few* ideas."

"It is a sight I have long craved," Safir admitted wistfully. "I am excited, I admit, but some of your uneasiness tugs at me as well."

"Am I uneasy?" Matt asked. "I suppose. I wish we had a little recon . . ." He avoided saying, *I wish we had the PBY*, for the ten thousandth time, but they all knew what he meant. "This steaming—I mean *sailing*—blindly into a situation we know nothing about reminds me too much of old times. I'd almost rather we had to chase down and pound on a few scouts. Besides"—he grinned predatorily—"it would be fun."

"'Fun,' he says." Garrett chuckled. "Remember what happened last time *I* had a little 'fun.'"

"But surely this is different," rumbled Rolak. "Even a large fleet would be no match for us now, and if there are no Grik to sound the alarm, the surprise of our arrival will be all the greater."

"In a perfect world," Matt agreed. He didn't elaborate on how imperfect he considered this world to be. "But they've had as much time to recover as we have. Okada didn't think they could bring anything forward for a while, but with what we know they left in Aryaal when they moved on Baalkpan, they wouldn't need to, to make it a damned bloody fight." He looked at Safir. "I've no doubt we'll win, but I'm always counting the cost. I have to. Besides, we know the Grik can surprise us—they've done it before—and if they didn't eat Kurokawa, he might've helped them arrange something . . . unexpected."

Two Marines tromped up the companionway. One was clearly Chack, still wearing his battered American helmet at a jaunty angle. The other seemed vaguely familiar, but Matt couldn't place him. He was uncomfortably aware that unless he knew them well and their coloration or dress was distinctive, he had a hard time telling one 'Cat from another. The two Marines drew close and saluted.

"Cap-i-taans," Chack said. "Lord Rolak"—he smiled slightly—"Your Highness. I beg to report the discovery of this . . . creature . . . in my own ranks!"

Rolak peered more closely at the Marine. "By the Sun God's tail! Lord Koratin, you have lost much weight!"

Koratin! Now Matt remembered. He'd been a big wheel in Aryaal and had even been an advisor to its murdering king, Rasik-Alcas! He'd met him briefly when they retook the city right before the evacuation. For some reason, Rolak hadn't hanged him and Matt had forgotten all about him.

"Indeed!" replied Koratin. "I feel like a youngling again! I have always maintained that martial exercises strengthen the mind, body, and character."

"Character!" Rolak huffed. "I have occasionally—and briefly—wondered what happened to you after our last meeting. I assumed you were aboard *Nerracca* when she was lost, since you hadn't been insinuating yourself in the business of the Alliance. Yet here you stand, proving once again your consummate skill for survival!"

"Here I stand, Lord Rolak," Koratin answered, suddenly less ebullient.

Chack cleared his throat. "It seems Koratin enlisted in the First Baalkpan as a private as soon as he arrived in the city. He doubted he would be popular in an Aryaalan regiment. . . . In any event, he distinguished himself in battle and was therefore eligible to apply for Marine training." Chack blinked irony. "He graduated 'boot camp' as a squad leader corporal."

As things now stood in the Lemurian Marine Corps, only combat veterans could be considered for promotion. If there were ever peace, that might change, but for now the system worked well.

Rolak glanced incredulously at the twin red "stripes" on Koratin's kilt. "You *earned* corporal's stripes," he said, astonished. "That is more than you ever did in any previous post."

"True," Koratin agreed, "and I cherish those two stripes more than the finest robe I ever wore." His voice was still soft. "I owed it to my younglings. To all the younglings of our people, Lord Rolak. This, at least, I think you will believe."

Rolak nodded and looked at Matt. "Koratin was never evil. Vain, venal, and grasping, but not evil. I did not hang him because I believed he truly tried to stop Rasik and warn us of his treachery." He grumbled a chuckle. "It did not harm his case that Rasik was trying to kill him when we entered the city."

"You trust him?" Safir asked, surprised.

"I trust his dedication to younglings. That was never in doubt. Even at his worst, he often told noble tales and performed dramas for younglings in open forum. Moral dramas that taught principles he never used to live by."

"I was corrupt," Koratin agreed. "I thought I controlled my destiny. I knew my failings, yet I tried to set an example of integrity beyond myself so the younglings of our city might become better beings than I." He looked at Matt. "I have heard the words of your Sister Audry when she has come among the troops and I know not what power guides all things, whether it is the Sun God, or this other God of yours. Maybe they are the same." He shrugged. "But now I know that no one can hope to control destiny; it has a will of its own, its own plans for all of us. We are but leaves swept into a whirlpool not of our making. We do our best; that is all we can do, but in the end, in this arbitrary new way of war, our fates are in the hands of whichever God truly watches over us. Ultimately, we can only hope He will consider us fit company for the ones He has chosen to reward."

Taken aback, Matt could only stare. He hadn't known Sister Audry's "ministry" had penetrated so deeply. She hadn't built a cathedral next to the Great Hall, so he figured she was keeping things low-key. He knew she'd helped many of his men who felt lost and confused, regardless of denomination, but thought she'd otherwise confined her discussions with Adar. He hoped they didn't return to Baalkpan to find it locked in a holy war. "Jesus," he whispered.

"Carry on, Corporal Koratin," he said at last. "You're dismissed." When salutes were exchanged and Koratin was gone, he looked almost helplessly at Chack and the others. "What were we saying about surprises?"

"Are you sure he can be trusted?" persisted Safir. "Perhaps this is another of his dramas, and he speaks . . . most strangely."

Rolak looked thoughtful. "I don't think he performs; he was never that good. He was always strange, however. Chack?"

Chack blinked and shook his head. "His squad respects him, even the Aryaalans among them. When I said he distinguished himself in battle, it was something of an understatement."

"Let him be," Matt decided. "I guess we'll see. He's right about one thing: none of us knows our destiny." He glanced toward the now barely visible passage between B'mbaado and the distant Sapudis. "Or what we'll find in that bay."

They pushed on through the day and into the night. Matt sent a detail of 'Cats to Jenks's ship to serve as pilots, and keen-eyed Lemurian lookouts spied carefully ahead for shoals or enemy ships. A quarter moon gave more than sufficient light for them to warn of any danger. All night, the tension ratcheted up, and Garrett shortened sail on Matt's orders so the fleet could consolidate. Two hours before dawn, he gave the order for all ships to advance in line abreast and come to general quarters. If they encountered the enemy, they'd execute a turn to port on a signal from the flagship, and form a battle line. *Achilles* would maneuver to keep the battle line between herself and the Grik.

With the sun, they were close enough to see the remains of distant Aryaal through binoculars. Matt raised his precious Bausch & Lombs and adjusted the objective. It was still too far to make out any real details of the city, but except for a few jutting masts here and there that marked the graves of some recent Grik wrecks—possibly survivors of the Battle of Baalkpan that could make it no farther—there were no enemy ships in the bay.

"They're gone," he muttered in wonder.

"Maybe not," Garrett warned. "Maybe their ships are gone, but they might still have an army here, waiting to pounce on us as we disembark."

Matt grunted. He wouldn't put it past them. Still, unless they'd known they were coming—and he couldn't imagine how they would—there would have been *something* here. Supply ships if nothing else.

"May I?" asked Sean O'Casey. The big, one-armed man had joined them by the rail. He'd been bored throughout the voyage and had asked to be used as an engineer on one of the steamers, but Matt wanted him close for his insights regarding Jenks. The Imperial commodore had come aboard to dine a couple of times and Matt always wanted to know what O'Casey had to say about what they discussed. O'Casey remained hidden whenever Jenks was aboard, but his insights regarding Jenks were confusing. He was clearly wary of the man, but there was a subliminal thread of respect intertwined with a deep-seated resentment that remained imperfectly explained. Matt was never sure how much of what O'Casey had to say about Jenks was colored by whatever had apparently passed between the two men. In any event, according to O'Casey, Jenks hadn't avoided any real questions except Matt's occasional attempt to get him to confirm his suspicions regarding the location of the Imperial capital. Even O'Casey still wouldn't divulge that, as a matter of principle, but he knew Matt's guess was essentially correct. Matt didn't ask O'Casey anymore and O'Casey didn't disseminate. It was understood.

Garrett handed O'Casey his binoculars and the big man steadied them against a stay. "Impressive fortifications," he admitted. "'Twould be a costly chore ta storm. There's little ta see beyond the walls, however. Naught but that one fancy structure."

"That was the king's palace," Rolak confirmed. He was old, but his eyes were still far sharper than the average human's. "We burned the rest in the face of the Grik advance," he added sadly. "We left them nothing upon which to sustain themselves." He shook his head and his eyes were moist. "Aryaal was once a mighty, beautiful kingdom."

"It will be again," Matt assured him.

More officers and important passengers began gathering by the rail for their first glimpse of Aryaal or B'mbaado City. Safir's city across the strait had been undamaged by the fighting, but they'd burned it too. Now all they could see were the sad ruins atop the cliff. The fleet continued its advance, the heavily loaded corvettes angling toward the front when Matt ordered the signal aloft. Smoke coiled from the steamer's funnels as their boilers were lit. When they had steam, they'd maneuver inshore with their troops as well.

It was almost surreal. They'd come expecting a savage fight, but as best they could tell, there was nothing to face them. The entire environ seemed too quiet, almost devoid of life. Everything had the look of recent abandonment, and the closer they drew, the more apparent it became. The docks were strewn with debris and every small boat had been dragged ashore and shattered. Nothing at all remained of the dockside shantytown that had once served the cities' modest fisheries. Nothing but bare, scorched ground.

Then they smelled it. It began as a hint, a tantalizing ghost, but as they continued to approach and the wind came more from the shore, they caught the stench of death. Matt had smelled death many times now, in all its ghastly varieties. He'd smelled the decomposing Grik carrion at Baalkpan and on the plain below the very walls he looked upon. He knew what human dead smelled like: burnt, drowned, festering in the sun. This was different. It was something like what he'd smelled in the belly of *Revenge* after they'd taken that ship from the Grik, although there, there'd been a slimy, humid, mildewed edge. Regardless, he now recognized the growing, all-pervading stench of putrefying Lemurians.

"Left them naught ta sustain themselves, ye say?" O'Casey whispered, and tried to hold the glasses still. Matt redirected his binoculars. There'd been a disconnect, he supposed. He'd noticed the thousands of stakes driven in the ground surrounding Aryaal's walls, but must have assumed they'd been some new entanglement or defensive measure constructed by the Grik. Now he saw that atop each stake was a severed Lemurian head. Some were mere skulls by now, and they were still too distant for details, but many hung, slack-jawed, with tissue still attached. Some were quite fresh. Safir Maraan, bold warrior that she was, nearly lost the binoculars she'd borrowed when she lurched to the rail and vomited into the sea. Chack went to her and murmured soft words.

"My God!" exploded Garrett. "We can't have left that many behind! We got them *all*, Captain! Mr. Ellis and I." His tone became pleading. "We took everyone we could—everyone who came to the rendezvous! Maybe some didn't make it, but . . . my God!"

"I'm sure you got all you could, Greg," Matt said, his voice wooden. "But they were here a long time. Long enough to scour Java clean of all the 'prey' we never had a chance to save. The people of Bataava, the other cities . . ."

Rolak jerked his sword free of his belt and desperately cast his eyes about for something to cleave. With a wail of anguish, he finally buried the point in the deck. Even Garrett didn't scold him.

"Do you think they're gone then?" Safir asked, stepping to face him. Her eyes were pools of horror and Chack supported her as though she might faint. Her usually immaculate silver-washed breastplate had been splashed with the contents of her stomach.

"Yeah. I think so." His lips curled in a snarl. "Why else do *that*?"

"What do you mean?" asked Chack. "We know they collect skulls . . . 'trophies' of their prey."

"But they didn't *collect* them!" Matt insisted. "They left them here like that! Maybe not all of them are gone, and keep that in mind when you go ashore, but I bet most are. For some reason, they've abandoned this place and they knew, eventually, we'd return." He gestured at the city and the literally thousands of stakes. "And they wanted to make sure, when we did, we'd see *that!*"

"Skipper," Garrett said quietly, "I think if Mr. Bradford were here, he'd say something profound, about the lizards being more sophisticated than we thought, or something like that. I bet they did this as a warning. To scare us. Make us stay away."

"You're probably right. Maybe they are more sophisticated, or maybe Kurokawa put them up to it. Doesn't matter." He looked at those around him, then forced himself to look at the city again. "I think they'll find it has an opposite effect than they intended. Just like Pearl Harbor." By now, most of the 'Cats knew the significance of that reference. "I want to exterminate them like the vermin they are." He paused, then spoke to Garrett. "Signal the corvettes to disembark their troops as planned. Form a perimeter around the landing area. The steamers will cover the landing with their heavy guns. Once we have a beachhead, we'll put the rest of the troops ashore, again, just like we planned. Whether the landing is contested or not, I want everybody acting like it is. Good practice. Finally, send a signal to *Achilles*, with my compliments, and ask Commodore Jenks if he'd care to accompany me ashore." Matt's face hardened. "I think it's high time our reluctant British friends saw the true face of our enemy."

Captain Reddy met Jenks's boat at the dock. Rolak was with him, along with the old warrior's staff. The only other human was Chief Gray, looming behind his captain with a Thompson submachine gun. The gun had once been Tony Scott's personal weapon and it hadn't saved him in the end—but he hadn't had it with him, had he? Gray was determined that Captain Reddy would always have him *and* the weapon at his back whenever he was at risk. Jenks stepped out of the boat with another white-coated figure. Both held perfumed cloths over their faces. Four of the red-coated, bare-legged Imperial Marines stepped ashore as well, bright muskets on their shoulders.

Jenks was watching the rapid, professional deployment of the Marines the 600, and the slightly less practiced arrival of the Army regiments. Once ashore however, the Army seemed as competent as the others. Matt sensed that Jenks was a little surprised and perhaps slightly daunted by what he saw. The Marines established a perimeter near where the old breastworks once had been, and Safir's 600—who trained with the Marines to the same rigorous standards—deployed across the road leading to the main gate. The Army regiments, in their multicolored leather armor and kilts, took supporting positions as the Marines broadened the beachhead. Four light guns were off-loaded and placed, by sections, in the center and on the right flank. Nothing stirred across the vast plain on the left.

Slowly, the steamers nudged their way closer to the dock. General Alden led the rest of the forces ashore and soon the area within the perimeter teemed with troops. In two hours, they had four thousand battle-tested, well-trained *soldiers* from every Allied power probing slowly forward and automatically preparing defensive positions around the perimeter. The steamers moved away and joined the frigates, where they could defend against any attack from the sea, while covering the ground force with their guns. It struck Matt how differently this landing was going from the first one they'd made on these very shores. Then, it had been dark and chaotic, and the Army was largely untested. It wasn't quite as big either. He was confident that if he'd brought these troops ashore back then, they could easily have defeated the nearly twenty thousand Grik despite Rasic's treachery, without any help from Aryaal at all. The weapons were the same as before, even though there'd been some familiarization training with the new prototypes. Full-scale production was just beginning when they left, and there was no sense "trickling" the new weapons in. The main difference between this Army and the old was, literally, a level of professionalism that came only with experience and confidence.

Alden and Chack approached and saluted. Alden was the overall field commander and the various regimental commanders would have already reported to him. "Skipper," he said, "we've pushed nearly to the gates." He scowled. "Close enough to get a good look at all the heads." He glanced at Jenks appraisingly. "Lord Rolak's supporting the Second Marines and the Six Hundred with the First and Third Aryaal. He begs the . . . ah . . . privilege of being the first to enter his city."

Matt nodded. "Very well. Chack, you and Queen Maraan let him through, but I want you both to support him closely. No telling what surprises the enemy may have left. Form a perimeter inside the gate, in that open area around the big fountain like we did last time. Use other supporting regiments. After the plaza's secure, proceed to secure the rest of the city. Once we're sure the enemy's gone, we'll form details to take those damn heads down."

"Aye-aye, sir," Alden and Chack chorused, and trotted off. Matt turned to Jenks, who'd remained mostly silent since coming ashore.

"A most impressive display, Captain Reddy," Jenks said. His tone held no irony.

"I guess you could do it better, though," muttered Gray sarcastically. Despite the slightly more cordial relations between Jenks and his captain, the Bosun hadn't thawed.

Jenks rounded on Gray, snatching the kerchief from his face. "It was a genuine compliment, *Mr.* Gray. I do grow weary of your attitude, however. You have harbored a grudge for long months now and perhaps I provoked it. If so, I sincerely apologize in the presence of"—he waved toward the countless pikes—"these tragic dead. That said, and the apology made, I will gladly oblige you if you insist on a confrontation." Jenks took a breath and suddenly gagged violently. "Excuse me," he muttered, and, stepping a short distance away, he retched. His companion, kerchief still in place, joined the commodore while he continued to heave and gasp.

Gray was stunned. "I'll be damned," he managed. "That Bakelite Brit can bend a little after all." He lowered his voice. "Even if it did break him to do it."

"Leave him be, Boats. He's been 'bending' quite a bit lately. More than you know. And seeing that"—he nodded at the city—"could break anybody. We've kind of gotten used to it," he said bitterly, "and it still makes me want to puke."

Jenks finally composed himself and returned to face them. His color was ashen. "My apologies again, gentlemen." His voice was rough.

"No need," said Matt, almost gently.

"I . . . guess I'm sorry too," said Gray. "I didn't mean to make you move your hanky . . . and . . . blow."

It was all Matt could do, even under the circumstances, to keep from cracking up. The Bosun had always had a talent for the backhanded compliment, apology, or . . . anything. Jenks looked at the big man intently for a moment before deciding to accept Gray's . . . statement.

"Actually, as I was saying," continued Jenks, forcing himself to keep the kerchief from his face, "your landing was most impressive. Very businesslike and coordinated. And somewhat ominous to a"—he glanced again at the heads—"a *neutral* observer such as myself."

"Surely you practice such things? Your Marines, for example."

"Certainly, but you have clearly had much more practice, on a considerably larger scale of late. My nation relies as heavily on naval power as does yours. Even more so, I'd wager, but we rarely engage in major land actions. The most recent of those was several years past. As you know, there are just under a hundred Marines aboard my ship, and I'm sure they could have come ashore just as creditably. But even their modern weapons might not have added much punch to your force."

Matt avoided commenting on Jenks's definition of "modern weapons" and the dubious advantage Matt considered muskets to be over the Lemurian's powerful longbows, but he knew his troops had won Jenks's respect. It remained to be seen whether that was a good thing or not.

The wind veered slightly and a gentle, merciful breeze diverted most of the stench northeast, toward B'mbaado. That or their noses were growing desensitized. Flags flapped and popped within the perimeter where the command staff awaited the first reports from the city. They'd heard no shots, but it was possible they might not have. The few rifle-armed scouts might have penetrated far enough by now that the ruins and the breeze could swallow the reports of their Krags. Eventually however, a runner appeared in the gateway and raced down through the ranks until he stood before Matt.

"General Rolak's compliments, Cap-i-taan Reddy," announced the 'Cat with surprisingly little accent. "The city is secure from the north gate, halfway to the south. There is no sign of the enemy other than a few . . . curious corpses. The Royal Palace has also been secured, and General Rolak begs you to come to him."

Matt arched an eyebrow. "Any resistance? Casualties?"

"No casualties, sir . . . but there *is* resistance—of a sort. Nothing to be concerned with," the 'Cat added with a snort, "but something my general prefers you see for yourself."

Matt shrugged and looked at Gray. "Very well. Tell him we'll be along."

Gray hitched his pistol belt and shouted for an orderly to assemble the rest of the Captain's Guard, some of whom were still aboard ship. Matt rolled his eyes, but knew it was pointless to complain. He looked at Jenks.

"Care to join us?"

They entered the city and the entourage was joined by an even larger security force that escorted them to the Royal Palace. Pete Alden met them there, reporting that Rolak and Queen Maraan were inside. Chack was leading his troops on a deeper penetration of the city. As the runner had told them, Alden confirmed that the only signs of the enemy were some "strange" corpses, but cryptically added that they *had* discovered a few Grik. Matt was curious, but knew if there was a threat, they'd have told him. They probably just wanted him to see whatever it was in the same context they'd first viewed it. Sometimes, context was important, and maybe they didn't want to prejudice his perceptions. The palace was filthy and full of reeking droppings. Matt wondered whether the enemy had done that deliberately. Surely even the Grik couldn't live amid such filth? The ships they'd captured hadn't been *clean*, but they hadn't been defiled to this extent.

Alden paused before a macabre scene. A Grik—or was it?—was

staked to heavy beams resembling an inverted cross. It flashed through Matt's mind that the thing had been *crucified* right here in the palace! Its tail had been hacked off and was nowhere in sight. All the claws were torn away, leaving mere jagged stumps of fingers and toes. It looked like even some of the creature's teeth had been knocked out. Both eyes were missing from the desiccated corpse but whether they'd been gouged out by scavengers or during the evident "entertainment" was impossible to guess. By the amount of dark, dried blood spattered all around, it had clearly been alive for at least part of the process.

"That's not an ordinary Grik," Gray said.

"Yeah," agreed Matt. "The fur color's wrong. It looks more like one of those aborigine Griks we saw on Bali."

"Wow," muttered Gray. "Bastards must not get along. Wonder why they didn't just eat him?"

"He's not the only one," Alden said. "And there's something else you need to see."

They followed the Marine up a long, winding stair that landed upon another wide chamber, not quite as filthy as the one below. Pete then advanced to a high-arched, guarded doorway. "Open it," he said to one of the guards, and the 'Cat pushed the heavy door inward. Pete glanced back, his face grim, and made a "follow me" motion with his head.

Rasik-Alcas, king of Aryaal, sat upon what had so briefly been his ornate golden throne. The throne had suffered the ravages of the Grik and was now somewhat the worse for wear—but so was Rasik-Alcas. His once elaborate robes were dingy and weather-beaten, faded and stained. His pelt was a loose shroud draped over what had been a powerful frame. His cheeks were hollow and his whiskers were long and shaggy. Within the well-defined skull, however, large eyes still shone bright with hatred and madness. Currently they were locked upon those of Lord Muln-Rolak, standing just a few feet away, his sword point held casually—and unwaveringly—less than an inch from Rasik's nose.

"My lord," Rolak said, addressing Matt, "we were mistaken. Somehow, the beast still lives. Clearly, the punishment we expected for him was far too mild." He grinned horribly. "Or perhaps even the Grik could not stomach the thought of eating him!"

Matt's first reaction was one of rage. He hated Rasik-Alcas more than any living creature—but he hadn't known he was living, had he? The bastard was responsible for the death of Harvey Donaghey, and probably Tom Felts and half a dozen other destroyermen as well. God knew how many Lemurian lives were lost to his treachery. Matt started to order Rolak to hack the miserable murderer down. Then his hand strayed to his Academy sword. He'd do it himself! Pulling the sword free with a snarl, he took a step forward.

"Ah, Skipper?"

"What, Pete?" Matt snapped.

"Well, hold on just a second. Please."

Matt paused, blood thundering in his ears, and looked back at Alden. The chamber was large, but much was in shadow. Large, arched passages that once opened upon a balcony were covered over with planks. The full heat of the day pounded against the wooden barriers, radiating inward. It was hard to see anything, though, except for Rasik and Rolak, who stood in a beam of light that must have been purposely channeled to rest upon the throne.

"We ain't alone in here, Skipper," Pete said.

For the first time, Matt peered hard into the gloom. Evidently, Gray did too, because there came a muttered, "Shit!" and the unmistakable sound of the Thompson's bolt being yanked back.

"My God," Matt said. He could now discern other figures in the chamber that he'd missed in his single-minded concentration on the Aryaalan king. Half a dozen forms stood stationary along the walls, each covered by two or more Marines. At first, he thought he must be imagining things, that the gloom was playing tricks on his vision, but he quickly realized that wasn't the case. They were lizards. Grik. He'd seen quite enough of the monsters to identify them at a glance. These were the real thing, not aboriginals or a different species like Lawrence. These were the exact same creatures they'd come here to fight, but here they stood, almost alone, and their reaction to the situation wasn't right at all.

"What the hell's going on here, Mr. Alden?" Matt demanded, pausing his killing advance on Rasik.

"Damned if I know, Skipper. We came in here and found 'em like this: Rasik on his fancy chair and a bunch of lizards standing around like guards. His guards. Lord Rolak went to kill the bastard and he told the Griks to defend him! It's been like this since: Rolak ready to stick Rasik and the lizards ready to fight. Wouldn't be much of a fight," he added, "but, well, I figured you ought to see it."

"Rolak?"

"The beast says they are his 'children,' his 'pets.' They do seem willing to defend him. Just as odd, he spoke to them in the language of the People, which he must have taught them."

"Ask *them* what this is all about!" Matt ordered.

"I tried. I think they even answered me, but I could not understand. They seemed to understand me, though, and I managed to get them to lower their weapons, at least."

Matt had never personally met the Aryaalan king, but that didn't matter. They knew each other through their deeds. He was glad he'd finally polished his 'Cat enough to vent his rage without an interpreter: "Rasik, you sick bastard! I figured when we left you here, you'd wind up on a stick! I thought that a fitting punishment for what you did. Even then, I never dreamed you'd collaborate with these monsters! They killed your people, your city! Have you seen what they did outside? Have you even *been* outside?"

Rasik turned his gaze upon the captain, the hate and madness still bright. "I did not 'collaborate,' you fool! I fled! I went into the wilderness with my few loyal guards and we evaded the Grik and sometimes killed them. We even fed upon them, on occasion," he added with some satisfaction. "But I *stayed* when all my people left me, left our sacred city to the Grik! *You* are to blame for what has befallen us! You led this evil here! If you had not come, all would be as it has always been. We would have defeated the first, smaller Grik horde and then turned our attention back to B'mbaado! Well, that city is mine now too, as is all of Jaava! None remain to contest me; even the Grik have fled! But I stayed. I *stayed*! All this land is *mine*!"

Rasik's rant was so wildly untrue and preposterous, Matt couldn't even bring himself to respond to it. Instead, he looked at the Grik guards. "Not all the Grik fled, it seems. If you didn't collaborate with them, why do they protect you?"

"A simple thing. They collaborated with *me*. They are not the same as the vermin that infested my city. They are some of those that scattered after the battle I so wisely kept my warriors"—Rasik paused and glared at Rolak—"*most* of my warriors from joining. My companions and I hunted them at first," he admitted, "like any Grik. We did not know the difference. When we discovered they *were* different, we . . . allowed them to enlist in our army of liberation! Never have there been such loyal troops! Lift a finger against me and they will strike you down and eat your bones!" Rasik chuckled and it sounded like a wood rasp dragged across a rock. "We came to hurl the invaders from my city and discovered it all but abandoned! The horde must have learned that I was coming to reap my revenge! All that remained were a few feral Grik, like are known to inhabit the islands nearby. Their masters must have left them here." Rasik flicked his wrist. "We disposed of them."

Matt wondered whether the crucified creature downstairs was one such Rasik had "disposed" of, and if all had been given similar treatment.

"Where are your other 'companions,' *king*?" asked Rolak. The word "king" dripped sarcasm.

"They were like you, *Lord* Rolak," Rasik replied matter-of-factly, with equal sarcasm. "They were disloyal. They disobeyed me *just like you* and I was forced to punish them."

"So," Matt said, taking a few steps closer. "Now you're the uncontested king of all Aryaal, all Java—with nothing but a handful of Grik for subjects!"

"My people will return!" Rasik hissed. "They will return now that I have driven the Grik away!"

"You didn't drive them away," Matt retorted harshly, unable to stomach Rasik's lies any longer. "'Your' people did!" He paused. "*They* did it, Rasik, and they *have* returned! They've come back to scour this city and make it their own again. They left you, sure enough, but they left you here to die."

"You did that!" Rasik screeched.

"Yeah, I did, and I'm sorry. I should have killed you then, like your people said I should!"

"Guards!" shouted Rasik, turning toward "his" Grik.

"Wait!" yelled Matt, in Lemurian. "You say you think they'll understand me?" he quickly asked Rolak.

"Yes, lord . . . if you are careful about your accent!"

Matt ignored the jibe. "You . . . you Grik warriors," he said carefully. "Listen to me. This creature is evil. . . . Do you know what that means?" Rasik prepared a shouted retort, but Rolak waved his sword point to regain his attention. "He has led you down a false path, a dark path . . . a wrong path. He does not want what is best for you, only for himself. He sacrificed his own people to his selfishness and he's ready to do it again. To sacrifice you." Matt rubbed his eyes, hoping he was getting through. "If you try to fight us, you will die. That's the truth. You won't even get any of us." He nodded toward the Marines covering each of the creatures. "If you put your weapons down and come with us, you'll be well treated; I promise! You'll never be 'prey,' and you'll never have to be afraid again. I'm the commander of the forces that defeated you to begin with, the forces that defeated your Invincible Swarm and finally drove your people from this city. I have the power to make this promise, and it *is* a promise! Think of it! Plenty of food, nothing to fear"—he looked at Rasik—"and no more dying at the whim of a wild, unfeeling traitor. A traitor that made prey of his own people and would do the same to you!" There was total silence. "*Think* on it!"

Suddenly, with what almost sounded like a whimper, a sword fell to the floor. Then another. Incredulous, Rasik squirmed on his throne to see, but anything he might have said was silenced when Rolak's blade caressed his neck. The rest of the Grik weapons hit the floor with a cacophonous crash and Matt felt a wild feeling of relief . . . and something else.

"Goddamn," muttered Gray. "Skipper, you just talked to Grik!"

I just talked to Grik! Matt screamed to himself. *What does it mean? What can it mean?* Quickly but carefully, since no Grik was ever unarmed, the Marines rounded up the prisoners—*Grik prisoners!*—and led them from the chamber. Matt took a deep breath and looked around. Pete still seemed speechless, as shocked as he was, and Jenks— he'd forgotten Jenks was even there—was looking at him with a very strange expression. He turned back to Rasik.

"Well," he said. "Left to die again. Somehow, you just don't inspire much loyalty, *King* Alcas!"

"Am I to die?" Rasik asked. His madness seemed to have passed with his illusion of power and his eyes had grown wide with fright.

"Just as soon as it can be arranged," Matt promised him.

"I would *so* enjoy killing him, my lord," Rolak crooned.

"Me too, but we need to do it right. For now, we've got a hell of a mess to clean up around here," he said grimly. "Then we've got to decide what to do next. Maybe even learn something from our prisoners." He stopped and shook his head. He needed time to wrap his mind around that. He wished Bradford were here! Or Lawrence. Maybe Rebecca's companion would have some insight. "I want to push on toward Singapore, see what things are like there. Maybe we can take it back too. For some reason, the enemy seems to be abandoning his forward outposts. Anyway, we'll be stuck here for a little while. There'll be plenty of time for a trial for 'His Majesty' and we'll boost morale for his former subjects with a proper, first-class hanging." He glanced at his watch and turned to leave. "Carry on, gentlemen."

"Wait!" cried Rasik. Matt kept walking. "*Wait!*" Rasik screeched with the voice of a terrified youngling. Matt paused in the doorway.

"What?" he snapped. "I've got a lot to do, and as far as I'm concerned, you're to blame for most of it. We might have *saved* some of those people out there on poles if it wasn't for you, damn you! The sooner you're dead, the happier I'll be!"

"After I'm dead," Rasik said, gaining a little control over his voice, "you will never know what I found while I wandered in the wilderness!"

"What you found?"

"Yes. I think you might find it quite interesting . . . possibly even worth my life."

C

ontact!" Ben Mallory shouted, warning Tikker that things were about to happen. Fast. They'd just completed the exhaustive, perhaps even mildly paranoid checklist he'd devised in the naive hope he'd somehow managed to foresee every glitch and imponderable characteristic his "creation" might throw at them. In spite of his excitement, Ben was more than a little nervous. He knew airplanes—particularly the high-performance pursuit planes he'd trained in—but in spite of the workmanlike proficiency he'd gained in the old PBY Catalina, he'd known it had a lot of idiosyncrasies he'd never figured out. Most of them probably had to do with its being a seaplane. His takeoffs and landings had never been all that hot, and that still bothered him. Now he was about to try to fly a seaplane that, essentially, *he'd* designed, without the benefit of any of the cumulative wisdom that had gone into the Catalina. Maybe "nervous" wasn't really the right word.

The water of the bay was a little restless, with a light, uneven chop, but the wind was right and the sky seemed docile enough. The X-PB-1, as he referred to the plane, or "Nancy," as everyone else had taken to calling it, after his first, ill-considered description, floated in the middle of the bay where it had been towed by *Mahan*'s launch, and all the area for a good distance in every direction had been cleared of harbor shipping. Other boats bobbed at regular intervals, ready to race to their aid if something . . . unpleasant happened. Ben hoped it wouldn't. Experiments had shown that if they crashed into the water, even in the bay, they had a life expectancy of between four and six minutes before the "flashies" arrived and tore them to shreds. Of course, they had to survive the crash itself before that little tidbit of information would be relevant.

Ben was unhappy about the seemingly universally accepted moniker. The plane hadn't ultimately wound up looking anything *like* a Nancy—one of the NC, or Navy-Curtiss, flying boats. It still looked more like a miniature PBY to him, although a comparison to a Supermarine Walrus was probably even closer. He was damned if he'd even mention *that*.

"Contact," Tikker confirmed, while Ben stood precariously and turned toward the propeller. He felt as if he were attempting the feat in a canoe. He almost fell when an errant wave bounced the port wing float and slapped the starboard float against the sea.

"Jeez!" he chirped, trying to brace himself. He reached back and grasped one of the blades. At least he felt confident about the propeller. They'd "tracked" it while the engine was on the stand, and run it at different RPMs to check for resonant vibration and balance. The first one flew apart and nearly killed "Mikey" Monk, but they quickly improved the design. Bernie and Campeti finally came up with a scheme for a machine like a Springfield stock carver that they could use to make perfect props every time, as well as musket stocks. He pushed the blade up as high as he could reach, then brought it down with all his might. Much to his gratification, his prototype engine coughed instantly to life, and with a burbling, liquid fart, the propeller blades blurred before him. His back screamed in agony as he pulled something important trying to keep from falling into the prop. *Improvement number one*—he winced—*some kind of rail behind the cockpit for the pilot to hang onto so the engine doesn't eat him!*

Painfully, he turned and tried to get in the seat, but tripped on the stick and sprawled forward, across the windscreen. The stick poked him savagely in the crotch. He had no idea what kind of sound he made over the suddenly coughing engine, but doubted it was very manly. Aft, behind the motor, Tikker sprang up like . . . well, a cat, and hosed fuel at the carburetor with one of *Mahan*'s bug sprayers. The engine farted again, ran up, then started to cough. Somehow, Ben managed to form an objective thought: *Okay. Have to figure out a whole new start-up procedure.* He slid down into his wicker seat and for a moment just sat there, gasping sympathetically with the motor while trying to re-member where the throttle was through the waves of pain. His vision cleared as the tears evaporated and he pushed the suddenly visible throttle knob forward. Tikker had been keeping the engine alive with the bug sprayer, but now it caught and settled into a healthy-sounding rumble.

Before he could grab it, Ben's six-page checklist flew past his face, into the prop, and showered Tikker with confetti. *Oh, well*, he thought. *Saves me the effort of tearing it up.* He settled in his seat, getting a feel for things, and put the control surfaces through their paces once more. So far, so good. The engine had settled down and sounded swell. He felt the plane begin to accelerate slightly beneath him and glanced up. *That's funny. What's the launch doing there?* The boat was racing straightaway, almost directly in front of him. *Oh. Damn. There's the city, too!* The plane must have bobbed around in a circle while he was concentrating on getting it started and staying alive. He pushed the right rudder pedal to the floorboard, and the plane began turning south again, completing the circle it had begun on its own. *Enough*, he thought. *The vaudeville show's over. Time to get this crate in the air!* He yelled for Tikker to hang on, but doubted the 'Cat heard him. He real-ized improvement number three was some kind of voice tube so he could communicate with his air crew.

Pointing roughly toward the mouth of the bay, he advanced the throttle. The propeller became invisible and the awkward-looking craft picked up speed. *Okay, fairly responsive. Let's give it some more!* He pushed the throttle to the stop. His creation had no flaps. The PBY hadn't had any and he'd hoped they wouldn't be needed. It was a sea-plane, after all, and runway length shouldn't be an issue. He'd hoped.

"C'mon," he muttered. The engine roared behind him, a little quieter now, and the prop was spinning—disconcertingly close—as fast as it could. The plane increased speed until it began to skip across the top of the water, but he couldn't seem to get it up. "C'mon!" he yelled, pulling back a little on the stick. The nose came off the water, but he *felt* it catch the wind! "Whoa!" he yelped, pushing back on the stick just a bit. His heart raced and he wondered how close he'd come to flipping the plane on its back. *CG*—center of gravity—*is too far aft. I was afraid of that*, he thought. *Too much ass in her britches, like a P-39.* He wondered why he'd done that. Was he trying to make a pursuit ship out of a floatplane? Chances were she'd be pretty nimble, but he was growing more concerned about the plane's stability. He concentrated on holding the stick where it was, still building speed. *Might need flaps after all*, he thought.

Suddenly, amazingly, the hull left the water and the contraption was in the air! He risked a glance back at Tikker, but the 'Cat was whirling madly on the crank that retracted the wing floats. He looked to the side. Sure enough, the floats were coming up—slowly. *Damn. Need a little more mechanical advantage there.* The floats had seemed to come up fast enough when they tested them, but that was on dry land, with no drag. *Number five.*

Once the plane was off the water, it practically rocketed into the sky. Again, he wondered if there was some seaplane mystery he was unaware of. He eased back on the stick and knew they had enough thrust at last to keep the nose from trying to flip them. He'd actually foreseen that to a degree, and intended that the high-mounted engine should counteract just such a tendency. He hadn't had any real formula to base his calculations on, but it seemed to be working . . . sort of. That might have been what kept them down so long too, though. *Oh, well, that's what test flights are for!*

He wiped his goggles and realized he was soaked. There'd been enough spray to wet him down pretty good. He'd never gone blind, per se, but a larger windscreen was in order. He'd also have hated to get this wet anywhere but in the tropics. Cold still might be an issue, depending on the ceiling. *Number six.* He started climbing and banking slightly left, intending to ease back toward the city. Slowly, his tension began to ebb. He'd done it! He'd designed and helped build the first airplane ever constructed on this world! A euphoric feeling began to take hold. He'd done it, and he was flying! When the old PBY folded up and fell into the bay during the battle, he'd never dreamed he would survive, much less fly again! He let out a whoop.

He didn't have an altimeter, but thought he was probably about two thousand feet up when he steadied the plane and aimed it at Baalkpan. With any luck, they'd have altimeters soon. There wasn't that much to them, and right then, anything seemed possible. He glanced at his instrument panel. They'd salvaged a few instruments from the Catalina and put them on the prototype whether they had realistic expectations of re-creating them or not. They had to know what the plane could do. All the new planes would have a few easy instruments: a compass, an artificial horizon—or clinometer, as the Navy types liked to call it. An airspeed indicator was easy to do. Several temperature gauges would be supplied: one for the crankcase and others for each cylinder head. An oil-pressure gauge had already been successfully tested and was in production. The fuel gauge, at present, was the time-honored floating stick bobbing up and down through a hole in the gas cap. The fuel tank was in the wing above and behind him and he could keep an eye on the "gauge" with a little mirror. They'd need more eventually. They already *had* more than most pilots relied on in the Great War. Ben fiddled with the stick. A little tight, he decided, and he'd like some trim tabs, but overall, the only real problem was a tendency to pitch. *CG, again.* He already hated the propeller so close behind his head. Maybe they needed to turn the engine around. Make it a pusher . . .

He read the gauges instead of just staring proudly at them. Airspeed was better than he'd expected. About ninety. The temps looked good. A little warmer in the rear cylinders, but he'd expected that. Oil pressure was steady, maybe dropping a little, but that was normal as the oil heated up. He looked back at Tikker and caught a huge grin splitting the sable face. A few particles of the checklist still clung in his fur. Ben returned the thumbs-up offered by the only other "experienced" aviator in the Alliance. That thought hit him again. It had been stupid to bring Tikker on this flight. Granted, the 'Cat wasn't *really* experienced, but he had guts and he *had* flown. He'd also done very well in the simulators they'd put together. *Shouldn't have done it*, Ben decided, *but the little guy* deserved *it*.

Tikker caught his attention again, made a swooping gesture with his hand, and pointed down. Ben saw they were coming up on where *Ajax* was moored. *Oh, no. Why did he have to do that*? Had he *known* Ben's pursuit instincts would kick in, like a dog seeing a rabbit take off? *Can't do it*, Ben decided. *Talk about stupid! No way should I do this! I really probably ought not to*. . . . With a wicked grin, he nodded exaggeratedly.

Pushing the stick forward, he pretended he had a gunsight in front of him and began a shallow dive toward the Imperial frigate. He knew Adar would get hot, and so would the captain when he found out, but what were they going to do? Ground him? The plane started gaining speed. One hundred, a hundred and ten, a hundred and twenty . . . The stick got even tighter, but he waggled his wings just a little and knew he had plenty of control. Closer they sped, and he could see figures running on the deck. He knew just seeing the airplane was probably giving them fits, but there'd been no way to fly it without them knowing, so no one had actually ordered him *not* to buzz the ship. Besides, they still had stuff to test. A hundred and thirty at this dive angle seemed about max, and Ben was really wishing for trim tabs now, but as the mast tops approached, he was pleased to note that when he pulled back on the stick, the strange little plane almost leaped back up into the sky.

Maybe just a little impulsively, he displayed a hopefully universal gesture and yanked the stick to the right, forcing the plane into a slightly tighter climbing barrel roll than he'd perhaps intended.

"Seat belts!" he shouted, as he went inverted. "Number seven!"

There was no danger he and Tikker would fall out—they were sucked *into* their seats—but they were slammed against the left side of their respective cockpits. The tight roll and sharp climb forced Ben's head back—where there was no rest—and he found himself staring right at the blurred propeller just inches away.

"*Shit!*"

Instinctively, Ben pushed the stick forward—maybe a little too much. The aft CG practically pitched the nose out from under them, causing a momentary—but terrifying—negative-G condition. This immediately levitated the fuel in the carburetor and closed the float, starving the engine—not to mention leaving Tikker to clutch the diagonal stringers in the fuselage for dear life. Recognizing that improvement number seven was of *extreme* importance, Ben somehow managed to ease back on the stick, finish the roll, and right the craft before he and Tikker were thrown from the plane.

Airspeed had kept the prop windmilling behind him, and within seconds, as the fuel in the carburetor remembered where to go, the engine coughed and sputtered back to life. Holding the stick in a viselike grip, Ben looked around. Everything was back to normal and the *Nancy* seemed to have survived the *stupid, stupid, stupid* gyrations with no apparent damage. He sighed, loosening his grip a little, and took a deep, shaky breath. He almost gagged. *Gas!* There was gas everywhere! He looked at Tikker and saw that the 'Cat was soaked. He was shouting something and pointing up. Ben spun to stare at the little mirror and saw the fuel gauge stick was gone. Worse, so was the gas cap it floated in. *What the hell?!* The pressure of the gas or the air in the tank slapping against it must have blown the cap off, he deduced. Judging by the amount of fuel all over everything, they must have dumped a lot—since most of it wouldn't have landed on them!

He looked down. They were over the city now, and he banked back toward the bay. *I wonder how much fuel we have left?* The engine coughed, gurgled, then roared back to life. *Shit! Not much!*

He turned back to Tikker and made a winding motion over his head. *Get the floats down!* Tikker was already spinning the crank. With a pounding heart, Ben Mallory concluded he was liable to have to attempt yet another stunt he'd absolutely *never* intended for this very first flight: a dead-stick landing on Baalkpan Bay.

Pointing the nose down to build some airspeed, he found he had to keep even more back pressure on the stick to keep the ship level as the engine burped and died completely. The sudden lack of any sound but the wind whooshing through the support struts and control cables was chilling.

"Slow down!" he heard Tikker shriek for the first time.

"Can't!" he shouted back. "Rule number one—when you start training those idiots who volunteered for this—airspeed is life! In our case, we need enough speed to land the damn thing on the water! If we're too slow when we flare out, we'll stall and pancake in. Liable to break something!"

"I thought rule number one was 'no stupid stunts that kill engine!'"

"I . . ." Ben fumed, and concentrated on keeping a steady, gliding descent. Ahead, the bay opened before them again. Damn, they were getting low! 'Cats were scurrying around on the waterfront, dodging this way and that, apparently expecting them to drop right on top of them. He eased back just a bit on the stick—and then held it tight against its tendency to come too far back. *Definitely going to have to change the CG*, he decided. They were over the water now, and he looked for a clear spot to set down. There wasn't much room. Many of the ships and fishing boats had gathered in this area to stay out of his way.

"A little speed help now?" Tikker demanded.

"Hell, yes. What . . . ?" Tikker hosed the last of the fuel in the bug sprayer at the carburetor. With a "pop!" and an explosive backfire, the engine roared to life and gave him just enough acceleration to level off and make a powered touchdown on the choppy water. He risked a quick glance aft when he heard a shrill cry, and saw Tikker pitch the flaming bug sprayer over the side like an arcing meteor. The backfire must have lit the damn thing!

Whump! The plane practically gouged into the sea, but it had just enough remaining speed and lift to bounce up and skip across a few little waves before settling down for good. The engine gasped, hacked, and the prop spun raggedly to a stop, leaving them bobbing peacefully on the light swells about three hundred yards from shore. Ben finally took a long, deep breath and forcefully released the stick. Tikker said nothing and the two of them merely sat floating on the bay, while the launch approached from seaward.

"Holy shit!" Brister cried when he was close enough to hear. "What the hell were you doing? I thought this was supposed to be a test flight!"

Mikey giggled. "I bet those Brits pissed theirselfs. Way to go, Mr. Mallory."

"It *was* a test flight," Mallory growled. "And it isn't over yet. Tikker, get out and help Mikey with that gas can. I'm taking her up again."

"Are you *nuts*?" demanded Brister, incredulous.

"Maybe, but I've got to figure out a few more things. See if you can find something to plug the fuel tank with. A hunk of that cork stuff you use for bumpers on the boat ought to do." Brister shook his head, but motioned for the man and 'Cat to comply. Shortly, the fuel tank was topped off again and Mikey had whittled a stopper for it. Tikker started to get back in the plane.

"No, you stay here," Ben ordered.

"You kidding?"

"Nope. I want to try her out without your fat ass in her tail. Get some idea how much we need to rebalance things."

"My ass not fat," Tikker replied. "Maybe my head. How you survive without me to save you?"

"See if you can find the bug sprayer. With it empty, maybe it floated." He flipped the switch and started to stand and prop the engine again. "Next one's going to be a pusher," he mumbled, then caught himself. "Hey, give me a piece of that rope while you're at it," he shouted across to the boat. "I need a seat belt!"

Commander Walter Billingsly had been utterly terrified and that just wouldn't do. His one response to fear had always been a killing rage, a need for whomever or whatever caused his fear to suffer the consequences. His terror now past, his rage had lost its heat. It still remained, however, and it would be vented, but it was a cold thing now, an icy ache inside him. By harnessing it and molding it from what it had been into what it was, he had made it a tool, a thing he could use. A thing that would help him when the time came, instead of controlling him.

When the bizarre contraption was towed past *Ajax* and into the open water of the bay, he'd watched with acute interest through his telescope. He'd known about the strange contrivances the Americans and their Ape lackeys were building, but his spies hadn't been quite sure what to make of the things. They reported that they were expected to fly, but neither they nor Billingsly put much credence in that. He'd supposed that was just a fanciful cover story meant as disinformation. Then he *saw* it fly. Amazing! How had these barbarians managed to accomplish something that all the greatest scientists in the Empire had proven was impossible?

He watched while the craft nosed higher and higher into the air and then turned back in his direction. He was excited at first that he'd get a better look at the thing. But then it dove toward him! It grew bigger and bigger in its downward swoop until he was sure it would collide with the ship. In terror, he'd scampered behind one of the great guns for protection, praying for the first time in years. Then, at seemingly the last second, it pulled away with a mighty roar and literally spun on its axis! For a moment during the shocking maneuver, it was silent. In light of what he saw later, he shuddered to think what might happen if such a machine came at them noiselessly in the dark.

He'd watched it zoom over the city, leaning back and forth, then making another silent, simulated attack upon the waterfront! After it was clear, he realized what the true purpose of the machine had to be: a flaming cylinder fell from it and dropped into the water! The machine was a weapon! Of course it was a weapon! It could just as easily have dropped the flaming bomb on *Ajax* as it swooped overhead! The very thought of such an insidious, unsportsmanlike—and utterly effective—device was what truly ignited his terror, beyond the fear he'd felt when he'd thought it was going to ram them. That it could have destroyed them in a single pass and hadn't done so was a clear indication of how the Apes and their Americans considered his presence there. They were not awed by Imperial power as he'd expected them to be. They were contemptuous of it.

They'd clearly intended to frighten him and they had. More significantly, they'd waited until Jenks was a week or more away, which meant they were not trying to frighten *him*. Billingsly's suspicion of Jenks was confirmed. The commodore *had* to have been shown the flying machine during his "tour," and he would have asked about it. Jenks was a fair scientist, to a degree, in his own right. Even if he'd doubted the thing would actually fly, he'd have known that his hosts thought it would. They couldn't have misled him about that. That left only a sin-

gle possibility: Jenks knew about the flying machine and had said nothing about it.

Billingsly's expression never changed, but inwardly, he roiled. Jenks
might command the squadron—such as it remained—and be in
charge of all things nautical, and even tactically military. But Billingsly
was the supreme representative of the Court of Proprietors, and in
matters of intelligence, foreign policy, and even long-term strategy, he
was in charge. Jenks had deliberately withheld critical information
that profoundly affected all those things. He could claim he hadn't really believed the machine would fly, and it might even be true, but
Billingsly didn't believe it. Such a defense might (probably would) get
Jenks off at an inquiry since, as a scientist, a respected explorer and
naval officer, he couldn't be expected to give credence to claims regarding the feasibility of powered flight.

Walter Billingsly knew better. He believed he understood Jenks
more perfectly than perhaps the man knew himself. Jenks would have
looked at the contrivance closely. If it was *possible* it might fly—as Walter now knew it irrefutably could—he would have known. And yet he
hadn't mentioned it. Did that make him a traitor? Yes.

Billingsly kept many secrets from the commodore, the real nature
of *his* "rescue" mission, for one, but Jenks was not supposed to keep
any from him. That alone was enough for a charge, if not a conviction.
But Walter had been suspicious of many of Jenks's activities of late.
This interminable delay, for example, waiting for the Americans to release the girl, was most unseemly. Then, instead of his getting steadily
angrier, as Billingsly had, Jenks's attitude toward their "hosts" had appeared to actually thaw somewhat. The most egregious was the tour
Jenks had received. The Americans had openly shown Jenks what
they'd kept guarded for long months from Billingsly and his spies.
Walter suddenly wondered darkly what *other* surprises Jenks might
have seen and not told him about!

Now Jenks was gone some hundreds of miles away, an "observer"
along to witness a foreign military adventure! Was he an observer?
Why did the Americans want him along in the first place? In Billingsly's suspicious mind, no one would show Jenks the things the Americans had without wanting something in return. What did Jenks

have? *Achilles*, of course, but the ship and her armaments were not substantially greater than anything the Americans were capable of. What then? Only information. The only thing Jenks had that the Americans could really use was information, and he possessed quite a lot of that.

All around Billingsly, the ship's company grew excited again as the bizarre machine roared by and took to the air once more. None of *them* were terrified, nor had they really been even when the machine came at them. Most shouted and good-naturedly returned the clear gesture the flying man had made. They were excited because a flying machine was a wonder, and they possibly even felt a strange kinship with anyone foolhardy enough to ride one. They were men as used to terrifying adventure as they were to the unending boredom of the last months. But they didn't see things the way he did. They never took the long view of anything. Whatever occurred after their next meal was the distant future. Walter Billingsly knew it was all up to him now, him and the operatives infiltrated into the ship's company. The contingency plan he'd been formulating was coming together nicely, and with some of the recent information he'd obtained, it was looking more practical as well. He needed just a few more pieces of the puzzle to fall into place and he'd be ready to proceed.

He strolled to the rail and watched the flying machine make lazy turns over the bay. His personal mission was more critical now than ever before, but even that had paled somewhat in comparison to the intelligence he'd gathered about these strange folk. He needed to get that intelligence home as soon as he possibly could. Things back there were already in motion and he had no idea how this might influence those long-secret plans. His primary mission was important to their success, but the threat posed by these folk—these other *enemies*— desperately required evaluation by his superiors.

He would no longer worry about Jenks. Surely he was a traitor? Besides, whether he was or wasn't was immaterial in the end. His allegiance was no secret and his presence might have been . . . problematic to the success of Billingsly's primary mission, in any event. Walter had often pondered how best to deal with him when the time came. Aside from the information he might give his American friends, it was probably just as well that he'd gone with them. Realistically, he'd expected a confrontation, a refusal to participate at least. He'd have been astonished if Jenks would have agreed to active cooperation and support. This way, it no longer mattered how Jenks would react. He was certainly in no position to interfere.

nconscious of any irony, newly minted Lieutenant Irvin Laumer stepped forward and extended his hand to Colonel Tamatsu Shinya. Without hesitation, the Japanese former naval officer took it and shook it briskly. The two had become friends, of a sort, during the long voyage, and there had existed a certain bond between them. Both were men driven to succeed and prove themselves, although Irvin didn't know what Shinya needed to prove. He was a loyal officer in Captain Reddy's cadre of companions. (Irvin was well-read and often compared Reddy's relationship with his officers and men to that of Alexander.) He admitted to himself that there might be just a touch of hero worship on his part that made the comparison more apt.

There was no doubt that there were two distinct groups within the Alliance: those who felt comfortable around Captain Reddy and didn't hesitate to express their views to him, and those who were almost afraid to be around the "Great Man." The former category was almost exclusively comprised of those who'd been with him from the start, regardless of race. Irvin still felt like he belonged in the second group. He'd had a tough ordeal—all the S-19s—had, but it wasn't a patch to what

Captain Reddy, *Walker*, *Mahan*, and all their crews and allies had been through. Laumer hadn't even been at Baalkpan during the desperate fight. Shinya had. He'd been there from the start like all the others, and he'd certainly earned the companion role, yet he didn't seem to realize it. If he did, he still seemed driven to continue earning it.

Maybe it was because he was a Jap. To this day, not all the Americans truly liked him. They universally respected him, but that wasn't the same. He'd proven he'd stand even against his own people in this war, if it came down to it, but during one of their talks, he'd admitted to Irvin that it still hurt him, even now. He had no compassion for the Grik, but maybe he needed to keep proving to himself that he actually belonged among his new friends.

"I'll miss you, sir, and our talks," Laumer said.

"As will I," Shinya replied. "I find myself speaking 'Cat so much, it is a pleasure to converse in a . . . human tongue."

Irvin knew what had caused Shinya's hesitation. He probably wished he could talk more with Okada, but he and the other Japanese officer didn't really get along.

"Yes, sir," Irvin answered. "And I really appreciate the 'Cat lessons, too. I'm still not too good at it."

"You will do fine. Besides, most of your command has at least a smattering of English now." Shinya chuckled. "I expect one day the two languages will intermingle!"

"That would sure be weird," Irvin said, imagining the bizarre combination. He took a breath and looked around, nodding farewell to others he recognized. He was awaiting the arrival of Saan-Kakja so he could officially take his leave. As his eyes swept over the massive ship, he was still overcome by the monumental ingenuity that had built her.

The level on which he stood, the battlement, occupied a single deck of the massive central superstructure, and the balcony went all the way around it like a giant wraparound porch. Even as high as he was above the surface of the sea and the ship's center of gravity, any sensation of motion was almost imperceptible. Unfortunately, the mammoth vessel's *forward* motion was almost imperceptible as well, by the standards he was accustomed to. With all her wings set and drawing nicely in the brisk morning breeze, *Placca-Mar*, Saan-Kakja's "Imperial yacht," or whatever it was, was barely making five knots. She was just so damn slow. There was so much to do, and he was anxious to get on with his mission.

Throughout the weeks they'd been at sea since departing Baalkpan, they'd crept northeast through the home waters of the Makassar Strait and entered the Celebes Sea. Their average, excruciatingly slow speed of five to six knots had slowed even further while they picked their way through the tangled, hazardous islands off the northeast coat of Borneo before making their island-hugging journey through the Sulu Archipelago. This tedious, circuitous route allowed them to avoid the abyssal depths of the Celebes and Sulu seas—and the monstrous creatures that dwelt there. Among those they were trying to avoid was one so huge that it actually posed a rare but real threat to ships as large as Lemurian Homes.

Mountain fish they were called by some, or island fish by others. Whichever it was, it made no difference. The name wasn't idle exaggeration. Irvin had seen one of the things before, when S-19 traversed nearby seas on her way to Cavite—only to discover the Cavite they remembered wasn't there anymore. That was when his now dead skipper decided they needed a place to hole up before their fuel was gone. The resulting odyssey was what had eventually left the sub stranded on Talaud Island.

Finally, after torturous weeks, Meksnaak, Saan-Kakja's Sky Priest, placed them off the western peninsula of Mindanao. Irvin had to take his word. They'd apparently missed the Sibutu Passage in the dark, but finally they'd reached a point where he and his little squadron could part company with the high chief of the Manilos and all the Fil-pin Lands. Despite the frustration goading him to get on with it, he had to admit the ship and the world around it were certainly a beautiful sight. They were on a tack that took them almost directly into the morning sun, and Irvin shielded his eyes against the glare. Lush, unnamed islands speckled the sea directly to starboard, and a larger shore loomed on the horizon. Mindanao, he presumed. Zamboanga. The water was an almost painfully brilliant blue, and was still touched by the golden glory of the new day. It was going to be a hot one, as usual, and eventually the bright, clear sky would give way to rain clouds. Even now, far to the south, a purple squall swept an empty patch of sea.

He hadn't seen the squall that brought the destroyermen and his submariners here. S-19 had been submerged at the time. He had only conflicting descriptions from the destroyermen as to what it looked like. Mostly, they'd said it had been green. He wondered sometimes what he would do if he ever saw one like it. Would he sail into it, hoping it would take him home? Or would he do everything in his power to stay the hell out of its way? He hoped the choice would never come. At least, not until he fulfilled his mission. Somehow, right then, making Captain Reddy proud of him was more important than ever getting home.

He shook his head and looked at his own ship, USS *Simms*. The former Grik Indiaman had been razed like many others and named for Andy Simms, who'd died at the Battle of Aryaal. She was now a United States corvette. She mounted twenty guns and with her once bloodred hull painted black, with a broad white band down her length highlighting the closed, black-painted gunports, she looked nothing at all like her former self. In spite of who originally made her, *Simms* was a heartwarming sight, loping almost playfully along under close-reefed topsails so she wouldn't shoot ahead of her lumbering charge.

She was Irvin's only warship; the other vessel keeping close company had been repainted, rerigged, and repaired, but her lines hadn't been altered. She was a transport, after all. A freighter. It was still a heady sight. He'd gone from an inexperienced kid, glad to have a subordinate take over when things got tough, to a commodore, for all intents and purposes. Deep down, he wasn't sure he was ready. This *should* be Flynn's job, he thought. Flynn was the one who'd brought them through. But Flynn wouldn't—apparently couldn't—do it. That left Irvin, and one way or another he'd accomplish his mission—if it was possible for anyone to—or die trying. He still believed this was a test of sorts and, for an instant, wondered if Captain Reddy understood the depth of Irvin's commitment to prove himself. He doubted it. Irvin didn't fully understand it yet himself. Besides, the captain had literally ordered him to be careful. Irvin appreciated that and he *would* be careful . . . but he *would* succeed, regardless.

"Well, Lieutenant Laumer," Shinya observed, "despite your . . . impatience . . . to leave us, you have one final nicety to perform. Saan-Kakja is here to bid you farewell!"

"Yeah, I'm a little anxious," Laumer admitted. "Is it really that obvious?" Shinya only chuckled.

Saan-Kakja approached, attended by Meksnaak and a trio of other functionaries. As always, Irvin was struck by her presence. She was so small, and much younger even than he was, yet she was beautiful. Not in a "girl" kind of way—at least, not a human girl—but like an exotically colored female tiger would be beautiful. Stunning, magnificent, but also a little "cute," in the fashion one might describe a young, predatory cat. Her eyes were something else too, unlike any he'd seen among all the 'Cats he'd met. Safir Maraan was just as beautiful in her own lethal way, but Saan-Kakja still inspired him with a strange sense of protectiveness as well.

"Lieutenant Laumer," she said, her English much improved, "my priests that chart our path tell me we have reached that point where you will leave us. I shall miss your company when we dine, and I shall miss the company and protection of your noble ships and crews."

Irvin blushed. Saan-Kakja's ship hadn't needed their protection. Hers was probably the most powerful ship left afloat in the world. She'd armed it with cannon before she ever left for Baalkpan, and between the guns Baalkpan lavished on her and the guns constantly arriving from Manila, *Placca-Mar* now mounted sixty of the big thirty-two pounders, and had a couple of the new fifty pounders as well. It would take something like *Amagi* to tangle with her now. "It has, ah, been my honor, Your Excellency. I'll miss you too." He blushed even deeper.

"Mr. Shinya says you will not be entirely on your own," she said with a concerned series of flashing eyelids, "but the transmitter you carry is not as strong . . . as powerful as the one Mr. Riggs has supplied to me. You will be able to receive transmissions, sometimes all the way from Baalkpan, but may not be able to transmit that far yourself. Rest assured, we will hear you and will routinely retransmit any message you send. If mischief of any kind should befall your mission or yourself, do not hesitate to call for help. My brother is High Chief of Paga-

Daan, and will receive a communication device similar to yours. He will come to your aid immediately. It will, in fact, be his ships that supply you, if your mission is lengthy."

"Thank you, Your Excellency. On all counts."

Saan-Kakja offered her hand, and for an instant, Irvin didn't know whether to shake it or kiss it. He settled for gently grasping the tiny thing in his own.

"Now, Ir-vin," Saan-Kakja scolded, squeezing firmly with her fingers, "you cannot break me that easily!"

"Of course not, Your . . . my lady."

Saan-Kakja grinned and, with an awkward bow, Irvin stepped away. He shook hands with Shinya again and climbed over the bulwark to descend the rope ladder to the waiting launch below.

"Hell," he muttered to himself, cheeks still hot. "She's not just beautiful; she's downright mesmerizing. Even in kind of a 'girl' way!"

Simms and her consort hauled away to the east, through the Basilan Strait and across the Moro Gulf. Meksnaak had suggested the gulf might be one of their most hazardous passages until they crossed to Talaud, but they met no danger there. A few large gri-kakka surfaced and blew, and some possibly related denizens with short, serpentine necks watched the ships periodically with large, somber eyes, but other than that, all they saw were the myriad seabirds, flying reptiles, and what looked like a cross between the two. Nothing unusual. The birds capered and swooped among the masts, occasionally even snapping at the top men, but the only real harm they caused was the reeking, fishy slurry they dropped and smeared all over the ships. Otherwise, the weather remained fine, the skies no more temperamental than usual, and the sea in no way stirred itself against them.

Irvin wasn't much of a practical sailor yet, and he relied heavily on *Simms*'s actual captain, Lelaa-Tal-Cleraan. She reminded him a lot of Silva's supposed Lemurian sweetheart, Risa-Sab-At, with her brindled fur and quick wit. Unlike Risa, however, Lelaa wasn't a born warrior, and she hadn't even seen action yet. Before getting *Simms*, she'd commanded one of the Navy feluccas. She *was* a born sailor, though, and

Irvin was learning a lot from her. She'd translated her skill with the fore-and-aft rigged feluccas to the primarily square rig of *Simms* with astonishing ease. She was a good, patient teacher and well liked by her crew. She lacked any of Saan-Kakja's cuteness factor, but she was young and still handsome in an experienced, practical way. Irvin had every confidence in her, and the two of them had become fast friends.

They tried to keep the Mindanao coast in sight as they worked east-southeast over the next few days. There were islands everywhere, and Lelaa was constantly worried about wind direction, something Irvin, a submariner, had never much considered. Truth be known, he was always more worried about how much water was under the keel and what sort of creatures might be in it. Lelaa was worried too; that was why they hugged the coast—a most unnatural act in a sailing ship. The depths here were unknown, however, and everyone was a little tense as they cruised the edge of the Celebes Sea.

"I like coffee," Lelaa said, staring into her cup with a surprised, wide-eyed blink. She and Irvin were on *Simms*'s quarterdeck enjoying another pleasant morning. "Everyone says it is vile and they don't know how you Amer-i-caans can drink it all the time, but I find it heightens my awareness . . . and I have even come to enjoy the taste. Does that make me strange . . . or even more Amer-i-caan?"

Irvin laughed, then took a small sip from his own scalding cup of "monkey joe." "Well, you've been in the American Navy for some time now, and everybody back home would swear the Navy couldn't function without coffee. I don't think we could've ever won a war without it."

"You have told me of the great battles in your . . . *our* Navy's past. Is that how they won? We drink coffee and our enemies do not?"

Irvin laughed again. "Maybe. If the only difference in a fight is that one side is wide-awake and alert, it might tip the balance. There are other variables, though, that coffee alone can't make up for. Crummy torpedoes, being outnumbered ten to one." His smile faded. "In the war we came from, we drank a lot of coffee, but it wasn't making much difference."

Lelaa took another sip. "I bet it would have, eventually. Maybe in that lost world, it already has."

Irvin grunted.

The alarm bell at the masthead sounded insistently and everyone's gaze turned upward.

"Island fish! Island fish! Three points off starboard bow! Two t'ousand yards! It just came up!"

"Clear for action!" Lelaa shouted, gulping the rest of her coffee and passing the cup to Midshipman Hardee. Hardee had been one of the kids on S-19 and had volunteered to return to her. Now sixteen, he was also the oldest boy who'd been aboard her. "Pass the word for Sparks to wind up his gear!"

"Aye-aye, Captain!" Hardee replied, clutching the cup in both hands. He raced away. "Tex" Sheider, also known as "Sparks," like every communications officer on any Navy ship, scrambled up the companionway from below. He was a small, skinny guy, as many submariners were, and had never seemed to fit his other nickname: Tex. Of course, that didn't matter either. All that mattered was that he was from Texas. There'd once been another Tex on S-19, but he'd suffocated in the battery compartment.

"Captain," Hardee addressed Lelaa. "Sir," he said to Irvin. "I heard the alarm. The guys are winding up the gizmo now." He looked ahead, trying to see the huge fish. A gray-black hump was just visible from deck now. "I sure hope this works," he added nervously.

The Anti–Mountain Fish Destruction Countermeasures, or AMF-DIC, after the British version of sonar—with a couple of extra letters thrown in—were a collection of mostly untried procedures it was hoped would scare the humongous, ship-eating beasts away. All had an acoustic pressure element, which they'd learned through experience might be effective. The first line of defense was literally a giant speaker activated by the ship's communication equipment. A wind-powered generator charged a primitive battery in the "wireless shack" that, when switched through a high-amplitude capacitor, allowed them to boost the output through the simple transmitter Riggs had given them. In this case, instead of routing the jolt of electricity to an antenna, it sent it to a crude speaker mounted firmly to the hull. The result briefly turned the entire ship into a resonance chamber meant to frighten the creatures away.

The second defense, one they knew *could* work when properly applied, was a device most of the destroyermen had been familiar with even though *Walker* and *Mahan* had never been equipped with them. It was a form of "Y" gun that used one of the old muzzle-loading mortars they'd employed in the defense of Baalkpan. A weighted barrel of gunpowder rested upon a rack positioned at the muzzle of the mortar, which allowed them to blast the depth charge into the path of an oncoming mountain fish. They knew the monsters didn't like depth charges at all, and they believed the "Y" gun would work fine—if it didn't blow up the ship.

They had a final defense that Jenks had told them the Imperial Navy used at close quarters: an indiscriminate, simultaneous broadside of every gun on the ship. The resulting concussion seemed to disorient the beasts, and although it made them *very* angry, only rarely did they manage to destroy a ship with their enraged convulsions.

"Stand ready to activate your gizmo, Tex," Irvin instructed. Lelaa nodded. "But wait for the word. I know we want to test it, but if that thing leaves us alone, we'll leave it alone. Right now it's just kind of wallowing there, catching some rays."

"Yeah, but it's right in front of us. What if it won't move? Do we go around it, or blast it?"

Lelaa looked at the sky and the set of the sails. "We blast it," she decided. "If we go around, we will lose speed, and I want us to be as fast as we can be if we are forced to use the gizmo." She raised her voice. "Signal our consort to lay aft and follow in our wake. Maybe it won't sense us both. No point in making it feel threatened by our numbers."

Irvin glanced at her and she shrugged, her tail swishing uncomfortably. "If there were ten of us, I might try it the other way," she explained, "but with only two, each less than a third its size . . ."

"It moving, Skipper," came the shout from above. "It know we here! It coming this way!"

Lelaa shook her head and looked at Sheider. "Stand by your gizmo, Tex." She gestured at the cluster of copper speaking tubes beside the wheel. "I will give the order."

"Aye-aye, Captain." With a nervous grin at Laumer, he disappeared below.

The giant was not on an attack run but seemed merely interested or curious, so their closing speed was not that great. Unfortunately, a mountain fish's curiosity often included tasting what it was curious about. At six hundred yards, Lelaa strode to the speaking tube and repeated, "Stand by." No one knew what the maximum range of the gizmo might be, but Riggs had figured it would become unpleasant at about five hundred yards. All they would get was one shot every several minutes. In a wind like this, it would take that long for the capacitor to recharge. If Lelaa had any hope of testing the device any closer, she'd have to try it at maximum range first. She started to say, "Fire," but that seemed inappropriate.

"Light it up, Tex."

For an instant, there was nothing. Then, with a jarring suddenness that surprised everyone, the whole skip began to tremble, accompanied by a dull bass rumble beneath their feet. The vibration was so intense, it blurred Irvin's vision. After only a few seconds, the sensation passed.

"What's it doing?" Lelaa shouted above.

"It pissed!" came the shout. "It swim in circle, go ape! Wait! It coming this way, fast! It pissed!"

"Ready the forward "Y" gun!" Lelaa commanded. The gun was already loaded and prepared in all respects, but Shipfitter Danny Porter tracked the oncoming target and shifted the weapon accordingly. The "Y" gun had no sights—it was an area weapon, after all—but Danny had a good eye and was a good judge of distance. He'd been striking for gunner's mate, and his surface action station on the sub had been her four-inch fifty.

"Ready when you are, Skipper," he announced tersely over the voice tube.

"Commence firing when you see fit," Lelaa said. Her voice sounded calm, but tinny. "Try to drop the bomb right on its nose."

For a moment, nothing happened. Danny waited, calculating the ship's slight pitch and the range to the target. He'd been allowed only a couple of tests with the new weapon and was no expert by any means. Suddenly, he stepped back.

"Fire!"

Simms's entire fo'c'sle was shrouded with white smoke and a loud, muffled *whump!* jarred the ship. The barrel-shaped bomb emerged from the smoke and tumbled upward into the sky. For a moment, it seemed to defy gravity as it hung there, wobbling, but growing smaller too. Then it began to fall. Everyone was tense, waiting for the plunge. It looked like Danny had missed, or worse, that the bomb might actually hit the back of the creature. Most supposed that if that happened, it might even die, but it would almost certainly lunge ahead and strike the ship before it did. A large concave splash erupted a hundred feet short of the monster, a little to its left. A pressure cap inside the bomb should detonate at about twenty feet. The sensitive nature of the detonator was always a concern when firing the damn things.

The sea spalled into shattered white marble, and almost immediately, a huge cloud of smoke and spray erupted in the charging fish's path. They saw the beast then, beyond the cloud, practically rear itself out of the water. Another momentous splash followed the first, and they glimpsed massive flukes pounding the sea—away from them!

"It worked!" came Danny's cry, all the way from the fo'c'sle. A huge cheer erupted, echoed by those on their consort astern. They hadn't seen anything, but they must have guessed the second aspect of the AMF-DIC defense had been a success.

"Outstanding!" Irvin said, stepping to join Lelaa near the wheel. Lelaa was smiling toothily. "Please accept my congratulations! We've got to get a message out right away and let everybody know it works!" Irvin's exuberance was tempered a few moments later when Tex appeared on the quarterdeck. His hair was singed and his shirt looked scorched. "What's the matter?" Irvin asked warily, a sick sensation in his gut.

"Transmitter's cooked. Kaput. All that juice was just too much for it. I *told* Clancy we needed a fuse! But nooo!" Tex shook his head disgustedly. "Damn Boston Mick! I'm gonna cool him off—to dirt temperature!—when we get home! One lousy fuse, but he says, 'You know how hard it is to make them?' Not as hard as it is to make a goddamn transmitter!"

"You okay, Tex?"

The smaller, dark-haired man shrugged. "Swell. A little scorched."

He looked at his shirt. "I threw the switch, but the transmitter was already on *fire*, so I stifled it with my shirt. Nearly choked myself to death getting it off. Did you know this was the last shirt I had that was made in the U.S. of A.?"

"I'm sorry, Tex. We'll get you another one."

"I want that bastard Clancy's, if he has one left!"

"What about the receiver?" Lelaa inquired. It was a question Irvin should have asked, but Tex was one of his friends. An old shipmate. One of the few left alive.

"I'll get in there as soon as the smoke clears, Skipper. I expect it's fine. It's just a glorified crystal set. Doesn't really even need power. If we didn't short the batteries, we'll still have juice, anyway. If we did short 'em out, once we get to Talaud and set up the steam generator, we'll have more juice than we need. For anything."

"Can you build a new transmitter?" Irvin asked.

"Could be. It ain't hard, and I've got what's left of Riggs's design to work from."

Lelaa looked at Irvin. "I command this ship, but you command the expedition. What are your views? Should we press on, even without two-way communications? This was a hazardous mission to begin with. . . ."

"We press on," Irvin almost interrupted her. "Captain Reddy knows how hazardous it is, and he knew there was a chance we'd find ourselves out of touch. We'll press on," he repeated, "and accomplish our mission. Tex will make a new transmitter. Even if he can't, we have a job to do. A lot of people are counting on us and I won't let them down."

Lelaa smiled. "As I suspected . . . but I had to ask!" She turned to the 'Cat at the helm. "Steady as you go. Our course remains one five zero."

"One fi' zero, ayy!"

alker was about to float again. All Baalkpan had turned out to watch the momentous event, it seemed, and no one really cared anymore if the strangers in the bay knew about it or not. It was a time of miracles. So incredibly devastated by the battle that had once raged here, Baalkpan had become a center of industry, connected with most of the known world by wireless communication! People had built aircraft and flown them over this very bay! Aryaal was retaken and Grik *prisoners* were on their way here! In the amazing dry dock, weeks of scraping, welding and riveting, heating and rolling Japanese steel into new plates, and a final, thick coat of red paint had resulted in this collective achievement. Even if anyone had desired to keep *Walker*'s rebirth a secret, it wouldn't have been possible. There was no question Imperial spies were present. In fact, knowing they would be, Letts had counseled Adar to *invite* the Imperial personnel. Their leaders might feel a little foolish learning the ship they'd been so concerned about had been underwater all this time, but the majority of the Imperial sailors who'd come to watch at least acted as excited as everyone else.

Water coursed into the dry dock and swirled muddily around the fresh red paint and wooden braces. Slowly, the polished bronze screws dipped beneath the torrent and constant shouts of encouragement came from men and 'Cats on the old destroyer's deck as they relayed reports from below that all was dry inside. There was a shudder, and the ship eased ever so slightly from the cradle that had held her upright since the water was drained from the basin. Cheers reverberated off the many new buildings when the support beams were heaved from the flood. Line handlers were careful to keep the ship positioned where she was, lest she bump against beams or pilings that were not yet free. Within an hour, all the beams had been withdrawn, and once again *Walker* floated free and easy, supported by her own sleek hull. The pandemonium the sight inspired was difficult to credit, and even more difficult for those who hadn't been there for the battle to understand. Tears erupted from hardened warriors from many clans, and many a Marine was misty-eyed as well.

In some ways, she looked like a different ship. Her guns and torpedo tubes had been removed, as had the big blower, refrigerator, and the tall searchlight tower. A temporary wooden deck was laid over the openings left from the complete removal of her shattered aft deckhouse. The short mainmast aft remained, defiantly flying the Stars and Stripes, but the tall foremast had not yet been reinstalled. The bridge was vacant and the fire-control platform was bare. Everything that could be removed and reconditioned ashore had long since been taken off, and she floated considerably higher in the water than anyone had ever seen her. Still, she floated. All her parts, possessions, and weapons would be returned to her, as would, ultimately, her crew. For now, she floated almost empty of the things that made her what she was; there was no roar of blowers, no machinery noises; she still slumbered, still resting from her grievous wounds, but she was no longer dead. She'd risen from the grave and it was only a matter of time before she'd awake once again.

"Look! Oh, look!" cried Sandra, tears streaking her face.

Beside her, Princess Rebecca hopped up and down, clapping her hands. "Oh, Lady Sandra! Is she not the most beautiful sight?"

Lawrence didn't understand his friend's attachment to the ship. It was but a *thing*. He was thrilled that it would again become the weapon it had once been, and *that* made him happy. He was also glad his friends were happy—for whatever reason. He hopped lightly and clapped too, imitating Rebecca's gestures. Dennis Silva stood beside him, fists clenched at his sides, a sheen over his one good eye. Suddenly, he raised a hand and blew his nose in his fingers. Absently, he started to wipe them on Lawrence's plumage.

"Mr. *Silva!*" Rebecca scolded, suddenly eyeing Dennis.

"A little snot won't hurt him! Runt's gettin' all frizzed out. Prob'ly oughta' comb a little grease in his hair." Under the princess's continued stare, Silva sighed and wiped his fingers on his T-shirt.

Unexpectedly, Lawrence had begun growing a crest on top of his head that Silva compared to a cock roadrunner's. Among the Grik, the only real "crests" of any kind they'd seen had been on dead Hij. Since it was now known the Hij were almost universally older than their Uul warriors, Bradford had ecstatically proclaimed "their boy" must be nearing adulthood, different species or not.

Letts, Adar, and Spanky moved through the throng to join them.

"A hell of a thing," Spanky said, his own eyes a little bright. "I never would've thought it."

"I had no doubts," proclaimed Adar. "Once you were over the shock of losing her and had a plan, I knew, sooner or later, *Walker* would float again. You Amer-i-caans are amazingly ingenious."

"Couldn't have done any of it without *your* equally amazingly ingenious folk," Alan Letts reminded him.

"Where's Karen?" Sandra asked. "She should be here!"

"She's not feeling too well," Alan said, a little self-consciously. "She's no bigger than you, and with her being somewhere around seven months along . . ."

Sandra laughed. "She's big as a house! I know. Don't worry; she's fine. But she is a little big." Her eyes twinkled. "I still say it's twins!"

Alan pretended horror. "Don't say that anymore!"

Over the tumult, they heard a rising drone and looked at the sky. Not to be outdone, the Air Corps was putting in an appearance. Three planes, or ships, as Mallory demanded they be called for some reason, wobbled overhead in a semblance of a formation. He'd finally won approval for his force to be called the Air Corps, even if most of its pilots were naval aviators. His insistence on the seemingly contradictory term confused everyone. Ben would be at the controls of one, Tikker another, and young Reynolds the third. The Air Corps had eight planes now, and with the implementation of Ben's improvements they'd been declared perfected as far as the fundamental design would allow. Within weeks, there'd be two dozen airplanes and they'd face the distinct problem of having more planes than competent pilots.

Sandra hugged herself. It was all finally starting to come together. After all their hard work and sacrifice, she was beginning to feel, well, optimistic. The war had really just started, but with all the new naval construction under way, the professional army they'd begun, the allies they had working along the same lines toward the same goals—they had airplanes, for goodness' sake!—and now with the resurrection of *Walker* . . .

"Mr. Chairman," she addressed Adar, "we must transmit the news to Captain Reddy at once! He'll be so pleased!"

"It has already been done, my dear, with careful observation to details! I expect he is watching the proceedings with us, through the eye of his mind, at this very moment." He grinned and blinked amusement. "I took the liberty of sending your warmest love as well."

Sandra blinked back more tears and hugged the tall Sky Priest.

"Now, ain't that the damnedest thing?" Spanky asked. They all turned to look where he stared. Sister Audry, surrounded by a few dozen 'Cats, was standing near the pier mumbling something none of them could understand. Adar caught a word or two, but over the hubbub, any meaning was lost. The nun finished speaking and brought the fingertips of her right hand to her forehead, down to her stomach, then to her left and right shoulders. The Lemurians with her copied the gesture.

"Say," said Silva, "does this mean our good sister's a 'Catechist?"

"You idiot," Spanky groaned, "you don't even know what that means!"

"Do so!"

"Yeah, he does," Letts confirmed. "And pun aside, he may be right." He looked at Adar. "Mr. Chairman, we've been promising each other a lot of 'talks' lately. Maybe we'd better have one this evening." He glanced around. "Lieutenant Tucker, please join us. Better invite Courtney too, or he'll pout. Spanky, you're Catholic. . . ."

"Sorta."

"I'd like you and Princess Rebecca to attend as well. Princess, you've stated several times that there are others of perhaps . . . similar faith to that of Sister Audry. I think it's time we sort that out, at least. I'll go invite the young nun to our little meeting."

Other eyes watched the proceedings discreetly, through eyelids narrowed with concern.

"I had heard rumors, but I could hardly credit them. Didn't dare to hope," Billingsly muttered to the man beside him. Linus Truelove was Billingsly's most trusted agent and a talented analyst as well. He doubled as *Ajax*'s third lieutenant, hiding his skills beneath a competent but unimaginative, almost oafish facade. His "cover" was easy to maintain. He was a large man, bigger even than the one-eyed protector who often escorted the princess, and even though he pretended drunkenness on occasion, he never drank enough to cloud his quick, devious mind—another advantage he had over the man called Silva, who appeared just as oafish as Truelove pretended to be.

"The enemy grows more capable by the day, and our window of opportunity may close before we are ready."

"We will be ready soon enough," Truelove assured him. "Curtailing our obvious activities has lulled them, I think. Even the guards at their industrial section are not as alert as they were." He grinned wickedly. "I think they are beginning to *trust* us, or at least they no longer have as great a care."

"Possibly. Regardless, when we move it must be as quick and silent as possible. They must not know what has happened for a good many hours and they must not be allowed to interfere once they discover the truth."

"You did not mention 'bloodless' as an imperative. 'Quick and silent' is almost never bloodless," Truelove observed.

"Quick and silent remains the priority."

"Bloodless," repeated Truelove, eyeing Silva. "I doubt that would be possible, regardless. That one, I think, hides behind much the same mask as I. I doubt he will accede 'bloodlessly.' Besides, he is the first I have seen among these barbarians whom I might enjoy testing myself against. He has a reputation."

"Put it out of your mind!" Billingsly snapped. "Perhaps he does, but your 'reputation' must remain secret!"

When the water level inside the basin equalized with the bay, the great gates opened and *Walker* was towed slowly, gently clear of the dry dock. Even as she was tying up to the old fitting-out pier, the dry dock's next inhabitant was being positioned to enter. Keje-Fris-Ar paced nervously back and forth on the strangely abbreviated battlement that remained offset, above the rebuilt deck of his Home.

"This is madness!" he remarked, eyeing the angle of approach. "The dry dock is too small!"

"It is *not* too small, Father," assured Selass, Keje's daughter. She strode each step right beside him and placed her hand comfortingly on his shoulder. "Really, you should not exert yourself so. Your wound..."

"My little wound is well healed, thank you," he said gruffly, but then looked fondly at his child. He and Selass had been estranged far too long. First, her choice of a mate had upset him—and then the self-centered fool had the effrontery to die a hero's death! Even before that occurred, she'd developed a hopeless infatuation for Chack-Sab-At, whom she'd first driven away, right into the arms of Safir Maraan! He'd despaired that she might ever become a sensible creature. Perhaps her friendship with Sandra Tucker had helped. She'd even grown civil to Chack's sister, Risa, who commanded *Salissa*'s Marine contingent. Whatever the cause, ever since the Great Battle, she'd been devoted to him and he admitted he was glad their rift had mended.

He stared the length of his ship. His Home was unrecognizable now. Where her great tripods and pagoda apartments once stood, there remained only a huge, flat deck. New quarters were under construction below that deck, but no more would *Big Sal*, as the Amer-i-caans called her, move with the power of the wind and tide that had controlled her every course since her very birth. She was becoming a machine, a ship of war! A thought once so alien to Keje he could never have imagined it. That anyone would build a ship just for war—besides the Grik—seemed unnatural. At least, it had before the Amer-i-caan destroyermen came. But these were unnatural times. *Salissa* had been all but destroyed by the Grik and their Japanese allies, just as *Walker* had. He pondered that a moment.

Was *Walker* not a live thing, even though she was a machine? Captain Reddy and all her people always behaved as if they thought she was. Keje *felt* she was. When they repaired her, would not her soul return to her? It must. Where else would it go? If a body lived, it must have a soul. If *Walker* had indeed been "dead" for a while, perhaps her soul was trapped within her. Or maybe it had rested in the Heavens above, with all the people she'd lost? It was all so confusing! *Salissa* had been nearly as "dead" as *Walker*, but Keje had never felt her soul had left her. That *should* mean her soul would remain with her whether she became a machine or was restored completely to what she was before. His tension ebbed a bit. He'd discussed this with Matt, with Spanky, Adar, and even his daughter. All had different thoughts regarding the soul of a ship, but all completely agreed that, whatever it was, *Big Sal* still had hers. Looking at her now, though, a mere naked hull with a long, flat top, he found it hard to imagine somehow.

"The wings are machines, Father," his daughter reminded him, easily guessing his thoughts. "By our construction and by our design, they harness the wind—a natural element—to our will. We make them, we control them, they move as we direct them. The wings are machines." She nodded toward the gaping hole in the aft center of the broad, flat deck. "The engines, when they are installed, will do the same." She pointed at the shipyard, where the massive contrivances lay covered with sailcloth, awaiting installation. "There they are, Father. They are not wings, but we made them and we shall control them. They will move us as *you* direct them! They will burn gish, yes, and we will no longer be independent of the land folk, but with this terrible war, that time was already past. Those engines will burn gish to make steam—merely heated water and also a natural thing—and that steam will move the engine and turn the propeller that will soon be installed. *Salissa* will move like *Walker*, the very same way!" She paused and chuckled. "Perhaps not as fast . . . but by the same means. If *Walker* has a soul, then surely *Salissa*'s is safe. It might even be proud!"

"Proud?"

"Indeed. Have you not seen the aar-planes? They will be *Salissa*'s! With the guns she still carries and the aar-planes to carry her strength farther than the eye can see, *Salissa* will be the mightiest ship in the world! Mightier even than *Amagi* ever was!"

Keje laughed. "You have been talking to Letts again!" He grew thoughtful. "But Captain Reddy says the same. As much as he loves his ship, he loves aar-planes just as much—and hates not having them!" He sighed, then laughed again. "Did you know I must go to school? I must learn how to handle my own ship all over again! And Mallory says we must form 'operational procedures'!" He shook his head at Selass's concerned blinking. Her tail was rigid with tension. "Fear not! I will be a model pupil! It does amuse me, though."

"What?"

"To 'relearn' how to handle my very own Home, I must practice by controlling their tiny launch!"

They stood together in silence as the great vessel was maneuvered entirely into the basin. Huge bumpers dropped into place and a tally was made of every object that had once supported the destroyer so they'd know nothing protruded from the flat, permanent trestle below. Only then were the pumps engaged.

"How long will it take?" Selass asked.

"A day. Perhaps more. Not as long as it took to empty for *Walker*. *Salissa* 'displaces' a great deal more water! Is that not a fascinating term? It has no real meaning in situations other than this, because *Salissa* cannot displace enough water to be even noticed in the wide ocean of the world, but here, because of her size, there is far less water in this dry dock, even though the level is the same as before!"

"I have heard the term," Selass admitted, "when the Amer-i-caans discuss the size of the new construction ships. Evidently, they do not weigh the ships themselves, but the water they push aside! How can they do such a thing?"

"Mathematics. They are fiends for it in all things. Everything you see that they have made involves mathematics and the most precise measurements imaginable. It is amazing and stirring, but it makes me somewhat sad as well."

"Why, Father?"

"Well, it is yet another example of how things have changed. Nothing will be built by eye again. Artwork may survive, but the talent, the skills passed down from one maker to the next, will be supplanted by mathematics! The guilds are howling, much like our wing clans did when they learned our Home would lose its wings! I am but an example. I have spent my life learning to move *Salissa* from place to place, and still I do not know everything there is to know about that. Now I must learn to drive a little boat before I will know the *first* thing about moving my Home again."

"You agreed."

"Yes, I did, and it is well. I will move her again, and when I do . . . I am informed"—he grinned—"she will be a weapon the Grik cannot match. I would . . . I *have* sacrificed much for that. So will Geran-Eras when she allows the same alterations to *Humfra-Dar*. But what of the builders, the makers of things? Soon, any leeching pit turner will be able to operate a machine that will quickly make things a shipwright has spent his life learning to build!" He shook his head, part in wonder and part in sadness. "What's more, that pit turner will be able to do it quicker and better and exactly the same every time."

"You sound as if you wish the Amer-i-caans never came."

"No. That is ridiculous. They have saved us. We would be filling Grik bellies if not for them. But in a way, as much as we fought to survive, we, the *People*, also fought for things to remain the same. I know that is what Nakja-Mur fought for, but deep down, even he knew it could never be. I will miss the old ways. It was a good, happy life. If this war ever ends, and it *must* end in victory, I know not what the world will be like. I do know it will be different. Let us just hope it will be different in a good way . . . and that we will live to see it."

"She's up!" Clancy shouted, racing up *Donaghey*'s companionway. Matt and those gathered with him on the quarterdeck turned toward the exuberant outburst. *Donaghey* was moored a short distance from the rebuilding dock and many of the AEF's officers were aboard for a conference of sorts. "She's up and floating and there're no leaks worth a mention! *Walker*'s off the bottom and Lieutenant Tucker sends her love!" There was a resounding cheer and Matt's ears heated just a little.

"Mr. Clancy," he said, unable to summon a frown, "that's wonderful news and I'm glad you shared it with us all, but the last part may have been meant as a private message."

Clancy halted his dash and his face went white. "Uh . . . oh. Ah, sorry, Skipper! I'm so sorry!"

"Oh, shut up," Garrett said, grinning. "That part isn't news!" There was more laughter. "What's the first part say?"

Jim Ellis retrieved the message form and scanned it. He looked at Captain Reddy and Matt nodded. "It's true. *Walker*'s been moved to the fitting-out pier and *Big Sal*'s gone in the tank." He chuckled. "Ben saw fit to celebrate with a flyover. One plane had to land on the bay and be towed in! Let's see. *Tassat* was launched and has been moved to the new fitting-out pier. The new generators are doing swell, but they've had a couple of engine casualties." He looked at Matt. "Hmm. Hope we don't have any out here. Says it wasn't much of a deal, but still." He looked back at the page. "Still no word from Laumer and 'Task Force S-19.' Palmer got that one signal that they were about to try the gizmo, then nothing. He figures it cooked the transmitter." He glanced at Clancy, who'd suddenly stiffened. He and Palmer had argued a lot over the design. "Anyway, they're probably fine. Saan-Kakja arrived safely at her brother's city and they made a successful test transmission of their set—"

"Yes, sir," Clancy interrupted. "I picked it up."

"Wow," said Jim. "Real long-distance comm. Why didn't you tell us?"

"Well, ah . . . you see, they were transmitting the raising of the ship in a kind of blow-by-blow sort of way. . . ."

"Anything else? What about our report of the Grik prisoners?" Matt asked. Jim looked down and chuckled.

"Yeah, it's got a postscript. 'Bradford excited.'"

"Ha!"

"I do wish we could speak to them," Safir mused.

"We can," Alden said. "They just can't talk to us. Maybe when we ship 'em home, Lawrence can talk to 'em."

"I doubt it," said Matt.

"Why not? Most of the 'Cats understand each other okay, except maybe a few of the ones from southern Australia."

"Yeah, but they've been in contact with one another. Look, we now know there's Grik all over the place, or something like Grik. They seem to fill the niche humans did where we came from. There's the Grik we fight, from Africa and Madagascar originally, but there's Grik-like lizards just about everywhere. Lawrence says his people are 'Tagranesi' or something. We've managed to squeeze enough out of Rasik to know the dead aborigines we found here were snatched from Java and the neighboring islands as slave labor and, well, food. I'm sure they don't call themselves Grik."

"I did not even know they were here," Rolak admitted.

"Maybe they haven't been for long, or at least not in any numbers. Our first and only meeting with them on Bali proved to us they were pretty smart. They didn't carry weapons, but then they didn't really need them, did they? They may have been leaking over here from Bali or other islands for a long time and just staying to themselves. As primitive as they were, compared to our enemies, they actually displayed even better tactical sense. Courtney's long believed that Grik behavior has more to do with societal conditioning than anything else."

"That might explain why the prisoners act so different," Ellis speculated. "After we licked them here, they wandered on their own for a while. Maybe they had time to think things over a little."

There was silence for a moment while everyone contemplated the significance of that.

"All the more reason we must not give the enemy more time to think things over," Safir said.

"If I were a member of this Alliance, I would tend to agree with the Queen Protector," Harvey Jenks said with a touch of irony. It was the first time he'd spoken, beyond civilities, since he'd come aboard. Something had changed in his demeanor ever since he went ashore and saw the aftermath of the Grik occupation for himself. Aryaal and B'mbaado were unusual cities, perhaps unique among Lemurians. Even before the Grik came, they'd been built of stone with stout walls to protect the inhabitants. The devastated architecture was more similar to Imperial construction than any other he'd seen so far, or than he cared to admit. It was as though he'd experienced a premonition of what would happen if the Grik ever threatened his home.

The rabidly gruesome nature of the enemy the Allies faced had been driven in to the hilt as well, and he felt he understood them and their motives much better now. The heads had been taken down and sent to the sky in the fires and much of the debris had been cleared, but the mental image remained. The thaw in his attitude toward the Allies, and Matt in particular, had continued at an accelerated pace. Still, he'd clearly been surprised to be included in this strategy session. He hadn't given any assurances that he was at their disposal or that he'd help them in any way. He *had* begun to consider himself on their side just a little, however.

"Jenks is right," agreed Rolak. "We cannot linger here. Has that vile creature"—he referred to Rasik-Alcas—"spilled any more beans?"

Matt shook his head. "He's told us all he knows about what happened here, and a little more about his activities while in exile, but he knows we've already measured him for a noose. No matter how fair we make it, the outcome of any trial is a foregone conclusion. He's guilty as hell and he knows everybody knows it. When he's not off in the land of Oz, he's sharp enough to be scary. The guy's a real psycho."

"No clues about what he found?" asked Ellis.

Matt shook his head. "The crummy thing is, I think there *is* something. Everything we thought we knew about the Squall that brought us here is changing all the time. First, we thought it was just us and *Mahan*. Then the PBY. Then we learned about *Amagi*. Why wasn't it there when the Squall passed? Okada said they came out of it in the *dark*, probably sometime during the night after we did. Unlike us, they were moving with it, not through it. Is it possible that by staying in it longer, they experienced its effects longer too?" He shook his head. "I doubt even Courtney has an answer for that. Anyway, we now know the sub came through as well. It was pretty far away, judging by the log we brought back, but close enough to hear our fight on the surface. How close was the PBY?" He shrugged. "Up till now, we've assumed we were it, but what if we weren't? That was a big squall and the track it took might have sucked up anything. Why some things and not others? No clue. Maybe the energy or local intensity had something to do with that. Anyway, we need to start thinking about the possibility that other stuff *did* come through, and if it did, we damn sure want to find it before the Japs and Grik do." He snorted. "His Nasty Highness did confirm that they watched a bunch of Japs get off Esshk's ship when it stopped here, roam around unattended, then get back on, so I guess they didn't eat the bastards after all."

"Pity," Ellis said.

"Yeah. The thing is, though, Rasik thinks if he tells us what he found, we'll just kill him anyway. He insists on *showing* us."

"We promised him clemency; what more does he expect?" spat Safir. It was the first time she'd agreed to the "deal" that had been proposed. She hated the very idea of letting Rasik live. Chack, who'd remained uncharacteristically silent, put a hand on her shoulder and stroked it.

"It does not matter," Rolak grumbled. "He still expects to be killed. He views all things in terms of what he would do in our place."

"I'll get it out of him," Alden promised.

Matt laughed. "Pete, I bet you and Boats could get him to confess he painted the moon, but that wouldn't do us much good." He thought for a moment, staring at the bleak shoreline. There was a lot of activity: building a new dock, erecting tents, and preparing materials for structures that would serve as forward supply depots. Few would remain at first, when the Allies moved on. They had more pressing business. Aryaalans and B'mbaadans would return, however, and begin the work of rebuilding.

"Here's the deal," he said at last. "We have to move. The scout we sent to Singapore reports the Grik are pulling out there too. We need to get there before they leave it like this." He gestured shoreward. "We also have to know if Rasik's pulling our chain. He says the things he found are accessible by sea, near Tjilatjap—Chill-chaap." He looked at Jim. "Not *at* Chill-chaap, but near it, so your guys would have missed it when they went ashore there."

Jim winced slightly. They hadn't exactly been *his* guys at that point.

"Here's what we'll do," Matt continued. "You take *Dowden* and a company of Marines and see what Rasik has to show you. If you can do it without puking, try to buddy up to him. He doesn't really know you, after all. Maybe he'll let something slip."

"May I command the Marine company, Captain Reddy?" Chack asked.

Matt hesitated. "I'd rather have you with me, but I guess so. Just don't remind the silly bastard you're the one who trapped him with fire and left him to be eaten by the Grik!"

"He cannot know that," Chack said.

"Right. Say, talk to Koratin. Maybe he can convince him he's on his side. Might get something out of him. Anyway, while you're doing that I'll take the rest of the fleet and all the troops we can transfer out of *Dowden* and head for Singapore. You meet us there if you can. Stay in wireless contact. If something breaks down you can't fix, come back here."

"Aye-aye, Skipper. We'll meet you at Singapore," Jim promised. "If there's a fight, I don't want to miss it."

Chack looked at Safir and caressed her furry cheek. They'd made no announcement at Aryaal after all. They hadn't had the heart. No one felt much like celebrating the reconquest of Aryaal and B'mbaado. "Do not fear, my love. I shall see you at Sing-aapore."

Matt looked at Jenks. "Commodore, if you'd care to dine with me, I'd appreciate it. Juan?" he called, summoning the Filipino who always hovered nearby, "if he has no objection, please escort Commodore Jenks to my quarters. I'll be along directly."

Knowing he was being dismissed, but not resenting it—he *wasn't* a member of the Alliance, after all—Jenks bowed and went with Juan.

Matt turned to Jim. "Take O'Casey with you. I think he's a good guy and he might be a help. Besides, I expect to be spending a lot of time with Commodore Jenks over the next few weeks, and O'Casey needs a break. He can't keep hiding forever."

One of the changes Adar had made during the reconstruction of Nakja-Mur's Great Hall (he still had difficulty considering it *his* Great Hall) was the addition of a number of separate chambers. Some of these were offices, such as the War Room, which was usually occupied by Matt when he was present. Letts had a small office of his own as well. There was also a conference room large enough to accommodate a fair number of attendees while still being relatively cozy. He'd been inspired in this by Keje. In Keje's case, the chamber on *Salissa* wasn't partitioned, but he often had informal, intimate meetings around a simple wooden table supplied with crude stools. In Adar's conference room, the table was bigger of necessity, and there were more stools, but there were also a number of the more traditional cushions for guests to lounge upon. The somewhat uncomfortable stools tended to keep those present awake and relatively alert, but Adar had discovered that often, people he met with needed to contribute only brief reports or accounts. There was no reason for them to suffer while others hashed things out. Many times, for example, he'd watched an exhausted Ben Mallory fall fast asleep on a comfortable

cushion while Captain Reddy and the members of his battle line discussed the ramifications of his aerial observations.

Mallory wasn't here for this discussion. Those present were essentially the same ones he and Alan discussed inviting earlier, with the
exception of Keje, whom Adar had asked to attend as well. Most of
them—Letts, Sister Audry, Rebecca, Sandra, and Keje—joined Adar
on stools around the table. Only Spanky and Courtney took advantage
of the cushions. Spanky was exhausted after his perpetual "watch-on-
watches," and claimed to be only marginally Catholic anyway. Adar
got the impression he didn't know why he was there. Courtney was
fascinated by the looming discussion, but he always accepted a cushion
(and the beer he preferred over seep) when the occasion allowed.

Adar had secretly hoped Alan Letts would start things off, but for
once, the light-skinned officer waited for Adar to begin. "Well," he said
at last. "I suppose we must hammer things out, as you Amer-i-caans so
aptly phrase it. Mr. Letts and I have long planned what he calls an economic discussion, but there appears to be a more pressing matter before us. The economic discussion will . . . *must* happen, I'm sure, but it
need not require the presence of some of you. What we must fashion
this evening is some sort of accommodation between what appears to
be a growing spiritual factionalism." He blinked at Sister Audry.

"I have long enjoyed our brief discussions concerning your faith
and how it may have . . . influenced ours historically, but until recently
I presumed you understood my fears that openly revealing that faith
might contribute to a schism of some kind among our people—right
when our growing unity is our greatest advantage. Aryaalans,
B'mbaadans, and even Sularans hold substantially different beliefs
from most sea folk, and even the People of Baalkpan, yet those differences are primarily matters of interpretation. The fundamental belief
system is quite similar. We all revere the Sun and the Heavens, even if
we place slightly different emphasis on one or the other, and our un-
derstandings of our lives beyond this one are somewhat different as
well. Still, the differences are little more profound than the color of our
fur. My dear Sister Audry, the differences you preach are far more
profound—and potentially more corrosive to the mutual trust and
understanding my people have achieved."

"I'm afraid I don't know what you mean," Sister Audry replied in her strangely accented English.

"Of course you do," Adar remonstrated gently. "I consider you a personal friend, and I thought we had an understanding. You assured me you would do nothing to undermine the solidity of the Alliance during this time of trial."

"I have not!" Sister Audry declared. She sighed. "My order is not given to radicalism. It is not even much given to aggressive evangelism. I come from a place that was mostly Mohammadan, after all. Immoderation of speech is not our . . . *my* way, except when it pertains to intellectual works and teaching."

"And yet your 'teachings' have gained a number of converts to your faith," Adar stated as fact. "Ordinarily, I would not concern myself. I cannot dictate faith . . . and I find myself curiously drawn to some of what you say myself. Much requires reconciliation, but it was my understanding that *you* understood our position and would allow me time to consider the merits of our . . . discussions, and decide how best to proceed with that reconciliation. These converts of yours have begun to be noticed, performing unusual rites. Rites that might be misunderstood. That which is strange and poorly understood can bring persecution and factionalism."

"It has not been my intention to abuse your trust, Mr. Chairman. I do what I may for the good of the people and you have my ungrudging obedience. But when people *ask* about the true faith, I must tell them. I cannot *lie!*"

"But there we have our difficulty." Adar drummed his fingers on the wooden tabletop. "Here in Baalkpan we have our own 'true faith.' It may be observed in different ways, but its basic tenets are a source of unity. You preach an entirely different true faith, and that creates doubt and possibly disunity. At this critical time, I fear your revelations."

"What if it's not really a different true faith," Sandra said slowly. "I'm not Catholic. I was raised Presbyterian, but Sister Audry believes much the same as I do. Only the practices are essentially different. Even among your people, there's a single Maker of All Things. I know many of your people believe He is personified by the Sun, and I guess that's understandable. First, there was apparently some misunderstanding passed down from the original tail-less ones, in which your people interpreted the 'Son' to mean the 'Sun.'" Also, even among my people, the sun—as the most impressive object in the heavens and the most obvious life-giving object visible above all things—is often venerated as the embodiment of the Maker. But generally, we believe the Maker, or God, is all-powerful, and as such, He made the sun as well. Why would that concept be so difficult for your people to grasp?"

"Yeah," said Spanky, rousing slightly. "As I said, I'm a little backslid, but I always figured if God *wanted* to be the sun for a while, nobody's going to tell Him He can't. Basically, we're talking a God with even greater powers than some of your folks have ever given him credit for. I like to think, if we can keep Him on our side in this war, the bigger and more powerful He is, the better. Think about it like this: if Sister Audry's right about her interpretation of this probably same Maker of All Things, maybe you shouldn't alienate Him by making her shut her trap. Maybe you should think more, not less, about incorporating her teachings and reconciling things *now* before He throws up his hands and leaves us on our own."

"Cover all our bases, is that what you mean?" demanded Letts.

Spanky shrugged. "Why not? No atheists in trenches—or engine rooms—when somebody's trying to shoot holes in them. What are you all worked up about, anyway?"

"I was always kind of a Mormon," Letts confessed.

"Jeez!"

"See what I mean?"

"What?"

Courtney finished his beer and belched politely. "The problem, Mr. McFarlane, is that there are at least as many different versions of Christianity as there are versions of the various Lemurian faiths. I won't even go into Islam, Hinduism, Buddhism. . . ." He shook his head. "For Catholicism to be the sole representative of human religion on this world might cause some dissent from our very own human ranks!"

Sister Audry glared at Courtney. "I'm sure I don't understand why *you* are even *here*, Mr. Bradford! I gather you are a Darwinist, and little I can imagine could be more corrosive to spiritual unity than the teachings you espouse—that you regularly, openly *engage* in!"

Courtney goggled at the nun. The sudden attack against him came as a complete surprise. He'd expected to have little participation in the discussion—thus the beer—and had accepted the invitation more out of curiosity than any other reason. He had to remind himself that Sister Audry really didn't know him well. "My dear sister," he began, imposing a moderate tone. "I am a Darwinist, as you put it, through evidentiary discovery and understanding, *not* faith. In faith, I do not recognize even you as my superior!" He glanced at Adar and raised a brow. "One of the discoveries, or rather rediscoveries, I've made since coming to your world is that I too am quite the Christian!"

"How utterly preposterous!" scoffed the nun. "How can one possibly be both an evolutionist and a Christian?"

"Quite comfortably and compatibly, I assure you," Courtney said. "In fact, I invariably find the one position complements the other! Even before I came to this fascinating world, I witnessed—*witnessed*, my dear—the endless, unstoppable force of evolution at work on a daily basis. In all of that, I saw the direction of the very hand of God"— he glanced at Adar again—"or the Maker of All Things." He looked back at Sister Audry. "How do *you* define evolution? I define it as physical and behavioral adaptation to any given species' environment or situation. Behavior can adapt quite rapidly. You have adapted somewhat to your circumstances here, have you not? Physical adaptations take more time, and there, I think—if you'll pardon the expression— is the rub between us. Particularly in respect to how those physical adaptations may have been manifested in humanity."

Sister Audry jerked a nod, and Courtney drew himself up on his cushion. "Personally, I do not believe I am evolved from an ape, although I am relatively certain my ex-wife's father was. Such a hairy, bestial, primitive . . . !" He shook his head. "In any event, I don't see that it matters. Why limit God's imagination? I believe He, like any master architect, would perceive the sundry ways in which His various creations might be better formed to suit their conditions. By His hand, those adaptations would begin!"

"Now you sound dangerously like a Freemason! With your notions of an architect!" Sister Audry scowled. The expression looked out of place on her pleasant features.

"In point of fact . . ." Courtney began.

With a look of horror, Sister Audry clutched the silver crucifix between her breasts as if a serpent had been revealed in their midst.

Courtney sighed. "You were undoubtedly taught and sincerely believe that man was made in the image of God. I must pose you some difficult questions: What *is* man? Are we upright apes like my former father-in-law, or are we sentient, spiritual beings capable of comprehending and returning the love of our Maker? What is the image of God? Is it the black one? The red? The brown, yellow . . . or just the white?" He nodded at Adar. "Or might He be covered in fur? You yourself observed no physical disqualification for salvation when you went among the Javanese and Malays to do His work! You continue it here. Does God have a tail? I submit that God is without form—or is of *any* form He chooses! The only 'image' we need concern ourselves with is the spiritual one!"

"But . . . you claim to be a Christian! How can that be? I grant you might be a deist, or some other species of heathen, but how can you claim yourself a Christian?"

"The same way you do, my dear: I have heard and believe the Word. But the Lord Jesus Christ, our *spiritual savior*, appeared only briefly, and his teachings and works were immediately known to but a very few. It was up to others, like yourself ultimately, to spread the knowledge of those works and teachings about. Certainly you don't believe that all those throughout the centuries who lived and died in ignorance of the Word are damned? The loving God I worship would not make beings such as we only to have them suffer such an automatic fate!"

Courtney shrugged, somewhat apologetically. He wasn't much given to proselytizing, or even to sharing his own beliefs so freely. "Perhaps that is your purpose here, my dear," he said more softly. "Your destiny, as it were. But do not reject the possibility that our savior might have come to this place already. If God is capable of creating other worlds such as this, as I certainly *believe* He is, as I believe He is *capable of anything*, perhaps he will send or has already sent his son here as well."

"I don't see the problem," Keje grumbled, surprising everyone. "As

I understand it, as Captain Reddy has explained it to me, this Christianity is just another path, another tack sailed to the same destination, to join the Maker of All Things in the Heavens, is it not?" Reluctantly, even Sister Audry nodded. "Chairman Adar is correct that all those who follow such different paths have put their differences aside, for now, at least, to work for the common good—our very survival. Yet, in his wisdom, he has not prevented the priests of Aryaal or B'mbaado or even Sular from ministering to those souls they tend. Why should Sister Audry be different? Her practices are strange, but to me, so are those of the other priests I mentioned. It seems that a simple statement by Adar that her path is yet another, different one leading to the same place should be sufficient to prevent this persecution he fears. And so what if a few people convert?"

"It is not that simple," Sister Audry protested.

"Let us make it so, at least for now, shall we?" Keje challenged her.

The nun sighed. "Very well. But I will not lie."

"No one is asking that you do," Adar assured her, "but I think my lord Keje has the right of it." He paused, grasping his hands in front of him on the table. He hoped this issue was solved, but he couldn't be sure. Why could nothing be easy? "If no one objects then, I will consider this a closed issue. I will make a formal statement recognizing this Catholic Church and, as has been discussed, proclaim it as yet another path to the Heavens, as far as the Alliance is concerned." Adar blinked imploringly at Sister Audry. "Is that sufficient? For now? Can you at least refrain from antagonizing those who believe differently?"

Sister Audry nodded. "I can. As I have said, I have much practice at that. I will extol the virtues of the Church, *ut in omnibus glorificetur Deus*, but I will say nothing against any other."

"Splendid!" Courtney boomed. "I do so enjoy consensus! Might there be more beer to be had?"

"Sounds okay," Sandra said, "in theory." She looked at Princess Rebecca, who'd said nothing at all during the debate. "What do you think?"

Rebecca looked uncomfortable. "Sounds swell to me," she replied reluctantly. She'd been picking up more and more Americanisms. Courtney sometimes joked that her people might declare war based solely on that. "But the issue may not be closed at all, once we visit my people."

Sandra nodded. She'd gathered enough from Rebecca to understand that the Empire's primary rival was still another human civilization that didn't seem very Catholic at all, despite retaining the name and some of the ceremonies. These others, whom Rebecca referred to only as the Dominion, had inherited many of the cruel and expansive methods and practices of a much earlier Church than was represented by Sister Audry. Apparently, they'd incorporated some radical elements of other "faiths" as well. Rebecca had come to know the nun and she knew a little history, so she understood there were substantial differences between Sister Audry's Church and what it had become under the Dominion. She wasn't at all sure her people would see any such distinction.

"I guess we'll see," Sandra said.

Marine Corporal Koratin, formerly Lord Koratin, renowned speaker, power broker, and counselor to kings, descended the companionway into the dark, dry hold. Despite his teetering conversion, he automatically thanked the Sun that he wasn't on one of the prize ships. No matter how their new owners tried, they could never quite cleanse the reeking stench of what the Grik had done in them. He'd helped capture a few and the dangling chains, emaciated "survivors," the slippery bones mixed with slimy ballast stones . . . all had been etched on his memory as with acid. In comparison, the hold of USS *Dowden* was a pleasant bower that smelled of fresh, well-seasoned wood, clean ballast, and the honest sweat and musty fur of her hardworking builders. There was only the slightest trace of rancid bilgewater from her new, seeping seams. That was nothing, he thought. *Dowden* was a tight ship, and her seams would only swell tighter.

Dowden's hold wasn't open from stem to stern like Grik ships either. It was highly compartmentalized. He understood the various compartments were even watertight to a degree, making the new steam frigate more difficult for an enemy to sink. He believed it. He was highly impressed with the construction techniques of the sea folk, and with Amer-i-caan designs to draw from, he accepted improvement as a given. He was most impressed by the Amer-i-caans in many ways. That didn't mean he loved them like the sea folk did, or even as the People of Baalkpan and other places had come to. He was genuinely intrigued by the teachings of their Sister Audry, but he didn't care much for their other strange notions of the way things ought to be. He hoped that somehow, the world might one day return to the simpler way it had been before.

The Amer-i-caans struck him as honorable warriors, but mere warriors they'd remained when they could have been kings. True, they'd helped establish a real alliance, the largest ever known, but it was a fragile thing in his cynical view. It would have been better for all if they *had* become kings. An empire was far more stable than any flimsy alliance. But simple warriors they remained—by choice—and all warriors were merely tools. As he had become.

Koratin entered a compartment where no gear was stowed. There was only a short bank of smaller compartments with barred doors across them. The common word was "brig," he believed. He passed the first and nodded genially at the inmate, an Aryaalan Marine like himself, who'd supposedly smuggled a quantity of seep aboard the ship. The prisoner did not react. Koratin came to the next cell and peered inside.

"Lord King," he whispered. "Are you well?"

Rasik-Alcas stirred slightly in the gloom. Confinement was even harder on Lemurians than on humans, but Rasik tried to appear disinterested. Only the slightest twitch of an ear betrayed his stress.

"Come to gloat, Koratin?" he asked at last. "I am king of nothing here, as you well know. This new ship does not yet even have enough vermin for me to rule."

Koratin squatted beyond the bars. "Still, you are a king. By blood. I served your father and I tried to serve you."

"By betraying me?" Rasik flashed, his eyes blinking rage.

"By trying to protect you from your . . . youthful impulses. You *are* young to be king, and when you attempted to destroy the iron ship of the Amer-i-caans, I foresaw the disaster that *did* result."

"You tried to warn them!" Rasik accused.

"I failed. You sent warriors to kill me. They failed. Still there was disaster. You angered the Amer-i-caans and instead of leaving to fight their war elsewhere, they took your city from you." Koratin didn't remind Rasik that they probably would have done it anyway after the Grik advance was discovered. Taking the city was the only way to save the people inside.

"So, you failed to betray me and I failed to kill you. That makes us even?"

"No, Lord King. You might say the one act cancels the other. That leaves us back where we started, if you wish it."

"What?" Rasik laughed. "You would be a king's counselor through iron bars? Why not be king yourself? I understand you have won glory with this ridiculous *Alliance*." He spat the word.

"I could never be king. I am not of the blood. The people would not permit it."

"So you have considered it?"

Koratin shrugged. "I am a political creature, as you know. You will also know I have considered many possibilities." He gestured at himself. "I was a *lord*! I had a great house, many servants, and enough retainers to defeat yours when they came for me! Do you believe I wish to remain a mere warrior? A soldier of lowly rank and status? Do you think me *mad*? I could never be king, but *you* could—and I could have back what I have lost!"

Rasik lowered his head in uncustomary dejection. "I could never be king again. The people hate me. I will be lucky to survive!"

For a moment, Koratin said nothing. He was almost stunned by Rasik's apparent bout of sanity. "Many do hate you," he agreed at last. "They blame you for the time that was lost in evacuating the city. Some think more might have survived and perhaps even *Nerracca* of the sea folk might not have been destroyed if . . . things had gone differently."

"What do you think, Koratin?"

"I think they may be right. I would have counseled as much, had you allowed me."

Rasik beat his hands against his head. "Easy to say now," he almost moaned.

"But true, Lord King. You know it is."

After several moments, Rasik finally nodded. "It *is* true. You and your love of younglings. I cannot doubt you. You *were* trying to help and I drove you away!"

"Yes, Lord King."

"Well . . . I know you, Koratin! You would not have come to me without a scheme of some sort. What is it? Tell me!"

"There *is* something the Amer-i-caans will want where we go?"

Rasik grew guarded. "Yes."

"Am I correct in assuming you mean to lead them a lengthy, round-about chase to find it?"

"Why do you ask?" Rasik demanded.

"It is what I would do in your place. You fear they will kill you when they have whatever it is, so you mean to lead them anywhere but where they must go until you have devised another plan."

"What if that were true?"

Koratin sighed. "All the Allied armies have left Aryaal. We sailed for Chill-Chaap this morning. The rest of the fleet moves on the Grik at the land they call Sing-aapore. The people of Aryaal will be returning and they will need a king!"

"But how . . . ?"

"If you have ever trusted me, trust me now," Koratin said. "You must lead the Allies directly to what you found! Give it to them quickly. They will be glad, they might even begin to trust you, and they will *leave*."

"They will kill me!"

"They will not! I have . . . arranged certain things, believe me. Do you think otherwise? That I would not have considered all contingencies? I swear to you, before the Sun in the sky, I will not let the Amer-i-caans harm you! You are my king! I cannot be king! How else will I have what I want?"

"If I do this, if I give them what they want and all goes as you say, how will I then be king again?"

"It is simplicity itself! You *are* king! King Rasik-Alcas! The Allies will leave and you will return overland and simply sit on your throne! I will be there, and you have many more supporters than you know! The first of our people to return to Aryaal will be among the most anxious to see you!"

"I am with you, Lord King!" came a voice from the neighboring cell. "I was in your palace guard! My sword is still yours!"

Koratin looked in the direction of the voice, then stared intently back at Rasik. "You see? When you sit your throne again with your people back in their homes—the homes *you* did not abandon!—who will oppose you then? Who will dare oppose *us*?"

Slowly, Rasik-Alcas grinned. "You always were clever, Koratin. Father said so as well. Too clever for your own good at times, but this time I think you are right. Who indeed will oppose me if I am already on the throne when our people come trickling back? It is not as if they will be great in numbers!"

"True, Lord King," Koratin said grimly. "Very true." He stood. "Is there anything I can bring you?"

"No," Rasik said, bright eyes searching the gloom as if looking for faults in the plan. "None must suspect our scheme. Do any know of our past . . . association?"

"None, Lord King. I am merely a soldier of low rank. No one knows who I really am, or what is in my heart."

"A brilliant subterfuge! Try to discover their plans if you can, but be discreet! Discreet! No one must suspect!"

"Count on it, Lord King."

As Marine Corporal Koratin turned to walk back the way he'd come, he nodded at the other prisoner again. This time, unseen by Rasik, the prisoner nodded back.

*T*alaud Island appeared much as Irvin Laumer remembered it when they'd approached it so long ago in S-19, her diesels gasping on fumes. They hadn't encountered another island fish in the crossing from Mindanao, and Irvin wondered if Silva had actually "sunk" the one that lingered there, as he'd claimed. Surely if he had, another had taken its place? *Walker* had picked one up on sonar, after all. Maybe they had been discouraged. Whatever the reason, he was relieved.

Island fish or no, nothing could protect them and *Simms* from the constant deluge of bird and flying reptile droppings.

"That is the place?" Lelaa asked, approaching him as she wiped at a greenish white smear across her dark fur with a towel. Irvin subdued a chuckle at the captain's expense.

"That's it," he said.

"Where to from here?"

"Around the eastern point. There's a broad lagoon, almost a tiny bay. S-19 was on the beach. There was a little protection but not much. . . . I hope she's still there." He voiced his greatest fear. They knew there'd been storms since they left. A high enough surge could have carried her farther inland, making complete salvage impossible, or it might have even carried her off to sea.

"The mountain on the island smokes," Lelaa observed. "Did it smoke this much when you were here?"

Laumer lifted his binoculars. It was a dreary, hazy, oppressive day. Still, he could see the dull, monochromatic outline of the distant volcano on the island. The smoke was blowing away to the south. "Yeah, maybe. Sometimes there'd be earthquakes—the ground would move. I don't know. It looks like the thing's a little taller than I remember it."

Midshipman Hardee and Motor Machinist's Mate Sandy Whitcomb were standing with him. Sandy said, "Nah," but Hardee remained silent.

Irvin looked at him. "What do you think?"

"Well, sir, I'm not sure. The top was usually misty when we were here before, and down in the jungle where we spent most of our time, one couldn't see it at all. That being said, I would have to concur with you. It does *seem* taller."

"Hmm. Well, shouldn't make a difference unless it decides to pull a Krakatoa on us." As soon as he said the words, Irvin wished he could take them back. He'd always prided himself on his rationality, but some of the men's superstition had rubbed off on him, he guessed. He noticed the accusing look Whitcomb gave him and smiled uncertainly. "Just kidding, Sandy."

"If it's all the same to 'His Highness,' the new commodore, I wish to hell you wouldn't say shit like that." Sandy gestured vaguely over his shoulder. "Me and the fellas who volunteered to come along did it because it's a job that needs doin' and we like you. We know you've got as much guts as Chief Flynn, but you had the sense to let him take the lead while you learned the ropes. You got more brains than he does, so you're better than him for this caper. As long as you use them brains to accomplish the mission and don't go jinxin' us, we'll get along fine."

Touched and chagrined by the convoluted and somewhat backhanded compliment, Irvin nodded. "Don't worry. Like I said, I was just kidding, but I won't kid about stuff like that anymore. If you want me to throw salt over my shoulder, scratch a backstay, or jump up and down, spitting on myself, I'll do it if it makes you feel better."

Sandy and Hardee laughed. "Nah," said Sandy, "It'ud be funny to see, but none o' that would work anyway."

"What is a Krakatoa?" Lelaa asked.

Sandy rolled his eyes. "A busted toe. A real bad one."

Late that afternoon, they rounded the point. The wind had shifted out of the south and they took in everything but the staysails. The wind cooled them but their progress slowed to a crawl. Irvin wasn't worried. The mouth of the cove he remembered so well was near, and he'd rather creep up on it than tack away and try to find it again from seaward. Better to approach it the same way S-19 had. A call came down from aloft and he knew they'd reached their destination.

"Any suggestions?" Lelaa asked.

"Ah, you'll want to aim for the middle going in. There's just sand, but it shifts around. The lagoon's shaped kind of like a cursive capital E. . . ." He looked at her blank expression and drew one on the bulwark with his finger. "We want the top of the E, the northern end. There's rollers, usually, but it gets calmer when we're in the point's lee. Water there was deeper too."

"Was?"

Irvin shrugged. "Was. Places like this can change every time a storm hits."

"Leadsmen to the bow," Lelaa commanded loudly, then looked back at Irvin. "You were saying?" she asked politely.

Irvin knew she'd just given him another tactful lesson in seamanship. "Ah, that's it. We sail in and anchor as close to shore as the tide will let us. We should see the boat."

Simms crept into the cove, her consort staying well back to avoid any hazards the flagship might encounter. Irvin and all the submariners were on the fo'c'sle staring ahead, passing the binoculars around and listening to the leadsman's shouted depths.

"Goddamn, we should see her by now!" Tex erupted suddenly. He had the glasses.

"Maybe," Whitcomb replied. The beach they'd left her on was still a mile or so ahead and it was hard to focus the binoculars while the ship passed through the rollers.

Hardee reached for the binoculars. "Here, let me have those a moment, please," he said, somewhat imperiously. Tex handed them over, but then made comic gestures behind the boy's back when he turned. He understood the concept of midshipmen just fine, but he wasn't used to taking orders from sixteen-year-old kids. Hardee put the strap around his neck and quickly scampered up into the foretop—no simple feat with the ship pitching so—and scanned the shoreline from a higher perspective. The Lemurian lookouts probably had better vision than he did, even with binoculars, but none of them had ever seen the submarine before. They didn't really know what to look for.

"There she is!" he suddenly cried down triumphantly.

"Where?" Irvin shouted back.

"About where she was, but . . . all I can really see is the conn tower! It looks like it's leaning toward the sea!"

Irvin looked at the other submariners. When they left, the boat was almost entirely exposed and leaning hard to port—away from the sea.

"Well," he said, "at least she's still here. I guess we'll know the score when we go ashore."

Simms and her consort anchored a quarter mile from the beach, where there'd be plenty of water under their keels even when the tide was out. Irvin was anxious to get a look at the task before them, but decided not to waste a trip ashore just for sightseeing. All the ship's barges went over the side filled with equipment; the disassembled steam engine was their "compact" model, but the parts were still heavy and bulky. The generator was one assembly, and although it wasn't very big, it was heavy. Other tools and equipment went as well, but no camping gear or foodstuffs. They wouldn't have time to establish their outpost that evening, and Irvin wanted to reimpress on everyone the hostile nature of some of the inhabitants of Talaud. Tomorrow they'd build a base camp, assemble the equipment they'd brought, and try to discourage the various predators he felt sure had returned to the area in their absence.

Rowing ashore, Irvin noticed few strikes at the boat. He'd gotten used to the incessant thumping of the flashies in the waters he'd crossed more recently and wondered why there weren't as many here. There were some really big, goofy-looking sharks, he remembered. Maybe that was why. Or maybe it was the deep water all around. He shook his head. Something else for the irrepressible Courtney Bradford to figure out.

His boat nudged ashore and he hopped into the calf-deep water, shoes tied around his neck. Once on the dry sand, he sat down and pulled the battered shoes on his feet. Even while he did so, he looked at the submarine—or what he could see of her. They'd realized, the closer they came to shore, that the boat had been virtually buried in the sand. Not just buried, but sunk in the sand as well. He could easily imagine how it happened. A big storm had lashed the island, maybe even the one that was brewing when they left it. The surge rolled the sub back and forth on the wet, loosening sand, slowly displacing that beneath her, and dragging her down into it. When she was almost level with the beach, the sand collected atop her until all that remained visible was the tower and the four-inch-fifty gun. Irvin stood and approached the boat with the other men.

Lelaa stared at what little was visible in wonder.

"You went under the water in *that*?"

"She's a lot bigger than she looks," Tex said defensively.

"Jeez. She's plumb *buried*!" said Danny Porter. "How the hell are we gonna get her out of *that*!"

Carpenter's Mate Sid Franks laughed. He'd been talking with some of the 'Cats in his division. "Hell, this is the best thing that could have happened!"

"What do you mean?" asked Irvin.

"Well, sir, if she was still high and dry, we'd have had to dig a hole out from under her. No way we could push or pull her in the water. We could have built rollers, I guess, but we would've had to run them out in water deep enough for stuff to eat us. We couldn't have made them stay where we wanted them either. This way, we just dig her out and dredge a channel into the lagoon!"

"Okay, I can see it's easier to dig her out, but how do we dredge your little canal?"

"Easy. Well, not *easy*, but simple, maybe. We securely moor the ships and use their anchors to dredge a trench! Actually, I'm sure one of you geniuses can come up with something better than an anchor—maybe a scoop or something. We scoop the sand, hoist the anchors, or whatever, into the boats, bring it back, and reposition it. Then we do it again."

"We'll have to 'do it again' a lot of times," Danny mused, "but yeah, that'll work better than if we had to relaunch her."

"Everybody hold your horses," Irvin said. The sun had touched the treetops at the jungle's edge. "First, you guys, all but Danny, help get that stuff ashore." He pointed where dozens of 'Cats were carrying crates from the boats to the beach. "Then we get to work tomorrow."

"What are you and Danny going to do?" asked Tex, a little irritated.

"We're going to climb up there"—Irvin motioned with his chin at the conn tower—"and crack the hatch." He took a battle lantern out of the pack he'd been carrying. "You can go on all you want about refloating the old gal, and that's swell, but the first thing I need to do is decide whether there's any point." He sighed. "Hell, fellas, all that banging around might have opened her up like a sardine can. She might be full of water, for all we know."

Suddenly, the ground shivered perceptibly beneath their feet and they heard a dull rumble even above the surf.

"What the hell?"

"Mr. Laumer, look!" Hardee almost shouted. He was pointing southwest, toward the volcano. From where they stood, they couldn't see the mountain itself—the coastal trees were too tall—but they easily saw the gray column of smoke and ash piling into the sky. It seemed to glow just a bit at the bottom, and Irvin wondered if the setting sun was causing it. With the wind now out of the south, they were likely to get some of that ash.

"I sure wish you'd quit doing that," Whitcomb said through clenched teeth. "Think positive, Mr. Laumer. The only thing the matter with her was she was outta fuel. She took a hell of an ash-canning by a Jap tin can. If that didn't open her up, a few little waves ain't goin' to."

Irvin nodded and took his eyes off the tower of smoke. "Okay. I'm sure she's ready for sea," he said, a little sarcastically, "but Danny and I will make that decision and we're going to make it fast. Tomorrow we'll start work on one of two things: refloating S-19 or breaking her up. Captain Reddy himself ordered me—*ordered me*—to make that determination as soon as I laid eyes on her, and that's what I'm going to do. If Danny and I come out of that boat and say we're taking her apart, there won't be any discussions or arguments. Tomorrow we start taking her apart. I know she means a lot to you guys—she means a lot to me too—but Captain Reddy's right. We need what she's made of a lot more than we need *her*. Is that understood?

A little taken aback by Laumer's sudden transformation from an easygoing shipmate to an officer who expected his orders to be obeyed, all the submariners nodded. Lelaa nodded too, in satisfaction.

"That said," Irvin continued, "it's my genuine hope that we can get her out of here in one piece. It would be easier, I think, and then we'd have all of her and not just the stuff we can get at. If we have to break her up, there won't be another trip to bring back more of her. Next time it might all be buried or gone and a lot will go to waste." He shrugged. "And who knows, Captain Reddy might decide we still need a submarine for some reason." He looked at Lelaa, then back at his men. "So now you know how I feel. One way or another, we *will* accomplish our mission and there *won't* be any bitching." He looked at the column of smoke. "And whatever we do, I think we need to do it quick. I have a weird feeling this island isn't too happy to have us back."

That went . . . okay, he thought as he and Danny made their way up the damp dune toward the conning tower. *They're all swell guys, but Captain Reddy's right.* Somebody *always has to be in charge.* Well, he might not be the best choice, but he was there. Now that the job was at hand and he was off Lelaa's ship, the time had come for him to step up.

There was a space between the four-inch-fifty and the conn tower that was free of sand, for the most part, and he eased onto the rotting strakes. They actually seemed to give a little beneath his weight. Somewhere beneath the sand was the top of the pressure hull but he saw none of it. He hoped it didn't look as bad as what he could see of the conn tower and the exposed areas of the gun. Apparently all the paint had been blasted away and everything was an almost uniform reddish brown. They'd sealed the gun as best they could before they left and he hoped the seal still held. He hoped the submarine's seals still held, for that matter, but his heart began to sink.

"Here," he said, pointing at the gun access hatch on the front of the conn tower, "let's see if we can get in that way."

"Sure," said Danny. The hatch was a new addition, not originally built with the sub, but like many of her sisters, S-19 had been upgraded—a little. Kind of like *Walker* and her Asiatic Fleet sisters, S-19 was literally generations behind the state of the art. They'd had so many accidents with the S-boats, however, many of them fatal, they'd been forced to make a few modifications over the years. The hatch was one. It was intended as a means to pass ammunition to the gun's crew, and as an emergency escape outlet. The ability to escape the dangerous boats had been deemed an important feature. Besides the infamous *Squalus* incident, Irvin remembered hearing about several S-Boat accidents. In one case, the sub sank, leaving nothing but her stern poking out of the open ocean and her surviving crew had to be cut out. Another sinking of a different boat had left the bow exposed, and the crew escaped through a torpedo tube! Regardless how many "escape hatches" the boats now had, far too many of the class had gone down with all hands before the war even started.

"Damn, it's stuck!" Irvin said, trying to undog the hatch. "Give me a hand!"

Danny moved to join him, and together they strained with all their might. No go. "Must've rusted shut," Danny said ominously. Irvin glanced up at a sound and saw Lelaa standing there.

"Let me help." Awkwardly arranged around the small wheel, the three of them gave another tug. To Irvin's consternation and Lelaa's delight, the dog finally spun.

"See? You just needed 'girl help.' I didn't really do anything but touch the handle. You Amer-i-caans say that ships are 'shes' even when you give them 'he' names. Maybe you're right. Girls always listen better to girls."

Danny made a rude noise and spun the wheel to its stop. Looking at Laumer, he raised the hatch.

After the better part of a year exposed to fresh open air, they weren't prepared for the stench that wafted out. It was ungodly, even to Danny. His submariner's brain instantly categorized most of the smells, however, and even as he almost retched and stepped quickly away, his mood brightened a little.

"Aggh! People live in that?" Lelaa gasped.

"No!" Irvin insisted. "At least . . . not this bad. We used to vent her out every day. She spent most of her time on the surface, not all buttoned up. There's months of stink down there that's been baking in the hot sun!"

"A little more than that, Mr. Laumer," Danny said. "There's mold and mildew and other things, but she doesn't smell any gassier than she did when we sealed her up."

Irvin looked thoughtful. Scampering up the rungs to the top of the conn tower, he tried the other hatch, and it spun freely. It had been the one they used most often when they were here before. It clanked open against its stops and he peered into the dark hole. Remembering the battle lantern, he shone it down.

"Doesn't look that bad," he murmured noncommitally. "Smells nasty, but what do you expect? No more gas, so water hasn't gotten to the batteries again."

"Are you going inside?" Lelaa asked. Irvin seemed to consider.

"Well, at first I figured we'd let her air out overnight. Even if it rains, it won't hurt anything, not really. Why?"

"I want to go inside," Lelaa announced. "All I can see is this little thing poking out of the sand. I want to see inside!"

"Okay . . ." Irvin hedged. "It *is* nasty. And it's hot in there too. Maybe not as hot as it used to be when it was in full sunlight . . ."

"Hell, let's go," said Danny. "You told the fellas we'd start to break her or get her out tomorrow, one or the other. They deserve an answer!"

Irvin nodded. "You're right. Let's do it."

One at a time, they descended to the control room below. The smell was ghastly and it felt like breathing a putrid soup, but eventually they grew accustomed to it, even Lelaa. Irvin shone the light around until he settled on the switch he was looking for. It activated the red emergency lighting Spanky had turned on months ago. To Irvin's surprise, the lights still came on, but just barely. There wasn't much juice left at all.

"If we get her dug out, run a cable from the generator, maybe we can charge her up enough to start an engine," Danny said.

"Maybe. Or if the compressed air tanks are still charged, we can turn one over that way. Just give her some fuel, and vroom!" He shook his head. "We're getting ahead of ourselves. Let's see what we've got."

"What are these big poles for, and what are those big, shiny wheels?" Lelaa asked, pointing to port.

"The poles are the periscopes. You know, those two things sticking up on top of the conn tower?"

"One is bent."

"Yeah, it was damaged when the Japs were depth-charging us. Giving us a treatment kind of like what we did to the mountain fish with the "Y" gun. We use them to see above the water when we're under it. Those wheels control the bow and stern planes. They make her go up and down underwater. That, and the amount of water we let in." She looked around.

"Water in here?"

"No. In the ballast tanks. We let water in to go down, and blow it out with compressed air to go back up. That big wheel at the front of the compartment controls the rudder, just like on *Simms*. It makes the boat turn from side to side."

"Sounds simple."

"Believe me, sister. There ain't nothing simple about it!" Danny quipped.

"Hey!" cautioned Irvin. "I don't think 'sister' is an appropriate way to address the captain of a United States ship!"

Danny blinked, then nodded. "Yeah. Sorry. Bein' back here on my old 'sugar boat,' it started to feel like old times."

Lelaa blinked in acceptance. "Then let us be about the business of determining whether we can make it more like old times by getting your 'sugar boat' off this beach!"

They decided to go forward first, since the bow was buried deeper than the stern. The crew compartment looked much like they'd left it: decks clear, racks chained to the bulkhead. They'd removed some of the mattresses for bedding on the island and the others had turned somewhat gray.

"Here's where some of the mildew's from," Danny said. "High humidity got the fart bags!" Irvin pointed the light, nodded, then looked around. It was the most spacious area in the boat and even some of the wooden folding chairs were still secured. A few had come loose, probably when the boat was rolling with the storm. Danny knelt and raised one of the linoleum-covered deck plates and Irvin shone the light.

"Forward battery looks just like we left it." Irvin glanced at Lelaa. "We lost a few batteries in here and had some water coming in. Had to seal off the compartment. Some good fellas died. Gas."

It was a simple statement, but Lelaa could tell the words still hurt. Irvin had already told her the story and explained what happened when seawater and sulfuric acid met. She also knew he'd been a junior officer and the decision wouldn't have been his. She wondered how she would have felt. Probably the same, she concluded. Not guilty, certainly, but pained that she'd survived as a result of such a decision.

"All the passengers were in the torpedo room." Irvin gestured forward. "No torpedoes, so it was the logical place to put them. There's racks in there too."

They moved to the hatch, which had been left standing open. Sure enough, there were quite a few more racks stowed in the compartment. There was also the most confusing conglomeration of pipes, valves, and instruments Lelaa had ever seen. She watched Irvin and Danny inspect a few gauges here and there and make approving or disapproving sounds. They inspected the bilge in the forwardmost area, in front of the fuel tanks.

"Well, she ain't dry," Danny announced, "but she ain't sunk either. Looks about like normal seepage to me."

"So?"

"So we look aft," Danny answered, shrugging.

The aft crew's quarters and officer's country looked much the same. The batteries under the plates looked okay too. There was water in the bilge under the engines, but it hadn't reached the huge machines.

"Those are the engines?" Lelaa asked. She'd seen the steam engines they were building, but the difference in sophistication was stunning.

"Yep," Irvin said. "Two NELSECO diesels. Twelve hundred horsepower combined. They'll move this tub at fifteen knots on the surface, if the sea's calm."

"And they were both running when you ran out of fuel?"

"That's right," said Danny. "They worked the last time we used them." Lelaa looked at him and twitched her tail. She had much to learn about Amer-i-caans, but the statement sounded . . . odd.

"What is in the next compartment?"

"The motor room."

Lelaa *was* confused now. "I have heard you, your people, use the words 'motor' and 'engine' interchangeably," she said. "Why would S-19 need engines *and* a motor?"

Irvin started to laugh, but then realized it was a perfectly good question.

"Motors, actually. Plural. Okay, here's the deal. Unlike the new Fleet Boats, S-19 can run her propeller shafts with a direct drive straight off the diesels. She's actually faster that way. The trouble is, she can only run them one direction—forward. She can't back up or use her screws for maneuvering with the engines. Since she has to use electric motors underwater—they don't burn fuel, make exhaust, or need air; that's how it works—we use the motors for reverse and maneuvering on the surface too. The new system's really better. They don't use the engines for anything but charging the batteries, and the motors do all the work. You've got forward and reverse and all the maneuvering you want all the time." He patted one of the NELSECOs. "But these babies do pretty good."

"I am anxious to see these 'motors,' but you did not answer my question: why is one a 'motor' and the other an 'engine'?"

Irvin and Danny looked at each other.

"Ask Sandy," Irvin said. "He'll know."

Danny nodded agreement, but then turned back to Irvin. "So what's the verdict, Skipper? What do we tell the guys?"

Irvin rubbed his forehead, looked at his two companions, and sighed. "Tomorrow we dig. And I want everybody trying to figure out the best way to dredge a canal this thing'll fit through!"

USS *Dowden*'s anchor splashed into the almost mirror-clear water off the Lemurian city of Chillchaap. Jim Ellis barely remembered having been there before—he'd had a fever at the time—and it wasn't exactly where its human counterpart, Tjilatjap, had been. The human city was east-southeast of the place the Lemurians had once chosen, and Jim remembered it as it had been in the early, chaotic days of the war they'd left behind. Some ships were still getting in and out when they'd seen the old cruiser *Marblehead* moored there after the pasting she'd taken from Japanese planes. Anyone who saw her was amazed she was still afloat. Her rudder had been jammed hard aport and she was still low by the head. They'd been transferring the wounded ashore, since nobody really expected her to make it out of the area alive. Ellis reflected that he'd never know if she had or not.

Tjilatjap was a dump. The fueling and repair facilities there were inadequate and there were no torpedoes to be had. Worse, from the crew's perspective, there was virtually zero nightlife. Even though it meant steaming back in the teeth of the Japanese storm, he'd actually been glad when they steered for Surabaya once again. He shook his head. That was another time, another world. Where the Tjilatjap he knew should have been, there was absolutely nothing, and never had been. Of the Chill-chaap their Allies had built on the other side of the peninsula, there was nothing left.

Even before the Grik came in force, a raiding party had sacked the city, eaten or taken its inhabitants, and razed much of what remained to the ground. Since then, a year and a half was all it had taken the jungle to reclaim a city almost as old and large as Baalkpan. It was a dreary, creepy sight. Vines and bizarre, spiderweblike foliage covered the ruins, and the old pathways were choked and impassable. From what Ben, Pam, Brister, and Palmer had told him, there were many bones as well. He figured rodents and other things would have eaten the bones by now, but he was glad they wouldn't have to make their way through the once-proud city. According to Rasik, what they sought was a number of miles up the estuary where the river became a swamp.

"Good morning, Cap-i-taan Ellis," came a voice from behind him. He turned and saw Chack standing there, neatly maintained Marine battle dress at odds with the dented American doughboy helmet he wore. He wore a sword suspended from a black leather baldric, and hanging by its sling, muzzle down on his brindle-furred shoulder, was his Krag.

"Morning, Chack. You ready for this?"

"Of course."

Jim nodded. Of course. Chack's steadiness and complete competence were among the constants he'd come to rely on. He still found it hard to believe the young Lemurian had once been a confirmed pacifist.

"Very well. You, me, half a dozen Marines, and Rasik-Alcas. I guess we'll take Isak Rueben in case this 'treasure trove' of Rasik's includes anything he might be needed to evaluate." Jim frowned. Isak had transferred to *Dowden* as chief engineer for the trip, since the ship would be on her own. Isak clearly understood the principles of *Dowden*'s machinery better than anyone else, but he wasn't a very good teacher. Once away from Tabby and Gilbert, he wasn't quite as antisocial as usual, but he didn't delegate worth a damn and tried to do everything himself. He probably needed a break from the engineering spaces as much as the engineering division needed a break from him. "One of the Marines will be Koratin?"

"Yes."

"Do you trust him?"

Chack's tail swished thoughtfully. "In a fight, as a Marine, I trust him. His status as a former Aryaalan noble causes some mild concern. By all accounts, he once lived a life of expediency, taking the tack of best advantage for himself." Chack blinked irony. "That is not necessarily consistent with the accounts of his performance in battle, so perhaps he has indeed changed." Chack shrugged in a well-practiced, very human way. "We will see."

The longboat went over the side and slapped the still water. The Marines escorted Rasik into the boat, followed by Isak, grumbling about the "stupid bulky rifle" he had to carry. Jim knew Isak was proficient with a Krag, but he also knew the wiry little Mouse didn't like wagging one around. The black powder and hard-cast bullet loads they'd made for the weapons had proved fairly effective on animals as big as a midsize rhino-pig, but even the precious few remaining rounds from the Rock Island Arsenal barely got the attention of something the size of a super lizard. No one but Rasik had any idea what sort of monsters they might encounter, and on that subject, at least, he'd remained cryptic.

After a brief word with Muraak-Saanga, his exec and "salig maastir," Jim was last over the side. He alone carried an '03 Springfield with "modern" ammunition and extra stripper clips. He also had his 1917-pattern Navy cutlass and a 1911 Colt. Besides Chack, the Marines he'd handpicked were all armed with their swords and the shorter thrusting spears they preferred. None carried shields. Without the numbers required to form a wall, they'd only get in the way. Two had longbows slung over their shoulders.

Chack barked a command and the oars came out. First and foremost, Chack would always consider himself one of *Walker*'s bosun's mates, and whenever he was in charge of anything on the water, he reverted to that capacity. He moved to the stern and took the tiller himself. Jim settled in for what promised to be a long trip, and with another command from Chack, the oars dipped in unison. "Well, Rasik," Jim said conversationally, "it's your show now." He grinned. "Don't disappoint us."

"You will not be disappointed."

"Swell. I'm glad you want to please. Just to remind you, though, I'll repeat the deal. You show us what you found. If it has any use at all to our war effort, you go free." He gestured to the south. "That's Nusakambangan. It's a pretty big island, and even on my world there was plenty there to survive on." He grinned again. "The Dutch used it as a prison, kinda like an eastern Alcatraz. For some reason, that strikes me as highly appropriate. Anyway, it may not be a palace, but if you managed to scratch out a living in the wild for nearly a year, you should have no trouble there. We'll even leave you weapons."

"I understand. Exile or death."

Jim shook his head. "No. You lead us *straight* to what you found or there won't even be exile, just death. If you try to give us the slip, I'll kill you. If I even start to think you're yanking my chain, I'll hang you in the jungle and leave you for the skuggiks or bugs, whichever get you first. Period. We've come here on your word when my ship's needed elsewhere—when I'd *rather* be elsewhere. If I find out you've been saving your miserable ass just to lead us on a wild-goose chase . . . you'll wish you were in hell for quite a while before you get there."

Methodically, metronomically, almost mechanically, the oars dipped and rose. They were following a major inlet north, and more than once, Jim wished they'd moved the ship farther inland. They didn't have a clue about depths, snags, or sandbars, though, and there was really nothing for it. Eventually the inlet, or river, or whatever it was, began to narrow. So far, they'd seen only the usual wild variety of lizard birds and an occasional crocodile. Once, something large and heavy exploded out of the water near shore and went thrashing into the jungle. No one saw what it looked like. The water eventually grew shallower and opened into a vast swamp filled with fallen trees and stumps. The jungle around it remained dense and apparently impenetrable, and high, misty volcanic peaks were visible in all directions. Jim had no idea if the old Java looked like this around here; he'd never been anywhere but Tjilatjap, but they were always discovering geographic differences here and there. Whatever had changed this world, whether subtle or momentous, was still slowly at work.

A herd or flock—he had no idea what to call it—of strange creatures marched sedately across the swamp some distance away. They looked kind of like giant, fat ducks through his binoculars, but they didn't have wings at all, that he could see, and their very ducklike beaks were proportionately much longer. Their necks were longer too, like a swan's, and their heads bobbed as they moved, swiveling in all directions. Finally, they must have collectively decided the boat was getting too close and they began moving away. Quicker and quicker they moved, with a kind of odd, rolling, waddling motion, and it seemed like the faster they moved, the more panicked they became. One suddenly slammed into an underwater obstruction, a tree or something, and heaved itself up to scamper over it.

"Holy shit, Mr. Ellis!" Isak exclaimed with as much surprise as his voice had ever carried.

The creature's long, gangly, almost delicate-looking legs must have been ten or twelve feet long! Apparently they weren't very strong either, because it was having a hard time clearing the tree. It just kept leaping up, scrabbling pathetically, and falling back to splash in the murky water. What happened next was almost too fast to register in their minds. All they got was an instant-long glimpse of a terrifying jaws clamping tight on the flailing legs and a swirl of some mighty tail. Whatever got the duck thing must have been under the tree, or maybe it came from nearby, drawn by the thrashing sound of distress.

"Holy *shit*!" Isak said again, as the ducklike creature practically capsized, the short, severed stumps of its long legs flailing madly. For an instant, the head popped back out of the water and it *mooed* piteously before the long jaws came again, clamped on the graceful neck, and pulled the head back under.

They kept rowing, a little quicker now, as the capsized corpse continued jerking and heaving as something fed on it from beneath.

"That was . . . a little spooky," Ellis said, controlling his voice. Isak was suddenly peering intently over the side at the dark water, Krag in hand.

Rasik smiled. "A 'spooky' place. You see why I and my followers"— he spit the word—"did not linger here despite our discovery."

"And just where is this 'discovery,' damn you?" Ellis demanded.

"You do not see it?"

"What do you mean? I swear I wasn't fooling! I'll pitch you over the side and let whatever got that big duck have you!"

"A little farther then. Perhaps just a bit to the left. You will see it soon."

They did.

"Sweet Olongapo!" Isak exclaimed when Chack suddenly pointed at something nestled against the western shore of the swamp. "It's a goddamn *ship*!"

Closer they rowed until it was clear for all to see. It *was* a ship, heavily corroded, daubed entirely with rust, and almost consumed by the vegetation along the shoreline. If she was one of theirs, she had to have been in pretty sad shape even before being abandoned here for more than a year and a half. She listed toward shore and was clearly a freighter of some kind, with cargo booms, a single funnel, and a straight up-and-down bow.

"Old," said Ellis. "About six, seven thousand tons, by the look of her. How the hell did she get here?"

"Same way we did, I figger," Isak muttered. "Captain, Mr. Bradford, and Spanky was all talkin' about there maybe bein' other stuff scattered around, got sucked here too. The Squall that got us woulda come through here first, maybe not as bad, maybe worse. Somebody said somethin' about local intensity or somethin'." Isak shrugged, but his expression was pensive. "She looks like a dead body that's bobbed up."

They steered closer until they passed under the dangling anchor. The water lapped gently against her rust-streaked side and Jim looked up at the raised-lettered name.

"*Santa Catalina*," he said. "Huh. Never heard of her. Never saw her. She sure wasn't in Tjilatjap when we were."

"She looks sorta like the *Blackhawk*," said Isak in a strange tone, referring to their old Asiatic Fleet destroyer tenderly.

"Yeah. Same as a hundred other ships," Ellis replied. "*Blackhawk* was built as a freighter and bought by the Navy. I bet she's thirty years old, though."

"So," interrupted Rasik. "Are you satisfied now?"

"So far. Don't give me reason to change my mind. Did you go aboard?"

Rasik shook his head and pointed across the swamp to the east-northeast. "We saw it from there. It does not look like anyone is on it, and it would have been a march of many days to reach. The swampland extends far to the north and there are rivers besides."

"So you don't know what she carries? Taking a lot for granted, aren't you?"

"There is much iron. That alone should be worth my life."

Jim grunted. "Where it is, it might as well be on the moon. I can tell she's beached, and probably flooded too."

"Do you want me to kill him, Captain?" Chack asked. "I would enjoy the . . . honor."

Jim shook his head. "No, a deal's a deal. She's worth *something*, even if it's just a boatload of bolts. Let's see if we can squirm through all that growth on her starboard side and try to get aboard."

It took much hacking and chopping, but they finally maneuvered the boat between the ship and shore. She was beached, all right, and that just added to the mystery of her presence here. A number of trees had fallen across her from shore, but there was a stretch of water as well. Also, eerily, rotten cargo nets draped her starboard side, as if the crew had used them to escape.

"Do we trust them?" Jim asked himself aloud, referring to the nets. Without a word, Chack sprang across to the closest one and scampered up. He disappeared over the bulwark. "I guess so," Jim said philosophically.

"You're heavier than Chack," Isak pointed out.

"Yeah, maybe a little. C'mon." He looked at two of the Marines. "You stay here with the boat. Keep your eyes peeled. You others, come aboard—but keep your eyes peeled, too!"

"What about Rasik?" Chack called from above, peering over the side now.

"He comes too. Might as well let him see what bought his life. What's up there?"

"Hard to say. There is much growth and many big boxes. Nobody seems at home. You can tell me what I see when you get here."

The four detailed Marines, including Corporal Koratin, swiftly climbed the nets. Rasik followed with apparent reluctance. Jim went next, followed by a less than enthusiastic Isak Rueben. When he gained the deck, Jim looked around. The ship was an ungodly mess. Vines crawled over everything and debris was strewn about as if large animals had been tearing into things.

"Stay on your toes," Ellis cautioned. "We might run into just about anything." Even as he spoke, his eyes were drawn to a number of large wooden crates still chained to the deck. They were about forty feet long, ten feet high, and maybe six feet wide. The paint had flaked off of most of them, and the wood underneath was black with mold. Other than the weights, around eight thousand pounds apiece, and faded arrows pointing up, the crates were unmarked. "Chack," he said, motioning the 'Cat to take two Marines and begin searching the ship. Isak and one of the Marines paced him as he approached the crates, looking around for something to crack one open.

There was a slight vibration, barely discernible through the leafy carpet and questing roots beneath their feet. Ellis paused, listening, feeling. "Heads up, Chack!" he called as the three Lemurians peered into the darkness beyond an open hatch. "Did you notice something?" Three heads nodded. "Either that was an earthquake or somebody . . . some*thing* is running around down below. Try to make torches or something. Don't go where it's dark without a light! Something might get you!"

"Somethin' might get *us*," Isak grumbled. He glanced nervously at the bulwark. "Somethin' that eats giant ducks with ten-foot legs!"

"Shut up. Just look around. Find a fire ax or wrecking bar or something!" Jim ordered.

Chack ran up the mushy ladder to the pilothouse. All the windows were gone and the whole space was badly overgrown. He wrenched open the door to what he assumed was the charthouse or the captain's ready quarters. On *Walker* and *Mahan*, the only two human ships he'd ever been aboard, the two had been one and the same, as well as serving other purposes. The compartment had survived severe invasion, and he snatched up a few rags that had probably been clothes. Shelves held moldy, insect-eaten books. He was beginning to read English a little, but not enough to tell what the books were about. No matter. All books contained precious information and his friends would want them. He kicked over the cot he expected to find and discovered the bottom of the mattress cover was intact. Wrapping up the books and grabbing some other fragments of the mattress cover, he descended back down to his Marines. One was holding a kerosene lantern he'd found by venturing a short distance into the darkness. He shook it with a grin and it made a sloshing sound.

"Kind of beat-up, but almost as good as the ones we make in Baalk-pan now, to burn gri-kakka oil. If we use your scraps for torches, we'll be in the dark before we go ten tails—if we don't burn up this dead ship!"

Chack chuckled and, removing his tinderbox from his pack, tossed it to the Marine. "You found it; you light it. Just remember, that's not gri-kakka oil! If it is like the stuff they use for aar-planes, it might burn *you* up!"

The Marine's grin faded, but soon he had the lantern lit and they entered the darkness beyond the hatch. They moved slowly, two facing forward and one walking backward behind them, all their spears out-thrust. Something was in the ship; Chack knew it. It might take forever to search the ship like this, but with its proximity to shore, it was probably unreasonable *not* to expect some kind of threat, whether they'd noticed the vibration or not. They descended a companionway with care and entered a dank passageway. Nothing grew in the darkness, but the deck was mushy and clammy beneath his sandaled feet. It stank and there were occasional large heaps of what might have been excrement.

He stopped and considered. The funnel was aft, so the engineering spaces were as well. Maybe the engine and boilers were salvageable, maybe not. Chances were, the spaces were flooded. He'd spent most of his life aboard massive *Salissa*, and if he'd learned to discern the subtle sensation of buoyancy aboard her, the utter lack of it now convinced him the water level within the ship was probably almost as high as without. That meant they wouldn't be immediately firing up her boilers and steaming out of here. That realization moved her possible cargo to the top of his list of priorities.

"Forward," he said, "to the hold."

He didn't know the layout of the ship, but some things were obvious. The main forward cargo hatch was ahead of them and one deck up. They should find an entrance to the forward hold if they continued down the corridor. There was another heavy vibration, longer this time, and accompanied by a shifting, sliding sound. He glanced at his Marines and saw them exchange nervous blinks in the lantern light. Whatever had infested the ship was big. They couldn't tell where the motion came from because it seemed to resonate through the vessel's very fibers. He handed his short spear to the Marine beside him and unslung the Krag. A hatch gaped before them and they eased slowly toward it. He nodded at the Marine with the lantern, who shone it through the opening. Chack poked his head around the lip and looked inside.

The hold was the largest iron chamber he'd ever seen. Nothing compared to the holds on *Salissa*, which held provisions, barrels of gri-kakka oil, and other necessities of the Home's long, solitary sojourns, but it was far larger than anything *Walker* could boast. In the meager light of the lantern he couldn't even see how far the space extended, but he imagined one could pile all the cannons yet made by the Alliance in the place. He looked down. There was water, but it didn't look too deep, maybe two tails by the curve of the hull. There were also many more huge boxes, just like the ones they'd seen on deck. He wondered what was in them. Smaller boxes, or crates, were stacked outboard on either side of the larger ones. Some were underwater, others partially so, but most seemed high and dry.

"Should we go down?" asked the Marine he'd handed his spear to. She was a female, young and attractive. Her real name was Blas-Ma-Ar, he suddenly remembered, after spending most of the day trying to recall it. He could never forget how and when she'd become a Marine, or the ordeal she'd once endured, but the name that always stuck in his mind was the one Chief Gray had given her: Blossom.

"I think not, for now," he answered softly. "Most of what is here looks to be much the same as what is on deck. Let Cap-i-taan Ellis discover what it is. If it is a good thing, we will know we have more of it." He shook his head. "I dislike moving any nearer the dark water below until we know what manner of creature dwells within this . . . human grave of a ship." The others nodded eager agreement and they retraced their steps. A trip through the engineering spaces seemed appropriate now, as they worked their way to the aft hold. In the corridor, they passed staterooms filled with decaying matter. Some doors were shut, and when they forced them open, they were gratified to see far less damage within the compartments. They found a few more books, in much better condition, and one such room even held a modest armory of unfamiliar weapons and rectangular tins of ammunition. These they carried up to the deck in two trips, along with their booty of books, before proceeding aft.

The boiler room was partially flooded, as Chack had suspected, but a meager light filtered through the grungy, vine-choked skylights, making visibility slightly better. They worked their way carefully along the highest catwalk. A sudden flurry of probably nocturnal lizard birds, disturbed by the lantern, frightened them, but Chack quickly recovered. He wanted to see where they went. They swooped around the space shrieking and flapping until they found a large gap between two twisted plates not far above the waterline. Like sand poured from a cup, they burst through into the daylight beyond.

"So she was sunk here," he surmised. "Or damaged elsewhere, and this is where she came to rest. Curious."

Unlike the boiler room, the engine room was relatively dry. There was water, but not much more than might be accounted for by a year and a half of seepage through riveted seams. They wouldn't be steaming her out of here, but the sight of the rusty but intact machinery was encouraging. Finally, they reached the aft hold and here they found their greatest surprise. More crates like those forward, and many smaller crates filled the space. Everything was a jumble, but Chack recognized hundreds of wooden boxes—maybe thousands—spilling rectangular, green metal cans like those that held ammunition for the big Amer-i-caan machine guns. Enough light diffused into the compartment through the murky water to indicate a substantial hole below the waterline.

"Another wound here then," he said. "Probably the fatal one. Still, though tossed about, many of the boxes are dry. Some are right below

us," he said, pointing. "It looks like each intact box contains several
ammunition cans. Let us claim as many as possible. Proof of the importance of our discovery!" The sight of so much clearly useful ammunition and the better light and visibility subdued his earlier caution.
They laid down their burdens and the Marine who'd been holding the
lantern descended a ladder to the top of a heap of boxes. Chack was the
strongest of the three, so he positioned himself halfway down the ladder, where he might pass the boxes up to Blas-Ma-Ar.

"Here's somethin' might work," Isak said, returning with a small hand
maul, a heavy, rusty chisel, and a piece of pipe.

"Sure," Ellis said. "Let's open this one." He'd been trying to choose
the worst of the rectangular monstrosities, hoping the mysterious contents were already damaged by the elements and opening it wouldn't
make any difference. The crates were unbelievably stout, built to take
significant abuse. He hated to crack any of them, fearing he might ultimately only expose the contents to further, more rapid corrosion. But
whatever they held, it would be a while before anybody could come
retrieve four-ton crates from a swamp! They had to know what was in
them.

"Here, give me that," Ellis said. Isak handed over the chisel and
Ellis positioned it on a seam. "Now the hammer. If I let you do it, you'll
knock my fingers off."

With deft blows, he drove the chisel in, moved it over, and did it
again. When he'd loosened an entire seam, he began prying at it with
the chisel until they could insert the pipe in the gap. "Give me a hand,"
he said, and Isak and the Marine leaned on the pipe with him. A tortured *greeech* sound came from the crate. "Again!"

They worked the pipe up and down, much as Jim had done with the
chisel, taking occasional anxious looks into the dark interior. "Once
more at the top and bottom, and I bet one of us can squeeze in there if
we hold it in the middle!" A little more effort and it was done. Jim inserted the pipe in the center of the seam and handed it over. "Pull!" he
said. The gap widened and he knocked a few nails over with the hammer. Then he stuck his head inside.

"Great God Almighty!" he said, his voice muffled.

"Well, what the hell is it?" Isak demanded acerbically, losing patience.

For a moment, Jim couldn't speak. Before him, as his eyes adjusted, he saw a bright, greasy metal spindle with only slight surface rust. Beyond was a triangular joint with bolts conveniently screwed into six holes. Still farther in he made out a radiator and the beginnings of a distinctive, Curtiss Green–painted shape that he'd never, *ever* expected to see again. Pulling his head back out, he looked at his companions with wide eyes. "Nail it up tight, fellas," he said. "As tight as you possibly can." He looked around at the other, similar crates and a slow grin spread across his face.

"Well . . . what the goddamn hell *is it*?" Isak demanded.

"Ah, they are pleased. I am so glad!" Rasik said to Koratin. The two had stayed back, near the bulwark, talking.

"So it seems. They also seem to have forgotten all about you."

"How convenient."

"Indeed."

"What is the plan?"

"Simple. Do you see that Marine with the Amer-i-caans? He is one of us. He will continue to distract Cap-i-taan Ellis and the wiry one while we take a boat ride."

"The other Marines?"

"With us."

"How delicious!" Rasik exclaimed. "They meant to maroon me, and I will maroon them! A shame we cannot kill them and take their weapons, but with half our group ordered to remain with the boat . . ."

"Precisely. It might prove dangerous. Now all we need to do is slip back down the net while they exult over their prize! After you, Lord King."

Down in the half-flooded aft hold, they heaved the heavy crates up one after another until Chack's shoulders screamed in agony and the others were panting with exertion. Through their increasingly concentrated toil, none of them noticed when it suddenly grew darker in the chamber for a moment as something moved through the light-giving rent in the ship's side. They felt it, though, another vibration like the others, but clearly *here*.

Chack looked down at the upturned face of his Marine on the diminished stack of crates. "Up!" he shouted. "Out of the hold!" He turned to race up the ladder, to get out of the way. Blas-Ma-Ar heaved frantically against the crates stacked above to make room for him to pass and so neither ever saw what got the other Marine. They heard a heavy splash and felt the entire ship judder slightly. More splashes came when the stack of crates collapsed into the water, but by the time Chack reached the top and spun to offer his hand, the other Marine was gone. There'd been no scream, no shout. Nothing but the splash. Chack snatched his Krag and frantically searched the water. He thought he saw a dark shape near the hole in the ship and fired, but all that apparently accomplished was to create an impenetrable haze of gunsmoke. He roared in frustration and fired again anyway.

"Cap-i-taan! Cap-i-taan!" Blas-Ma-Ar was pulling on his leather armor. "He is gone!" Chack shook her off and chambered another round. The almost youngling's voice turned hard. "Cap-i-taan Chack-Sab-At, we have lost a Marine. He died bravely doing his duty. How many lives is this ammunition worth? We still have our duty as well!"

Chack took a deep breath. "Very well. You are right, of course. Come, help me with these crates, but stay alert! There may yet be other dangers within this foul place!"

"Was that shots? That was shots!" Jim exclaimed. "Muffled in the ship. Chack!" He looked around. "Hey, where's Koratin and Rasik?"

"They left," the Marine with them said simply.

"*What?* Wait, never mind that now. C'mon!" Jim snatched his Springfield and raced toward the hatch he'd seen Chack and his party enter. "Chack!" he bellowed, and was relieved to hear an answering shout, still muted by decks and passageways. "Where are you? What did you shoot at?"

"We are here," came a closer reply. "We need help with some heavy objects. Most are still stacked in the entrance to the aft hold." Chack finally appeared at the base of the companionway they were looking down. It was dark as pitch.

"Where's your lantern?" Isak asked.

"Follow this corridor behind me, through the engineering spaces. It is not so dark back there. The lantern marks the spot." Chack paused, taking a breath. "Do not enter the aft hold. Something is in there. Something that got one of my Marines. You should be safe enough," he continued brusquely. "I do not think whatever it was can reach as high as the crates we retrieved."

Jim turned to face the Marine who'd stayed with them. "What's this about Rasik? What do you mean, 'they left'?"

Chack had reached the top of the companionway. He was puffing from exertion and repressed emotion, but he interrupted before the Marine could answer. "Cap-i-taan Ellis, we found much ammunition. Good ammunition for the big machine guns. I lost a good Marine to some monster getting it out. Please let us retrieve it while we know the path is clear. I will try to . . . explain the situation with Rasik as I see it when we are done."

Jim started again to demand an immediate explanation, but Chack had already turned to go back for another crate. "Come on," he said to the others.

It still took several trips by all five of them to retrieve the crates and drag them to the bulwark, where the cargo net was. There was indeed much ammunition. For some reason, Jim wasn't surprised to see the boat gone. "All right," he said at last, gasping from his effort, "what gives?"

Chack was breathing hard too, but when he set his last crate down, he turned to Ellis. "I learned a great lesson once, not long ago, from some very wise men." He glanced at Blas-Ma-Ar, puffing up behind them festooned with the odd-looking weapons and the sack full of books. "Sometimes, for their own sake and the sake of the greater good, there are things leaders keep from followers because they do not have 'need to know.' 'Specially if the knowing—and only the knowing—will cause grief or . . . make things harder." Chack's tail flicked dramatically from one side to the other in a gesture that meant much the same thing as "on the other hand."

"There are also some very few rare times when followers decide their leaders don't have 'need to know.' These . . . what-if—hypothetical?— decisions do not come from distrust, animosity, or for any bad reasons at all." His tail flicked again. "It is the esteem they feel for their leaders that makes them happen." He took a final deep breath and continued. "Sometimes, followers see . . . again, hypothetically . . . that a thing must be done. For reasons of honor, integrity, and the greater good of others, there is no choice." He held up a hand. "But, for those same reasons, leaders need not—*must not*—know about the thing that *must be done*."

"That's not good enough, Chack! What the hell's going on? Tell me; that's an order!"

"Very well, but forgive me if my explaining wanders. I've just lost a Marine and I'm maybe 'rattled,' as you say." He sighed. "I'm poorly prepared right now, but may I answer you . . . philosophically?"

"What is this bullshit?" Jim's 'Cat was good, but Chack was speaking English. He must have practiced saying "philosophically" for a while.

"I take that as yes. You of all people know that a leader's honor and authority must be maintained at all costs."

Jim blanched slightly, but he already knew Chack meant no insult.

Chack continued: "He cannot, *must not*, break his word. Not to his crew, or even his prisoners."

Jim's eyes went wide as he finally realized what Chack was saying. "So you're telling me . . ."

Chack shushed him. "A moment. I'm not *telling* you anything. For the sake of our 'philosophical discussion,' say Cap-i-taan Reddy, our supreme commander, was forced to make a decision . . . a terrible accommodation that must torture him . . . even though it was made for the greater good. You, as his friend and follower, are bound to honor that accommodation in his place. You have no choice, no matter how distasteful you find it, even knowing how much it cost Cap-i-taan Reddy to make it in the first place. You would be tempted as his friend to break the accommodation, but that would be against his orders.

That would reflect poorly on you and him as well. If, however, unknown to you, a small group of followers—who'd gravely suffered, I add—decided they could not bear this accommodation, and took it on themselves—knowing you would be bound to punish them—to break it without your knowledge . . ."

"They're gonna bump off that Rasik bastard!" Isak said gleefully.

Chack stared hard at the fireman. Under his helmet, his ears were probably slicked back in irritation. "I didn't say that. Nor as I understand it, is that their exact intent."

A short time later, the boat pulled back to the ship with Koratin and the two Marines. Immediately, all those on the ship besides Jim Ellis began passing crates and green metal boxes of ammunition down. Ellis fumed. He was relieved and infuriated at the same time. A plot had been hatched under his very nose—again—and although this time it was apparently done to spare him, he was still angry. Much to Isak's consternation, Jim hadn't revealed what he'd seen in the massive crates. It was just too big and it might be better if it remained a secret. Also, in this case, Isak's opinion wasn't worth much. A short time ago, it wouldn't have occurred to him to keep a secret from Chack, but right now he was mad and a little distrustful. Besides, he realized after he thought about it some more, they were going straight from this place into probable battle. If the Grik captured anyone, God forbid, it was best they have no idea what was in the wrecked ship north of Chillchaap. It wouldn't be difficult for the Grik to launch an expedition to destroy it, because who knew when the Allies would be able to come back themselves? No, this he'd keep to himself for a while until he had a chance to think more about it.

"We've done what we came here to do," he said. "We've found Rasik's 'surprise,' and I know what's in the big crates. This ammo will come in real handy. Hell, it's worth the trip by itself." One of the books Chack had retrieved was the ship's manifest. They'd lugged fifty-five thousand rounds of .50 BMG to the bulwark, and a few thousand rounds of .30-06. According to the pages in the book, there were *two million* more rounds in the ship. Quite understandable when one considered what they were for. A lot would be underwater and some might be ruined, but they'd have the brass and bullets. He tucked the manifest under his arm. He'd look it over some more on the way back to the ship.

He studied Koratin as the Marine corporal worked. It was hard to spot, but there was a little blood on his now slightly grungy white leather armor. "What did you do with Rasik, Koratin? I have to know."

Koratin paused in his labor. "He desired to be set ashore here, instead of on the island," he said simply. "As you Amer-i-caans would say, I owed him one."

Ellis clenched his teeth. "Is he alive?"

"Of course! We left him quite well situated, as a matter of fact." He glanced at the other two Marines. "We left him all our rations and even our spears! He should have no difficulty surviving for a considerable period. I swear to you now, before the Sun sinking yonder, Rasik will never die by our hands!"

Slightly mollified—Aryaalans didn't swear by the Sun lightly—Ellis frowned. "But he might wander back to Aryaal, damn it! That's why I wanted him on the island!"

"It matters little. If he'd wanted across, he could have built a raft. No, I think King Rasik will trouble the Alliance no more. He fully understands he is not wanted!"

"Well . . . you still disobeyed an order! Put yourself and these other Marines on report. I'm tempted to put Chack on report as well, as an accessory of some kind!" Jim looked at Chack. "Philosophical, my ass!"

"He had nothing to do with it!" Koratin objected.

"Maybe not, but he knew."

"He may have *surmised*, Cap-i-taan, but he did not know."

Jim looked at Chack again. Maybe Koratin was right. Clearly, Chack had expected them to kill Rasik. "Very well. For now. Let's hurry up and get the hell out of here. It'll be a long row home, mostly in the dark, and with that giant duck-eating . . . whatever it is, and with what got our Marine, that's kind of a creepy thought!" He shook his head. "What is it with this damn world, where everything wants to eat you?"

"Hey, Cap'n Ellis," Isak said suddenly. Once unaccustomed to making unsolicited comments to officers, the fireman blurted them out all the time now. "It just hit me. The ol' *Blackhawk* used to be *named Santa Catalina* before the Navy bought her! One of her snipes told me once when we was alongside." He shook his head. "Guy was one squirrely bastard. Used to run around ever'where tootin' on a duck call! That's why I remembered it all of a sudden. You know, the duck call . . . ? Well, anyway, it's still kinda weird."

Weird was right, Jim thought. Weird the way Isak's brain worked. A few minutes before, he'd been irate that Jim wouldn't tell him what was in the crates. Then he dredged up something like that.

Rasik-Alcas watched the boat pull away through small gaps in the canopy. They hadn't covered his eyes; they'd only gagged him. Now, through the searing waves of agony, he couldn't even scream. They hadn't taken him far, just a short distance beyond the jungle-choked shore. He'd actually been close enough to hear Koratin reassure Ellis that he wasn't dead! How could any creature lie so amazingly well? Rasik himself hadn't suspected a thing—but of course, he hadn't wanted to. Koratin would have known that! As depraved as Rasik knew himself to be, he'd certainly met his final, evil match—and all because of younglings!

He struggled feebly, but the movement only caused more agony. Koratin and the Marines had pinned his arms to the trunk of a wide subaa tree, right through the twinbones. He couldn't even tear himself free! Not that it would do any good. They'd done the same to the twinbones in his legs and then made a small incision in his belly. Not large enough to bleed him to death, but quite large enough to pull his intestines through. The squirming, tearing sensation had been more than he could bear, and he'd finally passed out. When he awoke, his murderers were gone. Food was scattered on the ground all around him— and his guts had been strung five or six tails away and hung on a limb.

He clenched his eyes shut as biting insects buzzed around his entrails. If only he'd known! How *could* he have known? Not only Koratin's precious, despicable younglings had perished on *Nerracca*—the Home the Japanese destroyed—but so had the younglings or mates of all his conspirators! He *should* have had a way of knowing that. *Would* have, if he'd been thinking clearly! Even so, what did younglings measure against the power Koratin could have had as King Rasik-Alcas's Supreme Minister? Younglings were simple to replace, even a pleasure, but the kind of power Koratin had denied was a priceless, precious thing. It was madness!

Even as Rasik-Alcas considered these imponderables and watched the boat grow small against the setting sun, the tiny, timid night predators began to gather around.

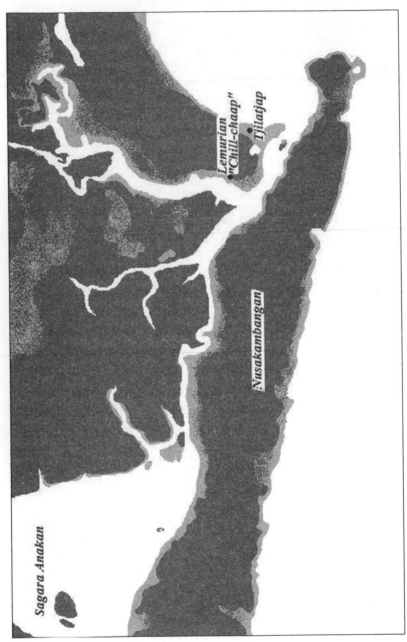

Environs of Tjilatjap

*M*att looked at the message form Clancy had handed him. The fact they now had relatively reliable communications was a godsend in many ways. He could keep track of all the various operations under way and he could even exchange semi-private correspondence with Sandra back in Baalkpan. He got daily updates—when atmospherics didn't interfere—on the progress made on *Walker* and all the other projects of the Alliance. He was a little worried about the silence from Laumer, but not *too* worried. The ex-Grik "tankers" they'd sent with both bunker-grade and diesel fuel should arrive there soon. Still, he'd received so much bad, sometimes calamitous news typed as neatly as their battered typewriters could manage on the dwindling message forms, he always accepted them with a trace of apprehension.

The news today was anything but bad. In fact, it was almost horrifyingly good. Jim Ellis had discovered Rasik's secret in the form of a battered freighter marooned in the swamps north of Chill-chaap. Clearly, the ship had somehow come through the same Squall they had. Jim hadn't found the ship's log, but her manifest told the story. She'd been attempting a mission similar to the one doomed *Langley* and a few old freighters had been trying to accomplish: a last-ditch effort to beef up Java's air defenses. *Langley* and the freighters—including *Santa Catalina*—had been ferrying P-40 fighters, spare engines, tires, parts, fuel tanks, and millions of rounds of ammunition to the beleaguered island. *Langley* was caught short and bombed into a sinking wreck. Matt had heard one of the other freighters made it to Tjilatjap, but since there was no nearby airfield, they'd actually assembled the planes dockside and were attempting to *tow* them overland on refugee-choked roads! He didn't know if they'd ever made it to an airstrip or not. Judging by Jim's report, *Santa Catalina* had been trying to do the same thing.

The only explanation for her condition, position, her very presence in this world, was that she too must have been damaged at sea, passed through the Squall, and arrived at a far different Tjilatjap. The Grik must have already sacked Chill-Chaap and the ship's captain, likely wondering where he was, proceeded as far upriver as he could to preserve his cargo and his ship from the deeper waters. Jim found no trace of the crew or the pilots who would have accompanied the planes. Maybe they were still out there somewhere, but more likely they hadn't survived their contact with this terrible world. Matt shook his head. Much the same would probably have happened to *Walker* and her crew if she hadn't made friends so quickly.

The existence of the ship and her cargo was an incredible stroke of luck, however, maybe even a war winner if they could salvage any of the planes. Jim thought it likely. The manifest totaled twenty-eight aircraft. Curtiss P-40Es! If they saved only half of them, they'd have more than the Philippines had after the first few days of the war. The reason it was horrifying was that Matt wanted those planes *now* and he had no way of getting them. Isak Rueben had said that the ship's engines were probably okay, but the fireroom was a shambles. She was also "kind of sunk," according to the report, so there'd be no salvaging her on a shoestring. An ecstatic Ben Mallory quickly fired back a suggestion from Baalkpan that they immediately launch an expedition to recover the planes. If they could hack an airstrip out of the jungle alongside the ship and somehow power her cargo cranes, they could simply assemble the planes and fly them out.

Matt knew there'd be nothing "simple" about it. The project would require a small army and there'd be no way to keep that secret. They'd also need a higher-grade fuel than the PBY had required and they'd have to cut airstrips everywhere they went to accommodate the planes. He'd been impressed by Jim's initial reaction to remain tight-lipped about the find, but realistically, it probably didn't matter. There was no risk of the Grik or even the Japanese infiltrating their ranks, and if they had spies on the island, they were just as likely to find the ship on their own. If the current Allied offensive was successful, they'd soon have the Grik pushed back almost to Ceylon, making long forays by enemy vessels into the Allied rear even more unlikely. Right now, every ship in Matt's squadron was essential where it was. They'd bottled up the approaches to Singapore and captured or destroyed a few ships— mostly leaving. His assault was essentially awaiting only Ellis and *Dowden*, and the extra weight of metal her broadside might add to the fight. He'd recommend to Adar that they send a small garrison to Tjilatjap and maybe at least begin recovery and stabilization efforts. That made good sense. But right now, his own plate was heaping full.

"A hell of a thing," Garrett commented, reading over his shoulder. "If we'd had those planes in the Philippines, we might still be there."

Matt grunted. "We had a hell of a lot more than that to start with and it didn't matter much. I don't know. MacArthur might have been some kind of Army genius, but he understood even less about his own Air Corps than he did about naval operations." He frowned. "I kind of wish we had him with us now, though. How's Pete's attack plan coming?"

"Pretty good, I think." Garrett looked at Matt. "Pete's done a swell job. I wouldn't be pining for that Army prima donna if I were you."

Matt laughed. "Not 'pining,' but I do wish I had someone else to bounce Pete's plans off of."

"Don't sell yourself short, Skipper. You've done fine onshore." Garrett looked thoughtful. "Besides, you have Rolak and Queen Maraan. Unlike our sea folk friends, they've been fighting on land all their lives. Pete and Safir did a good job chopping up that Grik force on Madura . . . I mean, B'mbaado."

"They sure did," Matt reflected. He took a breath. "Jim should be here in three days. Four at the outside—if the weather holds. Don't forget, this is the stormy time of year!" He chuckled grimly. Protection from the terrible "Strakkas" that struck the region was another reason they needed Singapore in their hands. "We'll pass the word via wireless or couriers for all ships to assemble just west of Bintan Island at that time. We'll have a final conference before we kick off the show."

"You want to invite Jenks?"

Matt nodded. "He's seen *why* we fight now and I think he's more sympathetic than ever before. He'll want to see *how* we fight. I think I'll give him a chance to get in closer this time, if he likes."

Captain Jim Ellis was piped aboard *Donaghey* and received a warm welcome. *Dowden* had made a quick passage, mostly under sail with the stout winds of some distant storm. He was a little surprised to be openly congratulated for his find—he still hadn't told his crew what he'd seen—and only his wireless operator and exec knew what the flurry of transmissions, prodded mostly by Ben Mallory, were about.

"Doesn't matter, Jim," Matt told him. "Adar has already sent a small force to secure the area. He wouldn't let Mallory go; he's still training pilots for the Nancys and he's fit to bust! But if we're successful, he'll have plenty of time to go play with his new toys."

"You're not going to give him a squadron, or wing, or whatever?" Jim asked.

"Hell, no! He's taught some guys and 'Cats to fly, but he's the only man we've got who's ever actually had real pilot training. He majored in aeronautical engineering at West Point, too. Even flew with Colonel Doolittle a few times. How do you think he got the Nancys up so fast?"

"I'll be damned."

"Yeah. He doesn't brag on it. I didn't know it either until he started pitching for the Nancys in the first place. In hindsight, we never should've let him risk his neck so much in that old PBY Catalina."

"But then we'd all be dead."

Matt nodded philosophically. "True. As a matter of fact, if we still had the damn thing, I'd tell him to take it up and scout Singapore for us."

"What do we know?"

"Not much. C'mon, let's adjourn to the wardroom. Juan'll fix you something cool to drink while the rest of the captains and commanders arrive."

Dennis Silva was hunting, as usual, during his free time. Besides being a pleasant diversion for him, it was an increasingly important chore. With so many foreign troops, artisans, and laborers in Baalkpan, the city needed more fresh meat than ever before, and the depleted fishing fleet was stretched to the limit. The ubiquitous polta fruit supplied a wide variety of nutrients the 'Cats, and apparently humans, needed, and other fruits and some vegetables were used as well, but both species needed plenty of animal protein. That left Silva with all the justification he needed to "go a-huntin'" regularly.

He did sometimes find himself craving some of the strangest things, though—stuff he'd always hated. Like beets. The killing grounds around Baalkpan had been planted with many different varieties of tuber and there was a root that tasted a little like beets that he sort of liked. It was odd. He'd always shunned vegetables as superfluous, useless things that took up space on his plate where more meat could have been. Now, some days, he figured he'd kill for a tomato—or a mess of black-eyed peas. Regardless, hunting was necessary. It got him out of the "house," away from the women, and let him kill things on a regular basis.

Pam and Risa were swell, but they had a tendency to coddle him. That could get old, despite the benefits. Technically, he was still sort of convalescing, but he felt as good as he figured he ever would. He was up to full speed working in the factory for Campeti or fooling around with Bernie's projects, but when he had any spare time at all, he headed for the jungle with the Hunter.

The Hunter was a scrawny, almost ancient Lemurian with a silver-streaked pelt and several missing teeth. He was barely taller than Rebecca, but like most 'Cats, he was incredibly strong. His weapon of choice was a massive crossbow that probably weighed as much as he did, and he carried it with a nonchalant ease Silva could only envy. He had guts too. Silva remembered when "Moe" (he called the Hunter Moe, since if the old 'Cat ever had a real name, he didn't remember it) had used *himself* to bait the super lizard that got Tony Scott so Silva could avenge his friend. They'd finally managed to kill the thing, but it was a close call and one of the reasons Dennis had built his massive Super Lizard Gun. So far, he hadn't found any super lizards to test it on. It killed the absolute, literal hell out of the big, dangerous rhino-pigs he and Moe pursued for their succulent meat, but rhino-pigs weren't much of a challenge for the thing. He'd taken to waiting for the creatures to bunch up so he could see how many the gun would kill with a single shot. So far, the record was four.

Enjoyable as any day in the woods was, Dennis and Moe rather doubted they'd get much chance to test the big gun's potential on this trip. In addition to the usual bearers they brought to deal with their kills, Courtney Bradford, Lawrence, and Abel Cook had tagged along. Lawrence's fieldcraft wasn't bad. His species were natural predators, and the little guy had an almost childlike desire to please. He also really liked Silva, even though the big man had shot him once. The fact that his adored Rebecca liked him and considered Silva a demented big brother was probably sufficient explanation. Lawrence wasn't the problem. Courtney Bradford and his young protégé, Abel Cook, still had a lot to learn.

The bearers hung back, letting Dennis and Moe do all the hunting, but Bradford and Cook stayed right up with them. It irked Silva a little, but he figured Abel needed to do more "man stuff" and Bradford was, well, Bradford. He didn't come along often. He was a busy, much-sought-after man. He could be a pain in the ass in the field, making too much noise or chasing after a lizard, but Dennis enjoyed it when he was around. Courtney was a hoot, and too much seriousness was hard on Dennis Silva. He missed the conversation Courtney provided, no matter how bizarre.

"What's that?" Silva whispered as a small, striped reptile that looked like a fat ribbon snake with legs scampered across their path. They were hunting the pipeline cut where they'd killed the super lizard, and the earth was thick and mushy beneath their feet. Moe murmured something unpronounceable and shrugged. Probably not something fit to eat then, Silva decided. Certainly not worth the abuse of a shot. He wondered what Courtney Bradford would have done if he'd seen it. Chase after it on all fours, most likely. At the moment, Courtney was absorbed by retelling the legendary Super Lizard Safari to Abel.

Moe held up a hand and they all froze. He'd sensed something. Motioning them down to the moldy turf, he beckoned them to follow on their bellies. Slowly scooching along almost soundlessly in the damp, rotting material, they moved ahead. Courtney's tale had ceased. Maybe he was starting to get it after all. Moe eased a little farther ahead of them, stopped again, then turned to look back, grinning.

"Rhino-pigs, many," he hissed. "Come up. We have wind so they not smell, but they hear good. Be quiet!"

Even slower, Silva crept forward. Lawrence practically flowed beside him, silent as death. Bradford and Abel brought up the rear. They began to hear the heavy thud of hooves and an incessant, contented grunting. Silva reached Moe's position and peered over a little mound that might once have been a tree.

"Quite a swarm," he acknowledged. "They're just rootin' along. Don't seem too worried. I guess you were right. It takes a while for another super lizard to move in on an old one's territory."

"Too far?" Moe asked.

Dennis calculated the range. It was only about a hundred yards to the pack of animals, but he wanted to get as many as he could with a single shot. That was part of the game as well as his stated "field test" rationale.

"Nah. It oughta do. If anything, we might be too close. Speed don't always mean penetration, an' it ain't like I can reduce my charge." Carefully, he eased the big gun forward.

Rhino-pigs looked much like their cousins back home. Sort of like giant razorbacks with bigger tusks and an odd-looking horn on the top of their heads. At first glance, Dennis hadn't really thought the horn would be good for much, but once he'd seen one take off like a hot torpedo, he'd realized that the forward-hooking horn would be bad news for a taller predator's exposed underbelly. The tusks would slash a man as wickedly as their Alabama brethren. Of course, at six hundred to a thousand pounds, they could just stomp you into paste, too.

"How exciting!" murmured Bradford, joining them at last. "Which one will you take?" Abel said nothing, but he was clearly fascinated.

Dennis eased the gun farther forward until the butt plate rested against his shoulder. He really wasn't looking forward to firing the thing from a prone position. He reached forward and adjusted the rear sight's elevation. As powerful as the weapon was, it had a markedly high trajectory and he'd sighted it in for fifty-yard intervals. When raised, the rear sight stood about four inches high, and the range markers were considerably farther apart the higher they went.

"I'll take 'em as they come," he announced. He was trying a new bullet today. It was essentially the same lead slug he'd used before, but it was capped and cored with a pointed bronze "penetrator." The penetrator made the bullet a little longer, to keep the same weight, and he wasn't entirely sure it would be as stable in flight. He settled in on the stock and peered through the sights. A mighty boar was shoveling great snoutfuls of turf aside as it searched for insects and roots. The clacking, gnashing sounds of tusks were constant.

"You go for big bull . . . boar . . ." Moe said. "I tell when most are best."

"Sure."

"Why not shoot now?" Abel asked. "There are half a dozen behind him."

"Gotta line up their vitals, not just their bodies," Silva answered absently. He checked his priming powder and thumbed the hammer to full cock. Settling back in, he caressed the trigger, waiting for the word.

The wait seemed interminable. A couple of times, Moe tensed, and it seemed like he was about to give the signal, but then he relaxed slightly. Through it all, Silva was as still as stone except for the tiny adjustments he made to his aim, following the vitals of the big boar. Sweat dripped unnoticed down his face and soaked the black patch covering his left eye.

"Now," said Moe, without any warning at all. Almost before the word was fully uttered, Silva squeezed the trigger. The flint leaped forward, scraping a shower of yellow-hot sparks from the frizzen and kicking it open to expose the priming powder. A jet of flame and white smoke erupted in front of Silva's face, and with a horrendous cracking roar, the main charge vomited the quarter pound missile from the barrel—and heaved Silva's shoulder a foot backward. There was a nightmarish shrieking squeal that reverberated in the cut, and through the smoke they saw the big boar perform an almost vertical leaping lunge. He collapsed in the turf, back feet kicking spastically. There was pandemonium among the rest of the herd. Two other dark shapes lay where they'd fallen; another was performing writhing cartwheels. The rest were thundering in all directions like small locomotives gone amok. One large beast came directly at them, and Moe let fly with his massive crossbow, driving a shaft through the charging creature's snout and probably straight into its brain. It collapsed in a heap perhaps a dozen yards short of their position. That fast, all the surviving rhino-pigs were gone, vanishing into the dense growth on either side of the cut.

Silva was standing, already pouring another charge of powder down the massive gun. "Whoo-ee!" he said excitedly. "Good stick, Moe! I figgered I was gonna hafta poke that last one off us with my rifle muzzle!" He shook his head and slapped the holstered 1911 Colt at his side. "Never would've even got my pistol out!"

Lawrence scampered forward with nothing but a short spear. With a peculiar cry, he plunged it into the one still-thrashing pig.

Dennis nodded toward him, smiling. "Junior's growin' up," he said, almost wistfully. "Come on, fellas. Let's see how many we got besides ol' Moe's there!"

Having heard the shot, the bearers were already approaching. They knew whenever Silva fired his big gun, there'd be work to do.

Abel stared at Moe's rhino-pig as they passed it. "Will they clean the beasts here?" he asked.

"Sure. No sense waggin' their guts back. Makes 'em lighter."

"I'd like to watch." He looked at Silva. "Not that I'm finished watching you, sir! You are every bit as fascinating as any entrails, I'm sure!"

Silva blinked. "Yeah, well, thanks." With his rifle fully loaded and at the ready, Silva marched forward to view the carnage he'd created. "Four for sure." He beamed. "Big sumbitches line up, little sumbitches bunch up!" He held out the Doom Whomper. "What a gun!"

"Two 'lood trails!" Lawrence announced. His voice was a little shaky, but he seemed excited. He was spattered with the blood of the pig he'd finished. Dennis sobered.

"Rats. We'll hafta go after 'em, and they're dangerous enough when they ain't hurt and sore at you. Mr. Bradford, why don't you and young Abel here stay and study these boogers while the bearers cut 'em up. Me and Moe"—he glanced at the "lizard"—"and Larry'll track these other ones."

They quickly found the first rhino-pig. It hadn't gone far and had probably bled out within moments of being hit. Silva wasn't sure which one it was in the lineup, but the entry and exit wounds were quite large and about the same size, so he figured it was toward the back. Moe trilled a call to the bearers and, returning to the cut, the three trackers commenced following the final blood trail. This one put them a little on edge, and they'd saved it for last for a reason. Moe said the color of the blood indicated a liver hit. A fatal wound certainly, but not necessarily *immediately* fatal. The more time they gave the beast to die in peace, the less likely it would be to kill one of them when they found it.

They advanced carefully. Rhino-pigs were notorious for playing dead when wounded. Sometimes, their last act was to charge a tracker, taking revenge with its final breath. Moe always said never to approach a "dead" rhino-pig lying on his belly. One that was *really* dead couldn't lie like that; it would always lie on its side. If it was on its belly, it was poised to strike.

They crept along a considerable distance, the blood trail clear and dark, the ground disturbance unmistakable. This was some of the densest jungle Dennis had been in yet. The path they'd once followed while tracking the super lizard was on the east side of the cut and had been fairly easy going, in retrospect. It had been made by an animal dozens of times as big as a rhino-pig. This path wasn't much larger than the animal that left it, and sometimes all of them were forced to their hands and knees. It was like following a shark down a tunnel, Dennis thought uncomfortably. At some point you knew you were bound to run into the bastard, and by then, he was probably turned around and waiting. Raucous cries permeated the jungle and harsh coughs and snorts stopped their progress occasionally. Dennis knew about super lizards and rhino-pigs and many other creatures by now, but only Moe had a real idea what other dangerous predators they were likely to meet. Lawrence proceeded, alert to every movement, his short spear held before him like a sword. *Little lizard's really a pretty good guy to have with you, times like this,* Dennis decided. He knew *he* was in over his depth. He'd never been this far from the cut before.

With considerable relief, they noticed the jungle begin to thin as they approached one of the many clearings probably created by lightning fires. This one was recent, and blackened stumps protruded through the lush, fresh undergrowth. The foliage was really a type of long-leafed grass, Dennis realized, and it was damp and clingy to walk through, even though it was barely calf-high. Lots of herbivores probably frequented places like this, he thought. They heard a squeal. Then another. Lawrence's fur bristled and his eyes became intense as he sniffed the air.

"Just ahead!" Moe told them.

"Not just rhino-'ig," hissed Lawrence with a note of caution.

"What else?" asked Dennis.

"Not sure. Strange, 'ut' a'iliar." He shook his head in frustration. "Like thing I should know."

As quietly as possible, they picked up the pace. There was a little rise, probably formed by burned and rotten deadfall, and they crept up to the peak.

Below them, little more than sixty yards away, three rust-colored Grik, or lizards . . . or something stood around a dead rhino-pig. Their clawed hands held spears that were no more than sharpened sticks, but the points were black with blood. They seemed to be resting from their exertions, or complimenting one another on their prowess, and for the moment, at least, their guard was down.

With a Lemurian curse, Moe brought his crossbow up.

"What the . . . Hey, wait a goddamn minute!" Silva said, pushing the crossbow down. "What the hell? There might be dozens of the bastards!"

"No, just those," Moe said, trying to wrench his weapon free. "They steal our meat! They just big skuggiks!"

"You mean they *live* here?" Silva whispered savagely. "You never said there was jungle Griks on Borno!"

"Like Griks, but not!" Moe insisted. "I tell. Others tell! There not many on Borno, but we kill them when we see them! Let them live on little islands! Not here!"

Suddenly, Silva did remember. He remembered Nakja-Mur mentioning that the Grik on Borneo were primitive and didn't know tools, and they'd been hunted to near extinction. Only on islands like Bali—small or far away—were they left alone. They *had* been told, but he, at least, had forgotten.

"*I* like Grik, 'ut not," Lawrence hissed.

The ground beneath them seemed to shake and the foliage near the trio of lizards exploded into the clearing. Within the confetti of leaves and brush charged a young super lizard! The "Grik," or whatever they were, scattered in three directions. Apparently more interested in live prey than the dead pig, the monster fixed its gaze on one rusty shape and bolted after it with the amazing speed Silva knew the things were capable of.

"Shit!" growled Silva, and rose to a knee. He cocked his big gun and pulled it to his shoulder, raising the stock to his cheek. For an instant, he honestly didn't know what he was doing, but he didn't really need to. Threat assessment had always been one of his strong suits, whether the question was whom to throw the first punch at in a bar, or which target to engage. There *was* that little incident when he'd shot Lawrence, but it was a perfectly understandable mistake and the little guy didn't hold a grudge. . . . His sights found the pocket behind the super lizard's right arm. He eased a little right to lead the target and squeezed the trigger.

The recoil nearly tossed him on his back. It *did* put him on his butt. It was the first time he'd ever fired the Doom Whomper from a kneeling position. Quickly, he reversed the rifle and blew down the barrel, sending a jet of smoke out the vent. Even as he reached for another charge, he was looking to see the results of his shot. At first, there seemed to be no effect. The rusty lizard running for its life dropped to the ground, cowering from the shockingly loud report, most likely. On the other hand, it may have been a final instinctive act of self-preservation. The super lizard was almost upon it. Suddenly, the huge monster just stopped running, as if remembering it had forgotten something in the woods. It swayed a little, caught itself, looked at its prey, and even glared around the clearing. With no further ado, the bulb went out and the beast plummeted to the ground with a rumbling crash.

"Hot damn!" Silva crowed, pouring the charge and seating the bullet atop it. "He may not be a trophy as such critters go, but one shot's one shot!"

"Have care," Moe cautioned. The red-brown lizards were gathering near the one who'd almost bought it, helping it to its feet. Dennis didn't miss the significance of that. All the while, the trio of lizards was staring at them inscrutably. "Those vermin is easy to kill at a . . . far. Up close, they dangerous."

"You leave them lizards be," Silva said.

"Why? We no kill them, them stay here. I told you, them . . . they steal! They dangerous scavengers. Dangerous to hunters. They stay, more come. Be dangerous to city."

"Did ol' Nakja-Mur know you was killin' 'em whenever you saw 'em?" Silva asked.

"Of course. We always kill them when get so close to Baalkpan. Borno is big; them no need be here."

"Does Adar know you're killin' 'em? Does he even know about 'em?" Silva asked. "Bradford woulda had puppies just to gawk at 'em if he'd'a known there was anything so much like Griks right here on Borneo."

Moe didn't answer at first. Even he seemed to realize Dennis was right. "I no see them," he said at last. "I no see 'ungle Griks,' you call them, for five, six seasons. They gone. Good gone, say me." He looked at Lawrence, comprehension dawning. "But they not Griks. Like Griks, but not."

"Larry here looks enough like a Grik that I shot him once," Silva said. "Here you are huntin' with him. Then you rear up and start to kill some lizards that look more like him than they do Griks. I guess I'm sorta confused. Did it ever occur to you to try to *talk* to one of them buggers?" he asked, pointing at the trio still standing, staring back at them. "Did it ever occur to *anybody*? Lord knows I'm not much of a talker myself and I sure ain't one to judge. Killin' a problem's a quicker, more permanent way to solve one than talkin' to it any day, you ask me, but knowin' Larry has made me a little more selective about the lizard problems I kill on sight."

The rusty lizards seemed to decide it was time to go. They gathered their spears but made no move to retrieve the rhino-pig when they went near it. They did look at their multispecies benefactors quite often, however. One of them, maybe the one Silva had saved, pointed at the super lizard with its spear and then pointed it at Silva, adding a resonant cry like a choking goat. Dennis nearly jumped out of his skin when Lawrence replied with something that sounded similar. All three lizards stopped then, looking back, black crests rising on their heads. Another moment passed and then they melted into the trees.

"Goddamn, Larry!" Silva exclaimed. "Don't do that! Most of the time, you talk better than me. That lizard lingo gives me the creeps!"

There was movement in the jungle behind them, but it was only the bearers coming to the sound of Silva's gun. Bradford and Abel were with them. All knew Moe would have finished the rhino-pig with his massive crossbow, so Silva must have found them a more substantial load.

"What did you shoot?" puffed Courtney, leading the others and hastening to join them.

"Teenage super lizard," Silva said offhandedly.

"Splendid, splendid! I do hope you didn't damage the skull this time! I so want an undamaged skull! I wish I'd been here to see it!"

"Honest to God, I wish you'd been here too," Silva said. He went on to describe their encounter.

"Amazing, remarkable!" Courtney looked at Moe. "Does Adar know of these creatures?" he asked, echoing Silva's unanswered question.

"Maybe yes, maybe no," Moe conceded. "Adar is of sea folk. Sea folk know lizards on Bali and other places . . . maybe not here."

"I must speak to him about an expedition to make contact!" Bradford declared.

"That may be a little tough," Silva said. "Ol' Moe here says he and other hunters been killin' 'em on sight for years. Kinda like Injuns." He brightened. "Injun jungle lizards!"

"Oh, dear!" Courtney exclaimed. He turned to Lawrence. "But you spoke to them! What did they say?"

Lawrence flared his new, longer tail plumage and tried to shrug. "I don't know. They could have said, 'Thanks 'or killing the 'ig lizard.'"

"Well . . . what did you say to them?"

"'Good day.'"

"So, what do we know, sir?" asked Chack. He was sitting as close as— probably closer than—was "decent" to Safir Maraan. His reunion with the Orphan Queen had been brief, but almost electric with suppressed passion when Safir arrived on the flagship for the conference.

Matt glanced at Jim and sighed. "Damn little. A week ago, we put a squad of Marines ashore here." He indicated the east-southeast coast of the island on a hand-drawn copy of a Navy chart tacked to the bulkhead. "They've moved to about here." He pointed to the vicinity where the map oddly showed the old British fortress garrison buildings. Whoever had drawn it had made an almost exact copy of *Walker*'s old chart. "Of course, none of this stuff is there." He paused. "In fact, the shoreline's not even exactly the same, and some of these little islands are bigger single islands now. Maybe more proof of Courtney's ice-age theory. Anyway, we'll have to watch the depth going in." He looked around the cramped compartment. "The Marines have set up one of Mr. Riggs's little generators and have been in intermittent contact. Intermittent because they have to move a lot. Evidently, supplies are running pretty low and the Grik are doing a lot of hunting. That doesn't mean they're not expecting us, but it does mean they're spread out a little. Maybe a lot."

"*Are* they expecting us?" Jim asked.

"They have to be expecting *something*. Most of the ships we've captured or destroyed were headed out, probably for Ceylon. Those ships were *packed*, friends. That's why most had to be destroyed. A few supply ships have tried to make it in, but to my knowledge, none has gotten past us. That alone is enough to alarm a savvy Grik Hij that we've cut his sea-lanes. Our spotters say there's a large concentration of enemy troops here." He pointed again at the chart, near where the British repair facilities would have been. "Apparently, it's a burgeoning port facility here as well." He shrugged. "You know, I used to wonder why Lemurians—and this was originally a Lemurian colony of Batavia, I understand—always seemed to pick the same spots for cities that humans did." He scratched his chin. "The old Scrolls might have had something to do with that, but mainly I figure if a place is a good spot for a city or a port, it's a good spot for a city or a port, no matter what species you are!" There were a few chuckles. "Anyway, the spotters also say there are a lot of ships anchored off those facilities, more than they can account for."

"What do you mean?" Jenks asked, speaking for the first time.

"Well, first you have to understand the sheer number of Grik we killed when they came against Baalkpan." He shook his head. "Lots of ships got away, but they were mainly the ones that offloaded their troops on the south coast. I bet they came home nearly empty. They didn't leave them in Aryaal, so they must have brought them here. Second, like I said, the ships we've destroyed were packed, maybe with twice their usual number. That convinces me our scouts have been right all along. They're pulling out of Singapore too."

"Well, that's excellent news, certainly," Jenks proclaimed. "All you need do is wait for them to leave and then take the place over."

"It's not that simple. First, and I really don't expect you to understand this yet, but the Grik don't act that way. They attack. Period. If they're pulling out, somebody up the chain has started thinking *strategically*, and that bugs me. If that's the case, it lends even more importance to our objectives, or eventually, we'll be right back where we started."

"And what are those objectives?"

"Foremost is to kill Grik, of course. The more we kill now, the fewer we'll have to face later. Second, I want as many of those ships as we can get. They may be foul and full of the . . . remains of their sick practices, but they're relatively well made. We need them and I'm afraid they mean to destroy them. Why else send so many troops out on so few ships? Some may have been damaged fighting us, but if they made it here, chances are they're fit for salvage. Third, again according to our spotters, the Grik spent a lot of time and effort on the port facilities.

They may not have a dry dock, or otherwise be up to Baalkpan's standards, but they're better than anything in Aryaal. I want those facilities intact." He looked around the compartment, meeting every gaze. "Finally, the spotters have seen a little compound where a few Japs are being held. We have to save them."

There were a few mutters of protest and others looked uncomfortable. A few tails swished indignantly. Matt held up his hands. "I know what you're thinking: what for?" He sighed. "Two reasons, really. No, three. First, chances are, if they were helping the Grik of their own free will they wouldn't be in a compound. Second, we might be able to get some information out of them. They've been to Ceylon and they know what the defenses are like. They've had a far different experience than Commander Okada, and they might even be willing to actively help us. Finally, and most important . . . we just *have* to, is all. If the spotters had seen a compound full of 'Cats, we'd have to save them, wouldn't we?"

"Of course," Safir replied. "But these Jaaps are the enemy too, are they not?"

"Maybe not. Just because some Aryaalans once followed an evil king, are they evil too? Maybe some are, and I'm sure Lord Rolak has his eyes out for any such, but not all. And personally, I'd rather kill each and every one of them with my bare hands than leave them to the fate they might face at the hands of the Grik."

Finally, there were nods in the room, and a few comments of support.

"Very well," Matt continued, "with that, I'll let Generals Alden, Rolak, and Safir Maraan enlighten us with their brilliant plan to accomplish all these objectives." He winced at Pete. "Sorry about the last addition, but I only just heard."

"It's okay, Skipper. I think we can add it in."

"Do you think, General Alden, you might add in some supporting role for *Achilles*?" Jenks asked.

Matt had actually been expecting the offer. He and Jenks might never become friends, but they'd developed considerable mutual respect and even admiration during the commodore's frequent visits aboard *Donaghey*. Matt also knew that the very savagery of their enemy had gnawed at Jenks since he first set foot on the Aryaal dock. He'd slowly come to the same conviction his princess had: sooner or later, the Empire he served most certainly had a stake in this fight.

Pete glanced at Matt and saw him nod. "Why, of course, Commodore. Always happy for another gun platform, especially one as maneuverable as yours."

"My Marines are at your disposal too," Jenks added, "as a reserve if you need it, or possibly as a flanking support of some kind?"

"That's very generous," Alden said, recognizing that the offer was smart as well. Throwing Jenks's untried Marines into a pivotal part of the plan at the last minute might wreck the whole operation, and Pete would never have done it. The Imperial clearly recognized the latter, at least. This way his troops could participate on some level and he avoided the insult of a refusal. Jenks was pretty sharp, Pete decided. "We could use a little more flank security, with all those Grik hunters running around," he said. He advanced to the chart tacked to the bulkhead. "Now, here's the deal. The operation"—he grinned—"is called Singapore Swing. At oh one hundred hours tomorrow morning, the fleet elements will be in position off these beaches, here, here, and here. . . ."

I t was long after dark when Silva's hunting party neared the environs of Baalkpan. The bearers had dragged the masses of meat on travois down to the original riverside fueling pier and transferred it to square, flat barges. From there, they slowly towed the barges to the city behind Scott's launch. As usual, Moe didn't accompany them past the pier, but disappeared into the jungle as soon as the hunt was done. Even Silva didn't know where he lived, and he was probably the closest thing to a friend the old Lemurian had. The sun went down quickly, as was its custom, and for a time the large, voracious insects pestered them as they traversed the estuary. The breeze of the bay protected them a little as they drew nearer the city.

"What the devil?" Silva asked as they caught sight of the old fitting-out pier. The city was lit up like it hadn't been in a long time, and a major party appeared to be under way.

"Most interesting," observed Bradford. "One would like to speculate that they've heard the news of our return after such an auspicious and successful venture as ours today, but I honestly doubt that's the case."

"Nobody invited you to a party neither?" Silva grumped.

"Indeed not. I can't imagine what might have transpired in our absence to cause such revelry. Perhaps the war is over?"

Silva grunted. "We musta missed *something*, but I doubt that's it. Besides, they wouldn't dare win the war without lettin' me in on it. I'm gonna personally poke that Sequestural Lizard Mother through the head with one o' Lanier's U.S.-marked butter knives. I told the skipper so. If she fell off the pot an' broke her neck, I'm gonna be mighty sore."

Abel stirred from where he'd been sleeping curled up next to Lawrence in the stern sheets. "Look!" he said a little blearily. "*Walker* is lit up! Her aft searchlight tower has been reinstalled and they are shining the light about!"

"Ahhh!" roared Silva when the beam rested momentarily on the approaching launch and its train of barges. He shielded his eyes from the painful glare. "Goddamn EMs are horsin' around! They musta managed to twist a couple o' wires together an' thought that was worth a hootenanny!" He chuckled. "Maybe Rodriguez'll point the light at Laney! He can't stand that stupid prick. 'Hey, Ronson, what's that smolderin' pile o' bones?' 'Oh, that's just Laney. Thought I saw a roach on deck!'" Silva laughed.

Abel looked at him in the reflected light—the searchlight beam had passed on—and wondered just how serious the big man was. There were persistent rumors that Silva had actually tried to kill Laney before. Abel usually doubted it. He'd discovered that Silva was particularly skilled at killing things that he *really* wanted dead. But he'd also learned Silva was only slightly more predictable than the weather.

"Hey," Dennis said, addressing the coxswain, "after we drop our load, take us over there, willya?" He was pointing at *Walker*. The coxswain was a Lemurian, one of Keje's officers learning powered-ship-handling skills so he'd at least have some sort of a clue when it came time for *Big Sal* to join the fleet. "Whatever's goin' on, it looks like it has to do with our ship, so I figure anybody that's anybody'll be there. We can report in and find out what's up at the same time."

"You betcha," came the high-pitched response.

The launch's nose bumped against the pier and Silva winced to think what Tony Scott would have said, but he sent Bradford and Abel up the rungs to the dock. Lawrence scampered up without assistance and Silva followed him. There was clearly a party atmosphere, and it seemed as if most of the city had turned out to see the show. It took Dennis only a few minutes to figure out what all the ruckus was about. Through the noise of the revelers, mostly Lemurian but a few human as well, a long-unheard but intimately familiar sound reached his ears. He turned and stared at the ship.

Smoke was rising from the aft funnel, the number four boiler, and the blower behind the still-stripped pilothouse roared with a steady, healthy, reassuring rumble. He'd expected it any day now, just not *today*. He knew the reconstruction of the numbers three and four boilers was almost complete and the starboard engine, that gloriously complicated Parsons turbine, had been carefully overhauled, but the blower motor and both the twenty-five-kilowatt generators had still been in the "powerhouse" when his hunting party set out that morning before dawn. For the longest time, all he could do was stand and stare.

Walker was alive again. She inhaled, exhaled, and her proud heart stirred once more. Her lifeblood flowed to the boiler, where hellish fires flared and water flashed to steam and sang joyously through the pipes to her turbines. At least one refurbished generator fed electricity to her blower and the spotlight. Silva's eye patch felt soggy and his good eye quit working right. Someone was calling his name, but it just didn't register at first. He noticed a slight weight land upon him, pulling his neck forward with small, strong arms. The passionate kiss suddenly inflicted on him finally brought him to his senses and he realized Pam Cross had jumped on him like a kid on a set of monkey bars. The small nurse clung to him and the curves pressed against him brought a smile to his tear-streaked face.

"Why, there you are, my little honeydew!" He still held the massive rifle in his right hand, but his left arm was more than sufficient to support the dark-haired, Brooklyn-born firecracker. "Where's Risa? I kinda missed you gals t'day. Killed me a super lizard! But I wish I'd'a been here, now!"

"Risa's on *Big Sal*, but she'll be heah." Pam giggled. "Probably give you the same kind of welcome . . . except I ain't going to lick you!"

"Always glad to oblige my adorin' ladies!"

Pam hugged him tight. "Gotcha a super lizard with your"—she gig-gled again—"big gun, huh? That's swell. I'm just glad you're back safe."

Silva pretended innocent confusion. "Say, where'd Bradford run off to? That reminds me. I need to talk to somebody. Mr. Letts or Spanky, I guess. I gotta make a ree-port. We saw somethin' kinda screwy today."

Pam kissed him again and climbed down. "He went over theah, with the kid and the lizard. They're talking to Mr. Letts and Adar al-ready. Hurry back, you big lug."

Silva bowed theatrically. "A hero's toil never ends, m'dear. I'll be back to perform whatever chore you require di-rectly!"

Someone pushed a mug of seep in his hand as he made his way to where Bradford, Letts, Adar, and now Spanky, Sister Audry, and Keje stood. Adar studied him intently.

"Why didn't you kill them?" Adar asked. "Mr. Braad-furd says they looked quite like Grik."

"Yeah, well, they wasn't, was they? Last time I shot somethin' only *looked* like a Grik, he wound up bein' one of my best buddies." Law-rence and Abel had joined them and Silva tousled Lawrence's young crest. The Tagranesi irritably shook his head. "Call me soft if you like, but I've decided shootin' fellas may not always be the best way to say how-dee-do. 'Specially with guns that won't leave much to get ac-quainted with." He hefted his rifle proudly. "A super lizard with one shot! This thing woulda spattered them little Injun jungle lizards all over the clearin'. Might coulda brung one of 'em back in a snuff can to meetcha."

"Injun lizards?" Spanky demanded.

"I discovered 'em!" Silva said, stubbornly. "I can call 'em what I want." He nodded at Adar. "Question is, what's the dope on 'em? Does his purple presidential holiness think we shoulda killed 'em, captured 'em, or left 'em be?"

Adar was highly accustomed to Silva's irreverent humor by now. He even shared it in good measure. Besides, if anyone had earned the right to make sport of him, or "josh" him a little, as the Amer-i-caans said, Silva certainly had. He wasn't the least offended now.

"Actually, I think you did precisely the right thing. As a Sky Priest of the sea folk who has just lately inherited a land domain, I confess I knew nothing of this species. Nakja-Mur never spoke of them, nor did Naga. I suspect your Moe and other hunters may have been carrying on this war of theirs for generations. Only he and others like him often venture into the wilds around Baalkpan. Nakja-Mur was a thoughtful, wise High Chief and a careful steward. I suspect if he had truly known of your 'Injun lizards,' he would have told us."

"Moe said he did."

"Nakja-Mur never left this city in his life," Adar said. "Naga did, but only by sea. Nakja-Mur also knew of the Grik threat from the west, but didn't truly *believe* it until it was upon him. The same is probably the case with those you saw today. All of us know there are aboriginal tribes of Grik-like creatures. Lawrence is proof of that. But no one ever considered the possibility they might not all *be* Grik in anything other than form. Captain Reddy has sent that they discovered the remains of Grik-like creatures in Aryaal that had apparently been used as slaves or worse. He believes they were like the ones that attacked your shore party when you first came to this world." Adar sighed.

"We have neglected studying these almost mythical creatures long enough—on the islands, and apparently here as well. Perhaps they are yet more enemies, as we have always assumed, but just perhaps"—he glanced at Lawrence and blinked fondness—"they are more like *him* than we could have ever dreamed. We learn more about even the Grik all the time," he added cryptically. He bowed to Courtney Bradford. "You will have your expedition. I want to make contact with these creatures. Perhaps we can even be friends, if they can forgive generations of violence most of us knew nothing about!"

"The only 'expedition' I want is back in the war!" Silva insisted.

"You'll get that," Letts said. "And before much longer." Subtly, during the conversation, Letts and Spanky had turned toward *Walker* so they could stare at the miraculously vibrant . . . living ship. Silva joined them, and eventually, so did all the others. They were here to celebrate her resurrection, after all. Even Sister Audry, who'd done everything she could throughout the day to prevent any spiritual significance from being attached to the event, was moved.

"She still looks a fright, Spanky," Silva said, "but you've done a swell job."

"Everybody has, you moron," Spanky replied gruffly. "Even you."

Silva belched loudly. Seep had that effect on him. So did the local beer, which he'd begun to prefer. Actually, Dennis Silva belched fairly often, regardless. "Try to be nice to a snipe," he grumped, "and what's he do? Slanders and insults." He shook his head. "Where's Loo-tenant Tucker and the munchkin princess? I woulda figured they'd be here for somethin' like this."

Spanky McFarlane looked around. "Well, they *were* here, just a little while ago."

"They went for a cool drink," Adar supplied, "and perhaps they have retired for the night. It is quite late."

"Yeah, well, me and Larry'd better find 'em and report in. I am one of the o-fficial pro-tectors of Her little Highness, after all, and I doubt Larry can stand it much longer without lickin' her er somethin'." Lawrence hissed at Dennis through his fangs, kind of a chuckle for him. "'Sides, Miss Loo-tenant Tucker's prob'ly worn out from dealin' with the little twerp all day!"

The others laughed. Not only did they know Silva was devoted to the girl and considered her anything but a twerp, but they knew Sandra loved the princess like a daughter.

"So long then." Spanky grunted. "And good riddance. Come back and brag when you kill a super lizard with your teeth!"

"That's the very next stunt on my list," Silva called back, heading toward Pam. "And I'll do it too, right after you build a battleship out of a beer can." Reaching the dark-haired nurse, he crushed her in another embrace. "You run along home now. Ol' Silva's kinda tired. Won't be good for more than three or four hours o' labor, I'm afraid. I'll be along directly!"

Pam giggled and moved away through the crowd.

"Mr. Silva?" asked a hesitant voice. It was Abel Cook. "May I accompany you, sir? That is, if you're going to see Lieutenant Tucker and . . . the princess, I would like to join you. To say good evening."

Silva belched at him. "Sure, I guess. What about Mr. Bradford, though? You're kinda his caretaker now, ain't ya? He'll be skunked in half an hour with all the booze down here—Captain Reddy would have a fit! Bradford's liable to puke on Adar or dance nekkid in the searchlight!"

"I'll come right back, I promise!"

"Hmm. You better keep yer grabbers to yourself! I seen how you look at her. You go to gropin' at Her Highness, me and Larry'll eat you!"

"No, sir, Mr. Silva! Never . . . ! I—"

"Oh, come on. If they went for a cold one, maybe they're at the Screw. Neither one's much for booze, but Pepper keeps some juice an' such."

They didn't find them at the Busted Screw; nor were they at the Fem Box, as the female bachelor officers' quarters was called.

"Say," said Dennis, "I wonder where they're at?" He wasn't really worried, but he was growing a little annoyed—and anxious. "Maybe they went to see Sister Audry? She ain't half bad for a gospel shark. Has some brains. Ever'body knows I'm as pious a critter as there is, but if you go jabberin' religion at folks all the time, without a break, pretty soon they'll tune you out—like a worn bearing. That, or they'll get sick o' hearin' it squeal and replace it with a new one."

"What did you say?" asked Lawrence, and Silva laughed.

The party had wound down considerably by the time they realized Sandra and Rebecca weren't at the little hut Sister Audry kept near the fishers' wharf. But Sister Audry wasn't there either. "Now, this is startin' to stink," said Silva. "Only place left they might be is *Big Sal*, in the dry dock, seein' Selass. She and Miss Tucker are pals." He shook his head. "Or maybe they're back where we started, oglin' the ship some more. I doubt it, though. It *is* gettin' late. Way too late for Miss Tucker to be sendin' love letters to the skipper at the wireless shack. *Must* be at *Big Sal*!"

Unconsciously picking up their pace, the man, boy, and Tagranesi headed back toward the shipyard. They met a few revelers on the way, but Baalkpan was a weary city. There were so many wildly different projects under way, employing such a large percentage of the populace, even the all-night bazaar that had once been the center of Baalkpan social life had shrunk to a mere shadow of its former size. Those not actively engaged in the war effort still had to labor: fishing and doing the chores of everyday life for more mouths with fewer hands. Others hunted, as they'd done that day. In any event, what had once been a city that never slept shut down almost entirely after dark these days. Even something as grand as bringing *Walker* back to life couldn't keep most from their bedding too long.

All that remained of the party at the dock were oil lamps and a few sozzled mounds lying on the planks. *Walker*'s blower still rumbled, but there was no light aboard. There was clearly still a lot of electrical work yet to accomplish, and besides the spare bulbs they'd stored ashore before the battle, few of those aboard the ship had survived the fight and subsequent submergence. Still, even darkened, she was alive. Silva noted as they passed her that a wisp of smoke rose from the number four stack and stars shimmered in the heat plume above it. He grinned.

Big Sal wasn't much farther, the once distinctive outline changed forever by the alterations under way. She was still lit and work continued aboard her. Keje was pushing her people relentlessly to finish the job so his Home might have water beneath her again. Silva knew the dry dock gave Keje the willies. *Big Sal* had often been flooded down for a variety of reasons, and she was built in something *like* a dry dock, but she wasn't ever *supposed* to be completely dry again. For her to be totally divorced from her natural element as she now was struck Keje and most of his people as an unnatural thing, worse even than the perverse changes their Home was undergoing.

"Least there'll be somebody there we can ask," Silva muttered. They were crossing the old, smooth ramp once used by the PBY to get her out of the water. There were several other ramps here and there, but this had been the one closest to the shipyard.

Almost across, Lawrence stopped and his head jerked toward the water. "Dennis!" he hissed, using Silva's first name. Usually he tried to say, "Mr. Silva," but it came out mangled. The others noticed the sudden difference and recognized the significance. They stopped.

"What's up, Larry?" Silva asked quietly.

"At the 'ater's edge, there is acti'ity—and the scent o' the ladies!"

Silva's heart pounded in his chest. He'd been using his big gun as a kind of walking stick, and he slowly brought it up, peering hard into the darkness. There was no moon and almost no light, but suddenly he *could* see something outlined against the gentle gray wave tops that lapped at the ramp. "Those Imperial sons o' bitches!" he seethed. "They're *swipin'* the gals!" He looked quickly around. Apparently, they hadn't yet been seen.

"'Kay," he hissed. "Abel, you stay put. If there's a ruckus, run like hell, screamin' your head off!"

"But—"

"Shut up. Larry, see if you can ease down the left side o' the ramp. I'll try to creep up on 'em from this side, close to the edge. We gotta see what's what before we raise the alarm. Don't want anybody panickin'! That said, if either of us sees a chance, we'll kill our way in to the girls. You move, I move, and vicey versey. Got it?"

Lawrence jerked a nod.

Abel was terrified, and a little indignant he'd been left out, but he was also chilled by how quickly and easily the jovial giant and servile, companionable Tagranesi became focused, single-minded killers. He stepped slowly back as the others all but disappeared in the darkness.

Silva began to hear muffled whispers as he drew near. Slowly, eight—no, nine—human shapes resolved themselves, gathered on-shore near a longboat. The white paint of the boat had been darkened. Three of the shapes stood a little apart, huddled together, while two others apparently watched over them. *That's gotta be them*, Silva thought. *One's shorter than the others.* He wondered who the third one was. *Must be Sister Audry. She wasn't home neither. Weird.* He paused and took a silent breath. *Them devils are actin' impatient. I wonder what they're waitin' for? They musta had the girls for a while. Why not just scram?*

Being a single-shot muzzle loader, Silva's big gun wouldn't be much use. Now, if the two guards would line up . . . Wait! One was moving away, fumbling with his trousers. With a wicked grin and a slow, fluid motion, Dennis slung the rifle and crept up on the man beginning to relieve himself. Dennis knew the human eye, like any predator's, keyed on motion, but it was always amazing how much movement one could get away with if the motion was slow and smooth.

The pissing man never had a chance.

From behind him, like driving his knuckles into his hand, Silva brought his left palm down on the top left side of the man's head and drove his right fist into the hinge of his jaw. There was a loud crunch, like a slick boot sliding on gravel, when the pointed part of the man's jaw crashed into his brain, but there was no other sound. "Sorry, sir," he hissed aloud, like an underling apologizing for making a noise.

"Silence, fool!" came the hoped-for muffled order.

Dennis eased the dead man to the ground, then slowly pulled his Pattern 1917 cutlass from its sheath. Like his giant rifled musket and his 1911 Colt, he never went anywhere without it. Trying to imitate the pissing man's stride, he moved back toward the prisoners. He had maybe a couple of seconds at best before he was discovered. For one thing, he was much taller than his victim.

A dark form fluttered in the corner of his good eye and he saw Lawrence pounce on the man farthest from him. In the same instant that Lawrence dug his hind claws into the man's chest, clamped his jaws on his throat, and launched himself backward into the darkness, Silva drove the cutlass into the ill-defined torso of the other guard. Both emitted hideous, wrenching screams. He yanked Sandra's gag down under her chin. "Surprise!" he said. "It's me!"

"Our feet first!" Sandra gasped. "It's Billingsly! He's trying to take the princess!"

"I figgered that!" Silva said, hacking at the ropes that bound their feet with just enough slack to walk or stand. A musket fired and a jet of blinding flame flashed from the boat. "Ow!" he said. The ball had grazed his hip. In the darkness, it could just as easily have hit one of the girls.

"Stop them!" someone bellowed. "They mustn't escape!" A pistol flared with a loud *ker-thump!*

"Help! Help!" screamed Abel's voice. "The Imperials are attacking! They are taking the princess! Help!"

Lawrence killed another man and a musket flashed in his direction.

With their feet free, Silva started working on their hands.

"No time!" Sandra shouted. "We're tied together too! We can't run like this!"

"Got to!" Silva replied. "Go!" He unslung his rifle and pointed it at the boat. With a mighty roar that anyone in the city who saw or heard it would recognize, he hoped he'd scuttled Billingsly's escape. Another musket fired from near the top of the ramp. Not the cavalry then, Silva realized. None of the new Springfield muskets had been issued yet. Must be the ones these others were waiting for! He heard Abel scream again, in pain this time. He dropped his rifle and pulled the Colt, flipping the safety with his thumb. "Get down, boy!" he roared, and emptied the magazine in the direction of the shot. "Run!" he shouted at the three ladies. "Run like hell that way!" He spun back toward the boat.

Evidently, he'd miscounted. Other men must have been *in* the boat as well, because there still seemed to be as many enemies as he and Lawrence had started with. He had only the cutlass now. "C'mon, Larry!" he thundered. "Kill 'em all! No pris'ners!"

Gilbert Yeager awoke from a happy, muzzy dream of happy, muzzy steam coursing joyfully through clean, tight pipes and leaping energetically at polished turbine blades. Something was booming somewhere and somebody had definitely stepped on him. Silly, rude bastards! Couldn't they tell he was asleep? Now somebody was shaking him, trying to get him off the miraculously cool pipe where he was listening to the glorious song of steam. "Whatcha fagarattin' ta da boomin' slip!" he demanded indignantly. He sat up, realizing he was still on the warm, damp dock where he'd apparently passed out. He blinked in the darkness. A bright flash not far away lit sparklers in his eyes. "Ahhhg!"

"Somebody's tryin' to swipe the princess!" Tabby said beside him. She was still shaking his head.

"So? Lemme alone!"

"No! We must do something! There is a fight, and Si'vaa and Larry are outnumbered! The princess and Minister Tucker, at least, are in danger!"

Gilbert blinked again. "Well, why the hell didn't you wake me up, goddamn it?" He leaped to his feet with a board in his hand, swayed, then brandished the piece of wood. "Death to whoever the hell it is we're fixin' ta kill!" he screeched. A probably errant pistol ball struck the board and slapped it into his face. He went down as though pole-axed. "I'm *keeled*!" he wailed through busted lips. "I knew it! Just a matter o' time!"

"You ain't killed!" Tabby shouted, trying to drag him to his feet. "But you are drink too much!" She dropped his arm. "Me too," she admitted. Leaving Gilbert where he lay, she ran toward *Walker*, trilling a cry of alarm.

There was much alarm already. Weary as Baalkpan was, most of her sentries were alert. Those who could be. A coast defense gun, situated to protect the shipyard, lit the night with a mighty roar. Another went off and a red alarm rocket screeched into the sky. Bronze pipe-gongs began sounding throughout the city. Spanky McFarlane ran past a still-babbling Gilbert dressed only in his hat and skivvies. There was a .45 in each hand. Mallory and Rodriguez wore only their skivvies, but they both had '03 Springfields. Keje rushed to the scene with half a dozen armed 'Cats. Blindingly, *Walker*'s searchlight flared down on the scene like an angered God. The tableau it revealed was stunning not only in its unexpectedness, but in the magnitude of the implications and the scope of the slaughter.

Commander Billingsly stood behind all three females, who were still tied together, and held a long-barreled pistol pressed painfully under Princess Rebecca's jaw. Another man with blood on his face held a cutlass across the throats of Sandra Tucker and Sister Audry. Five other men still stood, although all seemed wounded to some degree, but there were at least a dozen bodies scattered on the old seaplane ramp. One of them was Dennis Silva.

Silva, at least, didn't seem dead, but he was covered with blood and just sitting on the ground at the women's feet. Lawrence was there too, equally bloody, but apparently uninjured. He was supporting Silva and looking intently at the princess.

"Drop your weapons!" Billingsly demanded.

"Eat shit!" Spanky growled back. "Clearly you don't know who you're monkeyin' around with!"

"I admit to some uncertainty in that regard," Billingsly admitted. "Your man here, the big one, is not dead. I must say both his arrival and his courage came as a significant surprise. It is a shame you force me to kill him." Billingsly nodded at one of his remaining men, who pointed a pistol at Silva's apparently senseless head.

"Ronson, Ben," Spanky said quietly. "You got enough light on your sights?"

"Yeah."

Both Springfields spoke almost as one and the henchman's head geysered up and backward in what appeared an almost neon spray under the harsh light.

Billingsly flinched and drove the pistol more savagely into the princess's neck. "Well," he said, recovering himself. "Touché. A most impressive demonstration of marksmanship! You have saved your man, bravo! It changes nothing, however."

"How's that?" Spanky asked. "At one word from me, these two guys can do the same to you and your pals and this little game'll be over."

"That would be a most unfortunate word for you to give. You see, I have yet another hostage in the boat behind us, a young Mr. Abel Cook, if I don't mistake his name. He is lightly injured, I'm afraid, but he is also in the hands of a most dedicated friend of mine, a Mr. Truelove. He is perfectly prepared to cut that young man's throat, and you can't even see him." Billingsly shrugged. "Mr. Truelove is also performing a number of other tasks, highly specialized for this occasion."

Spanky glanced to his right as a winded Adar and Alan Letts arrived. He knew both would have enough sense to say nothing until they knew more about the situation. "Such as?" Spanky asked.

"Mr. Truelove is holding a hooded lantern over the side of the boat. As long as that colored lantern is visible to my ship, *Ajax*, she will not fire a full broadside of grapeshot into this very gathering. If you carry out your threat I will die, which would certainly disappoint me, but then Mr. Truelove would drop that lantern into the sea and everyone here, including many of you—who I predict are leaders of this ridiculous Alliance—would also die. A most tragic ending to what I had hoped would be a very peaceful little rescue."

"Kidnapping, you mean!" Letts snarled.

Billingsly shrugged again. "Semantics. A great hobby among philosophers, but quite tedious for me, I'm afraid."

"You're bluffing," Spanky declared. "I can still see your ship's lights, riding where they've been for months!"

"A regrettable subterfuge . . . Mr. McFarlane, is it not? A mere anchored raft with lights. I assure you, *Ajax* stands less than two hundred yards offshore this very moment. You could adjust your annoying light to see her if you wish. No? Well then, you should probably take my word."

"You can't possibly expect to get away with this!" Adar remarked forcefully. "We will chase you; we will hunt you! We will never give up! You are committing an act of war against a people who mean you no ill!"

"Oh, I certainly hope so!" Billingsly said. "War with you might suit our plans quite nicely just now! As for pursuit, what will you make it with?" He gestured at *Walker*. "Surely not that. It is not even armed and requires more weeks of repair before undertaking a chase. The bulk of your fleet is elsewhere, and that which is here and nearly ready to sail—your 'new-construction steamers,' you call them—are about to suffer a mischief." He looked about. "Does anyone happen to have the time?"

A red pulse of light engulfed the waterfront and a towering, roiling ball of flame gushed into the heavens. A moment later, there was a second flash, as large as the first, and the thunderous detonations reached them at last.

"My God! The fuel storage tanks!" Letts whispered. "They must have bombed the whole tank battery!" It was true. It also wasn't lost on anyone that the flash had indeed illuminated *Ajax*, just offshore.

"You son of the Devil!" Princess Rebecca finally screamed. "You filthy, vile, reptilian monster! These people needed that fuel to fight the Grik, not *us*, you pathetic fool! You've destroyed us all!"

Sandra, a bloody gag back in her mouth, struggled against the man holding her until he pressed the cutlass tighter, drawing blood. Billingsly silenced the princess with another jab of the pistol.

"There, now!" Billingsly exclaimed cheerfully. "No doubt you will replace the fuel shortly, but I am reliably informed that your new boilers do not thrive on wood or coal." He shook his head. "You may now regard that as an oversight in design, but perhaps not. The oil you use instead seems to have a number of advantages . . . but it *is* frightfully flammable, isn't it? In any event, you have little left with which to chase us! Your better-sailing frigates, gone with the fleet, alas, might have had a chance if the winds favored them, but your steamers will be no faster than we— and helpless if the wind fails! We would have a good start on them regardless. As for your 'prizes,' all the swifter variety of those are either gone as well, or their conversions are not yet complete."

"We will chase you, nevertheless," Adar warned grimly.

"Please do! Be my guest to try, but remember this: for each hostile act on your part, a hostage will fall into the sea with his or her throat cut! The one-eyed giant will die first. He has cost us much and spoiled what would have been a perfect plan. Next, the injured boy. After that, the Roman witch priestess will die, followed by your precious Minister of Medicine, Miss Tucker. I trust things will never proceed that far. If they do and if *Ajax* is ultimately somehow destroyed, the princess will, regrettably, die with the ship. Do as you will. Try what you like." He paused. "Test me," he taunted.

"We will chase you and we will watch you," Adar promised, "and we had better see our people alive when we do!"

"As you will. As I said, you are welcome to try. Beware if I tire of your company, however!"

Billingsly looked about for a moment, apparently pondering, then nodded to himself. Spanky recognized the look of someone who thought he'd covered all his bases. For the life of him, Spanky couldn't figure out what the man might have missed.

"Gather the giant's weapons," he instructed one of his men. He glanced at Spanky and raised his voice. "You will be safe," he assured the reluctant underling. "If they kill you, Truelove will kill the boy. Now hurry; we are leaving this place at last!"

"You'll regret this, Billingsly!" Spanky shouted. He saw Silva move a little and knew at last that the big man still lived. *Oh, Lord*, he thought, but it was something, at least. With a little more certainty, he shouted again, "I *guarantee* you'll regret this!"

"Perhaps," Billingsly replied. "I have few regrets, actually. I'm sure I *would* regret killing these poor souls now in my care. Pray, spare me that."

Somehow, Sandra must have worked her gag loose. Suddenly she shouted out, "Give Captain Reddy my love! Tell him to do whatever he must!" There was a loud slap and a muffled cry. The still-growing mass of warriors, sailors, and townsfolk pushed forward with a growl.

"Now, now!" yelled Billingsly. "That was sensible advice; do what you must! At present, you must let us leave and you must signal your fort to let us pass!"

"We *cannot* just let them leave!" Keje said, moving close to Spanky, Adar, and Letts.

"We have no choice for now," Adar replied heavily. He turned to Letts. "Quickly, have someone pass the word along the waterfront and to Fort Atkinson: do not fire; let them pass! We will save them somehow, but we cannot do it here or now!"

"What about Captain Reddy?" Letts asked. "He's going to flip!"

For a moment, Adar said nothing while he watched the hostages briskly moved into the boat. Someone was bailing water out of it as the oars dipped clumsily and it shoved off, away from the ramp.

"Cap-i-taan Reddy will be mounting his assault on Sing-aapore about now," he said woodenly. "Perhaps it would be best not to tell him just yet. He can do nothing but worry about our situation here, and his attack must proceed. Torn in two directions at once, he might behave rashly."

Keje grunted assent.

"I will never forgive myself for allowing this to happen," Adar continued, "and Cap-i-taan Reddy may not forgive me for keeping it from him, even briefly." He blinked beseechingly at Keje. "But if he is . . . distracted now, and somehow he or our effort suffers for it, our world will not forgive me—for however long it remains."

"And it was such a lovely plan, too," Sean O'Casey said as yet another seething mass of Grik infantry slammed into the shield wall of the 2nd Marines. Chack laughed. The 2nd Marines and 1st Aryaal had met virtually no resistance to their predawn landing in the shipyard district. Even now, in the dawn's dreary, overcast light, cutters and launches were securing the Grik fleet anchored in the harbor. As Captain Reddy had surmised, most of those ships had little more than caretaker crews aboard, and dozens were already making sail to join the Allied support vessels, blue streamers fluttering from their mastheads to identify them as prizes. The Marines and 1st Aryaal actually had plenty of time to deploy to defend the beachhead before the enemy finally "got their shit in the sock," as Alden put it, and gathered a significant force to fall on the defenders.

The Marines in front of Chack and O'Casey heaved back against the onslaught and the cacophony was beyond anything O'Casey had yet experienced. He'd been at Baalkpan and seen the terrible nature of this war firsthand, but never from quite this close. There was a constant, roaring screech of weapons on weapons and shields on shields and Grik cries of agony as weapons pierced or slashed their vitals.

"It is a phalaanx of sorts, or so Cap-i-taan Reddy calls it. He based it on an ancient human formation, but he modified it to better fit our different circumstances!" Chack shouted over the din. "The enemy uses nothing like it. They attack as a mob, without discipline. It seems to be all they know how to do. They *can* bash through by sheer weight of numbers, however." He nodded toward the left of his line, where it joined with Rolak's. "Can you heft that spear?" he asked.

O'Casey balanced the spear in his right hand, judging the weight. "Well enough," he assured Chack.

"Very well. Stay out of the front rank and beware the crossbow bolts!" With that, Chack called his staff, and together, they waded into the fiercest of the fight. O'Casey had been a soldier once, but he'd never been in a fight like this. The sheer scope was beyond his experience, and the type of fighting quite alien. The biggest battle he'd ever seen before Baalkpan had involved maybe a thousand men on both sides combined. He'd thought it was huge at the time. He'd lost that battle and been branded a traitor. His cause was crushed and he'd barely escaped with his life. Here, Rolak and Chack commanded nearly three thousand, and God alone knew how many Grik they faced. Many thousands more, at least. And yet Chack, whom he'd heard was once a pacifist, seemed unconcerned. He hefted the spear again and plunged ahead with the rest.

Six pounder field guns poked their muzzles through the ranks and spewed deadly, scything hail through the attackers, and two guns preceded Chack's reinforcements into the bulging line. With a pair of thunderclaps and a choking haze of white smoke, the pressure there all but vanished. Still Chack raced into the gap, giving the battered line time to re-form around him. He and his staff bashed with their shields and thrust with their short Marine spears at the regathering swarm. O'Casey found himself right among them, poking inexpertly and a little awkwardly with his own spear. More than once he felt it bite. Even so, he decided he'd probably have to become a pistol man, maybe with a few braces draped around his neck. A swordsman he'd never been. Maybe it was time he learned that art?

"Did you find that exhilarating?" Chack asked, when the last dribble of attackers was repulsed. Chack's white leather armor glistened with bright blood and the incongruous American helmet shone where a sword had skated across it, taking the paint. A slow, rolling, methodical broadside thundered from the frigates on the water. *Donaghey*'s eighteen pounders swooshed overhead to impact in the dense but confused enemy rear, while the fewer but heavier twenty-fours of the steamers moaned over the largely Lemurian force, trailing smoke. They detonated over and among the still-gathering Grik and the screams brought a wicked grin to Chack's face. "The new exploding shells, or case shot," he explained. "Wonderfully destructive things, though we don't have many yet. The fuses can be unreliable as well, which adds a . . . delicious uncertainty to their passage overhead!" He watched while another broadside erupted from the covering warships. "Glorious," he breathed happily and turned back to O'Casey.

"It *is* a lovely plan! What did you mean earlier? Do you fear it goes poorly?" Chack asked the one-armed man.

"What do *you* mean? Is this good?" O'Casey gasped.

Chack laughed again. "Everything's swell so far! You do not know *all* the plan, and I do!"

"I thought ours was ta be a blockin' force!" O'Casey seemed exasperated.

"It is! And we block well, don't you think?" He gestured around. "We have already accomplished much of our goal. We are ashore and well placed. We have seized most of the docks and much of the repair yard. We have drawn the enemy's focus and hopefully it will remain fixed upon us for some time to come." He pointed excitedly, watching several squads hurry toward them from the boats. "Ah! The new mortars! Soon we will see something, I think! Soon, but not yet!"

O'Casey had already seen quite a lot. He knew, for example, that he was glad these people were his friends, and he now knew how essential it was that they be friends of the Empire. He keenly suspected that this small force to which he was attached would have made short work of the Imperial Company regiment that had ground his own rebellion to dust. They had no muskets—yet—but they had something far more important: confidence, discipline, and the unwavering certainty that they were *right.*

"Oh, Jenks, ye fool!" he muttered under his breath. "Where'er ye be on this field this day, open yer eyes and do nae aggravate these folk!"

"Now, now, now!" shouted Pete Alden, lowering his binoculars. With the thunder of a hundred drums, the 1st Marines, the 2nd and 4th Aryaal, the 1st Baalkpan, 3rd B'mbaado, and 2nd Sular kicked off their sweeping, or "swinging," advance with around four thousand troops. 'Cats just couldn't do bugles, so they'd settled on drum tattoos and various combinations of short whistle blasts to control large forces on the battlefield. The first few fights had shown the need for something like that, and now they had it. The roar of the drums sent gooseflesh down Matt's arms.

"I agree," Matt said, "it's time." He grinned. "Not that it matters what I think! This is your show, Pete!"

"If it was completely my show, you'd be watching from *Donaghey* right now!" Pete answered harshly. "Promise me you won't wander off? We haven't really been engaged yet, but the pickets I threw out on the flanks report quite a few rambunctious Grik hunting parties, or the like. We expected that and our bowmen and a few of the NCOs with Krags are dealing with them, but I'd sure hate to have to tell Lieutenant Tucker I let you get conked from behind."

Chief Gray pointedly racked the bolt on the Thompson he carried. Gunner's Mate Paul Stites followed suit with a BAR. "Mind your own chickens," Gray grumbled. Besides Stites, there were four Lemurian Marines in the Captain's Guard detail, and Jenks had a pair of his own polished muskets on their shoulders.

Matt just smiled and shrugged. Harvey Jenks chuckled beside him.

"A magnificent show, Captain Reddy," Jenks said. "I, at least, fully understand your desire to view it firsthand!" He looked at his own distant *Achilles*, whose guns had remained silent thus far. "I almost regret not committing myself entirely to your support—not that it seems you need it!"

"I understand your reasons. It's hard to engage in offensive operations against somebody you're not at war with. I doubt the Grik will
notice any distinction, however. Besides, your Marines are on the far
left with General Maraan. They're yet another blocking force, but it
could be bloody work."

"There, if they must fight, it will be a defensive engagement," Jenks
said. "Defending oneself from attack is hardly offensive in nature."

Matt looked at the Imperial. "Again, the Grik will make no distinction. I doubt your own superiors will."

"You wanted us in this war," Jenks said more quietly, seriously. "I've
come to believe we belong in it, though God knows we have problems
of our own. We may need *your* help someday. How could we possibly
ask it of you if we did not make this small gesture?"

Matt grunted. "Your gesture could cost a lot of Imperial lives. Safir
says your Marine lieutenant Blair isn't particularly open to her tactical
suggestions."

Jenks nodded. "Well, there is little I can do about that. I command
my ship and I command the Marines to perform their duties. How
they perform those duties is up to Blair, I'm afraid. At best, if the Grik
do strike there, our people may learn from one another. At worst . . ."
He blinked. "Our people may learn a costly lesson from one another."

Matt shook his head, somewhat surprised Gray had held his tongue.
He surveyed the disposition of the troops and all seemed to be shaping
up nicely. All but the weather. Ahead, in the west, the general overcast
seemed darker as the day progressed. When he spoke, he sounded
slightly distracted. He was watching the sky. "I'd hoped your Marines
might bolster our lines, like spearmen behind the shields. I'm telling
you that a thin pair of ranks, even armed with muskets, *can't* stand
against the Grik."

Jenks's smile was brittle. "We'll see." He nodded forward. "Your
army will leave us behind while we discuss this, I fear, and General
Alden will scold us again."

Chack sensed a change in the Grik host before him. Another attack had
been repulsed, but for a long time now, nearly half an hour, there'd

been no assault. Leaving O'Casey with his staff, he trotted to where General Rolak directed his end of the line from the roof of a crude warehouse. Scrambling up the ladder, Chack saluted the old Aryaalan warrior.

"Quite a difference between this and our last meeting with these creatures!" Rolak enthused, returning Chack's salute. "Your Marines fight splendidly!"

"As do your troops, Lord. Any sign of Mr. Braad-furd's Grik Rout?" Chack asked.

Rolak frowned and his tail twitched with agitation. "Not yet. They do seem to have their shit in their sock, as General Alden so colorfully put it. This Hij general of theirs expends many lives, but he avoids allowing them to bunch up too deeply. If any panic, the panic spreads less far."

"True," Chack agreed. "But he has sacrificed mass to accomplish this. Twice they might have broken our line if they had supported their assault with greater numbers."

"They are hesitant, I think. Few of these warriors could have been at Baalkpan. All they know is that they lost there, badly. I believe they test new tactics here, within the constraints of their warriors' . . . capabilities."

"Do you really?" Chack asked absently, thinking. "Perhaps. There are no defensive works, other than gun emplacements for their limited artillery. They do not defend as we do, behind breastworks or terrain, or with careful discipline. They defend by attacking." He took a drink from his water bottle. "Do you think that is new? That they make 'spoiling' attacks hoping to slow our advance?"

"How can we truly know what is 'new' to them? Anything they do besides a mass attack is 'new' to us, but it is possible. It may also be that they think they have succeeded. We have achieved our objective, but perhaps they do not know that. Consider: would the Grik do as we have done? Land, attack, secure a defensive perimeter, then stop?" Rolak shook his head. "I doubt they can even comprehend such a strategy."

"You may be right, lord," Chack replied, eyeing the mass of enemies before them. Their numbers continued to swell, but they'd been badly bloodied and corpses were heaped along the length of the perimeter. "We seem to have affixed the enemy's attention entirely upon us. As best we can tell, they have no notion of the main force bearing down upon their left." Chack glanced at one of the Manilo couriers who'd arrived shortly before, mounted on one of the swift "meanies," as Silva called them. The beasts still gave him the "creeps." They looked like larger, more reptilian versions of their enemies, that happened to go about on all fours. The courier had reported only desultory fighting in front of the main force.

Rolak glanced at the darkening sky. "We are liable to have a storm today. A Strakka comes at last, I suspect. It is fortunate that we have secured a safe harbor for our fleet."

Chack had been looking often at the sky himself. "I wish our luck with the weather might have held a few more days. If the gust front hits during the battle, it will confuse things."

"More for them than us, I expect." Rolak grinned. "We have a plan and they do not. At least, what they have of a plan seems to depend upon what we do for a change."

Chack nodded noncommittally. He'd had some experience with plans now, and he knew how fragile they could be. So did Rolak, for that matter. Chack suspected the old warrior of practicing his dry wit upon him. "For myself, I would hope the Strakka holds off a bit longer so our plan might unfold unimpeded," he said.

"You are of the sea folk." Rolak waved his hand. "You would know that better than I." He gestured back to the front. "Perhaps you should return to your Marines. The enemy stirs. Does it appear to you, amidst that mob, that he is shifting his front?" Rolak's teeth appeared in a feral grin. "Perhaps he is preparing to attack in a different direction!"

"Good Lord!" Jenks exclaimed. "Do they always come on like that?"

"Yep," said Gray. The Bosun spat.

"Pretty much every time," Matt confirmed.

The closer Alden's army had approached what they'd identified as the Grik main force, fixed in front of Rolak and Chack, the more crazed attackers had charged headlong against Alden's overwhelming force.

At first, they'd come in groups of a dozen or less, shrieking defiantly and waving their weapons. Arrows cut down most of those before they ever came in range of a spear. Then, more Grik charged them from the jungle that bordered the clearing they'd started across. Matt had been secretly amazed they'd made it that far before being noticed, but Manilo couriers or cavalry—or whatever they were—had assured them Chack and Rolak had grabbed plenty of the enemy's attention.

They'd heard the cannonade grow louder as they neared and saw the warships in the bay jockey for more advantageous firing positions. Broadside after broadside sent roiling clouds of billowing smoke across the water. The new mortars were still silent for now, waiting for the Grik to wholly focus on the new threat. Then, shortly before, the dense peninsula of jungle ahead that stood between Alden's and Rolak's converging forces suddenly teemed with thousands of Grik shapes.

"They've finally turned to meet us," Matt had announced aloud, as much for Jenks as Alden. A number of horns blew together, their different tones jumbled and discordant, but they'd seemed a suitable accompaniment to the shrill, growling shrieks of the horde that had erupted from the trees.

Now Jenks could only stare in horror at the elemental force bearing down on them. It was a mob, to be sure, but a huge one, and this first look at a Grik berserker charge was most disconcerting. He wondered how Captain Reddy could just stand there like that, watching them come. Either the man was utterly fearless or his trust in his commanders and troops was truly that profound. Jenks realized that Captain Reddy and his guards had faced this before, but he couldn't imagine anyone ever becoming so inured to it. He stood as well. He was an officer, a gentleman, and possessed a significant measure of personal courage. He admitted to himself that he was terrified, though. Standing in the face of that seething, swarming mass of teeth, claws, swords, and crossbows couldn't possibly be done without some fear. And yet, glancing sidelong at the American officer, this Supreme Commander, he saw no sign of any emotion other than . . . anticipation.

"'Bout . . . now!" Matt said.

As if reading his commander's thoughts, Pete Alden bellowed at the top of his lungs, the order he gave repeated down the ranks and punctuated with whistle blasts.

"Commence firing!"

Twelve pieces of light artillery bucked and spewed dense clouds of smoke and double loads of canister. Arrows whickered into the darkening sky with a terrible, collective "swoosh." Untold hundreds of Grik warriors were swept away with as little apparent effort as the command had taken to give. Others screamed in agony and writhed on the ground, clutching wounds or festooned with arrows.

"Independent, fire at will!" Alden shouted, his voice already a little hoarse after the last command and the choking smoke that followed it.

There were a number of distinct thumping, popping sounds beyond the trees from the direction of the initial landing force. Whistling sounds, dozens, scores, like Jenks had never heard, were punctuated by fearsome but smallish blasts that sent gouts of earth into the sky right among the rear of the enemy host. A few of the "mortar bombs," Reddy had called them, though Jenks had never seen their like, erupted in the trees themselves and sent swarms of splinters into the Grik. The agonized screeching took on a desperate, terrified air.

Then, above it all, there came a roar. It wasn't like the roar of thunder or the marching surf; it was higher pitched, excited, almost gleeful. Despite its tone, it had a profound, unstoppable, elemental urgency that stirred his most primitive thoughts. In contrast to the increasingly agonized and terrified cacophony of the Grik horde, the roar from beyond the trees was confident, eager, remorseless. It was the sound of doom.

"That'll be Rolak and Chack!" Gray boomed happily. "They were the anvil. Probably got mighty sick of it too. Now they're the hammer!"

A large percentage of the Grik, where the mortars still fell, had been transformed from an unstoppable juggernaut into a wild, panic-stricken mass. Jenks looked on in amazement while thousands of Grik scrambled in all directions, slaying *one another* with wild abandon. Some ran back the way they'd come, smashing into the howling Lemurian troops and Marines that suddenly erupted from the trees. Others raced north or south, toward the jungle or the sea. Some crashed into the rear of the forward element, still charging the Allied line. Battle erupted there, among the *Grik*, even as the foremost berserkers slammed into the Allied shield wall.

The slaughter was incredible. The mortars stopped falling and the field guns were pulled back to avoid inflicting casualties on the Allied forces now closing on the still-larger Grik army caught between them. The relative sizes of the armies lost all meaning, however, since growing numbers of Grik were now murdering one another. It was insane. The fighting at the shield wall was still wildly intense; the Grik that struck there as a relatively cohesive force still outnumbered Alden's entire command, but that was when the qualitative difference between the combatants was most plainly demonstrated. Nowhere did the shield wall break. It stood like a monolithic cliff in the face of disorganized breakers, and the killing was remarkably one-sided.

Spears thrust and jabbed over, under, and around the front-rank shields, whose bearers pushed with all their might against the battering Grik. Inexorably, General Rolak's force swept through the chaos of the Grik rear, killing any who stood even momentarily. Those who fled from between the closing pincers were mostly ignored, but few seemed to realize this and even fewer had the wherewithal or initiative to take advantage of the fact. Within an hour of the first mortar blasts, the jaws of the pincers clamped shut and all that remained of the battle was a prolonged, remorseless butchery.

Captain Reddy must have noticed Jenks's expression. Perhaps his face was pale?

"Maybe you're wondering why I don't put a stop to it?" Matt's words came in a fierce monotone. "On some level, maybe I still wish I could. But those down there"—he gestured at the dwindling Grik—"won't quit fighting. Hell, half of them are still killing each other!" He shook his head. "I don't know how or why they act the way they do, and frankly, that's not my concern right now. Maybe we'll know someday. Maybe the prisoners we took at Aryaal will help with that. But right now, we'll use this clear weakness of theirs against them as often and mercilessly as we can. There may come a time when they get wise and it won't work anymore." He looked at Jenks again. "Or maybe you're wondering *if* I could stop it?"

Almost without thinking, Jenks jerked a nod.

Matt shrugged. "I don't know that either. You probably can't comprehend what's driven these people, *my* people, down there, to become what they are from what they were. Mostly, they used to be almost instinctively unaggressive. There were exceptions, but all of them have suffered loss like you can't imagine. At least, I don't think you can. Hell, I couldn't have until I came to this world. Maybe the Rape of Nanking comes close . . ." He saw Jenks's uncomprehending blink. "Skip it. Anyway, like you saw at Aryaal, we aren't fighting a civilized enemy, and this isn't anything like a civilized war. The very wickedness of our enemy is what's allowed us to build this army, these *soldiers* I'm so proud of. I don't think anything else would have done it."

Captain Reddy sighed. "*Could* I stop them from hacking the life out of every last Grik down there? Maybe. I tried once, you know, and it didn't work. The Grik give no quarter and *never* ask for it. I don't think they know how. Faced with an enemy like that, what do you think? Even if I could *make* Alden's troops stop killing, the Grik won't. I don't know what made 'tame' Griks out of the ones Rasik had, but it didn't happen in the middle of a fight. Maybe they need time to think things through, and some of the ones who get away will come in later, all peaceable and contrite. For now . . . I have a rule. It used to be 'Never give an order you know won't be obeyed.' 'Know' has become 'believe,' but it still works pretty good. That's my little concession to the gray area of command, and given a choice, I'd much rather err on the side of my people than those monsters down there."

He looked away from Jenks, back at the dwindling fight. There were cheers now. Cheers of survival, pride, and relief. Cheers for Captain Reddy too. "Besides, to answer the last question you never asked: no. Deep down, I don't *want* them to stop. Not after Baalkpan. Not after all *I've* lost."

A meanie galloped up. Well, "galloped" wasn't exactly the right word, but it was blowing hard through flared nostrils and would likely have been panting if its jaws weren't cinched tightly shut. It stared malevolently around. "Cap-i-taan Reddy," cried the Manilo cavalryman from its back. "General Rolak's most fervent compliments and affection! He begs to inform you that when they made their charge, another, smaller Grik force was assembling on his flank. He had no choice but to ignore it when this show kicked off. Since it did not attack his rear as he advanced, he fears it may have wind of the blocking force to the west." The courier motioned toward where the clouds were growing positively malignant. As before, when Matt had seen a growing Strakka, black tendrils had begun to radiate from the dark, brooding core.

Matt looked at Jenks. "After seeing this, are you sure you don't want to urge Mr. Blair to consider General Maraan's suggestions a little more carefully?"

Jenks eyed the semidomesticated beast the rider sat upon. "Is there room up there for me?" he demanded.

"Of course."

Jenks turned to Matt. "Thank you indeed for a most . . . illuminating experience. I believe I would like to . . . strongly counsel Lieutenant Blair to do just that. By your leave, Captain Reddy?"

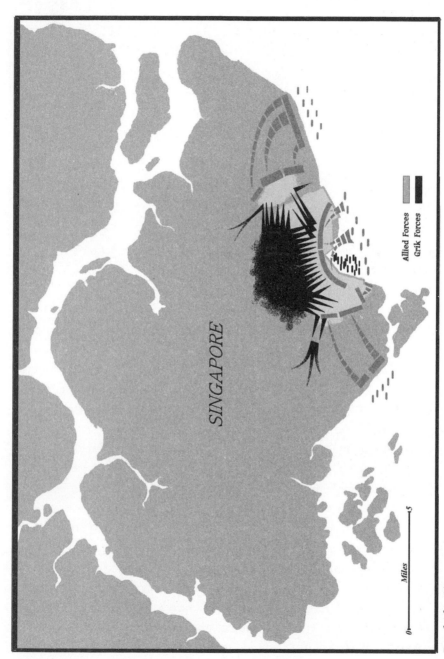

SINGAPORE

Allied Forces
Grik Forces

Miles
0————5

Battle for Singapore

*T*he mood in *Donaghey*'s wardroom was mixed that night. The island of Singapore was theirs, essentially, and almost without exception, all the objectives outlined in the plan had been achieved. Casualties were light, considering the relative sizes of the forces involved, and that was reason enough for most of the commanders to feel proud of and comfortable with the victory.

Lieutenant Blair was anything but comfortable. Not only did he suffer from a painful wound across his ribs, but his losses had not been light at all. Jenks and the Manilo courier astride the meanie had arrived at the left-flank blocking force too late to counsel, cajole, or issue orders, and in contrast to the other leaders present, Blair stared at the bulkhead with a stricken, opium-slacked expression.

His Imperial Marines had stood bravely in the face of the Grik tide that swarmed across them. The two aimed volleys of musket fire they'd managed had forced the charging Grik into Safir Maraan's shield wall, but meeting that immovable object, they'd swarmed back around it— and over the left flank "secured" by Blair's Marines. Caught in the process of reloading, and helpless in the face of an enemy the likes of which they'd never faced, the Imperial Marines either broke or were slaughtered where they stood. It was a horrifying thing to see, Safir later confessed to Matt, and she was as furious over the senseless waste of Blair's Marines as she was over the utterly avoidable losses her own flank had suffered before she could pull it back. In her practical, slightly bloodthirsty way, she'd insisted that Blair be hanged.

He wouldn't be, of course. Matt secretly suspected Jenks had far more control over Blair's tactics than he'd confessed, and the Marine Lieutenant had probably just been following orders: orders not to integrate his force with the Lemurians or take *their* orders under any circumstances. Jenks's own horror over the aftermath and his hesitation to censure Blair confirmed as much. If Blair could recover from watching half his men shredded before his eyes, he might be a better officer for it.

Otherwise, all the major port facilities had been secured and the remaining Grik driven into the jungle. Chack's 2nd Marines had joined with Alden's 1st, and together the two regiments stormed the stockade where the Japanese prisoners were held. They were just in time, too. Apparently, some final order had been issued by the now dead (by suicide, as usual) Hij commander that none of the Japanese be taken alive. More than a dozen of the thirty-odd advisor/prisoners had already been killed before the Marines slaughtered their captor/allies. With Matt's permission, the Bosun had accompanied the effort in case his Thompson was needed, and to his reported incredulity, one of the Japanese prisoners actually killed *himself* when he realized that Americans were among their rescuers! The rest of the Japs seemed appropriately grateful for their rescue, after witnessing their comrades die and recognizing their own ultimate fate.

The wardroom heaved and the gimbaled lanterns cast eerie shadows. The leading edge of the Strakka was upon them at last, having waited until the battle was over before descending in all its savage fury. The army still ashore had taken cover as best it could, mostly in the newly constructed Grik warehouses along the dock. Some pickets were still out, and the meanie-mounted Manilos were scouring the jungle for any large Grik concentrations they'd missed. Most reports had any semicohesive groups heading north. No one knew if there was any kind of causeway connecting this Singapore with the Malay Peninsula or not, but one way or another, the overriding imperative of the Grik survivors seemed to be escape. Even the enemy force that broke through on the left was reportedly moving north now, in disarray.

Matt was guardedly optimistic. They'd know more when the storm passed and the weather cleared, but the 2nd Allied Expeditionary Force seemed to have won the first purely offensive battle of the war. They'd engaged in an ambitious multipronged amphibious assault against territory the enemy knew better than they did, and utterly crushed that enemy on his own ground. It was a heady moment and an auspicious beginning to the complex strategic plan he, Adar, Keje, and Alden had initially conceived.

Matt was speaking to Rolak. Unlike Pete, who'd remained ashore, the old warrior wasn't too proud to retreat to the comforts of a warm, dry bed. "Too proud" probably wasn't the best way to put it, Matt decided, seeing the signs of fatigue the day had left on his friend. "Too practical not to," was probably the better choice of words. Chack remained ashore in his stead. The ship tossed on the suddenly malicious sea, jerking up short as her carefully laid anchors kept her in place. The wind screamed through the rigging and was even audible in the wardroom, over the pounding rain that lashed the skylight. It was a *hell* of a storm, Matt thought, but the Allied ships and their rich haul of prizes rode relatively easily in the protected harbor. It was a slow-moving Strakka, and any ship caught on the open ocean would have been in for it. In spades.

"What now?" Jenks asked. He'd come out to *Donaghey* with Matt before the storm struck with all its fury. He was essentially stranded aboard until the sea calmed enough for him to return to *Achilles*.

"Now we wait," Matt replied. "Clancy's been transmitting our action report to Baalkpan, but in this weather, who knows if they'll get anything. He said he's picked up pieces of a reply, but can't make any sense out of it." Matt shrugged. "Not only are we trying to transmit a message through terrible atmospheric conditions, but we can't run the wind generator in weather like this, so he can't even boost the gain on the output. Cheesy, primitive batteries are all we have."

"'Cheesy' to you, perhaps, but exciting technology to me, I assure you!"

Sean O'Casey suddenly burst into the compartment, waving a wet message form in his hand. His face was hard, enraged, and newly damp dried blood was running down his face like reconstituted tomato soup. Clancy trailed close behind. He looked a little apologetic, but overall his expression was much like O'Casey's.

"Ye must read this, Captain; read it now! Proof at last o' the heinous Empire that creature serves!" He was addressing Matt but his murderous glare was fixed on Jenks.

Matt was momentarily taken aback, but Jenks could only goggle at the one-armed apparition who'd appeared in their midst. Recognition spread across his face and it reddened with discovery and outrage.

"You!" Jenks shouted. "By all that's holy, how . . . ! That you should be *here*!" He turned to Matt. "Captain Reddy, I *demand* an explanation! This man is a wanted criminal—never mind the missing arm; I would recognize him anywhere! He is a traitor, sir, and his appearance here not only confirms it, but for him to appear now, after all these months, is sufficient proof to me that you *knew* he was wanted and yet kept the knowledge of his presence from me!"

"Ye *demand*!" O'Casey almost choked. "Captain Reddy, *I demand* that . . . monster be clapped in irons, his ship seized, an' he be hoisted kickin' to the end of a yard on the first sunny morn' we're granted! Of all the perfidious, lyin', spyin', goats o' the world! I hope ye choke all the day long afore ye gasp yer last!"

"As I said," continued Jenks, his tone ominous, "Mr. Bates is a wanted man. He is a traitor to his emperor and has risen in arms against him and his lawful subjects! I demand that you arrest him at once, or there will be consequences!"

"This is *my* ship," Greg Garrett suddenly exploded, "and *I* demand somebody tell me what the hell's going on here!"

"Yeah," Matt said angrily. "Let's all find out, shall we? What are you even doing here, O'Casey? You were supposed to be on *Dowden*!"

"He was ashore for the fighting today, Captain," Rolak answered. "Chack brought him and said you had told him to 'let O'Casey entertain himself,' or some such. He came aboard here with me."

Matt groaned. "Commodore Jenks," he said, "I was and am aware Mr. O'Casey—or Bates, as you seem to know him—is a fugitive from your government, but he's also the man most responsible for the survival of Princess Rebecca. He lost his arm in the act of saving her, and it was he and some of our submariners who protected and cared for her long before you ever came to call. I'm personally convinced he's not a traitor to your emperor or his household, although other . . . elements within your government might not agree. Ask the princess yourself for her opinion of the man!"

"Aye, that's the problem, Captain Reddy, the blackguard cannae do any such thing!"

"What the hell are you talking about?" Matt demanded. In answer, O'Casey held forth the message form.

"I been trying to clean it up, Skipper," Clancy supplied. "It just didn't make any sense! Finally, O'Casey here comes in the shack wanting to check on things back home. He used to do that now and then when he was here. . . . Anyway, we went over it again and again. There's no mistake!" Clancy glared at Jenks.

Matt took the page after a final glare around the wardroom, and looked at the words.

```
TO ALL MEMBERS OF THE SECOND ALLIED
EXPEDITIONARY FORCE X FROM ADAR COTGA
X GREETINGS AND CONGRATULATIONS ON
YOUR NOBLE VICTORY OVER THE EVIL FOE
X THE GRATITUDE OF YOUR PEOPLE AND
YOUR RACE KNOWS NO BOUNDS X AS
CHAIRMAN OF THE GRAND ALLIANCE
PLEASE ACCEPT MY MOST HUMBLE
APPRECIATION FOR YOUR VALOR AND
SACRIFICE X YOUR SLAIN AND WOUNDED
ARE IN MY PRAYERS X END MESSAGE

    ADDENDUM:

EYES ONLY M P REDDY CINCAF X DISTRIB-
UTE FOLLOWING AS YOU SEE FIT X AT
APPROX 0230 THIS DAY CMDR BILLINGSLY
AND IMPERIAL FRIGATE HIS COMMAND
```

COMMENCED OFFENSIVE OPERATIONS
AGAINST BAALKPAN—THE UNITED STATES
NAVY—THE GRAND ALLIANCE X SEVENTEEN
ALLIED PERSONNEL KILLED IN DIRECT
ACTION AND BY DELIBERATE DESTRUCTION
OF BAALKPAN HARBOR READY FUEL RE-
SERVE X APPARENT MOTIVE FOR ASSAULT
IS ABDUCTION OF PRINCESS REBECCA X
REGRET TO INFORM THIS OBJECTIVE
ACHIEVED X ALSO PROFOUNDLY REGRET TO
INFORM THAT OTHER HOSTAGES TAKEN
INCLUDE MINISTER OF MEDICINE SANDRA
TUCKER—SISTER AUDRY—ABEL COOK—DENNIS
SILVA—TAGRANESI LAWRENCE X SILVA AND
COOK BOTH WOUNDED CONDITION UNKNOWN X
UNABLE TO MOUNT IMMEDIATE EFFECTUAL
PURSUIT DUE TO DESTRUCTION FUEL RE-
SERVE AND THREATS AGAINST HOSTAGES X
COURSE ENEMY SHIP AJAX 050 CONSTANT
CONFIRMED BY AIR X REQUEST DIRECT
ORDER BEN MALLORY CEASE INCREASINGLY
EXTENDED OBSERVATION FLIGHTS X CANNOT
EXPRESS DEPTH OF SHAME X ADAR X END
TRANSMISSION

For a long moment, Matt could say nothing. The expression on his face must have told something of the nature of the tale, however, because the shouts and accusations in the wardroom ceased entirely and the only sounds came from the groaning hull, the confused sea, and the moaning storm outside. A rage as pure and hot and black as boiling pitch roiled up inside him as he reread the stilted words. They'd taken Sandra! That was all that registered at first. That maniac Billingsly had taken the one thing he truly cared about on this entire, mixed-up planet! No, that wasn't completely true. He cared about many things; he cared about their friends and the work they'd started here. He cared about the war and defeating the Grik so their friends and works might thrive. He cared about Rebecca, Sister Audry, Abel, and even Silva . . . but almost from the beginning, it had always been Sandra who gave him the strength and will to continue in the face of . . . anything. With her love, understanding, and healing way, she'd been the one who brought him back from the brink of despair when he lost his ship. She'd tended his battered, bleeding soul and restored it to something that *could* care again despite the horrors and agonies it had seen and endured. He couldn't lose her! She had become his life! When all was said and done, ultimately, she was *why* he carried on. *As God is my witness*, he swore fervently to himself, *I'll have you back, Sandra! And those who have done this, no matter who they are or where it takes me, are going to pay!*

He flung the sheet at Jenks, who picked it up and started to read. Matt waited a moment longer until he was sure he could control his voice. "Mr. Clancy," he said at last, "write this down." His tone was calm, but iron hard. Clancy fumbled through his notebook until he found a blank page and poised his pencil. "From Matt Reddy, et cetera, to Adar, et cetera. No shame. Even the best hunter can step on a viper." He paused to decide if the analogy was appropriate. Oddly, there were no snakes on Borneo that they knew of. There were deadly poisonous lizards however, and he'd heard them translated and referred to as vipers before—once in reference to Jenks himself, come to think of it. He nodded and continued, thinking hard as he spoke. "I want tankers sent out *today* from the new refinery at Tarakan Island. Use every available ship. We're going to start stockpiling fuel on Mindanao at Saan-Kakja's brother's place. Lots of it. We'll probably leapfrog it east of there as well. Meanwhile, if the Baalkpan tank batteries can't be repaired, we'll start a reserve at the refinery dock up the river, if we have to. I don't care if we have to fill Grik hulks with the stuff. We took enough ships today to make up any supply issues that might arise." He paused and Jenks tried to speak. "Shut up," Matt said, and turned back to Clancy.

"No matter what, we still have to keep the pressure up out here. Baalkpan is to redouble its efforts to get all the steamers, troops, supplies—everything—to Singapore as fast as possible. Keje's got to step on it too. We need *Big Sal* and her planes to scout if nothing else.

Finally"—he paused again and took a deep breath—"if Spanky honestly doesn't think *Walker* will be ready to steam ten thousand miles and fight a battle within thirty days, I want all work on her suspended. We don't have the time to waste resources on her."

Everyone in the compartment was flabbergasted. Most still had no idea what had occurred, but if Matt was willing to write *Walker* off, it must have been something . . . astonishing. Sensing Captain Reddy's sudden hostility toward the Imperial, Garrett snatched the message form from him.

"General Rolak? I want Chack and a company of the Second Marines," Matt said.

Rolak glanced at the hull and, by implication, the storm outside. "Now, lord?"

"Right now." He looked at Clancy. "As soon as we're finished here, anyway. Signal 'em to be ready, if you can." Glancing at Garrett, he saw the rage and astonishment begin to spread across his face. "I love the old *Donaghey*, but she's helpless right now," he said, still talking to Clancy. "Signal Mr. Ellis on *Dowden* and have her come alongside as close as he dares. Somebody wake up the Bosun and assemble the Captain's Guard. When *Dowden* arrives, we're going across. We'll try to swoop in close to the dock and pick up Chack's Marines."

"What are we going to *do* about this, Skipper?" Garrett demanded.

Matt's gaze finally fell on Jenks. "First, we're going to take that bastard's ship."

There was an uproar then, with everyone grabbing for the message form and shouting for explanations.

"Enough!" Matt bellowed, and when there was silence, he calmly summed up the situation.

Sensing his position was precarious at best, Jenks cleared his throat. "Captain Reddy, may I speak now?"

"Knock yourself out."

"Captain . . ." Jenks's hand encompassed all present. "Gentlemen, I assure you that none of you is more shocked and horrified by this outrage than I. I swear before God that Commander Billingsly has acted not only independently of, but utterly against my direct orders!" He faced Captain Reddy. "Think upon it, sir! We were upon that field together today! Think upon what we discussed! Think of the *blood* that was shed by my countrymen! I accept that it may have been shed foolishly, and that is for me to bear, but it is no less precious or sacred for all my pride! Upon *that blood* I swear I am sincere!"

O'Casey balled his single fist and took a step forward. "Sincere, are ye? How sincere were ye when ye crushed me effort tae destroy the likes o' Billingsly long ago?"

"*You took up arms against the throne!*" Jenks shouted. "What was I to *do*? I fancy we were friends once, you and I. The governor-emperor himself called you friend! He tried—*I* tried to make you see reason, to seek accommodation, but *no*! It has always been all or nothing with you! We could have pushed the Company back, reined it in, but you had to have it *all*; you wanted it *dead*! Instead, by *your* actions, your *rebellion*, you won sympathy for their cause! It was *you* who gave them a majority in both courts and marginalized the governor-emperor to near impotence! It is you, ultimately, who has brought us to *this*!"

O'Casey took another step, but instead of striking Jenks, he suddenly seemed to deflate. It was as if years of self-righteous anger and purpose just drained away and left nothing in its wake. Nothing but a man. He began to sob. "Oh, ye divil, ye prob'ly have the right o' it!" he managed through his tears. "God damn me fer a fool! An' now the very beast I'd hoped ta slay has our sweet princess! God *damn* me!"

Jenks's hand seemed to strain to comfort the big man, but didn't reach quite far enough. "No," he said softly. "God damn *me*. You were right all along, as it turns out. The Company *is* a beast to spawn men like Billingsly. I doubt now that we could have controlled it in the end, regardless. Damn *me* for not joining your cause!"

Stiffly, Jenks faced Captain Reddy. "You have my surrender, sir, and that of my ship." He fumbled at his side for his sword. "I will not fight you. As that note will attest, your people and mine would seem to be at war. *My God*, but this is a stupid, terrible world we live in! In any event, your people are clearly the aggrieved party and I will require none of those under my command to shed their blood in defense of the actions of a lunatic. Or a nation gone mad."

Matt shook his head, as if to clear it. Too much too fast! "Keep your sword, Commodore Jenks," he said at last. "It would seem I'm not at war with *you* after all. But I'm kind of like O'Casey, or Bates, or whoever he is, in one respect: all or nothing. From now on, you're on our side all or nothing, and we're on yours the same way. We're still taking some of the Second Marines aboard *Achilles*, though, you and I. If there's anyone you or anyone you trust even *suspects* of being a Company spy, they'll be sent back here to *Donaghey*'s brig."

Matt looked at Clancy. "Make those signals now, if you please." He turned to Rolak. "Commodore Ellis will assume overall command here until Keje arrives with the rest of the fleet. At that point, Keje will assume strategic command, but you and General Alden will still command the ground troops. Jim will be Keje's exec and chief of staff. Standing orders are and will remain to keep up the pressure on the Grik. Stay focused *here,* on the job that's *here,* and push the bastards any way you can. Follow the plan, but stay flexible; the ability to do that has always been our biggest advantage."

"But . . . of course, lord. But where will you be?"

Matt jerked his chin at Jenks. "I'm going home. With him."

Rain battered Adar's Great Hall, where the grim meeting was under way. The air was dank and musty with the smell of wet fur and burning gri-kakka oil. A broad, hand-drawn map covered a large table in the gloom, and all the major leaders of the Alliance were gathered around it. All who weren't absent or taken from them, at least. Kathy McCoy stood in for Sandra and Karen Theimer Letts. Karen had taken the news of the abductions hard, and with her increasingly difficult pregnancy nearing its peak, Alan had convinced her to let him put her on light duty.

"But surely they're not coming *now*," sputtered Geran-Eras, high chief of *Humfra-Dar* Home. *Humfra-Dar* had been with the Alliance almost from the first, and Geran, the first female High Chief the Americans had known before they met Saan-Kakja, was particularly fond of Matt. Now young Tassana was a High Chief too, and she nodded agreement with Geran's concern.

"It is madness to ride the Strakka!"

Adar nodded miserably. "I fear Captain Reddy has gone quite mad—in that dangerous, special way we have all come to recognize— and it is my fault!"

"Bullshit," Spanky growled. "For the last time, Adar, it ain't your fault! And Captain Reddy hasn't gone mad, he's just mad as hell. I am too—we all are." He paused, watching the nods. "I don't know what kind of seaman Jenks is, but the captain's not going to let him goof around and get them sunk, either. *Achilles* might take a beating, but she's running with the storm. My bet is they just get here faster."

"Your confidence is reassuring," Adar said, "both in Captain Reddy and myself." He sighed. "But what of these other issues? What of *Walker*?"

It was Spanky's turn to sigh. "We'll have her ready," he said simply. "As much as she means to you, she means even more to me. I'm not about to give up on the old girl now. Besides, the skipper's going to need her."

"What remains to be done?" Keje asked.

"About a million things," Spanky admitted, "but we're already working on most of them. If we just quit, the guys working on that stuff will waste a lot of time twiddling their thumbs before they can get up to speed on other projects anyway." He held up his hand, counting off on his fingers. "Just about everything on *Walker* runs on one twenty DC. That's what we've standardized all our industry for. Even if we hadn't rebuilt her little generators, we could probably stick one of our homemade jobs in her. We're still soaking her AC generator, the one she needs for the gyro and a few other things, but we're almost done with it too."

They'd discovered yet *another* use for the ubiquitous polta fruit and the seemingly endless applications to which it lent itself. In this instance, the fermented form of the juice that became the popular intoxicant seep would turn to a variety of vinegar if its ultimate journey toward becoming the curative polta paste was interrupted. They'd made diluted vinegar baths for the generators and other electrical equipment to deoxidize the nonferrous components. The solution was weak enough that it did that nicely without unduly attacking the ferrous parts. This rendered the assemblies clean and corrosion-free for their ultimate disassembly and restoration.

"Thank God at least the gyro itself was dry," Spanky added. He nodded at Rodriguez. "Ronson and his EMs have been running all over the ship, refurbishing distribution panels, breakers, switches, and all that magical electrical shit. Act like a buncha spiders spinnin' wires everywhere instead of webs."

Rodriguez arched his eyebrows, which matched his Pancho Villa mustache quite well. "Come into my parlor," he said, in a passable Bela Lugosi imitation.

Spanky rolled his eyes, but inwardly he was satisfied. Like all of them, Ronson Rodriguez had come a long way. "Hull and structural damage was repaired before we refloated her," he continued. "Her turbines ain't new, or anything like it, but they're in at least as good a shape as they were when she went down. We hadn't been able to do proper maintenance on 'em in forever, so we still had plenty of spare seals and bearings and such. For them, at least. Numbers three and four boilers *are* practically new. Completely rebuilt and clean as a whistle inside and out." He shook his head. "Those Mice . . . Anyway, we're starting on number three. I wanted to put a new boiler where number one used to be, one that *could* burn something besides oil if it had to, but I guess she's still going to need that extra fuel capacity after all. We'll get started on a new, better bunker in there. Thanks to Letts's gaskets, her steam lines are tight as a drum. We're still having trouble with the steering engine, but we'll get it sorted out."

"That is all very well," Keje said. "She can float and she can steam, but what will she fight with, at need?" Spanky looked at Campeti to answer.

"Uh, well, there's good news and bad news. The numbers one, two, and three four-inch fifties are ready to go back aboard. Even made a new, thicker splinter shield for number one outta Jap steel." He looked at Rodriguez. "Your guys'll have to wire 'em in to the gun director, which, thank God, never even got wet." Rodriguez nodded and Campeti went on. "The number four gun and the three incher on the fantail are practically junk. We can save the tubes and breeches, but that's about it. No way can they be ready in thirty days. Same with the torpedo tubes and mounts—not that we have anything to stick in 'em. Three and four were already gone. We can make the number one triple mount work now, if we swipe parts from number two, but without torpedoes, what's the point? I say we leave 'em off for now and fix 'em at our leisure. Who knows? Maybe someday we'll have some torps.

"I do have a little good news. All the old girl's machine guns survived. That gives us two thirties and two fifties to start with. Add the two fifties we fished up from the PBY and all the ammo the skipper's bringing that Ellis found, and we're actually better off there."

"What about putting some of the Jap guns from *Amagi* on her?" Spanky asked.

"Yeah, I was coming to that," Campeti said. "We've got just about all *Amagi*'s secondaries ashore now, and most are in decent shape. There's a fair amount of ammo for 'em, too. Some was wet, but some was in ready lockers above the waterline." He shrugged. "Some cooked off in the fire. Anyway, the only ones I know we could tie into our fire control are the five and a halfs. They have about the same velocity as our own guns, according to what Shinya told Bernie, but they're way too damn heavy to stick on *Walker*. The dual-purpose four-point-sevens are just a little heavier and only a little slower. They might work—at least in local control. They're the best bet, actually. They were mounted higher up and we've already recovered more ammo for them than *Walker* ever carried. If Brister can get the aft deckhouse rebuilt in time, we could mount one of those suckers right where number four used to be."

"You said they're slower, but with us feeding the four-inch fifties black powder, that's not so, is it?" Spanky asked.

"Not right now," Campeti defended, "but we have to standardize on what we have the most of. 'Sides, Mr. McFarlane, hope springs eternal. We still haven't got the new propellants sorted out, but we will someday. Then we can tie 'em all together."

"What about the antiaircraft stuff?"

Campeti looked thoughtful. "We might stick a few of those Jap twenty-five millimeters on the old girl, just for hoots. They're kinda clunky and don't seem good for much. They're not heavy, though, and we've got 'em. Lots of bullets, too."

"Do it," said Letts. "I want the skipper to have as much firepower as we can give him."

Ben Mallory had been murmuring something to Tikker during the exchange. He was utterly exhausted, having flown all day. Captain Reddy never did order him not to fly, but the Strakka had him grounded for now. By the time the storm was past, *Ajax* would surely be out of range. "I got an idea," he said suddenly. All eyes turned to him. "Yeah," he said, thinking fast, "I got a *swell* idea. When you get the ship all put back together, what's going in that empty space where the torpedo tubes used to be? I know the searchlight tower's there, but what else?"

"I don't know," Spanky confessed. "Maybe those popguns Campeti was talking about."

"Why not give her one of the Nancys!" Ben said triumphantly. "Skipper's always going on about recon," he said a little smugly. "Let's give him some!"

Spanky, Letts, Adar, and Keje all looked at one another.

"Would a davit lift one of those cockeyed contraptions of yours?" Letts asked.

"Sure! They don't weigh much. Might have to rig an extension boom. But with all the weight we're saving, even with the Jap stuff you're adding on, there'll be plenty of margin for a plane, fuel, spares and such as well!"

"And I guess you just happen to know somebody who'd volunteer to fly it, too?"

"Well . . . sure." Ben grinned.

Letts looked at Adar, then shook his head. "Great idea, Ben, but not you. We need you to train pilots, not go tear-assing off on your own. Besides, don't forget what Mr. Ellis found. What would we do about that without you?" Ben slumped, but brightened again at the prospect of an expedition to Tjilatjap. Tikker grinned hugely and his tail swished expectantly. "Not you either," said Letts. "As our only other combat-experienced aviator, you'll command *Big Sal*'s air wing, or squadron"— he shook his head—"whatever you're going to call it."

"Then who?" Ben and Tikker demanded simultaneously.

"You said Ensign Reynolds is competent to commence independent operations. We'll ask him if he'd like to volunteer."

"This is all very excellent, but this discussion has strayed somewhat," Adar said. "You have convinced me that *Walker* will be ready. Good. What else must we do? There are other issues at hand."

"Well," said Letts, "*Big Sal* will soon be ready for sea. The new frigates too, as soon as we can fuel 'em. They're finished. We'll put the planes we have on *Big Sal*, and send the fleet off against the Grik. *Humfra-Dar* can then go in the dry dock. We'll send a couple other Homes with the troops we can't put in the frigates. Otherwise, we keep doing what we're doing." He looked around. "Making the tools for them to do the job."

"Indeed," said Adar, "that is as I hoped. We must push the Grik! Whatever support Captain Reddy requires in the east, Saan-Kakja has promised. Already, ships are leaving Manila to intercept and shadow this *Ajax*. We have finally contacted Lieutenant Laumer on Talaud—his transmitter was damaged—and Captain Lelaa's sloop will attempt to intercept *Ajax* as well. We have addressed all we seem capable of, yet *one* serious issue remains."

"Ah!" Courtney Bradford declared, speaking at last. He hadn't had anything to add to the military and logistical discussion, but now his turn had come. "I presume you refer to a certain . . . ticklish physical and somewhat spiritual notion?"

"It is not a *notion*!" Adar insisted. "For such a learned creature, you are so very cavalier with the most fundamental laws of things!"

"Physics," Bradford agreed. "And I assure you Mr. Chairman, I'm not in the least cavalier about that at all! The problem is, as I've so often told you—and not to put too fine a point on it or to intentionally insult you in any way—your understanding of some physical aspects of the world are . . . well . . . wrong." He pointed at the map before them. "According to Captain Reddy's last transmission, Commodore Jenks has at last freely revealed what many of us have long suspected: this Empire of New Britain Isles is centered in a chain we called the Hawaiian Islands! It is quite distant indeed. It is, in fact, according to your, um, *mis*understanding, quite an impossible place for anyone to be, or even exist. You recognize the world is round, like a cannonball, but since gravity pulls *downward*, you believe we here stand either near or upon the very top of the world! I assume this tradition is due to our proximity to the equator and the fact that the midday sun passes almost directly overhead. On its face, that would seem a most sensible and understandable position. I take it, however, from our discussions and a few old sayings I've heard, that you believe anyone who ventures too distant in any direction will plummet into the void of the heavens!"

"That is a simplistic summation, but essentially correct. Of course, one may venture quite far before that occurs. You have shown me maps of where this Mada-gaaskar lies. You insist it is our ancestral home and I doubt it not. The distance and description are consistent with the Scrolls. Clearly one can exist even that far away, since we once did ourselves. The Grik dwell there still, and in places even more distant. But this . . . Ha-waa-ee . . . It is so far! It is in the Eastern Sea, where monsters even more terrifying than the mountain fish dwell! You cannot lightly ask anyone to venture that far."

"We must, and so will you," Alan Letts said, "because that's where *Ajax* is going."

Bradford pondered a moment. "My dear Adar, I know we have asked much of you and your people in matters of faith. We popped in here and, in some ways, stood many things you've always believed upon their heads. I personally apologize for that. Having one's beliefs constantly under assault is always traumatic, and I *do* respect your beliefs even if they are wrong." He cleared his throat, realizing that didn't come out quite how he'd intended. "I shall ask you a rhetorical question. You are of the sea folk. You have wandered far indeed throughout your life. Perhaps, at times, you have even wandered far enough that you feared you were getting, oh, at least a little close to the dropoff point. True?"

"Perhaps," Adar reluctantly agreed. "Once we voyaged around the bottom of the land you call Aus-traalia. I admit I grew somewhat concerned."

"Tell me, as you drew farther south, did you notice anything extraordinary?"

"It . . . was less warm."

"Yes, yes, but what I mean is, did you notice any tendency at all to walk strangely, or lean? Did you feel any sideways pull of gravity at all?" Adar didn't answer, but he seemed frustrated and even a little irritated. "I must point out that we, these other humans and myself, have little better understanding of what gravity *is* than you do. We *have* learned that it works quite well and it is surprisingly consistent wherever one goes, whether here, Australia, or even the other side of the world. No matter where one goes, gravity always pulls downward, toward the center of the world! This, sir, is a fact. When Captain Reddy told you and Keje that he was born and raised on the 'bottom' of the world, he was quite sincere. Most of our American friends are from a land situated on the far side of this globe. I have never been to America, but I can assure you the Americans have, and they did not have to hang upside down, clinging to their land with their fingers!" He looked thoughtful. "Your beliefs are correct in the respect that the sea returns to the sky, but it does not pour off the side of the world to do it; it evaporates and travels upward, much like the smoke of your pyres carries the souls of your dead to the heavens! It is always dreadfully humid here, but surely you've experienced a day or two in your life when the air seemed less thick, less heavy?"

Adar nodded speculatively.

"Then there you have it! That thickness of the air is water being carried into the sky!"

"If this 'gravity' works so well, then why does it not prevent that?" Adar demanded.

Courtney sighed. "It's a long story. I can and certainly will be more than happy to demonstrate the experiments required to prove it to you, but for the moment, I ask only that you trust me—trust us. The ultimate fact remains that, in order to retrieve those who have been taken from us and deal with this . . . situation in the east that threatens to distract us from our bigger business, Captain Reddy will chase them when he arrives. As you have had faith in us before, have faith now; those who go east will *not* fall off the world. They"—he looked defiantly around the chamber—"*we* may well face unknown dangers, but falling into the sky is not one of them!"

Achilles arrived in Baalkpan Bay on the very heels of the Strakka, after what must have been a record passage. She'd sustained some minor damage, but Matt could find no fault with Jenks's seamanship. Stony stares greeted her arrival and the flag she flew as she steamed into the bay and eased up to the dock. Only when Captain Reddy, the Captain's Guard, and Chack's Marines disembarked was there a marked decrease in the hostile tension. Many people still tried to get at the ship and the people aboard, but the company of the 2nd Marines with Chack was more than sufficient to keep the crowd at bay.

Matt strode to meet Adar, Keje, Letts, and Spanky, flanked by Gray, Stites, O'Casey, and the rest of his personal guard. "It's good to see you, Adar," Matt said, receiving the customary embrace. Keje embraced him as well. "I wish it were under better circumstances."

"As do I, my friend. I cannot express—"

"Skip it," Matt interrupted. "It's done. Quit beating yourself up. Now we have to decide what we're going to do about it."

"Yes," Adar agreed. "All has been prepared as you have specified. The wood and charcoal have been brought, as you ordered." Adar pointed at a massive heap. "That is for *Achilles*, I take it?"

"Yeah. Jenks wants to get under way as soon as possible. Can't say I blame him." He looked at Adar, at all the faces present. "And yes, I do trust him. What's weird is, even O'Casey trusts him now. You wouldn't believe the mess they've got at home." He paused. "Or maybe you would. It's sort of like Aryaal and B'mbaado, except it's all mixed-up in one government." He shook his head. "Anyway, that doesn't matter. Jenks might catch them, but I doubt it. He has to try, though, and we might need him." Suddenly, Matt looked at *Walker*, tied securely to the pier. Her upper works had not yet been repainted, except for a few spots where the weather had allowed the painting of some welds and seams. She looked like a patchwork quilt, but she was *whole*, or mostly so. Smoke rose from two stacks and workers shouted and scrambled over her. A strange-looking gun was being lowered onto her rebuilt and slightly reconfigured aft deckhouse. Her force-draft blower gave the distinct impression she was breathing on her own.

"I didn't believe it," he confessed quietly. For a moment, the hard expression he'd worn melted away. "I couldn't let myself." He looked at Spanky. "Mr. McFarlane, my compliments—and my most heartfelt appreciation."

Spanky looked uncomfortable. "Shucks, Skipper, wasn't just me."

"No, but you're the ramrod. Always have been. Looking at you, I doubt you've slept since those bastards took the girls."

Spanky shrugged, glancing down at his stained and filthy self. "Not many have. You're gonna need your ship for this one, Skipper. She's the only thing in the world fast enough to catch them. You've pulled more than one trick out of her hat. I figure she's got plenty more where they came from."

Matt clasped the skinny man's arm. "You bet. How long?"

"Two weeks, Skipper. We'll have her good as new by then. Might be a few quirks—we've basically rebuilt her from the keel up—but that's still a week ahead of schedule."

"I doubt it, if you count the man hours!" Matt chuckled grimly. "Give the guys a little more time off if you can. Don't worry; I'm not going to stop you now!"

Spanky—everyone—grinned relief. They'd been afraid the captain would want to leave immediately. Undoubtedly he did *want* to, but he also knew a fully repaired *Walker* would catch *Ajax* regardless of the head start over the vast distances they were contemplating. One thing bothered Keje, however, and he had to ask.

"What will this Billingsly do with the hostages? He has threatened to kill them if he is harassed. Might he not do that anyway?"

Matt shook his head. "I don't think so, and neither does Jenks. Taking the princess was his objective. According to your accounts of the events, everybody else he took was basically an accident. If he just wanted Rebecca dead, he could have assassinated her many times and just left before anyone got wise." He shook his head. "No, he wants her alive, or this Company he works for does. Probably as a bargaining chip to wring even more power from the governor-emperor. If I know the princess, she's going to be making life miserable for Mr. Billingsly about now. See, not all of *Ajax*'s crew are Company men. Even her captain is a loyalist, according to Jenks. Billingsly wouldn't dare even clap her in irons without risking an open break with what has to be a very divided crew. I bet that will put the princess in a position to demand decent treatment for the hostages."

"I hope you are right," murmured Adar.

"Me too," Matt admitted.

Jenks joined them, saluting. "Please let me express my most abject apologies," he said sincerely. "If I had only known—"

"You stow it too," Matt interrupted. "Everybody's sorry. Okay. We're all on the same side now, so let's get on with it. What do you need?"

"Very well. Some assistance loading the fuel aboard my ship would be appreciated. Our victuals should suffice, but a little more couldn't hurt. Also, after observing the healing effects of your wondrous polta paste, I would beg some of that from you as well."

Adar, still eyeing Jenks suspiciously, motioned to one of his staff standing a discreet distance away. "See to it," he commanded.

"How are we fixed for transmitters and receivers?" Matt asked.

Spanky looked around. "I'll have to ask Riggs. Most have been going in the new ships as soon as they finish 'em."

"See if we can spare a set for Commodore Jenks. I want a couple of spares aboard *Walker* too. I never want to be out of touch again."

"Who'll operate it?" Spanky asked, referring to the one meant for *Achilles*.

"Clancy told me Mr. O'Casey has become fairly proficient. He didn't have much else to do on the voyage out, after all. At least until we transferred him to *Dowden*." Matt looked at Jenks, who was staring at his old nemesis.

"Under the circumstances, I believe that would certainly be acceptable, if Mr. O'Casey—Bates—would be kind enough to agree. In fact, with the discovery that my second officer was one of Billingsly's creatures, I have an opening there as well."

With a strange expression, O'Casey nodded. "Aye, 'twould be . . . interestin' ta sail with ye again, Commodore. On the same side."

Dennis Silva groaned and opened his good eye. He'd actually been awake and alert for some time, but playing possum was a skill he'd learned in China once upon a time, and it had come in handy more than once. When, oh, Chinese gangsters, for example, thought you were down for the count, they were less prepared when you suddenly resurrected yourself and beat them to death with a goofy jade Buddha you didn't know why you had. Life was weird that way, and it always helped to have an edge. He groaned again, making sure the ladies knew he was awake. He hadn't learned much during his possum phase, but he did know everyone was alive, where they were, and that, for the moment, they were alone.

"What hit me?" he grumbled. That was still a mystery. He'd been doing well enough, him and Lawrence, when everything just . . . quit. He knew his head hurt—badly—so something must have conked him. He didn't remember anything else from then, until a short time ago.

"Strange. I would have wagered on 'where am I?' came Sister Audry's voice.

"Wagerin's a sin, Sister," Dennis proclaimed piously. "'Sides, any fool can tell we're at sea, an' I been in enough brigs to recognize one for what it is, even if I never been in it before."

"The weapon was a bag of musket balls," Princess Rebecca said, moving quickly to sit beside him where he lay on a pair of moldy blankets. "But the man who hit you was a particularly revolting and traitorous coward named Truelove. He seems to be Billingsly's chief minion." She caressed his forehead and then gingerly inspected his wound. "Healing nicely, at last," she pronounced. Silva hadn't yet tried to rise, but he suspected it would be a disorienting procedure.

"Truelove, eh? Big guy? I remember him. Hafta make a point outta returning the favor. I hate leavin' obligations like that undid." He paused, a thoughtful expression on his face. "Knew it had to be a sneak attack. Ol' Abe the newsboy mighta whupped me in a fair fight, but by the time I met him, it wouldn't have been fair. Good fella. Readin' about him's practically what got me in the Navy. Practically."

"You fought splendidly before that coward struck you down!" Rebecca gushed. "Splendidly!"

"Well . . . of course I did! Ol' Larry helped a little, though. Say, how is the little lizardy guy?"

"I okay," came a familiar voice from the gloom.

Sandra Tucker moved into Dennis's field of vision. "Lucky for you, you showed enough sense to keep some polta paste in your shooting bag. Rebecca got it for us. She pretty much has the run of the ship. You probably would have come out of it—you've got a bad concussion, by the way—but we might have lost young Mr. Cook. Before Truelove hit you, he'd evidently fired his last pistol at the boy. The ball took a big hunk out of the top of his shoulder, close to his neck. Not normally a mortal wound, but it became infected quite quickly."

"Well. Yeah, I keep some o' that stuff in there case o' scratches an' such. Be kinda stupid, after all we been through, to die o' some infected scratch. How is the little bugger? Abel, right?"

"I'm here, sir," came a weak voice. "I'm well enough. I did what you said. I yelled and ran for help!"

"And was shot for his efforts too, the brave, silly boy!" Rebecca scolded.

"Oh, well. Ever'body gets shot sooner or later in the Navy. Seems like it, anyway. You done good, boy." Silva finally tried to sit up, but it just wasn't going to happen yet. He growled and lay back down. "So," he said, "what's the scam? Why ain't we been rescued?"

"We're hostages," Sandra said simply. "They've threatened to kill us if our forces molest them. For a couple of days, one of our planes came and buzzed around, but we haven't seen it since the storm."

"A couple o' days! A storm! How long have I been out?"

"Several days. I believe you were in a coma."

"Huh. Damn, no wonder I'm so hungry. Several days on this bucket and we could be anywhere. That's the first thing we gotta figure out: where we are. Then we gotta keep track of our position."

"Why?" Sister Audry asked.

"So we'll know when to get off, of course! If they're keepin' us hostage, our folks won't blow the hell outta this tub! Besides, Dennis Silva ain't *nobody's* hostage!"

"What's your plan?" Rebecca asked eagerly.

"Ain't got one yet. I just woke up, remember? Gimme a minute or two to figure the angles. So, Miss . . . Lieutenant . . . Minister . . ."

Sandra laughed. "Lieutenant will still do."

"Thanks, ma'am. Lieutenant Tucker says you got the run o' the ship?"

"Essentially," Rebecca replied. "That porcine beast must preserve the fiction he has rescued *me* from *you*. No one actually believes it. I spend most of my time down here, after all, but he dares not put me in irons. My behavior is controlled by threats against your well-being."

"You figure there's anybody aboard we can count on?"

"I'm sure of it. There are more Company men aboard *Ajax* than any ship that sailed with the squadron, but not all are traitors. Why, even the captain, Captain Rajendra, is a loyal man! He fairly chafes! He does not know what to do, however. Less than half the crew stands with him."

"The captain himself, eh?" Silva pondered. "Sure you can trust him?"

"Absolutely."

"Then get our position from him. We need maps too. Charts."

"What have you got in mind?" Sandra demanded.

"Well, I'm still conjurin' it up, and me and the boy have a little healin' to do, but it strikes me the last thing we want is to wind up wherever this ship is goin'. Once we're there, there won't be any use for us. There may not be any use for the princess. So somewhere between here and there, we have to switch trains."

Irvin Laumer's eyes jerked open and he leaped to his feet when he heard the scream. Everyone was exhausted and he'd been taking a short siesta in the shade of a leafy lean-to on the beach. Only an idiot would do such a thing under the standing trees on Talaud Island. It took him an instant to realize the scream had come from the workers near the sub. Sprinting through the loose sand, he yanked the .45 from his holster and jacked a round into the chamber.

"What the hell's going on here?" he shouted. The screaming had stopped, but there was still a lot of shouting and confusion around the work site.

"One of the 'Cats was just walking across the gangplank to the boat," Danny Porter said excitedly, "when this jet of water, like a high-pressure hose, knocked him off into the water! As soon as he fell in, something . . . got him!"

Irvin looked at him incredulously, then eased a little closer to the basin they'd begun excavating around S-19. There was a lot of water down there, and nothing they could do about it. Some soaked in through the sand and more came in with the tide when the sea was running high. Sometimes the boat actually floated. "What was it?" Irvin asked.

"How the hell am I supposed to know?" Danny demanded. "There's all kinds of weird, murdering critters running around on this place! It's a miracle we survived here as long as we did before, and we were idiots to come back to it!" Danny brought his voice under control. "And if that ain't enough, we've got *that* thing scaring the water out of everybody!" He pointed at the mist-shrouded volcano in the distance. When they'd been marooned on Talaud Island, the volcano occasionally rumbled and made the ground shake, but for the past few weeks, it had been venting almost constantly. Sometimes it belched heavy clouds of ash that settled on them and got into everything when the wind was right. Sometimes it just made creepy noises. A time or two, they'd had spectacular light shows in the middle of the night. Nobody in their group really knew squat about volcanoes, aside from a few historical accounts, but the overwhelming consensus was that the Talaud volcano was building up to something big.

The problem was, they were stuck there—marooned again, in a sense. *Simms*'s consort had been little more than a freighter, and once she'd off-loaded the equipment, machinery, fuel oil for the steam boiler, and the hopefully required diesel, she'd sailed for Manila for more supplies. *Simms* had remained, lending her crew to the labor and as a safety measure in case, for any reason, they had to abandon the expedition. But even *Simms* and Captain Lelaa were gone now. They'd sailed two days before to rendezvous with a little squadron of feluccas led by Saan-Kakja's brother to intercept and at least pinpoint *Ajax*'s position.

Irvin understood why Lelaa had to go, but it left him and his crew in a pickle. *Simms* had taken the newly repaired transmitter, and the set on the boat was irreparable. Tex was trying to build another set like Riggs's design from the parts at hand, but it was slow going. In the meantime, they were at the mercy of all the terrors *Walker* had once rescued them from—the dangerous predators including the nocturnal tree git-yas, as Flynn had called them, bizarre creatures that looked and acted like a cross between a Grik and a sloth that dropped on unwary prey from above. There were other things, almost ghostly things no one had ever really seen or had a shot at, that could snatch a man and run faster than anything ought to be capable of. Then there was the mountain, of course. Now . . .

"Did anybody get a look at it at all?" Laumer asked of the creature that got the 'Cat.

"Well, it was kind of blotchy," Sid Franks volunteered. As the carpenter, he would now have to repair the damaged gangplank. The jet of water had enough force to blow off the handrail. "It swirled up when it . . ." He stopped, staring at the water.

"So whatever it is, it's still in there?" There were nods and Irvin sighed. "Must be a sea creature. Came out of the water last night when nobody was looking and moved in." He shrugged. "Only one thing for it." He turned to Midshipman Hardee, who, along with a 'Cat who'd been dubbed Spook, had increasingly taken on their ordnance duties. "We have to get rid of this thing before we can get any more work done today. Get some of the grenades and all the small arms. Make sure you issue them to guys who know how to use them."

The armed guards who protected the workers from the denizens of the jungle were summoned, and with the distribution of the four other Krags and the single Thompson (all the small arms had been retrieved from the submarine on *Walker*'s previous visit) a total of eight riflemen, one submachine gunner (Danny), and Irvin Laumer armed with his pistol prepared to face whatever was in the water. Six grenadiers had simple, ingenious devices quite similar to the grenades the Americans were accustomed to. They were virtually identical in form and function, although the fuses weren't as reliable. There could be as many as ten seconds or as few as two before the things went off, so there was never any goofing around after the spoon flew.

Irvin nodded at the first 'Cat grenadier. The idea was to chase the creature aft, toward the screws, where the water was shallower. There they hoped to get some shots at it. The grenades weren't powerful enough to damage the pressure hull of the submarine, but Irvin told them not to throw the things too close to it anyway. With a returning nod, the first 'Cat pulled the pin and dropped his weapon in the water. A few seconds later, a geyser of spume and white smoke erupted into the air with a dull thump, and this was the signal for the next grenade. A high, splashing column of water that dissipated downwind followed another *ker-plunk*. A third grenade went off. Then a fourth. Suddenly, out of the spume of the fifth grenade, something . . . terrifying . . .

scrambled up out of the excavation directly at Tex Sheider. At first glance, it looked like a mottled black-and-green spider, but it had a tail sort of like a lobster and long, thin claws to match, making it at least ten feet long. One of the claws clutched the partially shredded body of the 'Cat workman.

"Holy shit!" was all Tex had time to screech before it blew him off his feet with a concentrated burst of seawater. Instantly, the monster lunged at him.

"Well . . . fire, damn it!" Irvin yelled.

Danny opened up with his Thompson, spraying chunks off the beast in all directions. The black powder loads under his bullets created a fog bank of white smoke around him. The thing recoiled from the impacts and writhed in agony. The other riflemen had recovered somewhat from the sudden appearance and attack and were scrambling to shoot without hitting one another. Irvin stepped forward, firing his pistol. He'd never fired any of the new loads before and was surprised not only by the smoke, but by the significantly greater recoil and loud boom that came with every shot instead of the usual sharp bark. The hideous creature turned to face him and he steeled himself for another blast of water. This time, however, there was only a meager, bloody splurt, and as he emptied his magazine, the creature suddenly flopped on its back and began to spasm violently. Irvin ran to Tex and grabbed him by the shirt, dragging him farther from the dying beast. Tex seemed unconscious, and where his shirt had torn, Irvin could see a dark red impact point on his chest.

"Cease firing!" he shouted at the men and 'Cats who were still shooting at the creature. Any twitching movement was sufficient proof to them that more bullets were called for. "Get over here! Help me with this man!"

Irvin was feeling for a pulse when Tex suddenly groaned. "Oh, Jesus, that hurts." He gasped.

"What does?"

"What do you think! It feels like that thing squirted a fourteen-inch shell at me!"

Irvin gently tore the rest of the shirt away. The red mark was already turning black. "Lie still! You may have some broken ribs! No

wonder it was able to knock the 'Cat off the gangway! You're lucky it
didn't stop your heart."

"I think it did, for a minute."

"Well . . . we don't have a real doctor. Sid knows a thing or two.
Should be able to tell if anything's broken. You'll be taking it easy for a
while, anyway." He motioned for some 'Cats to move Tex under the
lean-to he'd been napping under. "Danny, form a detail to bury our
man," he said, referring to the half-eaten 'Cat. "And get that damn
nasty thing's corpse out of my sight!"

"Yes, sir," Danny said. Only later did it occur to Irvin that the man
had called him "sir." He raised the 1911 Colt and looked at it. Filthy.
The new rounds might work okay, but they sure dirtied up a gun. "Mr.
Hardee, you and Spook gather up all the weapons that were fired and
clean them thoroughly. Step on it, too. No telling when we'll need them
again."

Irvin sighed and looked at the submarine while workers either resumed their tasks or performed the duties he'd just ordered. Somehow,
he'd managed to last until no one was looking before the shakes over-
took him. For a long moment, he just held his trembling hands tight
against his sides, waiting for the spell to pass—hoping it was just a
spell. He'd been wondering more and more whether he was ready for
this. In the past, he'd always had someone to turn to, to turn things
over to when it started getting rough. Now he was *it*. He had to come to
grips with that. Ultimately, that was the real test Captain Reddy had
given him, and in an even greater sense it was the test he'd set
himself.

So far, in spite of everything, they'd made a lot of progress. S-19
hadn't been badly damaged before it wound up here, just out of fuel.
Time and the elements had treated her more harshly than the Japanese
did. "Task Force S-19" had done good work and with any luck, they'd
get her off eventually. The trouble was, did they have time? Would the
island even *let* them go? One thing was almost certain: they'd lose
more people before they were done. He hoped it would be worth it, and
he hoped he wouldn't lose his mind—or his nerve. He wished Lelaa
were here!

Without noticing when it happened, he realized that his hands had stopped shaking. It was just a spell after all, he decided. This time. He looked at the lean-to, where Sid was inspecting Sheider. They were talking in low tones and he even heard a faint laugh. He shook his head and started back toward the sub.

Lelaa was mad as hell. She'd had *Simms* heaved to, just as the commander of the steamer had instructed. Her orders were not to fire on the Imperial ship for any reason, and while she understood the orders, she was still frustrated. Not that it would have done much good. The Imperial frigate was more than a match for her and both sides knew it. Still, this order to heave to only added insult to injury. Two feluccas, the ones she'd been dispatched to meet, had also loosed their sails.

Their mission had been to avoid contact, to observe from a distance and report, but the wind had died away and the steamer came to them. Helpless now, all they could do was what they were told. The enemy (she could think of it as nothing else) steamer closed the distance until she saw a form raise a speaking trumpet.

"I am impressed by your people's persistence," an amplified but distorted voice called, "but this is becoming ridiculous. I can't have you hounding us all the way to our destination! This is the last time I will suffer any interference! The next Allied vessel that crosses my path will be destroyed."

Lelaa quickly motioned for a speaking trumpet as well. Raising it to her lips, she caught herself wishing Irvin were there. She knew her English was better than good, but he'd always just seemed to have a way about him. "Excuse me, please," she called back. "We have neither the desire nor the ability to interfere with your progress. It is you who closed the distance with us. Our mission is merely to ensure that the hostages are safe and well. This is no more than I understand you invited us to do!"

"That is all? You don't mean to menace us with your mighty fleet?" mocked the voice.

Lelaa's tail swished with rage, but she managed a civil reply. "That is all, I assure you."

The man across the water didn't speak for a while, as if he were considering something. Finally he raised the trumpet again. "Since, as I said, this is the last time I will be bothered by you or your Alliance, I will allow you to come across and interview my guests. Come aboard alone. If I see any weapons, you will be fired upon!"

Lelaa lowered her trumpet, stunned. "Hoist out a boat," she said.

Clambering up the side of the Imperial frigate, Lelaa was not met by the sort of side party she'd grown to expect. Instead, a pair of armed men essentially took her into custody and escorted her to a small gathering by the rail. She'd never actually met Princess Rebecca, but she recognized her on sight. She bowed. "Greetings, Your Highness," she said in her most respectful tone. "I trust you and your companions are well?"

"Look. The monkey talks!" muttered a large, dangerous-looking man in the group.

"There, there, Mr. Truelove! Let's attempt to be civil!" admonished another, probably Billingsly, Lelaa decided.

"Well enough," the girl replied. "For now." She seared the one who must be Billingsly with a glare. "But one takes these things day by day."

Lelaa addressed Billingsly. "And what of the other hostages? She says they are well, but where are they? Have you any idea how important they are to us?"

Billingsly smiled. "Honestly, at first I did not. I expected my resolve to be tested and I'd be forced to, um, release a few of them over the side, as it were. Imagine my surprise when that did not occur! We quickly learned the truth of the matter. We knew who the Roman witch was, but good gracious! You *cannot* imagine how amazed we were to discover one of our guests, the noble Minister Sandra Tucker, is practically affianced to your Supreme Commander!" He chuckled. "Honestly, I confess to a professional lapse. I never had any idea, yet the young princess let it slip as if it were common knowledge!"

Rebecca loosed a glare of perfect hatred at Billingsly.

"I'll wager your Captain Reddy was a tad upset? I understand you have some means of rapid communication, so I expect he has been informed."

"He knows," Lelaa admitted, "and I submit that *you* cannot imagine the wrath you have brought down upon yourself!"

"Oh, splendid!"

Lelaa was confused. "In any event, if any of the hostages have been mistreated . . ."

"Not a hair on their heads! They are confined, of course—no end to mischief in a couple of them—but their wounds are healing nicely and they thrive in their accommodations. It *is* a bit cramped, and I'm afraid privacy is at a premium, but no one would say they've been mistreated!" A strange expression crossed Billingsly's face. Unlike most Lemurians Lelaa was good with human face moving, but this was . . . different. "Nor will you be, so long as you behave."

"What . . . what do you mean?"

Truelove laughed and Billingsly's lips quirked into something like a smile. "Why, you will be joining them, of course." He turned to a darker-skinned man with a graying mustache. "Is that ridiculous ship still there? I believe I gave them fair warning that I did not wish to be pestered again! Open fire!"

"What! Wait!" cried Lelaa, struggling against the two guards who'd suddenly seized her arms. "You said 'the next time,' damn you!"

Billingsly turned to her. "When you had the insolence, the gall to raise your speaking trumpet and answer back at me . . . at *me*! You who are not only a lesser species, but a *female*!" Billingsly barked an incredulous laugh. "That *was* the next time. Captain Rajendra, I gave you an order!"

The dark-skinned man replied, clearly forcing his voice to remain calm. "Commander Billingsly, firing on that ship would be an act of willful murder. They are completely unprepared. . . . Their guns are not even run out!"

"Then that should make destroying them all the easier. Destroy one of the other little ships as well; I don't care which, but you may allow one to escape."

"But, Commander!"

Still facing away, Billingsly spoke very clearly. "Destroy those ships, Captain Rajendra, or place yourself under arrest. Which will it be?"

"*Simms!*" Lelaa shrieked at the top of her lungs, hoping someone on the nearby ship might hear. "Hard over! Run!" Truelove backhanded her to the deck.

"Captain Rajendra?" Billingsly prodded.

Rajendra's expression seemed almost desperate as he looked at those around him. This was beyond anything, beyond even the questionable seizure of the princess. This entire episode had been engineered to paint the Navy with the same guilt the Company wore. He could not be part of it! But what of the princess? He feared for her and her friends, and he knew the Company had an unwholesome agenda regarding her. If he was relieved, he would be unable to help her. His eyes sought hers and he saw . . . pleading. She would think him a monster and might not trust him when she absolutely had to. And yet, the ships were doomed. If he refused the order, another would carry it out. Presently, he at least retained command of his ship's movements, if not her actions. He had to preserve that!

"Commence firing," he whispered, barely audible, eyes locked on the princess, pleading for understanding.

"What was that, Captain? I'm a bit hard of hearing today."

"Commence firing, God damn you!" Rajendra bellowed, not caring if Billingsly knew he was shouting at him and not the crew.

CHAPTER

22

Matt stood on *Walker*'s port bridge wing and, for just a while, allowed himself to feel the pure joy of the moment. At long last, his ship was alive again. He felt her sinews coiling for the rush in the vibration of the newly painted rail beneath his hands. Her hasty, impatient breath was in the blower behind the pilothouse. Her muscles were the men and 'Cats who scrambled on the fo'c'sle, a little awkwardly and out of practice perhaps, to single up her lines. Her heart was her own and always had been, but as he stood there, he almost felt her mind merge with his once more, becoming a willing tool for his purpose. Oh, if only Sandra were there, it would be the *perfect* moment. A measure of her old vitality restored, the ship fairly strained against the bonds that clutched her to the land. She was ready for the long voyage ahead, come what may. Together they'd get Sandra back: the old destroyer and her captain.

"Take in the stern lines," Matt commanded, and he waited while the task was performed. "Left full rudder," he called to Kutas, the scarred helmsman. "Port ahead one-third." The dingy water alongside the dock boiled up through the propeller guard and thunderous cheers reverberated from the crowd gathered to see. Matt scanned the crowd for faces as *Walker*'s stern crept away. They were the ones who'd done this, the people of this city he'd grown to love. Partly they'd done it because this ship was their protector, the almost holy talisman that saved them from the Grik. They owed it to her; they needed her still—but the quality of the work they'd done and the inhuman hours that work had required bespoke a labor of love. Matt nodded his thanks to all of them, not only for what they had done for his ship, but for what he knew they'd done for him.

Some of the faces he saw were less jubilant than others. Adar appeared thoughtful, but he waved encouragingly. Judging by his posture, Keje was downright morose. He'd badly wanted to come, but *Big Sal* would soon join the fleet at Singapore. He couldn't be in two places at once. Besides, his daughter Selass was sailing as *Walker*'s medical officer. They'd become quite close again and he would miss her. Letts looked anxious. He'd complained that he never got to go anywhere, but as Matt had once told him, he'd worked himself out of a job. He had a bigger job now and a very pregnant wife. Riggs looked stoic. Ed Palmer could do his job on the ship, but he couldn't take over ashore. Perry Brister made an obscene gesture at somebody aft and Matt chuckled, spotting Spanky McFarlane waving cheerily from where the number one torpedo mount used to be. Spanky had left Brister in charge of his division in Baalkpan because there was no way *Walker* was steaming off without *him*.

Gazing farther aft, the incongruity of an *airplane* lashed carefully to the deck behind the searchlight tower struck Matt again. Besides never having seen such a thing on a four stacker before, the Nancy just looked so strange and fragile. He knew it would be great having it along—if it didn't fall apart. Mallory had assured him the "ships" were tougher than they looked. Matt hoped the same was true for poor Reynolds. The young aviator seemed somewhat lost and all alone standing near the plane.

"Rudder amidships," Matt called. "Take in the bowline." A few moments later, he added, "All astern, one-third." The old ship groaned a bit as the turbines' gears reversed their thrust, but she did seem . . . tighter than he remembered. As they backed away, the crowd cheered again and Matt kept looking for faces as they grew smaller. Bernie was there, waving happily with the others. He liked his job ashore. Laney was some distance away from him, sitting on a stanchion, probably wondering if he was happy or sad. He caught sight of Pam Cross and Risa standing side by side. Whatever . . . relationship . . . they shared with Silva, they were worried about the big ape, and his heart went out to them. The final face he recognized was that of one of the Mice— Gilbert Yeager—standing all alone with his hands in his pockets. Tabby knew *Walker*'s systems as well as anyone now, and she'd won the toss. Matt was secretly amazed Gilbert hadn't just sneaked aboard anyway. He'd done it before. Still, he was probably the most forlorn figure *Walker* was leaving behind.

"All stop. Right full rudder, all ahead two-thirds!" Matt commanded. The old ship's stern crouched down and water churned. Almost immediately, she began a looping turn to starboard. "Honk the horn, if you please," Matt said, and with a shriek of her whistle that drowned any further cheers, *Walker* sprinted for the mouth of the bay.

"Feels good, huh, Skipper," said the Bosun as he and Chack appeared on the bridge. Back aboard his Home, Chack had immediately reverted to his role as bosun's mate. He would have other duties too: his company of Marines would augment the crew, but it also had to drill with the new muskets they'd been issued. Bernie had insisted *Walker* get the first batch.

"Feels good," Matt confirmed. "We'll let things shake down a little; then we'll start running a few drills."

"Gonna be a comedy at first," Gray warned.

"I know. Say, where's Mr. Bradford? I figured he'd be on deck to enjoy the send-off."

"Oh, he's below, still stowing junk he says *you* said he could bring along, for experiments an' such."

Matt laughed. "He hit me with a list and swore he'd stick to it, but I guess I don't really care what he brought as long as it stays out of the way." He shook his head, watching as they left the feluccas and fishing boats in their wake. "God, it feels good to be *moving* again!"

"In case you didn't notice, we were moving along pretty well on *Achilles* in that Strakka!" Chack said dryly.

"Mmm. That was quite the thrill ride, but we were being pushed. It's nice to move that fast on our own!"

They talked amiably until they passed below Fort Atkinson and the report of a gun interrupted their conversation. Then another.

"A salute," Gray said. The guns kept firing. As the number mounted, Matt turned to Gray, who was staring expressionlessly ahead. When they finally stopped at nineteen, Matt's tone was ominous.

"Nineteen guns? *You* told them to do that! Are you out of your mind? That's nuts . . . and think of the wasted powder!"

Gray looked at Matt. "Yeah, Adar asked and I told him. And it ain't nuts! The Secretary of the Navy gets that many, and if you ain't at least that, what are you? You'd better dip the flag or you'll disappoint the boys an' girls in the fort."

Walker turned north-northeast after clearing the point batteries and islands beyond. Sprinting at the glorious speed of twenty-six knots, she reached the refinery island of Tarakan at dawn the next morning. The growth was beginning to reestablish itself after the vicious but comparatively small battle once fought there, and the ensuing great fire that had ravaged the place. To Matt, it still seemed a little odd to see the Stars and Stripes flying over an island where not a single human currently dwelt. All the workers there were 'Cats—Navy 'Cats, and thus Americans—still. . . . *Walker* topped off her bunkers and sped on.

A week before *Walker* sailed, they'd heard the news of *Simms*'s fate, when a lone felucca returned to Paga-Daan, Saan-Kakja's brother's home. The transmission had told how *Simms* was approached and destroyed without warning of any kind. Worse, a felucca under the command of Saan-Kakja's brother himself was also destroyed. Other than a few of *Simms*'s crew who'd apparently rowed Captain Lelaa over to *Ajax* to confer with the hostage takers, there were no other survivors. Saan-Kakja was in a frenzy, understandably, but she was also ready to declare war on the Empire of the New Britain Isles. Matt had to send his personal assurance that the Empire itself might not be to blame, and they'd secured a strong alliance with at least one element of the Imperial Navy. He then had to beg the Paga-Daans to replenish Jenks's ship when it arrived instead of firing on it. Things were spiraling out of control and, for Matt at least, the all-important war in the west had assumed an almost back-burner status. Meanwhile, he spent more time trying to smooth things over between his Allies than he did running his ship—all while pursuing the criminals who had taken Sandra, the princess, and at least three more of their people. Those hostages might now include *Simms*'s captain.

Just as they turned west to cut across the Moro Gulf of the Celebes Sea, they received confirmation that *Achilles* had indeed reached Paga-Daan and had her fuel replenished. A subsequent transmission from *Achilles*—O'Casey had apparently finally figured out the device he'd been given—asked why the Paga-Daans had been so unfriendly. Matt had Palmer send a message that explained the new situation—and the Paga-Daans immediately replied that they had not been rude to Jenks. Matt finally summoned Bradford and put him in charge of the diplomatic situation and insisted that it had been his job in the first place.

Walker steamed on, her repaired sonar blasting the depths before her. The sonar had been a major concern, but all the delicate equipment had been above water in the charthouse, so it hadn't been as difficult to fix as originally feared. They'd installed a pair of the "Y" guns—thanks to *Simms*, they knew those worked—but it was good to be able to cross deep water at speed. With Bradford finally dealing with diplomacy, Matt was free to drill his crew and get his ship ready to fight.

"Sound General Quarters," Matt said for the third time that day, and cringed. Of all the things no one had thought to repair, the general alarm was becoming the most obvious. Everything else seemed to be working fine so far, but the alarm, always ill-sounding, now reverberated through the ship like a goose being choked underwater. Despite the comical sound, the crews immediately sprang to their stations. The automatic response had already returned to *Walker*'s veterans, and her new draft was quickly picking up the pace.

Fred Reynolds was the talker (he had to have something to do when he wasn't fussing with the plane) and he began to call out readiness reports from the various stations.

"Engineering reports manned and ready," he said. "Main battery is manned . . . and mostly ready. They're still having a little trouble figuring out who stands where on that Jap gun—I mean, number four." He quickly recited the rest of the litany. Matt noticed that the young ensign visibly paled when he reported for the plane-dump detail. Matt hoped it would never come to that, but if the plane ever caught fire or was otherwise interfering with the performance of the ship or crew in battle, they had to be ready to throw it over the side. He glanced aft and almost barked a laugh. Once again, he saw a pair of 'Cat mess attendants solemnly, carefully, carrying the Coke machine forward to the companionway under Earl Lanier's fierce, watchful supervision. Apparently, Earl was determined that providing for the iconic machine's safety should become as instinctive as any other preparation for battle. It had been severely wounded in action before, and after Earl lovingly and painstakingly restored it to health, he wasn't going to risk it again.

"Lookouts, machine guns, and damage control, all manned and ready. All stations manned and ready, Captain!" Reynolds finally reported.

"Very well," Matt said, controlling his voice and looking at his watch with a dissatisfied frown. The time had actually been pretty good, but he had to maintain appearances. "Secure from General Quarters. Continue steaming as before but maintain condition three. I want a few fingers close to a few triggers. There *are* sea monsters out there, after all."

"Aye-aye, Skipper. Secure from General Quarters and maintain condition three."

In the short bustle that followed, while the crew secured their helmets and other gear, and men and 'Cats slid down the ladder from the fire-control platform above the wheelhouse, Courtney Bradford appeared on the bridge. "How invigorating!" he wheezed after the effort of climbing the steps aft. "The old girl seems as good as new and ready for a scrap! It does my heart a world of good, I must say. It feels almost like old times!"

Matt turned to look at Bradford. "You weren't here for the old times, back before the war. We had some damn good men and we've lost an awful lot of them since, but the few who remain, from *Walker* and

Mahan, and a few from S-19, have become something a little more than just damn good men. With them, and their Lemurian shipmates, this old can probably has as good a *crew* as any four stacker ever had!"

"Quite," Courtney agreed. "I have always noted how, in the various navies I've grown familiar with, each crew contains all the wildly different varieties of specialized skills to operate and maintain their ship at sea and on far-flung deployments. Oddly, however, I've also seen how the men who possess those skills set themselves apart from one another as distinctly as, well, different races sometimes do. Aboard here, all those different skills have become wonderfully diffused through necessity. Your crew has become much better educated than is the norm, Captain Reddy, and they have accomplished that feat largely on their own."

"You're right, but they've had a lot of help," Matt said. "These 'Cats! They're smart as a whip, but teaching them stuff has helped all the fellas. I've often heard it said that teaching makes a smart man wise. I'm not sure that's true in a classroom, but out here?" He shrugged. "It sure shows you what you *don't* know, and in our situation, you'd better find an answer. Chances are, somebody has one. That's what's caused your diffusion of skills." He waved his hand. "There'll always be rivalries. The 'snipes' and 'apes' wouldn't have it any other way, but that's good for morale. The thing is, after all we've been through and what this crew went through to get this ship back in action, there's probably not a deck ape aboard who couldn't lend a competent hand in the firerooms if it came to that. And vice versa. They might gripe, but they could do it and they *would*."

"Speak for yourself, Skipper," said Chief Gray, joining the pair. "Spanky's still mad that I missed most of the slop work. Says I'm *banned* from the engineering spaces! Hell, I wouldn't go down there to piss on him if he caught fire!"

"You see?" Matt said, laughing. "Boats, you're the exception that proves the rule!" He shook his head. "What does that mean, anyway? What a stupid thing to say."

"Indeed," Bradford agreed, lowering his voice. He glanced around as if checking to see who was in earshot. There weren't many secrets aboard *Walker*, not anymore, but Bradford had learned that his theories and observations were sometimes prone to . . . upset sensitive ears. Some of those sensitive ears were already somewhat agitated. Everyone knew *Walker* was steaming inexorably east and there was a very good chance she'd ultimately pass into waters no Lemurian had ever been. The fact that all the humans and a fair number of the Lemurian old hands seemed so unconcerned kept the edge off among the more strictly pious or superstitious. In this case, however, Bradford himself had become suddenly and surprisingly sensitive to the imperative that they minimize stressful contemplations among certain elements of the crew.

Apparently assured there were no panicky types present, he proceeded. "I have in fact been giving that a great deal of thought. As you know, I've been overwhelmed with stimuli, overwhelmed, sir! This world is a cornucopia of delights for a man of my interests. Forgive me if, on occasion, I've been diverted from some fairly obvious conclusions that would've ordinarily struck me with the greatest importance! It's the sheer volume of wonders that's crippled me and I'm but one man. . . ." He paused. "I do hope we may rescue young Mr. Cook. He's been such a great help. . . ."

"Courtney?" Matt prodded.

"Of course. Where was I? Oh, yes. A mere trivial example of my preoccupation is my failure to extrapolate beyond a few observations I made when we first came to this world. Surely you remember when Miss Tucker and I dissected the creature we killed on Bali?"

The day Marvaney died. "Yeah, I remember," Matt said.

"Well, you may recall that Miss Tucker and I disagreed about the physiology of the beast? I said it was more like a bird, with its furry feathers and hollow bones, et cetera, and she said its jaws made it a lizard as far as she was concerned—oh, please don't take this as criticism of the dear woman—but, well, I was right, you see. I admonished her to judge them more by what they *were* like and less by what they *looked* like . . . and I promptly fell into the same trap myself. We bandied the term 'lizard' about for so long, I failed to pursue my original course of study. We *were* a bit busy at the time, as you'll recall.

"In any event, it was the boy Abel who brought it back to my mind; he was quite fascinated with dinosaurs before his unpleasant experiences turned him slightly against them. But the point is we, the scientific community of which I consider myself a part, have always assumed dinosaurs were cold-blooded reptiles! Monstrous beasts, plodding along, lying in the sun like lizards on a rock, but we were wrong! If the fauna of this world is truly descended from the same fauna as our own, there would be a lot of egg on a lot of faces at the Royal Society, if I could ever report!"

"Well . . . that's amazing, Courtney," Matt said dryly, "but what's your point? I'm afraid 'lizards' has pretty much stuck as slang for 'Grik.' I doubt you're going to get folks to start calling 'em 'birds' at this point. Be happy with your win over 'Lemurians.'"

"No! That's not what I'm saying at all!"

"Then for God's sake, for once in your life, say what you mean!" hissed Gray, exasperated. Matt looked at the chief and raised his hand, but couldn't help agreeing with him.

"I'm trying to! Aren't you listening at all?" Bradford asked forcefully, and Gray rolled his eyes. "The thing is, all my various preoccupations pushed some rather more important thoughts from my head. One such was retrieved by your ridiculous comment that the 'exception proves the rule.' I know you don't believe that," he hastened to add, "and neither do I. That brings us to some rather disturbing thoughts I've had regarding our arrival on this world. We already know we must have been given, or been the victims of, some exception to the rules we knew, because, well, here we are."

"Clearly," Matt said.

"We also now know that exception wasn't necessarily an exception at all."

"Shit, Mr. Bradford—'scuse me, Skipper—but just spit it out. I'm getting an 'exceptional' headache trying to figure you out!" Gray whispered, but Matt shushed him. He thought he knew where Bradford was going.

"Very well," Courtney continued, a little stiffly. "Jenks's ancestors came through a . . . phenomenon much like the one we did. They call it the Passage, and it occurred in relatively close geographic proximity to our Squall. We also agree there may have been other similar such episodes over the centuries. Maybe it happens quite often, in fact, but the transportees are otherwise in smaller, more vulnerable ships with smaller crews, who have no means of protecting themselves in this more hostile world. They either don't survive the event, or are lost before locals like the Lemurians discover them and give them aid. The mysterious fate of the crew of the Tjilatjap transport, *Santa Catalina*, and even the original crew of our own lamented PBY would seem to support that theory. As noted, a few men in a fishing boat would have poor prospects of survival.

"We still don't know what all else might have come through our Squall with *us*. Four ships now, counting the transport, plus a submarine and an airplane—that we know of. Now we learn of this Dominion that controls a portion of the Americas. Princess Rebecca is a dear child, but her history is not up to that of Jenks or Mr. O'Casey. They told me that this Dominion was founded by some bizarre combination of survivors from an 'Acapulco' or 'Manila' galleon and remnants of an even older, possibly pre-Columbian American tribe. I won't go into the details of that twisted union at present, but it was the Acapulco galleon that rang the first warning bell."

"What are you talkin' about?" Gray asked. "What's a 'Aca-poolco galleon'?"

"What I'm talking about is that whatever phenomenon transported us to this world may not be nearly as unique as we first believed. Whatever conditions arise to trigger it might—*might*, I say—also ensure that it is a one-way transfer. I don't begin to understand the mechanics of it yet, but that at least seems certain, since we've never encountered any lumbering Lemurian Homes or mountain fish on *our* world." He paused. "Or maybe *that* is the key!"

Captain Reddy and Chief Gray looked at each other. Evidently, Courtney was on one of his stream-of-consciousness rolls, and they might as well let it run its course.

"What key?" Matt prodded.

"Metal! As far as we know, only recently—relatively speaking—has any quantity of *metal* been abroad on the oceans of this world! Perhaps large quantities of iron contribute some form of electromagnetic aspect to the phenomenon—or the superior conductivity of the bronze guns, copper fittings . . . precious nonferrous metals of our predeces-

sors. . . . Oh, dear me, Captain, an entirely new avenue of contempla-
tion has opened before me!"

"Well, let's finish our little trip down the avenue you were already
on, for now," Gray almost pleaded. "What's Aca-poolco got to do with
anything?"

"Oh, dear, I do apologize! Let's see, yes. Only that our little Squall was
not unique. Probably not even *regionally* unique! There might well be
other human civilizations beyond those we know of scattered about this
hostile world. Perhaps many more. Now you understand, of course!"

Finally Matt understood. Bradford was right. The question had
been sitting there in front of all of them, but they'd just been too busy
to notice it and ask. The possible answer chilled him in spite of the
warm day. "Acapulco galleons were Spanish treasure ships, Boats," he
explained. "They sailed once a year or so to Acapulco from the Spanish
Philippines loaded with loot. We studied Commodore Anson's cir-
cumnavigation at the Academy. He captured one of the things with a
fifty-gun ship—*Centurion*, I think it was—and the loot set most of his
crew up for life. At least, that's the story."

"So? I mean, it's a neat story and all, but what good is a bunch of
Spanish treasure to us?" Gray still didn't get it.

"None," Matt said. "None I can think of now, anyway." He grinned,
but then his expression turned serious again. "The problem is, no Acapulco galleon would have ever sailed into the Java Sea. If that's indeed
what it was, that means whatever happened to us could've happened in
other *places* and not just other times, all over the world. Might happen
again. To think otherwise would be expecting an exception to these
screwy *new* rules."

"Indeed," Bradford said again. "I would think it's inevitable. Something, some force, connects this world with ours. In the past, our
world's oceans were vast, mostly empty places, yet there have been
many unexplained disappearances there. Perhaps some of those un-
fortunates wound up here as well. But right now, on our earth, a global
war is under way and the seas are packed with many thousands of
modern, quite seaworthy vessels. If my theory is correct, I fear it's just
a matter of time before we meet another lost traveler like ourselves,
and it could happen anytime, anywhere."

For a long moment there was silence on the bridge. Chief Quarter-master's Mate Norman Kutas at the wheel, who'd clearly heard at least the gist of the conversation, finally broke it. "Well, if we do run into somebody else," he said, "I hope to God they're on our side. We got enough folks mad at us as it is."

Glaring at Kutas, Bradford lowered his voice still further. "There is yet another quite bizarre possibility," he said.

"Oh, no," moaned the Bosun.

Bradford ignored him. "Just as we've discovered beyond any serious possible debate that there are *two* earths, as it were, how can we assume there are not many, *many* more?"

Walker put in briefly at Paga-Daan, long enough only for Matt to go ashore and express his sympathies and for his ship to fill her bunkers from one of the tankers moored there. There were two so far and more on the way. Most would probably take their time, creeping along the archipelago and down the Mindanao coast. Matt couldn't blame their captains, but he wanted to make sure the commanders and crews of the ships already there, that had taken the more danger-ous route across the Celebes Sea, were recognized. Bunkers full, *Walker* steamed away before sunset, haze blurring the tops of three funnels.

Churning south-southeast, Matt now had a choice to make. He could continue in Jenks's wake until he caught the Imperial within two or three days at most, or he could lose another day and swing south to Talaud. Irvin Laumer and his crew had been out of touch since the loss of *Simms*, and Talaud was a dangerous place. Once he caught up with Jenks he'd be slowed down, regardless, and they had to be closing the gap on Billingsly. *Achilles* was bigger and faster than *Ajax* and she'd been replenished periodically, allowing her to steam ahead in the face of contrary or indifferent winds. But where could *Ajax* refuel? She might have stopped and cut trees for her boiler on any number of is-lands, but that would have slowed her even more. Matt doubted Billing-sly would have done so initially, but chances were the man considered himself safe from pursuit by now. He knew the Alliance had nothing beyond the Philippines, and *Simms* and the feluccas were the last gauntlet he had to pass. He would be in for a surprise.

But what of Laumer? With the full concurrence of his officers, Matt decided he had to check on the young lieutenant's situation and at least leave him a transmitter. They recrossed the Celebes Sea in the dark of night and a severe rain squall, sonar pounding the depths. It was in these very waters, this bottleneck to the vast Pacific—or Eastern Sea— that *Walker* had once encountered *two* mountain fish in close proximity. The sonar had chased one away and they were pretty sure they'd killed the other one, but there was something about the area apparently, maybe the food-bearing currents, that allowed a higher percentage of the monsters to coexist than usual. In any event, in addition to the sonar, they made the crossing with extra lookouts, keen-eyed Lemurians scanning the sea for basking behemoths under the glare of the searchlights. None were seen.

Dawn revealed Talaud's hazy outline under an oppressive gray sky. Campeti was serving as *Walker*'s gunnery officer for the voyage and he had the deck. He knocked quietly on the charthouse hatch and opened it a crack. Matt had taken to sleeping on a cot inside, intent even in sleep on the green flashes that lit the quiet sonarman's scope. He liked to be handy if he was needed, but also, even though the new mattresses they'd made for the ship's crew were comfortable, nobody had gotten around to fixing the fan in his stateroom. It got awfully stuffy in there.

"Captain, you awake?" Campeti asked.

"Sure," Matt said, sitting up. He glanced at the sonarman. A 'Cat was usually in the chair, but Fairchild, *Mahan*'s chief sonarman or sound man, had taken the watch for this stretch. "Anything?" he asked.

"Nothing, Skipper. We're going too fast to really tell, but since we're trying to scare stuff off instead of hunting, I guess that's a good thing."

Matt grunted. "What's up, Campeti?"

"Talaud's off the starboard bow. It looks . . . kinda queer."

"I'm on my way."

Staas-Fin, one of Ronson's best electrician's mates, stood behind the big brass wheel and Courtney and Spanky were on the bridge when Matt joined them, putting on his hat. He hadn't shaved. Of all the crew, Matt always tried to keep himself clean-shaven, but that was hard to do, sleeping in the charthouse. He needed to see if Staas-Fin, or "Finny," could fix his fan. Otherwise, he might as well give up and grow a beard like the rest of the men. He wasn't ready to let Juan shave him on the bridge in the captain's chair. "What's up?" he repeated.

Spanky pointed at the island. "Well, it looks a little different, for starters," he said.

"Wow," Matt muttered, agreeing. The quiescent volcanic mountain he remembered had grown significantly since he saw it last and the thick haze either came from it, or was the aftermath of some action on its part. The air had an acrid taste. The top of the mountain was lost to view, but there were occasional flashes of light, either from lightning or maybe even lava arcing into the sky.

"Fascinating!" Bradford exclaimed.

"Yeah. I hope our guys are all right," Matt said.

"Hey," said Spanky, "where're all the damn birds?" On their previous visit the ship had been swarmed with lizard birds and even some real birds that pestered them constantly and defecated all over the ship. Nobody replied. They had no answer.

Just before noon, *Walker* rounded the northeast point of the island and entered the wide lagoon where they'd found the submarine. The sky was even blacker, but the air had cleared with a northerly breeze. At least they could breathe. Anchoring in almost the exact spot as before, they swung out the launch and steered for shore. Matt, Spanky, and the Bosun were accompanied by Stites, Chack, and six Marines. The Marines were the ones Chack thought had gained the most proficiency with their muskets.

At first glance, the camp around the submarine looked deserted. A lot of work had clearly been done and the sub itself actually seemed afloat in a basin on the beach. No smoke rose from the generator engine boiler, however, and as they drew near they could see a literal swarm of what looked like bizarre lobster corpses on the beach.

"What the hell?" Gray murmured. The launch's engine seemed to attract someone's attention, because as the bow nudged against the sand, a figure stood up from behind hasty-looking breastworks.

"Captain Reddy, is that you?" came a cry. The men and 'Cats jumped out of the boat and advanced. Other faces, eyes drooping with fatigue, peered over the breastworks as they approached.

"My God, Lieutenant Laumer?" Matt asked incredulously. The scruffy beard and tattered clothes left the man almost unrecognizable.

"Yes, sir, it's me!" Laumer said, grinning. He looked out at the Lagoon. "*Walker*, sir! There she is! Boy, is she a sight for sore eyes! Looks almost new!"

"What happened here, Lieutenant?" Matt asked, glancing at one of the dead creatures. It did look something like a lobster, although it was skinnier, proportionately, and appeared less heavily armored. The head was different and the leg arrangement looked more like a spider's. The pincers were long and tapered like a scorpion's. Most of the corpses looked like they'd been blown open fairly easily with bullets.

"Well, sir, we've been making decent progress on the boat. She should be ready for sea before long. We put diesel in her tanks and have one engine running. The problem is getting her off the beach. We were going to use *Simms* to dredge a channel, kind of kedge it out, but Captain Lelaa hasn't returned from her mission to intercept Billingsly." He looked down. "I was sorry to hear about . . . what happened at Baalkpan."

"Yes, well, chasing him is our business now. I hate to tell you, but Billingsly and *Ajax* destroyed *Simms* and a felucca commanded by the High Chief of Paga-Daan. Captain Lelaa may have been aboard *Ajax* when it happened, but there were few survivors otherwise. I'm sorry," he added when he saw Laumer's stricken expression.

"But . . ." Irvin straightened. "That leaves us in kind of a tight spot," he said.

"I'll say," said Gray. "What the hell happened here?"

Irvin rubbed his nose. "A few weeks ago, one of these things got in our basin. Killed one of our guys. We killed it, but it wasn't easy. Scary as they look, they're not only quick on their feet, but they can squirt a jet of water like a cannon shot!"

"Indeed?" muttered Bradford, stooping to examine the head of one of the things.

"Yeah. Anyway, we didn't see any more for a while, but then, day before yesterday, the mountain let loose, bigger than it has yet. We had critters coming at us out of the woods and we figured we'd better fort up. Next thing we knew, all these spider-lobsters, or whatever they are, started charging up on the beach. It started slow, just a few at a time, but it kept growing, so we threw up another breastwork here until we had a little fort. Dug like maniacs! We finished just in time, because the next thing we knew, there were dozens, hundreds of the things! Just about shot ourselves dry." He shook his head. "The situation looked pretty bleak without more ammo. The new loads work okay, but they sure foul up a gun. The Thompson completely seized up a couple of times and we had to dump it in water."

Matt took a breath and looked longingly at the submarine. "You've done a great job here, Lieutenant, but I think you should prepare to evacuate. We have some ammunition we could leave with you, but not much more than it would take to drive off another assault like this one. Another supply ship is on its way, but it may not arrive in time to kedge out your channel. This mission has already gone above and beyond what I ever expected of you."

Irvin set his jaw. Later, Matt would realize that he probably hadn't chosen those last words very well. "Sir," Laumer said, "with all respect, I think we've earned the right to finish this job." He looked around at the nods of his crew. "We don't know if the spider-lobsters will even come back. It might have been a onetime deal. Lots of weird stuff going on." He gestured at the mountain. "I think it has something to do with that. The thing is, if it blows its top, we'll never get this boat out of here!"

"If it does that, there won't be enough left of any of you to catch in a butterfly net!" Gray said.

Irvin nodded. "Maybe. But damn it, Captain, we're almost done! All we need is a couple of weeks with a ship, an anchor, and a windlass!"

"And no storms to fill everything you've done in with sand!" Gray added.

"That would be nice," Irvin admitted.

Matt rubbed the stubble on his chin. "Like I told you once, we need that boat, but we need you and your people more. Here's the deal. We'll leave you a transmitter and a receiver. If things get hairy, there'll be no goofing around! You call for help, understand? Paga-Daan can have a felucca here to pick your people up in just a few days. Leave all the equipment. The same goes for when the supply ship arrives. Use it however you need to, but if things get bad, get the hell out, understood?"

Irvin sighed with relief. For a moment, he'd seen failure staring him in the face and only Captain Reddy could have pronounced that sentence upon him. No storm or spider-lobsters or even a volcano was going to stop him, but Captain Reddy could have. He saluted. "Thanks, sir. We *will* succeed!"

Matt was moody as *Walker* steamed out of the lagoon and into the open Pacific. He'd begun to realize the effect his words might have had on Laumer, and even though he hadn't meant to, he'd practically challenged the young lieutenant to stay. He felt like a heel. He got up from his chair and stepped to the chart table. Kutas had marked the spot where they should rendezvous with Jenks, according to the latest position fixes O'Casey sent. One more day, maybe two, and they'd slow their sprint and take station with the Imperial frigate, maintaining visual contact, but sweeping east while covering the widest possible area. Apparently, the Empire had a few settlements in the Marshall Islands, but according to Jenks, they were notoriously independent places. Billingsly would find no haven there. He must be making for one of the main islands of the Hawaiian chain, probably New Ireland, as Jenks referred to it. The island was a Company hotbed and the center of its administration. New Scotland—was the primary naval base, and Hawaii itself was New Britain. None of the islands seemed "right" to Matt, when he'd looked at Jenks's charts. Their shapes were distinctly changed from what he remembered. Most geographic differences they'd discovered so far were subtle, but the "Hawaiian" chain was more radically altered. He wondered why that was.

Walker could just barely make it to Hawaii before her bunkers ran dry, but what then? Matt was counting on the tankers following them to the Marshalls—if their crews didn't chicken out or if mountain fish didn't eat them. Regardless, *Walker* would be stuck there until she could refuel. He didn't know what awaited them in New Britain, but he wasn't going to arrive with empty bunkers. All he and Jenks could hope to do was catch Billingsly somewhere in the wide expanses that separated the Carolines.

"We're coming for you, you son of a bitch!" he muttered under his breath.

"You may tell Captain Rajendra he can ask to speak to the moon if he likes," Princess Rebecca retorted sharply, "and he will be much more likely to get what he wants than by asking to speak to me!"

"But, Your Highness!" the boy in the passageway whispered urgently, "the captain had no choice! If he had refused the order, he would have been placed under arrest! How then could he assist you and your friends?"

"He is a dispassionate murderer," Rebecca proclaimed. "A stain upon the honor of the Navy and the Empire!"

"Now, hold on just a second," Silva whispered in the darkness. It was almost pitch-black in the brig. They were supposed to be asleep, and no lights were allowed at this time of night. "Rajendra wants us to trust him, does he? How does he mean to make us?"

"What do you mean?"

"I mean *why* should we trust him? We need proof. Real proof, not just a extra piece o' cheese."

"Well . . . what do you want?"

"I want my goddamn guns, but I bet they'd be missed. They keepin' 'em in the armory? The magazine?"

"The aft magazine," replied the boy. "It is the most secure place on the ship. The Marines' arms are stored there as well, with ready ammunition. Besides, your largest gun would not fit in a weapons locker."

"Hmm. You're prob'ly right, at that. Tell you what. I want three things. First, I want a key to this here lock."

"But—"

"Lookie here, you want us to trust him or not? It ain't like we're gonna break out an' run loose all over the ship. I just want a key to where I can get us outta here if the time comes. 'Sides, what if the ship gets ate by one o' them big fish? We'd be stuck in here." That thought actually gave Silva the creeps. Earlier that day, the great guns had opened up, firing furiously for some time. Three full broadsides. At first they thought a battle was under way, until they heard the guns had been used to frighten off a mountain fish.

"Very well. I will see what I can do."

"Next thing I want is our position. Our exact position!"

"Why?"

"Never you mind. If we take to trustin' you, we'll tell you why. One other thing. I want a lantern. A little one so we can look at our map in the dark. It's too hard to go over it in the daytime 'cause you never know when somebody's peekin' in the door at us."

"I have a one-sided lantern in my quarters," said the boy. Dennis knew he was a midshipman or something and he actually did trust him, at least. For one thing, the little guy was clearly terrified of Billingsly.

"That sounds fine, just fine. You do that, and maybe I can talk the princess into speakin' a word or two to Rajendra if he happens to mosey by."

"Thank you, sir!"

"You bet. Now run along before you get caught—but before you go, there's one last, final little thing."

"Sir?"

"I want all that stuff tonight, see?"

"I . . . I will do my best," whispered the boy a little shakily. They heard his quiet footsteps retreat.

Silva turned to the others in the brig. He couldn't really see more than dark shapes in the gloom, but he knew where everyone was. "Good work, li'l sister," he said to Rebecca. "He seemed ready to pee himself. I figger somethin's up and Rajendra thinks he'd better do somethin' before it's too late."

"It does seem that way," Sandra said in a worried tone. "Maybe they think they're safe enough from pursuit that they can get rid of the 'extra' hostages."

"I fear that may be the case," Rebecca said. "Billingsly no longer even pretends to care what I do or where I go. Nor does he seem to think it important to maintain the fiction of my status aboard. He may plan to eliminate more than us."

Silva doubted Billingsly was through with Rebecca yet, but she might be right about the rest. "Cap'n Lelaa?" he asked.

"Rajendra is a murderer," she said miserably. She'd been badly traumatized by the destruction of her ship, and for quite a while, all she'd done was lie curled in a ball in a corner of the cell. Finally, however, she'd begun to take some interest in their situation. She was a naval officer and she couldn't indulge in self-pity forever. Silva was glad she was snapping out of it. When things hit the fan, they were going to have to move fast. He knew Sandra, Rebecca, and Lawrence had plenty of guts, but though he didn't dislike her, he considered Sister Audry a deadweight. He didn't need another one to worry about when the time came.

"Yeah, I guess he's a murderer," Silva said, "but so am I, by most lights. If the kid's right, he did what he *thought* he had to so's to stay where he might help Rebecca. I'm not plumb sure that *is* what he had to do, but I'll give him the doubt for now, 'cause I wadn't there. Somebody else mighta just blown your ship to hell if he didn't, an' then where'd we be? He *did* give us a map, even if it's kind of crummy."

They'd spent many days explaining maps to Lawrence, describing them as pictures of the world from high in the sky, as if drawn by some bird that could fly higher than the eye could see. It finally began to sink in, and then they showed him places they'd been: Talaud, the Philippines, even as far west as Baalkpan, though the map was so out-of-date in that respect as to be almost useless. Between Lawrence and Rebecca's imperfect memory of how long and in which directions they'd drifted in her boat with O'Casey, they pieced together which island or atoll they thought they'd found Lawrence on in the first place. Finally, from that, Lawrence was able to pinpoint roughly where he thought his home island was. "There is no land called Tagran on the chart, though," he'd accused, "and I ne'er saw it fro' the sky. I think it is this, though," he'd decided, pointing at a rough rendition of what Silva thought was Yap Island. He'd never been there, but he'd seen plenty of charts and the screwy name had always stuck with him.

"Okay, I hope you're right," Silva had replied. "So long as they don't eat us."

Lawrence had glared at him and hissed. "They'll take care o' all o' us. La'rence 'riends their 'riends! You all heroes, ring La'rence to Tagran Island land," he'd said.

It wasn't much, but it was a chance. An escape attempt to Talaud or even Mindanao would have been their best bet, but Abel had still been weak, and tension before and after *Ajax*'s confrontation with Lelaa's ships had made any attempt then impossible. Now that Billingsly knew there were no other Allied outposts, security surrounding them had grown lax. They were down to only two choices: they could stay aboard and risk whatever fate Billingsly had in store for them, or they could try to get off the ship and hope Lawrence's Grik-like people would take them in.

For some reason, Silva didn't seem particularly concerned with the mechanics of escape. He apparently thought Rajendra could be trusted, for selfish reasons at least, and believed his assistance might be handy, if not necessarily essential. Evidently, he didn't even think he needed the key he'd asked for. He'd probably just thrown in the request as a further test of Rajendra. Ever since he started feeling more like himself, he'd given the impression that escape was just a matter of Sandra deciding when. According to the map, their approximate speed and position, and Lawrence's best estimate regarding which island was his home, "when" would have to be the following night. That was when *Ajax* would pass most closely to the island where he thought his people dwelt.

Their discussion was interrupted by more footsteps in the passageway, followed by a quiet voice at the door. "Your Highness, it is I, Captain Rajendra. Midshipman Brassey is here as well. He says you might speak with me. I tell you it is of the utmost importance that you do. All our lives are at risk."

"What of the lives of Captain Lelaa's crew?" Rebecca hissed.

"I could not stop that!" Rajendra insisted. "I had hoped you would understand!"

So it was as Brassey said and Silva had speculated. There was no doubting the torment and sincerity in Rajendra's tone. Either he was telling the truth or he'd missed his calling as a stage performer. Silva still thought there was one way Rajendra might have prevailed, but there was little point in bringing that up now. "Did you bring the stuff we asked for?" he asked instead.

"Yes. I will open the door and pass them through. . . . Please make no attempt at the moment; I would prefer to help coordinate an escape by being elsewhere when it begins!"

There was a tiny clack as the tumbler in the lock disengaged and the door opened a fraction. A hooded lantern, already lit, preceded a piece of paper with some numbers written on it. Finally, Silva felt the large brass key pressed into his hand.

"Well, you done what we asked," Dennis said, announcing the key transfer. "Whaddaya say, li'l sister?"

"I will trust him," Rebecca replied. "Captain Lelaa?"

"I suppose we have no choice," she said ominously. "For now. But if there is further treachery of any kind—"

"Hush now," said Silva, and his tone hardened. "That goes without even sayin'!" He paused. "Loo-tenant Tucker?"

Sandra cleared her throat. "Tomorrow night, Captain Rajendra, providing the position you gave us corresponds with our calculations, we'll be leaving your ship one way or another. If you can facilitate our escape, it would be appreciated."

"Tomorrow night should work well," Rajendra agreed. "Much later than that might be too late." So. Rebecca was right. "This is what I have done, and can do. You may incorporate as much of it into your plans as you see fit. The carpenter has repaired the launch Mr. Silva shot such a gaping hole through. Tomorrow, I shall have it swung out to tow, to swell the wood. I would prefer the pinnace because it is larger and will carry more, but I have no excuse to put it in the water."

"Sounds fine, but why would we need room for more?" Sandra asked.

"Midshipman Brassey has overheard a certain conversation," Rajendra said stiffly. "Most of you are to be hanged for abducting the princess and holding her against her will. My loyal officers and myself will then be hanged for committing a crime against humanity when we fired on Captain Lelaa's ship without warning." Rajendra's voice was full of irony. "Clearly both are legal fictions concocted by Billingsly to eliminate any story but his own should things at home be different than he suspects, but there it is. Some of us will be coming with you."

"Why not just rise up, take back your ship from these Company bastards?" Sandra asked. "We would help!"

"Impossible. I count perhaps seventy loyalists among my crew, opposed by two hundred. It would be a bloodbath and would ultimately fail."

"There've been longer odds," Silva prodded.

"True, but how could we coordinate any effort? I need be wrong about only one of the seventy and our plans will be undone." He shook his head in the darkness. "I cannot let those who are loyal die to no purpose."

"Okay," Sandra said, "we've got a boat and a few extra passengers. We'll need provisions, a compass, sextant, weapons . . . and a means of getting to the boat in the first place."

"The carpenter is one of us. Provisions and navigational aids have already been stowed in the boat," said Brassey. "If a 'sextant' is like a 'quadrant,' that has been included as well. As soon as night falls, I shall bring sufficient ship's clothing to disguise you all." He cleared his throat. "More care than usual must be taken with Captain Lelaa and, uh, Mr. . . . . Lawrence, I presume." Lelaa bristled, but knew it was true. What would they do? Tie her tail around her body?

"Otherwise," Rajendra said, "I will adjust the watch so we will have the greatest number of known loyalists on deck as possible. They will sway out an anchor beneath the bowsprit and allow it to fall back against the hull as though we have struck a leviathan. Action stations will be sounded and we should find our chance in the general confusion."

"Silva?" Sandra asked.

"Not bad," he answered, somewhat distracted. He was mentally adjusting certain elements of his own plan to fit. "Sometimes it's better to do sneaky stuff right out in the open. Slinkin' around in the dark always *looks* sneaky." He spoke in Sister Audry's direction: "Guess you'll have to ditch the nun suit!"

"I will not!"

"Well, you'll have to cover it up somehow, or stash it in something." He turned back toward their visitors. "As for weapons"—he found Brassey's form in the gloom—"I figger the boy an' me an' maybe a few other hands can take care o' that. I want my guns back!"

"Very well," Rajendra said, sounding a little unnerved by something in Silva's tone. "Shall we regard the blow against the bow as our signal to begin, then?"

"I suppose that would be best," Sandra said. "But we must move quickly after that. Where will we gather?"

"On the starboard quarter. The first thing that will happen is that the engine will stop and steam will vent. It will be noisy and add to the confusion. The boat will already have been drawn alongside and each will go over as they arrive. I and some other officers will provide security there by sending anyone whose loyalty is unknown to perform some task or other."

"Sounds swell then," Silva said. "You do your part and we'll do ours. Okay with you, li'l sister?"

"Swell," Rebecca replied.

"Um, there is one other thing," Rajendra said. "Our destination. After we escape, assuming we do, where are we going? Our lives are as much at risk in this venture as yours and it is a terrible sea. You have determined a safe landfall, have you not?"

"Yes," Sandra said, but offered nothing more.

After an expectant but disappointed pause, Rajendra straightened. "Well. Then I suppose we must all trust one another."

"Guess so," Lawrence answered in his distinctive voice.

*   *   *

Late the following night, during first watch, according to Silva, they felt a distinct and surprisingly violent blow strike the ship. Already dressed as Imperial crewmen, with both Lelaa's and Lawrence's tails secured as well as possible (far more difficult in Lawrence's case, and he could hardly walk), they began their escape by evacuating the compartment that had been their prison for weeks. Quickly, they scrambled or shuffled down the corridor, Rebecca and Sister Audry helping Lawrence. Lawrence had a nightcap pulled down over his face, but it was so misshapen the disguise wouldn't stand close scrutiny at all. Lelaa might pass as a ship's boy in the dark, but, of course, neither she nor any other female must speak. Other forms began appearing in the corridor, but Silva burst through them shouting, "Gangway!" in a terrible accent. About then, the alarm bells began to ring, and if anyone noticed the strange, hurrying group in the dark, their attention was quickly diverted.

Up a companionway they lurched, now heading aft across the gun deck as *Ajax*'s crew began assembling at their action stations. Most were confused, barely awake. A few had felt or heard the bump and there was a cacophony of wild, almost panicky speculation. Silva grunted with frustration and suddenly swept poor Lawrence up in his arms. The Tagranesi was slowing them down and Dennis thought he'd draw less attention if he appeared to be injured. There were a few lanterns on the gun deck, but only enough for fighting light—enough that the gun's crews could serve their pieces, but not enough to damage their night vision a great deal, or provide much fuel for a fire. Again, if anyone had begun to grow suspicious of them as they made their way through the building, only slightly controlled chaos, the sudden roar of venting steam distracted them. Reaching the quarterdeck companionway, they ascended and rushed to the starboard rail, where several men were heaving on a line. "Get that boat in, afore somethin' eats it!" one shouted. "I didn' spend two days fixin' it ta pre-vide a toothpick fer one o' them divils!" Clearly the carpenter.

"No, damn your vitals!" Rajendra's voice rose toward another group. "Get you and your party down in the forepeak! Check for sprung timbers! We'll be taking water after a thump like that, I shouldn't wonder!" He raised his speaking trumpet. "Run out the guns! Handsomely now! We must fire before the monster returns!" Another man, burly and dark, approached the captain. "The safety valve has suffered a mischief, I fear," he said in a satisfied tone. "There's no fixin' it either, more's the pity. She'll vent steam till the boiler's cold enough to replace the valve!"

Rajendra glanced about. "Very well. Into the boat with our guests! It will add to the confusion if our engineer cannot be found!"

"Aye, Captain!" The man rushed to the rail. "Over the side with ye, Yer Highness!" he said. "There's a man waitin' below ta catch ye!"

"But what of Lawrence?"

"I can 'anage!" Lawrence said. "As soon as this huge creature puts La'rence down!"

"Dee-lighted, you ungrateful little turd," Dennis said. "Snatch onto that line. You can turn your tail loose in the boat! Maybe you'll be good fer somethin' then." He looked at Rebecca. "After you, li'l sister!"

With only the slightest hesitation, perhaps reliving old memories, the far different person who'd become Princess Rebecca grasped the rope and disappeared into the darkness below. Lawrence went next.

"Now you, Sister Audry!" Dennis ordered, after the engineer disappeared.

"I . . . I'm not sure I can!"

"Sure, you can. It's a cinch. Besides, if you don't go, I'll just drop you over the side and hope you land in the boat."

Audry looked at him, utterly uncertain whether he was serious or not. He'd spoken with the flat firmness of fact. "Very well, *Mr.* Silva," she said sharply.

"Prepare to fire!" Rajendra roared.

"You're next, Loo-tenant Tucker!"

"No. You must get weapons. Where's Midshipman Brassey?"

"Here, ma'am!"

"Good. Lead Mr. Silva to the magazine. Take two of these other men. We need weapons and ammunition! We'll pass well enough up here for now, Mr. Cook and I."

Silva knew she meant to guard against treachery. He wasn't sure how she'd do that, but he also knew it would be pointless and time-consuming to argue with her. "All right, Miss Tucker, we'll be back in a flash!" He turned to Brassey and two of the men who'd been hauling the rope. "C'mon!"

"Fire!" bellowed Rajendra. With a stuttering, rolling, earsplitting bark of thunder, *Ajax* vomited an uneven broadside port and starboard. Silva and his pickup team of commandos vanished in the swirling smoke.

"Follow me," Brassey cried. As he'd explained, *Ajax* had two magazines. The one they sought was aft, beneath the orlop and essentially below the waterline, which afforded it some protection from enemy shot. They met a steady stream of grim-faced, sweaty boys hurrying back to the guns, charges in their pass boxes. Reaching the magazine, they found it virtually deserted, the powder boys having already come and gone. The first compartment had a lantern illuminating racks of muskets. Silva was surprised and joyful to see the Doom Whomper secured at the far end of one rack along with his shooting pouch and belt. From the belt still hung his holster, magazine pouches, cutlass, and '03 bayonet in its scabbard. The bayonet was a respectable "sword" in its own right.

"Hot damn!" he hissed, wrapping the belt around his waist and clipping it in place. He then grabbed his massive rifle. He could see movement in an adjoining compartment through a thick pane of wavy glass. The gunner and his mates, most likely, preparing charge bags.

"Whose side's the gunner on?" Silva asked.

"I don't know," Brassey confessed.

"Okay. You fellas get a double armload o' them muskets and some cartridge boxes. Anything in 'em?"

"There should be a battle load of forty rounds apiece," one of the men supplied. "The door is usually locked and guarded."

"Huh. Well, gather all you can carry and take 'em up." He grinned. "If anybody asks, say it's Billingsly's orders!" While the men did as he said, Silva turned to Brassey. "Loose shot and powder? How 'bout musket flints?"

Brassey pointed. "Those small kegs hold balls and flints, but powder will be in there," he said, referring to the space where the gunner was.

Silva nodded. Taking off the Imperial ordinary seaman's striped shirt, he quickly knotted the sleeves and dropped two thirty-pound kegs of shot and a single keg of flints into it. Tying it all together, he handed it to Brassey, who staggered under the weight. "You handle that?"

"I'll manage," said the youngster.

Seeing the other men festooned with muskets, cartridge boxes, and a few baldrics with cutlasses and bayonets, Silva sent the group on its way. "I'll get powder," he said, shooing them off.

Another shattering broadside shook the ship. Any minute now, the compartment would fill with powder boys again. *Hmm.* Backing out of the magazine, he slipped into a compartment across the passageway, leaving the door open a crack so he could see. He smelled something pungent and glanced behind. "Well, well," he muttered. "Rum, by God!" One of the short, thick black glass bottles must have cracked and soaked the padding around it. There was a sack hanging on a hook and he filled it with the bottles, leaving two aside. Pulling the cork on one, he took a long swig. "Ghaaa!" he hissed appreciatively. Not great, but not bad. He wondered what they used for sugar? Lowering the bottle, he took a length of light line that had probably once bound the padding together and stuck one end into the bottle. Then he wrapped it around the open mouth and tied it. Nothing to do now but wait.

Soon, the boys had all apparently come and gone and he slipped back across the passageway. He held both bottles by their necks between the fingers of his left hand, and drew the cutlass with his right. Anyone who saw the cutlass would know *it* didn't belong. It was longer, straighter—and much better—than anything like it on the ship. He shrugged. Time to do his thing. He'd behaved himself long enough.

"Open up!" Silva growled at the inner door. A short man with spectacles and the almost universal Imperial mustache opened the heavy door and peered out. Silva drove the cutlass into his chest and pushed his way inside. Without a sound, the man slid off the blade and onto the deck when Silva lowered the cutlass and regarded the other man. He was bigger and might require more exercise.

He screamed shrilly.

So much for first impressions, Silva thought, and pinned the man to the bulkhead. The gunner, or mate—whichever he was—screamed even louder. "Well, shit!" Dennis hissed indignantly, skewering the man again. "I've seen *bunnies* make manlier noises when a dog gets 'em by the ass!" Still sobbing, but mortally wounded, the big man fell to the deck when Silva freed the blade.

Quickly, he laid the cutlass on the gunner's table and hung the rope and rum bottle from a hook on the beam overhead. Snatching up a fifty-pound keg of powder, he hurried to place it in the passageway. He knew he was running out of time. Imperial drill for deterring mountain fish seemed to be three broadsides, and the next would fire any minute. He didn't know what would happen after that. He doubted the powder boys would return the pass boxes to the magazine—there was limited space inside, after all—but *somebody* was liable to come down. He ran back inside, picked up another barrel of powder, and smashed it against the deck.

"I thought I might find you here," came a voice from the armory compartment.

Silva looked up. "Well, how do, Mr. Truelove," he said. "For some reason, I thought you might too." He nodded at the pistol held casually in Truelove's hand. "You gonna shoot that in here?"

Truelove grimaced at the pistol and slid it on his belt, where it hung by a hook. "I don't suppose I really need it. I'm actually quite good with a sword. I've seen you use one, you know, at Baalkpan, before I gave you that little tap on the head. You fight quite . . . dynamically and enthusiastically . . . but your sword work is just that: work. To me, it is play."

"Why'd you conk me then?"

Truelove shrugged. "Unsportsmanlike, I know, but necessary at the time. Perhaps now we might meet each other properly?"

"Sure. Just a couple o' questions first. 'Twixt gentlemen."

Truelove nodded. "Of course. Adversaries should know each other at times like this, and I already know a good deal about you."

"How *did* you know I'd be here?"

"Oh, I don't know. Call it intuition. You *are* a resourceful man. I thought it likely you might take advantage of the situation facing the ship. I don't know what you hope to accomplish, but I've no doubt you have a plan. I almost regret thwarting you. I view you as a fellow professional in a way, and suspect I would have enjoyed seeing your plan unfold."

So, thought Silva, *he's here on a whim. Everything else might still be going swell.* He had no doubt Truelove was better with a sword, since Silva had no proper training at all. A real fight wouldn't do, and besides, it might take too long and draw too much attention. A moment earlier he'd been in a rush. Now he needed to stall. "Why Billingsly?" he asked conversationally. "A fella like you'd go just as far on the right side, I figger."

Truelove laughed. "Well, let us just say that I had gone quite as far as I could in His Majesty's Secret Service, and I like money. Yes, indeed." He nodded at Silva's cutlass and reached for his sword. "Shall we be about it then?"

"Sure, but there's just one thing you may not know about me," Silva said, shaking his head with a conspiratorial grin and a prolonged display of being a man with a great secret.

"Oh?"

The third broadside erupted, jarring the ship and making the lantern in the adjoining compartment jump. Silva launched himself like a torpedo and struck Truelove in the chest with his head before the man could clear his blade. They sprawled together in the armory compartment, and quicker than his opponent could recover, Silva's mighty fists were already slamming into his face like pile drivers. Truelove was still trying to free his sword, but with six inches of the blade free, Dennis paused long enough to grasp the man's hand in his and wrench it to the side, breaking several of Truelove's fingers against the guard and snapping the blade off at the top of the scabbard. He pitched the twisted guard in among the musket stocks. The last thing Truelove might have heard before darkness took him was Silva's final, gasping explanation: "Sometimes I can be a little unsportsmanlike too."

For the moment, Truelove was out. Sore from his leap, Silva struggled to his feet and dragged the heavy, limp form into the magazine. Tearing off a piece of wadding made of something he didn't recognize, he stuffed it into Truelove's mouth and propped him against a heavy upright beam. Finding a spool of slow match, he fiercely tied the man's head to the post, across the gag, then proceeded to secure him quickly and professionally against any attempt to escape. Tearing away a piece of Truelove's shirt, he lit it from the lantern and carefully lit the rum-soaked cord that held the bottle suspended. He had no idea how long the cord would hold, five minutes or half an hour, but he needed to be *gone*.

As he fled the armory, as an afterthought he snatched Truelove's pistol from where it had fallen from his belt, then shut the outer door and locked it with his heavy brass key. He'd taken a chance the same key would work, but he'd expected it would. He knocked the top off the second rum bottle and liberally doused the passageway on both sides of the magazine, taking pains not to spill any right in front of it. Finally, he slung his big rifle and hoisted the keg of powder onto his shoulder. He lit another piece of Truelove's shirt from the lantern in the passageway and pitched it onto the far splash of rum. It lit with surprising fervency. Beyond the sudden flame, he saw a boy's panicked face appear and then quickly vanish, yelling, "Fire!" *Oh, well.* Dropping the lantern on the nearest splash, he hoisted his sack of rum bottles with a clinking sound and dashed up the companionway.

Things on the gun deck had calmed significantly when the leviathan they'd apparently struck failed to reappear. He even caught a snatch of a rumor that the starboard anchor had been discovered hanging in the sea. Maybe it was all just a false alarm. Silva paid no heed. His old maxim of doing sneaky stuff right out in the open seemed to be holding up. If a guy with a strange-looking gun came running by with a keg on one shoulder and a canvas sack on the other . . . he must have a good reason—or whoever had ordered him to did. Cries of "Fire!" began to increase, further distracting the crew. The alarm bell was sounding again when Silva reached the quarterdeck—and saw Billingsly pointing a pistol at Sandra, Rajendra, and Cook.

He was dressed in a probably stylish robe, with clashing colors and frills, and stood in stocking feet. He must have finally emerged from his spacious cabin to investigate all the commotion. Like Truelove, perhaps he suspected something and armed himself. Or maybe he was just paranoid. Regardless, there he stood with his long pistol aimed at Sandra. Again. He was shouting for guards, Marines—anyone—but no one could hear him over the alarm bell, the renewed uproar, and the still-venting steam. He didn't hear Silva either, when the big man stepped up behind him and laid him flat with the sack of rum bottles. To Silva, the wild pistol shot was only slightly more alarming than the mournful crash and tinkle of an unknown number of the little prizes in the sack.

"Silva!" cried Sandra. "Thank God! I don't know whether to yell at you for taking so long, or hug you for showing up when you did!"

He flashed a grin. "A hug'll do, but later! We'd better scram! Over the side with you!" He ran to the rail. "Here, somebody strong'd better catch this!" he said, and tossed the powder barrel at the boat. Next went his sack, and he heard someone cry out when they must have found some broken glass. Sandra and Abel were sliding down the rope.

"You next, Mr. Silva!" Captain Rajendra said. "I must be last to leave my ship!"

"I know that sounds all noble an' shit, but not this time," Silva replied. He nodded at a group of men approaching, cutlasses out. Billingsly was beginning to revive as well. "I can handle 'em a lot quicker than you." Rajendra hesitated; then, with a nod, he left Dennis Silva alone on *Ajax*'s quarterdeck. Almost nonchalantly, Silva popped open the holster flap and drew his beloved 1911 Colt. He'd considered it—and all his weapons—as much a hostage as the rest of them. There was a magazine in the well, but if he remembered, he'd emptied it. Besides, the weight was wrong. Depressing the magazine release with his thumb, the—sure enough—empty magazine clattered on the deck at his feet.

"Stop him, you fools!" Billingsly screamed at the swordsmen. "That is a *repeating* pistol of some sort!" The crewmen hesitated. A few more scampered up the stairs; one was an officer. "Kill that man this instant!" Billingsly shrieked.

Silva fished another magazine out of a pouch on his belt, inserted it, and racked the slide. "Too late," he said, and shot the officer. A large red hole appeared on the white jacket, exactly in the center of his chest, and he toppled backward onto the gun deck. Methodically, he then shot the three closest men and they sprawled on the deck around Billingsly. The other crew, who'd arrived with the officer, fled into the waist. Silva pointed the Colt at the Company warden and grinned hugely, his single eye gleaming. Smoke was beginning to coil up out of the ship and there was a growing panic.

"Well, *Mr.* Billingsly! Just you an' me!" He gestured with the pistol. "'S a wonder you didn't fiddle around with this thing, learn how it works. A fella like you coulda used it—at a time like this!" He laughed.

"Just do it!" Billingsly shouted. "Do you mean to mock me to death? Shoot! I *swear* I will kill you and all your pathetic friends! I'll *hang* that precious princess of yours, damn you!"

Silva's grin vanished and something akin to . . . regret crossed his face. "I already *have* killed you, you stupid, measly son of a goat! And at least you *deserve* killin'. You know, I was kinda groggy at the time, but seems I remember ol' Spanky yellin' somethin' about you not knowin' who you was monkeyin' with." He shrugged. "Now you do."

With that, Silva slid down the rope to the waiting boat below. "Cast off!" he said. "Out oars! Get us the hell outta here!"

"They'll fire on us!" Brassey shouted.

"No, they won't. Row."

Rajendra gave Silva a strange look. "Do as he says. All together!"

"I want this ship turned in pursuit of that boat this instant!" Billingsly shouted.

"There's no steam!" returned *Ajax*'s first lieutenant. "Someone has wrecked the emergency valve! We'll have to let the boiler go completely cold before we can fix it!"

"Then make sail! I want that boat! Where's Truelove? Has anyone seen him?"

"No, sir. We have almost extinguished the fire in the orlop passageway. It is very strange. The fire was deliberately set, but also set in such a way as to make it difficult for us to reach the magazine! With all those flames that close . . . it makes me shudder to think!"

Billingsly's eyes went wide. "Has anyone inspected the magazine yet?"

"No, sir. It is locked, would you believe it? Locked!"

"Quickly! Who has a key?"

The executive officer was taken aback, both by the line of questioning and by Billingsly's intensity. "Why, Captain Rajendra, that traitor, would have one."

"Who else?"

"Only the master gunner."

Billingsly covered his face with his hand. "Get axes! Every man who will fit in that passageway this instant, with axes! You must chop a way into the magazine! There isn't an instant to lose!"

The officer raced off and Billingsly turned to face in the direction the boat had pulled away. It was invisible in the darkness, but he knew they would be watching. Probably that fool Rajendra had no idea, but Silva would be watching . . . and waiting. As he'd said, Billingsly was a man with few regrets, but one nagging little minor regret—letting the hostages live as long as he had—suddenly lunged to the very top of his list.

Truelove managed to open one eye but the other was swollen shut. For several moments he couldn't figure out where he was, why he was there, or why he was so uncomfortable. Slowly it all returned to him. *Unsportsmanlike!* He would have chuckled if he didn't hurt so badly and if something painfully large and well secured wasn't stuffed in his mouth. He'd been in the business long enough to appreciate the work of a professional, even at his own expense. Sometimes, given the nature of that brilliant fool Billingsly and the treacherous cause they served, Truelove couldn't help but appreciate a fellow professional, *especially* when it came at his expense. He'd been at it too long and he'd grown jaded. He *did* like the money, but his heart just wasn't much in it anymore. Another thought would have made him laugh. He'd told his adversary his swordsmanship was work while Truelove's own was play. It suddenly occurred to him that, though that may be true, Silva's . . . "professionalism" was still play, while his own had become work. Such irony.

He could barely move his head, but with his one good eye, he gazed around the compartment. Two dead men. A lot of blood. Wait! He was back in the magazine itself! There were no muskets, just barrels of powder secured all around. *If I'm in the magazine, where is that flickering light coming from?* He looked up, but couldn't quite see. After much wriggling, he managed to force his head back just far enough.

Oh, bravo! he said to himself as the charred rope parted and the burning rum bottle dropped.

The current ran swiftly here and the men and women in the launch had rowed for their lives. All knew *Ajax* might turn at any moment and chase them down, but a couple of those on the boat suspected there might be further reason for gaining distance while they could. *Ajax*'s own momentum and the prevailing wind kept her pointed east, while the current carried the launch and its occupants west-northwest. Therefore, they'd gained almost two miles' distance from the ship when the night suddenly lit with a blinding flash that drew all their stares.

The entire aft half of *Ajax* erupted amid a yellow-red ball of fire, scattering masts, beams, yards, timbers, shards of burning rope and drifting canvas far across the sea. There was little steam left in her boiler, but a great steamy plume shot skyward when seawater touched the hot iron. Another similar blast demolished the forward part of the ship when the other magazine went. The bowsprit was launched entirely out of view like an enormous javelin. *Ajax*'s death took only seconds, but to those in the distant boat, it seemed to last much longer. The rolling, staccato, thunderous punch of the blast finally reached them with a physical jolt, and for what felt like whole minutes, flaming debris, blocks, an entire gun and carriage, bodies—or parts of bodies—rained down to splash amid the already vanishing flames.

"My ship," murmured Rajendra.

"My God, Silva, what have you done?" Sandra whispered.

Dennis stood up in the boat and glared around at the dozen or so survivors. "Why is it ever' time somethin' like this happens, it's 'Lawsy me, what's ol' Silva done now'? I'm sick an' tired of it, hear! Might give a fella the benefit o' the doubt now an' again!"

"Did you . . . do something . . . that might have destroyed that ship?" Rebecca asked quietly.

Dennis looked harshly at her for a moment, then glanced at his feet. "Well . . . what if I did? What were we gonna do? *Row* off from 'em? That wadn't ever gonna work, not after Rajendra and his bunch decided they wanted to come with us! Sneakin' off ourselves was one thing. They wouldn'ta noticed us gone till they came to feed us the next day, and we woulda had a lot of ocean to hide in." He glared at the men from *Ajax* again. "A ship's captain, engineer, carpenter—an' who knows what else—disappear in the middle of a distraction like was necessary to get so many off, somebody's gonna take notice! Somebody *did*!"

Rajendra stood too, slightly jostling the boat. "You . . . murdering filth! You *murder* my ship and all her crew and then have the nerve to say you did it because of *us*? Because we came with you? How would you have escaped without our help—without the help of some of the men you killed this night who had to stay behind?"

"It wadn't *your* ship no more, genius!" Silva bellowed. He was fed up. "You were in the same fix we were. Don't you *dare* stand there an' act all sancti-fidious at *me* when you wouldn't even rear up on your hind legs an' *try* to take your ship back! When *you* blew Cap'n Lelaa's ship outa the water with all *her* people on it! You coulda saved your ship then, if you'd pulled your pistol an' shot Billingsly square betwixt the eyes! That prob'ly woulda been the end of it right there, because whatever else you are, or your crew was, you were the *goddamn captain*! Instead, you said, 'Yes, sir! You're the boss!' an' killed two hundred of *our* folks! Then you slunk around whinin' how it wadn't your fault!"

Silva looked at Sandra, knowing she, at least, would believe his next words. "I had me a little plan to get us off the ship. Mighta worked. We mighta got off without killin' hardly anybody"—he shrugged—"or I mighta still blown up your ship. That was always plan B. When I heard your plan, I figgered it 'ud be easier—an' safer—for *us* an' the *princess*. But only if I dusted off plan B an' made it part o' plan A! Well, the plans worked, yours an' mine, an' here we are. I'm sorry if I killed some good fellas, but I ain't *that* damn sorry." He pointed at the pistol on Rajendra's belt. "You can try to shoot me now, an' maybe that'll prove you ain't as yellow as I think you are, but I'll kill you an' you'll just be dead instead o' helpin' out now, when your princess needs you. Or you can prove you weren't never yellow at all—just confused an' a little scared, in a fix you hadn't come upon before. I've heard that happens to folks. You can prove that by bein' a good captain for what's left of your crew, an' by helpin' Larry an' Captain Lelaa—if she'll have you—navigate our way to the boosum o' Larry's lovin' home."

Slowly, Rajendra sat. Some of what Silva had said must have struck a chord, because he lowered his eyes and then stared at the few distant flickering fires that marked the grave of his ship and crew. His expression was desolate. "Who is to be in charge, then?" he finally asked, controlling his voice.

"Lieutenant—rather, Minister—Tucker," Princess Rebecca said in a tone that brooked no argument. "Now that we're all on the same side, she is the highest-ranking official present, myself excluded. If you prefer, you may consider her as my proxy, but you *will* obey her."

"What about *him*?" asked the engineer, referring to Silva.

"As has been most . . . eloquently . . . presented, if Mr. Silva is to be arrested, I must have Captain Rajendra arrested as well. What purpose would that serve? Mr. Silva will retain his position as my chief arms-man and personal protector—provided he at least consults me before destroying any more of His Majesty's property."

Dennis looked at the girl. He'd more than half expected her to despise him for what he'd done, and the relief he felt was indescribable.

"Well," he said, a bit huskily, "I'll sure try."

Sandra took a deep breath. "All right, let's get on with it. Captain Lelaa, you have the helm. Lawrence, assist her with the compass, if you please. Captain Rajendra? I assume this vessel has a sail?"

"Report from the crow's nest, Captain," Reynolds said. "Sail on the horizon, bearing zero one zero."

"Very well. Helm, make your course zero one zero, if you please," Matt ordered. He raised his binoculars.

"Making my course see-ro one see-ro, ay!" replied Staas-Fin at the wheel.

"Uh, Skipper?" Reynolds continued. "Wouldn't this be a good time to put my plane in the water and let me fly over there and have a look?"

Matt restrained the grin that tried to form. Reynolds took his new calling as a naval aviator very seriously, and by all accounts he was a good pilot. He and his small flight and maintenance crew cared for the Nancy meticulously. They'd even worked out a number of the problems associated with stowing, rigging out and recovering the plane, and protecting it from the elements. They still hadn't had a chance to actually fly the thing yet, and partially that was due to the time it required to launch and recover the aircraft. Mostly, Matt admitted to himself, he personally didn't want to risk the valuable, fragile resource the plane represented, or the young, excitable, but steady ensign he'd grown so fond of. So far, in addition to his Special Air Detail duties, Reynolds had been stuck in his old job as bridge talker, for the most part. He was starting to feel a little put-upon and it showed.

"Not just yet, Ensign. The sea's got a little chop to it. Besides, I expect that'll be *Achilles*, based on our position. If we spot anything on the horizon we're slightly less sure of, you can risk your crazy neck in that goofy contraption then."

"Aye-aye, Captain," Fred replied, a little wistfully.

The sail was indeed *Achilles*, and they easily overhauled her at twenty knots by early afternoon. Both ships flew their recognition numbers as they approached, even though each captain would have known the other's ship anywhere. It was a procedure they'd agreed on in advance among themselves—just in case. *Walker* slowed to match *Achilles'* nine knots. It was a respectable pace, considering the wind and the drag of the freewheeling paddles. Jenks was undoubtedly conserving fuel, and running the engine wouldn't have given him a dramatic speed increase in any event. Matt recognized his counterpart standing on the elevated conning platform amidships, between the paddle boxes. Stepping onto the port bridge wing, he raised his speaking trumpet.

"It's good to see you, *Achilles*!" he shouted, his voice crossing the distance between the ships with a tinny aspect.

"You cut a fine figure, Captain Reddy," Jenks replied. "Your beautiful ship is quite the rage aboard here! To have you so effortlessly come streaking alongside within an hour of sighting you has been a marvelous sight to behold, while we here labor along and toil for every knot! I must protest your choice of such a drab color for such an elegant lady, however! Gray, for heaven's sake! And I do fear I perceive a streak or two of rust! Clearly you've had a difficult passage!"

Matt laughed. He couldn't help it. For the first time, perhaps, he caught himself *liking* Jenks.

"Rust, he says!" the Bosun bawled on the fo'c'sle. "Did you hear that, you shif'less pack o' malingerers? If there's a *speck* of rust anywhere on this ship, I want it chipped and painted if you have to hang over the side by your useless *tails*!"

Lord, thought Matt yet again, *in spite of* everything, *some things never change. Thank God.* Of course, in his own way the Bosun was a genius. The man was a hero to the crew—to the entire Alliance—and even "Super Bosun" was an inadequate title. He had the moral authority of a thundering, wrathful God, and his increasing harangues were probably carefully calculated to keep the Lemurian crew from dwelling on the now obvious fact that they'd steamed beyond where any of their kind had ever traveled. Possibly only two things kept the more nervous 'Cats diligently at their duty: the persistent and familiar sense of normal gravity that proved they weren't about to *fall* off the world, and the absolute certainty the Bosun would contrive to *throw* them off if he ever caught them cringing in their racks.

"Maybe we should steam in company for the day and through the night," Matt shouted across. "Then spread out tomorrow. In the meantime, I'd be honored if you and your officers would join us for dinner. Juan"—he smirked slightly—"and Lanier have been preparing something special in anticipation of your visit."

"Delighted, Captain Reddy. It would be *my* honor."

Dinner was served in the wardroom with as much pomp as Juan could manage. He hovered near the guests with a carafe of monkey joe in one hand, towel draped over his arm. His wardroom breakfasts had become legendary, but he rarely got a chance to entertain. For this dinner, he was at his most formal best, and though mess dress hadn't been exactly prescribed, everyone managed as best they could. Matt's own dress uniform was one of his few prewar outfits Juan had managed to maintain. He'd even sent it ashore with other important items before *Walker*'s last fight.

Earl Lanier entered with as much dignity as possible, carrying a tray of appetizers. He'd somehow stuffed his swollen frame into his own dingy mess dress and wore a long, greasy apron tied around his chest and under his arms that hung nearly to his shins. Laying the tray on the green linoleum table, he removed the lid with a steamy flourish. Nestled neatly around a sauce tureen were dozens of smoky pink cylindrical shapes, decorated with a possibly more edible leafy garnish. Matt's face fell, as did the faces of all the human destroyermen. In his ongoing effort to use the damn things up, Lanier had prepared an appetizer of Vienna sausages, or "scum weenies," as some called them. Juan almost crashed into Lanier, forcing him into the passageway beyond the curtain, where he proceeded to berate him in highly agitated Tagalog.

"Ah, cooks and their sensibilities!" Jenks said, spearing an oozing sausage with a fork. After dipping the object in the sauce, he popped it in his mouth. "Um . . . most interesting," he accomplished at last, forcing himself to swallow.

"Yes, well . . ." was all Matt could manage. The "appetizer" remained little sampled except by Chack and some of the other 'Cats, who actually seemed to like the things. Sooner than expected, Juan returned with the main course: a mountainous, glazed "pleezy-sore" roast. He quickly removed the offending tray. The excellent roast was much more enthusiastically received and consumed with great relish. Juan also brought in some other dishes: steamed vegetables of some sort that tasted a lot like squash, and some very ordinary-looking sautéed mushrooms. There were tankards of fresh polta juice and pitchers of the very last iced tea known to exist on the planet. The ice came from the big refrigerator-freezer on deck behind the blower, and Spanky and Lanier themselves had teamed up to repair it. Ice, and the cold water that came from the little built-in drinking fountain, was always welcome, and of course the truck-size machine allowed them to carry perishables.

The dinner was a huge success, and to Juan's satisfaction, everything was much appreciated and commented on. He might kill Lanier later, but for a time, he was in his favorite element. After the last remove, Jenks spoke up. "A most flavorful dinner." He patted his stomach. "Perhaps too flavorful!" He turned to Juan. "You and Mr. Lanier have my heartiest compliments! Even the iced tea! How refreshing! We usually take tea hot, you know. Even if we had a means of making ice at sea, I don't suppose it has ever occurred to anyone to ice tea before!" He paused, and everyone looked at him with keen interest. Of *course* the Empire would know tea! Planting and growing some of the "founder's" cargo would probably have been one of their first imperatives!

Jenks continued. "I am given to understand that you do not imbibe strong drink aboard your Navy's ships, Captain Reddy. Perhaps that is not a bad policy. In case you might consider an exception, I did bring a very mild, dry port to commemorate our rendezvous. There is just enough for a single short glass for all present, and I intended it as a means for proposing a toast."

Matt nodded. "In that case, Commodore, I'll allow an exception. It's not unheard-of in situations like this when 'foreigners' are aboard. Juan, would you be good enough to fetch glasses?"

A few minutes later, glasses had been positioned and filled by Juan's expert hand. Jenks raised his glass. "It is customary at this time for our most junior officer to offer the first toast to the governor-emperor. I do not expect you to participate, under the circumstances, but I do beg you to give His Majesty the benefit of the doubt in this matter. It is his own daughter who has been taken, after all."

"Very well," Matt agreed. "The benefit of the doubt . . . for now." One of Jenks's midshipmen stood, and all those present, everyone, stood with him.

"Gentlemen," he said, "His Majesty!"

All, including Matt, took a sip. The port was interesting, fruity, Matt decided, and as mild as Jenks had promised. He held out his own glass. "The Grand Alliance, and the United States Navy!" All drank again, but Matt noticed there was the slightest hesitation among a few of the Imperial officers. Inwardly, he sighed.

Jenks held forth his glass. "Hear, hear!" he said forcefully. "And a most formidable Navy it is. We have joined together to embark on a venture essential to both our nations." He paused. "May it ever be thus: that we will forever cooperate as friends, and never meet as enemies!" On that, Jenks emptied his glass, and with no hesitation at all, everyone else in the wardroom followed suit.

"Captain!" Reynolds exclaimed excitedly. "Lookout reports surface contact bearing one two five degrees! It's a sail, Skipper! More than one. He says it looks like three or four!"

"Course?" Matt snapped. *Sails! Here?* Other than Billingsly, who else would be in these waters? According to Jenks, they were still a considerable distance from the closest Imperial outpost. Possibly *four* ships! Could others have *joined* Billingsly?

Reynolds relayed the course request and stood, waiting anxiously for several minutes before the lookout in the crow's nest replied, "Almost reciprocal, Skipper. Lookout estimates contact course is two eight zero! Four ships for sure, sir, under sail!"

"Well," said Courtney Bradford, "of course we all presume those are Imperial ships? If not, personally I'd be willing to lay a wager to it."

"What makes you so sure?" Gray asked. "'Specially after all that stuff you were goin' on about the other day."

Bradford looked oddly at Gray. "Why, I will gladly wager my . . . my *hat* that they are indeed Imperials, coming in response to the ship and message Jenks dispatched when he first arrived in Baalkpan! Considering the time it would have taken that ship to travel to the Imperial homeland, spread the word, outfit another expedition . . . that expedition would be about, well, *here* by now!"

Gray looked at the bizarre sombrerolike hat hanging from Bradford's hand (he wasn't allowed to wear it on the bridge) and shook his head. "I wouldn't want that nasty thing as a gift. 'Sides, when you put it that way, you're probably right."

Matt was already convinced. He'd forgotten all about the ship Jenks was allowed to send away, with news of the princess's survival and rescue. He rubbed his chin, looking at Reynolds. Oh, well, he'd promised. Besides, there were other good reasons. "How do you like the sea, Ensign?" he asked.

Reynolds studied the swells. "Looks fine, Skipper. You'll need to heave to and set us down in the lee. The hard part, actually, will be moving away so we'll have the wind again—without sucking us into the screws."

Matt sighed. Another danger he hadn't really thought of. "Very well. Sound General Quarters and call your division. Have Mr. Palmer signal *Achilles* that we'll reduce speed and await your report."

"Aye-aye, sir!"

After all stations reported manned and ready, Reynolds announced shipwide: "Now hear this, now hear this! The Special Air Detail will assemble and make all preparations for flight operations!" Those members of the Special Air Detail not stationed at the plane as part of the Plane Dump Detail during GQ sprang from their various battle stations and hurried to their new posts. Matt had decided that the ship would always be at general quarters whenever the plane was launched or recovered so everyone would be at their highest state of readiness in the event of an accident. It was then easier to call the larger air detail from their normal battle stations, which, with the exception of the designated observer, were all close by. Observers came from Lieutenant Palmer's comm division.

"Mr. Reynolds, you are relieved," Matt said, gesturing for Carl Bashear to take Fred's headset. Kutas was at the helm, so Fred couldn't hope for better ship handling.

"Aye-aye, sir! Thank you, sir!" Reynolds said, and slid down the stairs behind the pilothouse. Hurrying past the galley under the amidships deckhouse, he heard the diminutive Juan Marcos and the monstrous Earl Lanier still arguing about the night before. He chuckled. He didn't care—he was going to fly! His division, almost entirely 'Cats, had already cleared the tarps from the plane and were arranging the tackle to the aft extended davit when he arrived. This Nancy was his own personal plane, the one in which he'd finished his training. It was one of the new, improved models, infinitely better than Ben's prototype. It looked incredibly frail, but Fred knew appearances were deceiving. He'd botched a landing or two, and it had held together under stresses he'd have thought would tear it apart. He had confidence in the plane and himself. Shoot, he had almost thirty hours in the thing! He climbed up to the cockpit and, as always, looked at the large blue roundel with the big white star and smaller red dot with a mix of pride and a sense of incongruity. The roundel contrasted well with the lighter blue of the wings and fuselage/hull, and all the colors looked right, but the contraption they covered was, while in his eyes a thing of beauty, still strange enough to cause a disconnect between its shape and the familiar colors. He shrugged and climbed in. "Who's my OC?" he shouted, referring to his observer/copilot.

One of Ben's improvements, besides turning the engine around, had been installing auxiliary controls for the observer. It only made sense. Observers didn't have to be pilots—yet—but they had to be familiar with the controls and able to demonstrate at least rudimentary flying skills. Of course, their main job was to observe and transmit those observations via one of the small, portable CW transmitters (originally meant for airplanes) that all the new transmitters in the Alliance were patterned after. There was no battery—Alliance-made batteries were still too heavy—but the "Ronson" wind powered generator and a voltage regulator the size of a shoe box gave them all the juice they needed with little weight. An aerial extended from a faired upright behind the observer's seat to the tail.

Fred looked aft and saw Kari-Faask scrambling into her position. She was a niece of the great B'mbaadan general Haakar-Faask, who'd died so bravely in a holding action against the Grik. Kari wasn't quite as bold and fearless as her uncle, but Fred knew she had plenty of guts. She never made any bones about the fact that she was afraid to fly, for example, but she went up anyway and performed her duties without complaint. Also, despite her still somewhat stilted English, she had a good fist on the transmitter key.

"You okay with this, Kari?" Fred called back to her.

"I good. You be good and no crash us!" she hollered back.

Reynolds could tell *Walker* was heaved to by the sudden wallowing sensation. He quickly checked the function of all the control surfaces and shouted down to the chief of the air detail, "All right, Chief, pick us up and swing us out! Set us down with plenty of slack but don't cut us loose until the engine starts, hear? And keep an eye on those line handlers!"

The Nancy lifted. 'Cats strained at the taglines to keep the plane from swinging with the rolling motion of the ship. Reynolds knew Ben had been hoping to construct some kind of catapult, a sort of abbreviated version of what *Amagi* had had, but there just hadn't been time. Now Reynolds better appreciated Ben's scheme. It wouldn't have made any difference with recovery, but with a catapult, they could have just flown right off the ship. A couple of times, the Nancy swung dangerously close to the davit and Fred clenched his eyes shut, expecting a splintering crash, but somehow, fairly quickly, the plane was over the water and headed down. Now the only immediate concern was giving the plane enough slack that the roll of the ship wouldn't yank her back out of the water and smash her against *Walker*'s side.

Suddenly, Reynolds felt the independent motion caused by water under the plane. There'd been no thump or splash at all. "Switch on!" he yelled, and Kari leaped up to lean against the little railing that kept her body away from the prop. Reaching as high as she could, she grabbed a blade and yanked it down. There was a cough, but nothing else. She repeated the process and was rewarded by a loud, muffled fart and the blades blurred before her. Reynolds advanced the throttle while she fell back into her seat and strapped herself in. This was the signal for the detail on the ship to pull the tagline pins that released all ropes from the plane. Kicking the rudder hard left, Reynolds advanced the throttle still more to gain some distance from the ship.

"All right!" Reynolds shouted, tension ebbing away. "We're on the loose!" Behind them, the ship slowly eased forward, exposing them to the westerly breeze. Turning the Nancy's nose into the wind, Reynolds advanced the throttle to the stop. The new liquid-cooled engine was heavier than Ben's makeshift prototype, but the power-to-weight ratio was actually a little better. It stayed uniformly cooler too, which could be good and bad. They'd need better spring technology before they could do a proper thermostat. The big, exposed radiator behind the cockpit also negated any potential speed increase, but having flown a couple of times in the prototype, Fred liked "his" Nancy a lot better. Unlike Ben, Reynolds had also quickly figured out a major secret to seaplane flying. Maybe it was because he'd had no preconceptions and just did what came naturally, but he'd amazed Ben on his third flight by "bouncing" his plane into the air off a wave top with half the speed and in a third of the distance with which Ben had ever managed it. Ben had been flabbergasted, amazed, annoyed, and proud all at once. After he got Fred to first figure out what he'd done, and second explain— and ultimately show it to everyone else—the practice became SOP.

Fred used the procedure now, and within moments of his applying full power, the plane was in the air. "Whooee!" he shouted, banking low over the water. He gradually pulled back on the stick. The Nancy's CG was still just a little aft, and Ben had constantly pounded it into them not to fool around with the stick, particularly at low altitude. Slowly, the plane climbed. In the distance, about ten miles away, he saw *Achilles*. He knew no one on the Imperial ship had ever seen a man fly, and he was tempted to cruise over and buzz her. He resisted the impulse, realizing it probably wasn't appropriate to goof around in the air the first time the skipper let him fly. He grinned, thinking about what it would be like—Ben had told him of the chaos he'd caused on *Ajax* that one time. Shaking his head, he banked a little sharper and flew back toward *Walker*, gently waggling his wings as he flew over.

In all the wide expanse of the world around them, there was nothing but sea. He'd never flown over the empty ocean before, at least not beyond sight of land, and it made him a little queasy. Worse, it was a dull, humid day and the higher he flew, the more difficult it became to tell where the sky and the horizon met. He looked at his clinometer and steadied his wings. As far as he could see, there was no sign of land at all. Just the hazy, grayish sky and the hazy blue sea below. *Achilles* and *Walker* were there, of course, and that comforted him, but the only other things in view were the distant ships the lookout had spotted. It was time to get to work.

"Definitely four ships," he shouted to Kari through the speaking tube, knowing she would report it, although by now *Walker* and *Achilles* would probably know that already. There were no ships beyond those, however, and that would be news. He reported that as well. Closer and closer to the unknown ships he flew, gaining altitude. Still nothing beyond them but maybe an atoll or something. He couldn't tell for sure, and it might even have been a distant squall. But the four ships were clearly alone. "Tell 'em they're sailing steamers, like *Achilles* . . . and *Ajax*. All have those paddle box things on their sides. When we get a little closer, I'll take her down a little and see if we can get a look at their flags. They've *got* flags; I can see that much from here."

A short time later, he was kiting a few thousand feet above the strange ships. He still couldn't see what flag they flew, but they must have noticed him. He couldn't tell if his flying machine had caused any consternation below, but they were taking in sail, and puffs of smoke began streaming from their tall, slender funnels.

"Say, Kari," he shouted, "I don't know what it means, or if they're reacting to us or our ships, but they've lit their boilers. Seems that would mean they want to be able to maneuver. Better send that; then we're going down for a closer look."

"Yes, I send," Kari said. "But stay out of musket shot! If they Jenks people, they muskets are no as good as our new ones, and no *near* as good as you rifles, but they plenty good shoot holes in this 'crate' you get close enough!"

"Don't worry. I plan to stay well clear." He eased the stick forward and began a slow, spiraling descent. "Let's see," he said, mentally kicking himself for forgetting a pair of binoculars. He'd have to remember that in the future. Surely Kari could hold the plane level while he took a look—or he could do the same for her. She was the observer, after all. Maybe with her better eyes . . . "Hey, Kari, if you get a good look at the flag, describe what you see!" he yelled.

Still closer they flew, swooping down to within three hundred feet of the water. The ships looked just like Jenks's, for the most part. One had more gunports, the others fewer, but all followed essentially the same lines and rig. Sooty black plumes rose thick from all four ships now.

"I see flag! Imper'al flag!" Kari confirmed. "Is same as Jenks . . . I think." Something about it, she didn't know what, didn't look exactly right.

A single puff of smoke belched from a gun on the nearest ship.

"They shoot at us!" Kari shouted. "With cannon! We out of range their muskets, but not cannon!"

"Relax," said Reynolds, a little shaky himself, as he banked abruptly away. "We probably just spooked them. That had to be a warning shot telling us to keep our distance. If they were shooting *at* us, I doubt if they'd have used just one. Think about it: they've never seen an airplane before in their lives. They don't know if we're dangerous or not. I can understand them not wanting us too close." He rubbed his windblown face. "From what I could see, they looked like Imperial flags to me too. Send it. Tell Captain Reddy we're coming home and ask him to fly a signal saying what he wants us to do." Fred would be glad when they could make headsets for the observers. His Nancy had one of the simple receivers, and the little speakers Riggs had come up with worked fine, but they couldn't compete with a droning motor. For now, they had to rely on visual instructions from the ship.

"Wilco!" Kari shouted through the speaking tube.

*   *   *

"He says—En-sin Reynolds says—they Imperials, all right. Chase plane off with warning shot," one of Ed Palmer's comm strikers reported. "He ask we hoist signal flags, tell more instructions."

Matt was thoughtful. "A warning shot, huh? Very well." He turned and spoke to the Bosun. "Have him orbit us while we meet the strangers, fuel permitting. He should have plenty and it won't be long. The main reasons I let him fly in the first place were to test his procedures—we had to do that sooner or later—and to get the plane off the ship when we meet these guys . . . just in case."

"Aye-aye, Captain," Gray said, and he strode the short distance to where the signalmen and signal strikers stood, just aft of the charthouse.

"That's most odd," Courtney observed.

"What, the warning shot?" Matt asked.

"Well, that too, but I suspect even our Harvey Jenks would have done that when we first met, had we flown an airplane at him. Imperials do seem to have a rather well-defined societal arrogance. Mr. Jenks has mellowed rather satisfactorily, I think. Actually, though, what suddenly strikes me is that presumably they can see us as well as we can see them by now."

"Sure . . ." Matt glanced at the approaching ships and saw the black smoke above them. They *were* much closer, maybe only six miles away. Under steam and sail, they were probably making ten or twelve knots. *Walker* had slowed to five when the plane took off, but she'd accelerated to fifteen as the Nancy swooped back over the ship, reading the flags they'd hoisted. Matt peered past the port bridge wing and looked north-northwest, where *Achilles* had been keeping pace. He saw that Jenks's ship had closed the distance to about seven miles, and smoke was streaming from her stack now too. "What the hell's going on here? Those ships are clearly heading toward *us*, not Jenks. And why did everybody light their boilers all of a sudden?"

Palmer himself appeared on the bridge. His voice had an edge when he spoke. "Message from *Achilles*, Skipper."

"Okay. What's it say?"

"Commodore Jenks suggests that we not, repeat *not* close with the approaching squadron alone."

"Why not?"

"He doesn't say."

"Well, find out, damn it, because they're sure as hell closing with *us*, and they'll get here before he does!"

"Aye-aye, sir," Palmer said, and left the bridge.

"Slow to one-third," Matt ordered. "Maybe we can reduce our closure rate, at least. I'm not sure showing our heels will make the best impression."

"We ought to go to flank and steam circles around the buggers," Gray muttered to Bradford as he returned.

"While perhaps highly satisfying," Bradford whispered back, arching his eyebrows, "it may also be deemed provocative." He raised his voice. "I think I know why they are concentrating on us, Captain," he proclaimed. "When Jenks dispatched his message, he surely must have reported that Her Highness desired *us* to take her home on *this* ship. No doubt Jenks would have described *Walker* as she had been described to him: a dedicated steamer with an iron hull. No sails. I shouldn't wonder if that's why they are converging on this ship; they believe the princess is aboard!"

"Maybe you're right," Matt replied. "And if it hadn't been for Billingsly's stunt, that would make me feel a lot better. Even so . . . Even if they're all as big a pack of jerks as Billingsly, I can't imagine they'd fire at us and risk hurting the girl. Billingsly took her—and the rest of our people—'cause he wanted her. He could have just bumped her off at any time."

"Not and lived," Gray growled.

"Good point," Matt agreed. He rubbed his face again. "If they've got twenty four-pounders, like *Achilles*, they can punch holes in us out to what, five hundred yards? Six?"

"I'd think about that, Skipper," Gray agreed. "Probably dent the hell out of us to a thousand. But round shot loses a lot of energy quick. It's buckin' a lot of wind for the weight." He shrugged. "If they've got anything even a little bigger, though, the weight goes up exponentially for just a little more wind resistance. A thirty-two's not buckin' much more wind than an eighteen pounder, like *Donaghey* carries, but it'll punch a hole in us at a thousand!"

Matt made up his mind. "Okay, at two thousand yards, we heave to, broadside. We'll fly a white parley flag, but all batteries will remain loaded, trained, and aimed for surface action starboard. The gun director will concentrate on that big boy that must be their flagship. If they close to fifteen hundred yards, we'll fire a warning shot of our own with the Jap gun aft. Have Chief Gunner's Mate Stites lay it himself, in local control. Tell him to use HE for a really big splash and put it close enough to rain on 'em without hurting anybody, clear?"

Chief Bashear understood that the tactical conversation was over and that orders had been issued. He quickly passed the word. "Skipper?" he asked when he received confirmation. "I oughta be aft." Chief Gray might be the "Super Bosun" of the fleet, but Carl Bashear was *Walker's* official chief bosun's mate now. Since Gray's self-appointed battle station was the forward part of the ship, near the captain, Bashear's post was aft, near Steele, on the auxiliary conn. Chack was a bosun's mate too, but since he also commanded the Marine contingent, he oversaw things amidships, where he could remain close to his Marines.

"Of course, Boats . . . Bashear," Matt said with only a slight hesitation. Gray would always be "Boats" to him, but "Boats Bashear" had seemed to make Carl happy. "By all means, round up a relief and take your post."

Staas-Fin, or "Finny," quickly arrived to take his place and Carl Bashear was gone. Time passed while all the ships gradually converged. *Achilles* was really cracking on, but even with *Walker's* speed reduced to slow, Jenks clearly couldn't arrive until shortly after the Imperial squadron reached the two-thousand-yard mark and things began to happen. The squeal of the halyard behind the charthouse announced that the parley flag was on its way up. Reynolds's Nancy flew by ahead, just a few hundred feet off the wave tops. Matt had to admit the thing looked a lot better in the air than it did strapped to his ship.

"I see a white flag going up on the biggest Imperial ship," cried Monk from his lookout post on the starboard bridge wing. About that time, the same report came from the crow's nest.

"Sir," said Palmer, gaining the bridge again, "Jenks says firing the boilers is Imperial SOP when they clear for action! He asks if we are

certain the ships fly the same flag he does, *exactly* the same? The Imperial Naval jack is basically the same as the national flag—thirteen red
and white stripes with red on top and bottom, and the union blue in
the field! The Company flag has white on top and bottom with no blue,
just a red cross of Saint George! He says the Company revived an older
flag to show a distinction!"

"Goddamn, what a crock!" Gray said.

"Not a crock," Matt retorted. "There's definitely historical prece-
dence, and it makes sense. Can anybody tell if there's any blue on those
flags? If Jenks thinks it's that important, we'd better find out!"

"Can't tell!" shouted Monk. "All their flags are streaming aft
and they're headed right for us! I can see stripes now and then, but
that's it!"

"What's on top, red or white?" Matt barked.

"Two thousand yards!" cried Finny.

"Very well, left standard rudder. When we're in position, we'll heave
to and maintain position. Flags?" he prompted again.

"I can't *tell* what's on top!" Monk yelled.

"Crow's nest?" Matt demanded.

"White!" said Finny. "No, red! Jeez, Skipper, crow's nest no tell either! Campeti say coming to fifteen hundreds!"

"Gun number four will prepare to commence firing. One shot
only," Matt said.

"Fifteen hundreds!" Finny almost squealed.

"Fire number four!"

From aft, they heard the bark of the Japanese 4.7-inch dual-purpose
gun. Even over the sound of the blower, the *hssssshk* sound of the pro-
jectile in flight was distinctive. A large geyser of spume erupted one
hundred yards off the port bow of the largest approaching ship, and
spray did indeed collapse upon the fo'c'sle.

"Pass the word to Stites," Matt said. "Well-placed."

For a long moment, there was no response from the ships. Matt was
about to order a second shot when Monk reported that the target (odd
how it had suddenly become "the target") had begun reefing sails. Still,
though, the ships continued toward them.

"I don't like it," Gray said.

"Me either," agreed Matt. "They're reducing sail like they're re-specting the warning shot, but they're still steaming right at us. I don't like it at all." He looked to port. "Where's Jenks?"

"Coming up hand over fist, but he's still a couple thousand yards off the port quarter. Sir, he's hoisted a really big flag!" Matt looked. Sure enough, a much larger than usual Imperial national flag had been run up to the peak of *Achilles'* maintop. It was clearly a battle flag, and Matt had seen something similar done a long time ago. *Walker* even had her own battle flag now. Meticulously repaired after the Battle of Baalkpan, and with the name of that battle added to the others embroidered upon it, it lay folded in a place of honor in the center of the signal flag locker.

"Run up our battle flag," Matt said resignedly. "Obviously they understand what it means. That ought to impress them more than another warning shot!"

"Skipper! They're turning!"

Matt looked back to the front. At about eight hundred yards, the four ships executed a very tight turn to port that only paddle wheels would have allowed. They still had the wind, and for a moment, the flags all streamed forward from aft. They were red-and-white flags, without the slightest touch of blue, and just as that realization dawned, the starboard side of all but one of the ships erupted in a solid bank of white smoke.

"All ahead flank!" Matt shouted. "Main battery, commence firing! Somebody yank that white rag down and get our own flag up there!"

Fireman Tab-At, or "Tabby," felt the ship squat down and lurch forward as the throttlemen poured on the steam. She almost fell against the aft bulkhead of the fireroom. Access plates on the deck popped up out of their grooves and slid toward her like big, rectangular blades, and she hopped as they went by to keep from losing her toes. They clanged against the bulkhead behind her. "Feed 'em!" she shouted. "Open 'em up!" They had to increase the flow of air, water, and fuel to keep up with the sudden enormous dump of steam. An instant later, she felt like somebody had put a bucket on her head and started beating it with a stick. As quickly as it began, the heavy drumming ceased, but *Walker* kept picking up speed. The air lock cycled and Spanky emerged from the forward engine room. He was covered with dark fuel oil from head to foot, but his eyes were white as they darted around the compartment.

"Everything okay in here?" he shouted.

"Yeah . . ." Tabby started, then amended, "Yes, sir! A few loose plates. What happened?"

"The bastards fired at us!" Spanky bellowed. "The goddamn sneakin' *bastards*!"

"Who shoot?" Tabby asked, her drawl and English slipping a little.

"Those goddamn Company Brits. Who else?"

"How you get so oily? Engines okay?"

"Yeah. Somethin' punched a hole through one of the saddle bunkers, somethin' *big*. Must be rollin' around in the bilge, 'cause it didn't go out the other side, but it blew oil all over the place. Damage control's on the way. Any of 'em come through here, tell 'em to pump the bilges into one of the two empty bunkers aft. It'll be full of crap, but we can't spare the fuel. Maybe we can separate it out some." He started forward. "Gotta check the forward fireroom!"

"Commander McFaar-lane?" Tabby asked. "Spanky? You okay?"

Spanky stopped and looked back at her. "Swell, kid. Just gotta check on the old rice bowl." He wiped at the oil burning his eyes. "Might be your rice bowl too, now. Chief Aubrey's dead. Whatever came through just kinda smushed his head." He wiped his face again. "Chiefs don't last long down here. Never shoulda picked him. He started out as a torpedoman, for God's sake! Shoulda left him at home!" Spanky sneezed, still wiping his face on his oil-soaked sleeve, and disappeared forward through the swirling, steamy heat of the fireroom.

"Damage report!" Matt bellowed over the rapid salvos of the numbers one, two, and four guns.

"Buncha big dents, three big holes," Finny replied. "One hole through for'ard engine room, make big leak in fuel bunker. One dead, two injured. 'Nother hole through wardroom, spray Selass with few steel pieces, but she okay. Hole through for'ard berthing space not hurt anybody."

"*Damn* them! Their flagship better be a wreck by now!" Matt growled. He raised his binoculars and stared hard at the geysers erupting around the distant ship. Actually, as he thought about it, it would be a miracle if they'd hit anything with their first salvo. They had explosive rounds now, using a black-powder bursting charge just like in the Great War. It was a lot better than the solid copper bolts they'd been forced to use before, and way better than nothing. The problem was, Bernie was still working out some issues with his cordite. They had all the formulas, but the organic material they had to work with was different and produced different properties and burn rates. For now, they were still using black-powder propellant charges, and it took time to work out the differential math on the gun director. Their sudden acceleration to flank hadn't helped. Unconsciously, he opened his mouth, trying to pop his ears. They'd installed one of *Amagi*'s alarm bells to replace the dead salvo buzzer, but Campeti had forgotten to push the button. "Cease firing main battery," he called. "Left full rudder! Come to course one eight five!" He needed to give his fire control crew a break, and the only thing that would allow that was a constant course and speed.

"Left full rudder, aye!" answered Kutas. "Making my course one eight five!" Another enemy broadside churned the sea behind the ship, skating across the wave tops and looking for all the world like a giant shotgun pattern in a duck pond.

"They can't hit a moving target, at least one moving this fast," Matt observed with satisfaction. "Where's Jenks?"

"Starboard quarter. He'll pass astern of us on this course," Gray answered. "He's still headin' right at 'em!"

"Course is one eight five degrees!" Kutas exclaimed.

"Main battery may resume firing as soon as they have a solution," Matt ordered. He'd opened the range and given his gunners a stable platform. *Crrack!* Three guns spoke together and smoke gushed aft from number one. *Shssssssssh* . . . Splashes rose.

"Down fifty!" they heard Campeti shout from above. "Match pointers . . . Fire!"

"Good hits, good hits!" cried the lookout in the crow's nest. New splashes erupted around *Walker* and she shuddered from a heavy, booming impact forward.

"Trying to lead us," Matt observed with grudging admiration. That had taken quick thinking and steady nerves. "What's the condition of the first target?"

"She hit pretty bad, it look like. She steam in circle, out of line."

"New target, designate far left steamer," he ordered.

"Campeetee say we can't shoot at her," replied the talker a moment later.

"Why not?" Matt raised his glasses. *Damn, what's Jenks up to? Achilles* was still steaming forward, broad battle flag streaming, and she'd moved almost directly between *Walker* and her target. Splashes began to rise around Jenks's ship.

"Come left to one five zero! Redesignate far *right* enemy ship!" Matt ordered in frustration.

"Making my course one five zero, aye!"

Matt didn't want to close the range and risk any more serious hits, but he *needed* to be closer to support whatever it was Jenks was up to. He studied the enemy battle line through the lingering haze of the day and the gun smoke of battle. What was *left* of the line. The enemy had opened the battle—*started* it, he fumed—in an extremely disciplined fashion, but in the face of *Walker*'s salvos, that discipline had fallen apart. The far left ship he'd meant to engage was rushing headlong for *Achilles*, just as the far right ship had turned toward *Walker*. The largest, presumably most powerful, had made a wide, looping turn to port that now had her steaming away, off the starboard beam of the ship *Walker* was bearing down upon. The only ship that had maintained her position in the original formation seemed to have struck her colors! At that moment, no one was firing at anybody. What a mess.

"Guns one and three will bear on the advancing ship!" shouted the talker.

"Commence firing!" An instant later, the two four-inch fifties boomed.

At a range of only six hundred yards, it was almost like engaging the smaller, slower Grik ships they'd fought; but unlike the Grik, the enemy had at least one heavy gun that would bear forward. Even as *Walker* fired, smoke bloomed on the enemy fo'c'sle. Matt never knew where the roundshot from the big smoothbore went; it didn't hit the ship, but *Walker*'s two exploding rounds found their mark. The first detonated against the fo'c'sle with a thunderclap they eventually heard. Large splinters flew in every direction and the bowsprit dropped into the sea, pulling the foretop down with it. The second shot must have exploded inside the ship, because gouts of smoke gushed from the gunports. Bernie's new shells weren't as devastating as the old high-explosive rounds, Matt decided, but they could still make a mess of a wooden ship. He was about to call, "Cease firing," when the next salvo streaked toward the target. One round struck a paddle box and spewed smoke and debris far across the water. The other went down the throat again, and again there was little apparent effect.

At first.

Suddenly, for an instant, the entire center of the ship seemed to bulge as if her seams were straining against some horrendous inner pressure. In the blink of an eye, the seams burst open like an enormous grenade and the ship blew apart amid an expanding, scalding cloud of sooty steam.

"Cease firing, cease firing!" Matt yelled. "All ahead, flank! Have the boats swung out and rig netting along the sides! Stand by to rescue survivors!"

The Bosun started to dash for the stairs. "Uh, Skipper? Maybe we'd better have some of Chack's Marines handy. If there *are* any survivors, they might try to pull some kind of fanatical Jap-like shit. Remember that one crazy Jap . . ."

"I remember, Boats. By all means, keep a squad of Marines at the ready." He glassed the floating debris that had once been a ship. There *did* appear to be survivors. If so, they didn't have much time to get to them. He looked beyond the wreckage. The bigger ship was still headed away and was piling on sail. With her damaged paddle wheel, she probably hoped to escape with the wind alone. He shook his head. Turning, he saw that the one ship that had apparently "surrendered" was still hove to, and was beginning to drift. Turning still farther, he saw that Jenks and the final enemy combatant would soon pass alongside each other, and they were already going at it hammer and tongs. Gun smoke drifted between them and he could feel the periodic pounding of their guns in his chest. "Signal Ensign Reynolds, if you can get his attention," he said, referring to the pilot still circling the battle overhead. "Tell him to buzz the enemy ship engaging *Achilles*, but stay out of musket shot! Maybe he can distract them or something."

"Holy cow!" Reynolds yelled when the ship about fifteen hundred feet below suddenly just . . . blew up. Kari shrieked when debris peppered the plane and a slender, three-foot splinter lodged in the port wing. "Holy *cow*!" Reynolds shouted again, and then struggled for control when the shock wave hit.

"I got hole between my feet!" Kari cried over the voice tube. "We leak when we land!"

"Yeah," agreed Fred, "I bet that's not the only one either. Who knows what it was. Maybe a nail."

"Big damn nail!"

"Hey, look! *Walker*'s coming up fast. Maybe she's going to pick up survivors. She's running up a new signal too. What's it say?"

Kari strained to read the flags as they went up the several halyards on the destroyer's foremast. "Ahh, they spell it. I not so good at spell yet. I know standard message flags good. Not so good with spell flags. They too many!"

Reynolds pushed forward on the stick and banked slightly left. "I'll have a look. Just be sure they know we're full of holes and our gas is half gone. When we set down, they'd better fish us out in a hurry!" He flew closer to the ship, squinting his eyes. "Okay." He paused. "They're not *all* letter flags," he accused.

"What they say?"

"They say, 'Buzz enemy still fighting. Distract from Jenks. Beware mu . . . muskets.' Acknowledge that, will ya?"

"Okay."

Reynolds stood on the rudder and banked right, then began a slow climb. Several minutes later, still gaining altitude, he passed over the ship that wasn't doing anything and continued toward where

Achilles and her enemy were now locked in a deadly, smoke-belching embrace. "Wouldja look at that!" he exclaimed. The ships had apparently damaged each other's paddle wheels and all they seemed able to do was steam in ever-tightening circles around each other. Both looked shattered, and *Achilles'* foremast was down. The funnel on the enemy ship had been shot away and her deck was choked with smoke.

"Here we go!" Reynolds shouted, and pushed on the stick. The new planes had altimeters, but they weren't very accurate or quick to adjust, so he ignored his now. The airspeed indicator worked just fine and his was starting to crowd the red-painted line. A few hundred feet above the enemy masts, he pulled back on the stick and the Nancy swooped up and away. Something smacked the plane and he heard a low, humming *vooom!* whip past him in the cockpit.

"Captain say you stay *away* from muskets!" Kari shouted.

Fred started to reply that he'd meant to; that he hadn't really realized how low he'd been. Now he was mad. He spiraled upward, gaining altitude for another pass. Pushing the nose over, he lined up on where he thought he'd have a bow-to-stern approach by the time they got there. Fumbling at his holster with his left hand, he pulled out his Colt. "I'll teach you to shoot at *me*, you screwy Brits!" he muttered. He laid the pistol on his lap, then took the stick in his left hand and the pistol in his right. He flipped the safety off.

"We go too low again!" Kari scolded.

Grimly, Fred pointed the pistol over the windscreen, in the general direction of the ship he was diving on. With nothing but ship in front of him, he started yanking the trigger. Drowned by the noise of the engine, all the pistol made was popping sounds, but he suspected the men below might hear it better. The ship was coming up fast and he knew he had to pull out. Easing back on the stick, he heard several more *voooms!* but nothing hit the plane—until he accidentally shot it in the nose himself as the target disappeared aft.

"Crap!"

He'd shot his own damn airplane! It wasn't much of a hole, really, although he knew there'd be another one below, where the bullet came out. But with the obvious powder burn on the blue paint in front of the windscreen, there'd be no way he could blame the hole on enemy fire. He was lucky he hadn't shot his own foot off!

"Crap, crap, *crap*!"

"What you say?" Kari cried from behind.

"I said 'crap'!"

"Get those men out of the water!" bellowed the Bosun. "I don't care if they *are* sneakin', bushwhackin', traitorous sons o' bitches! The more you let the fish get, the fewer we'll have to *hang*!"

The Bosun's words were meant more for the men they were pulling from the water than the men and 'Cats who were saving them. Oddly, the usual swarm of flasher fish hadn't yet arrived to tear the survivors apart. He couldn't account for that. Maybe the explosion of the ship had driven them away, or maybe there just weren't as many of the damn things in really deep water like this. Regardless, he expected something with an appetite would be along eventually, and judging by the panic with which the Imperial Company survivors were trying to get aboard, they must think so too. They'd made them send the most badly wounded up first and fifteen or twenty horribly burned and scalded men had already been sent to Selass in the wardroom. She'd appeared briefly on deck and seemed fine other than a few glistening spots where she'd applied some polta paste to her "scratches," as she'd called them. Now the less injured were coming aboard and a handful already squatted, hands behind their heads, clustered around the steam capstan. Some simply stared back at the, to them, ridiculously small but unfathomably destructive maw of the number one gun.

"Hurry it up, you pack o' jackals!" the Bosun berated. He pointed at the continuing distant fight between *Achilles* and her foe. "We got friends over there dyin' and more scum like you to kill! You got one minute before I yank these nets and we leave you here!" There were moans and cries from the water, but somehow the men, many still injured, managed to climb or splash along a little faster.

"You are consistent, at least," Chack remarked softly. He'd appeared beside the Bosun still holding his Krag instead of one of the new Springfield muskets. "You are merciless to everyone."

"I ain't merciless," Gray murmured through clenched teeth. "I actually feel sorta sorry for the bastards. I just want 'em scared of us before they come aboard. Make 'em easier for your boys to handle."

For a moment, Chack said nothing, possibly digesting the Bosun's words. "It is . . . strange," he said at last.

"What?"

"All the hu-maans we have ever really known have been our benefactors. They have helped us. It is very . . . disconcerting now to have fought them, and killed . . . so many."

"You helped us kill Japs, and they're sorta human, I guess."

"True, but these"—he gestured at the last of the survivors climbing the cargo netting—"these are more like you. They speak the same language, and more important, to us at least, they are the very descendants of the original tail-less ones, the ones who came before." He paused. "It is . . . hard to know they can be bad, and maybe a little hard to know *you* can kill them without remorse."

"I said I felt sorry for the bastards, didn't I?" Gray demanded quietly. He shrugged. "Hell, I felt a *little* sorry for them Jap destroyermen that got ate—before we met you. But war's war, and it's a damn strange world—whichever the hell world you're from." It was Gray's turn to pause. "Just remember, *they* started this fight here today, and it was friends o' theirs who took Lieutenant Tucker, the princess, your buddy Silva, and all the rest. Friends o' theirs who slaughtered *Simms* and all the 'Cats on board. It's a strange world, sure, but strange as this fight today may seem to you, it's crystal clear to me."

He motioned at the bedraggled survivors, maybe thirty in all, not counting those in the wardroom. "There' a lot more of 'em than I expected, and that's a fact." He turned to Chack. "Take charge of your prisoners, if you please."

C aptain Reddy and Commodore Jenks met that evening aboard HNBC *Ulysses*, the captured enemy
flagship. Except for her starboard paddles, she
hadn't suffered much. *Achilles* had been badly
mauled in her fight with HNBC *Caesar*, and had
suffered over seventy killed and wounded. She'd
require significant repairs before she could con-
tinue on. *Caesar* was in worse shape, and once all her wounded were
moved to *Ulysses* and *Icarus*—the ship that surrendered early on—
Caesar would be allowed to sink.

Jenks's fight was practically over by the time *Walker* steamed to her
aid, but the destroyer's appearance had ended any further resistance.
Matt then turned his ship in pursuit of *Ulysses*. He'd wondered at the
time why she would abandon her consorts so readily, but when she too
surrendered as he drew near, and he was forced to endure the sniveling
apologies and explanations of the squadron's admiral, he understood.
Chack and his Marines remained aboard *Ulysses* while *Walker* towed
her back to the other somewhat assembled ships.

Meanwhile, Jenks had gone aboard *Caesar* and *Icarus* and gained a
little information. To everyone's complete surprise, the ship *Walker*

had destroyed was *Agamemnon* herself, the very same ship that Jenks had dispatched home so long ago. He'd also discovered his own loyal Ensign Parr aboard *Icarus*. *Icarus* had been another Navy ship "pressed" into Company service, and was considered the least reliable in the squadron. It was to her that most of the known Imperial loyalists had been sequestered. The young ensign had recognized *Achilles* and risen up with some trusted men, seized the ship, and promptly surrendered her before she could fire a shot. It was Parr who confirmed the terrible news that only the Company had ever learned the results of Jenks's mission, and more important, that they'd discovered the governor-emperor's daughter alive.

Now Matt and Jenks strode *Ulysses*'s quarterdeck, talking quietly, while both men's guards stood watchfully by. From amidships came the cries of the wounded *Walker* had picked up, as they and the other prisoners were transferred aboard.

"How come you took *Achilles* in like that?" Matt finally asked. "We could have destroyed all four ships from beyond their range."

"That's why I took her in," Jenks replied. "I'm reliably informed that you have a temper, and I feared you would destroy them all once they'd fired at you. Was I wrong?"

Matt shrugged. "I don't think I'd have fired on the ship that surrendered," he said, a little defensively. "I didn't destroy *this* ship."

"Ahh, but by the time you caught her, your passion had faded!"

"Mmm," Matt said noncommittally. He pointed at the wounded and the prisoners coming aboard. "What're we going to do with all of them?"

"I suppose we must convene a court-martial," Jenks replied. "We have many repairs to attend and I understand even your ship was slightly damaged?" Matt nodded, thinking of poor Aubrey. "That should give us sufficient time," Jenks added. "If you've no objection, I think Imperial forms might be most appropriate. Three officers will preside as judges. I would be indebted if you yourself would sit, as well as two other officers of your choosing. I know you're not disinterested, but you have no personal knowledge of any of the defendants. I expect you will also assume not *all* are guilty, as Mr. Parr was not."

"Why don't you do it?" Matt asked. "Even some of your loyalists might object to a foreigner."

"As prosecutor, I cannot preside."

"Oh. Okay then. I'll appoint a couple of others. I don't think taking volunteers would be a good idea just now."

"Perhaps not."

For a while, they just walked together and an awkward silence hung about them.

"How's it feel?" Matt finally asked.

Jenks looked disdainfully at the bloody sling supporting his left arm. "It hurts a bit," he confessed with a grin, "but that wondrous ooze your medical . . . person applied has dulled the edge."

"Good. Shouldn't get infected either. How's O'Casey?"

"Hmm? Oh, Bates. Ha. Utterly insufferable. He wasn't hurt at all, but I confess at times I wished for a ball to take off his head."

"I guess he came up with a number of ways to say, 'I told you so'?"

Jenks looked blank for a moment before realization dawned. "Oh! Oh, yes. An infinite number of ways, and without pause, I might add." Jenks shook his head. "He was right all along. I think I even knew it back then, but the politics of New London are considerably less clear at home than they are out here, at the ends of the earth. I hope someday he will forgive me and we might be friends again." Jenks gestured at his arm. "Now that I know where the *true* infection lies."

"So it would seem," Matt said, and sighed. "And here we are, over a thousand miles from where I ought to be fighting who I ought to be fighting. We still don't know where Billingsly and my people—and your princess—are, but we do know your governor-emperor never knew we even had the girl. This Honorable New Britain Company did, though, and fired on the ship—my ship!—they suspected she was on. The only explanation for that is that now, they want her dead! Apparently, this Company is pulling a major power grab, and everything and everyone both of us cares about might depend, one way or another, on how that turns out. Jeez, if that doesn't put us on the *exact* same side at long last, I don't know what ever would."

"I apologize for all of this," Jenks said quietly. "Everything."

Matt became angry. "Damn it, Jenks, I don't want your apology! Maybe that'll make you feel better for being such a jerk once, but all it does now is cheapen everything we've done—and have to do! I still think we need to be friends, your people and mine, because—as I've been trying to pound into that thick skull of yours—there are bigger threats out there than either one of us can handle on our own. There may be stuff we can't even imagine yet! On top of that, I want my people back, the ones Billingsly took! Maybe you didn't know, but Sandra Tucker, well . . . she's my girl . . . and I want *her* back!"

"I am aware of that," Jenks said softly.

"Yeah? Well, be aware of *this*! That night on *Donaghey* during the Strakka, right after the fight for Singapore when we heard the news, I swore an oath. As God is my witness, whoever took her, whoever's *responsible* for taking her and the others, and for the unprovoked attack on Baalkpan . . ." Matt took a breath and his green eyes were as remorseless as the sea. "You can add *Simms* and my ship here today to the list now, but whoever put all this in motion, *no matter who he is*, is going to *pay*!"

*H*alik stared greedily at the map laid before him on the table in the brazier-lit chamber. It was a map of all the known world, and the chaotic jumble of mountains and coastlines, rivers and islands fascinated him. He dully remembered, even as a young Uul warrior, occasionally wondering how his Hij commanders could know how the world was shaped and how they knew where to take them to fight. Now he could see, *look down upon*, where he was, and many of the places he'd been before. He'd learned much in the months since his unexpected elevation, but maps and the terrain they depicted still held him almost spellbound. Matching terrain in his memory with what he saw on the maps was like scratching a crude drawing of a beautiful sculpture in the sand, and yet the value was in knowing where that sculpture was. Somehow he could sense that, for his purposes, terrain would become vitally important. It was like the different parts of a shield. Some areas were best for countering the blows of an enemy, while others could be used to great advantage when striking out.

He tore his attention from the map and focused again on Regent

Tsalka's words. Words that, in all their infinite variety, he'd learned to understand!

"Singapore will surely fall, if it has not already, and my own province, my very own Ceylon, my beloved India, will be next on the list of the prey!"

"You must stop thinking of them as *prey*, lord. That is essential!" General Esshk scolded—quite harshly, Halik thought. "They are no longer even Worthy Prey, as we began to suspect, but have become hunters themselves, in their own right! Hunters perhaps as cunning as ourselves who fight in a new, unexpected way! Hunters like we have never met or faced before!"

"Yes, yes," Tsalka hissed angrily. "I know your views on this. Perhaps you are even right. But what are we to do? Though we argued for it, it destroys me to concede my very home!"

"We must," said the strange creature Halik knew as General of the Sea Kurokawa. "But we must do it slowly. As slowly as we can possibly manage. We will lose territory, yes, but we have much of that. Time is what we lack. If we can trade land for time, and balance the exchange in our favor, the magical weapons I am preparing will be ready before the enemy—they are *the enemy*, my friends!—before the *enemy* can push beyond the frontier into what you consider your ancient Sacred Land! The invaders will not sully the pure realm of the Celestial Mother herself! If a few regencies or frontier territories must be strategically sacrificed to prevent that, that is what must be done! We *will* reconquer them!"

Halik understood that it revolted Tsalka and Esshk when Kurokawa called them "my friends," but he wasn't sure why. He did know Kurokawa was growing in favor with Her just now. The miraculous weapons he'd begun utterly delighted the Celestial Mother, and she was even beginning to appreciate his strategies. Still, he knew Tsalka in particular thought Kurokawa took too many liberties.

"Enough debate, My Lord Tsalka." Esshk hissed. "She has decided— and in favor of our arguments, for now," he added ironically. "Would you try to change Her mind?" Tsalka said nothing in reply. "Well, then," Esshk growled, "that still leaves us with the issue of *how* we will trade land for time."

Kurokawa's gaze slowly shifted to Halik. "That is a question perhaps best asked of our newest general, is it not? You yourself said he survived the entertainment battles far longer than any before him. He is not old, but he is not young anymore either. He could not have prevailed so long on strength and ferocity alone. My few *Rikusentai*, or naval landing forces, that survived the loss of my ship think he has much promise. Look! Even now he studies us, evaluates us, considers . . . and no doubt forms opinions! I think he is learning that map by heart!" Kurokawa paused, and when he spoke again, he addressed Halik directly.

"Tell us, General, based on the map before you, how would *you* trade land for time? The enemy will come, and for now, we cannot stop him. How would *you* slow him down and bleed him white?"

Even to Rebecca, who had little experience with such things, it hadn't really been much of a storm, but it had been a challenge for an open boat on the wide expanse of the Eastern Sea. After two weeks of diminishing stores, sunburn, and increasingly doubtful navigation, the sudden storm afflicted nearly everyone, particularly the Imperials, with a sense of near hopelessness. Lelaa ignored them as much as possible. She was still confident that if Yap—or Tagran—was where the chart showed it to be, they'd find it.

Whatever she felt inside, Sandra remained a diminutive pillar of strength and steady authority. Her skin was red and peeling and her hair was bleached to a platinum blond, but by force of will alone she managed to maintain discipline and keep Rajendra and his men at work. Sister Audry took solace in her faith and remained stoic, if not cheerful, and set a further example for the men. Dennis Silva, as always, seemed unconcerned about anything. He was the only one among them, with the possible exception of Rajendra, who didn't even seem sunburned. His tanned skin only grew darker and his beard and unusually long hair became almost white.

Rebecca herself maintained an unwavering faith in Sandra Tucker—and Dennis Silva. She did worry about Lawrence and Abel, who, along with the Imperial engineer, suffered cruelly from the heat. Lawrence wasn't accustomed to being in the sun all day without recourse to shade, and Abel was still troubled by his wound.

The Imperials did as Sandra said, but they weren't happy. They feared they were doomed and they hated Dennis. Rebecca watched him become the focus of much of their misery and frustration. He'd destroyed their ship and killed their shipmates, and regardless of their current situation, that was something they all had in common. The reason he'd done it, and even the very reason they'd taken to the boat in the first place, became a blurred and distant memory. Slowly, through the long, miserable days and endless, terrifying nights when strange creatures bumped the boat or distant leviathans blew, it all became Silva's fault.

Outwardly, Silva didn't care. Rebecca considered it possible he even deliberately encouraged their animosity to keep them focused on *anything* but giving up. In reality, she suspected he was more deeply troubled by what he'd done than he'd ever admit. At least, she rather hoped so. Then the storm came.

Proper navigation became impossible, but Lelaa and ultimately Rajendra steered the boat as best they could, following a heading they adjusted constantly based on their calculations of leeway and current. It was an imperfect solution, but by working so closely together they at least temporarily made a sort of peace between them. For four days they fought the storm, reefing the sail to a mere sliver of canvas and shouldering through long, westerly swells. Then the wind shifted out of the south and they scudded along, pitching horribly on the confused, tumultuous sea. It had been Silva, standing in the bow of the boat, inundated by spray, who saw the breakers ahead.

It was probably the swell that saved them. That, and Silva's almost earsplitting bellow of, "Drop the sail *right goddamn now* if you want to live!" Without thought, his order was obeyed, and the boat rode a mountainous wave right over the worst of the shoals. They still struck something, probably coral, that tore a terrible gash in the bottom of the boat. It almost broke the keel, but the boat carried on, quickly filling, until the wave deposited them upon a sandy beach.

Leaping in the surf right along with Silva, Sandra ordered everyone who could move out of the boat. They used each new wave to help them heave their burden farther up the beach. Finally, they could go no farther and they collapsed in the sand. After a while, Sandra roused everyone and had all their stores and weapons taken near the edge of the trees, where the waves shouldn't reach. Then, before she would allow anyone another rest, Sandra ordered that the lightened boat be moved farther from the water as well, and secured to a tree by a stout cable. Only then did everyone collapse again, utterly exhausted, and sleep until the light of day.

Rebecca woke to the sound of surf. Her eyes didn't want to open and seemed glued shut with some sort of crust. She wiped them with her hand and grainy particles fell away. She tried again and this time she could see.

"Mornin', sunshine!" Silva said, and grinned at her. He was sitting cross-legged in the sand with his huge rifle across his lap. On a piece of canvas beside him lay the disassembled parts of his pistol. His cutlass was thrust into the sand nearby.

"Good morning," Rebecca replied. She felt disoriented. She was on dry land at last, but it still seemed to be moving under her. She also wasn't where she remembered being, lying in the sand beside the boat. She was under the shade of a large, strange tree and covered with a scratchy blanket. Beyond the shade, she saw that the storm was entirely over and bright sunshine played upon a much moderated, sparkling sea.

"I hurt everywhere," she complained, sitting up.

"Course you do. You been cooped up in a little room for weeks, then sittin' on yer butt in a boat. Takes a while to get the muscles all loosened up again."

"All is well?"

Silva's grin faded just a bit. "Mostly," he hedged.

"What do you mean?" Rebecca fought down an almost panicked concern. "Is everyone all right? What of . . . What of Lawrence, and Mr. Cook?"

"Oh, ever'body's okay, I guess. Cook's over there, still sleepin'. I fig-ger Larry must've perked right up, 'cause he was already gone, trompin' around, I expect, before I even came around. Most o' them Imperial fellas is still sleepin' too, 'cept Rajendra. Him and Cap'n Lelaa's over there inspectin' the boat." He looked up. "And here comes our overall captain o' everything now."

"At ease," Sandra said sarcastically. "Don't bother to jump up and salute!" She was smiling when she sat in the sand next to Silva. "How do you feel, sweetie?" she asked Rebecca.

"Okay," replied the girl. She glanced warily at the nearby tree. "Are you quite sure there are none of those creatures such as were on Talaud? The ones that climb trees and drop upon prey from above?"

"Ain't seen any," Silva assured her, "and there's no scratch marks like they make." He shrugged. "Who knows, though? Don't worry; I been keepin' my eye out!" He chuckled at his little joke. Suddenly, his face went blank and he stiffened. Seeing his reaction to . . . whatever, the two girls froze as well. Slowly, Silva eased around to look back in the jungle behind him. "Damn you, Larry," he said, "what are you doin' sneakin' around in the bushes? You mighta got shot. Again."

Lawrence practically *slithered* up among them, his eyes darting about. "Quiet!" he insisted. He looked at Rebecca and lowered his head. "I *so* sorry!" he moaned. "I so, *so* sorry!"

"What? What is it, my dear?" Rebecca asked, alarmed.

"I just learn charts and I guess I didn't learn so good, or I did learn good, and still not right!"

"What the hell's that supposed to mean?" Silva hissed.

"I think he means that we are where we set out to go, this Yap Island, but, with Larry not knowing charts or being familiar with all the hundreds of islands around here, Yap isn't the same place as Tagran after all," Rebecca said carefully.

"Yes, yess!"

"How does he know?" Sandra asked.

Lawrence hesitated. "I here . . . again!"

"Before?"

"Yes!"

"You're positive?"

"Yes!"

"Well," said Sandra, relieved, "if he's definitely been here before, he should know where the real Tagran is. Isn't that true, Lawrence?"

Lawrence lowered his head again. "Yes," he hissed.

"Whoa, wait a minute!" said Silva. He fumbled behind him in a pile of things he'd brought from the boat. In a moment, he had the chart in his hand. He pointed at a spot on the map. "This here's Yap, what you thought was Tagran. That's where we are, right?" He pointed southwest. "This here's that scary island you said was the place you went through your trial, where there's all sorts o' boogers you wouldn't ever tell us about." He looked at Lawrence. "There *ain't* nothin' south-west of that but empty ocean, so it *can't* be Tagran."

"No," Lawrence said.

"So if that ain't it and this ain't it, your home must be this spot, northeast of here, right?" Lawrence nodded miserably, and Rebecca and Sandra both looked at Silva questioningly. He exhaled noisily. "What the hell. Whatever doesn't kill you is a hoot, I always say."

"What do you mean?" Sandra asked, but she knew.

"Ladies, Larry here's been beatin' around the bushy fact that we're marooned on Boogerland itself." Silva looked hard at Lawrence. "I ain't scared o' Boogerland. I ain't scared o' much at all anymore. The only thing that *does* scare me is threats to folks I care about. You mighta noticed I tend to react violently to those. Now, I know you ain't sup-posed to blow about what's runnin' around here, but we're talkin' Princess Rebecca and Miss Tucker now! I don't give a furry shit what you promised or swore to; *I* swear I'll twist your head off your skinny neck if you don't cough up everything you know about this damn place!"

That evening they had a big fire on the beach. In spite of every-thing, Lawrence had still refused to tell Dennis what he wanted to know, but he had told Sandra and Rebecca. They were females, after all, and no female was ever expected to undergo the trial. Sandra promptly told Silva roughly what they could expect—and it *was* scary. Evidently, they had some time, though. Not much, but apparently, the most dangerous time on the island reached its peak at a certain "sea-son" of the year: the mating season of the semi amphibious "shiksaks" that sometimes even troubled Tagran. It wouldn't be a cakewalk, but maybe, just *maybe* they could be gone by then. In the meantime, they had a lot of work to do, and this first full night on Shikarrak Island, or

Boogerland, as Silva continued to call it, would be devoted to a much-needed, watchful rest.

Rebecca was drowsy, but it suddenly dawned on her that she didn't see Silva among the group gathered around the fire. She stood and walked a short distance away, and as her eyes adjusted, she could just make him out, standing short of the surf line.

"Mr. Silva?" she said quietly

"Hmm? Oh."

"You frightened me," she scolded. "I looked about and you were nowhere to be seen!"

"Sorry, li'l sister," he said. "Most o' those fellas over there don't like me much, and I had a little thinkin' to do."

Sandra joined them in the darkness. "What were you thinking about?" She huffed. "Anything besides the obvious?"

Silva actually laughed. "Well, yeah, prob'ly. You know the skipper—Captain Reddy—will be lookin' for us by now."

Sandra sighed sadly. "I know. No matter what else is going on, he'll have dropped everything to come after us."

"After you," Silva stated the fact. "And maybe the munchkin queen here. Don't hurt my feelin's none. I bet he's got *Walker* back by now, and I can almost see her steamin' by out there in the dark, with a fine, big bone in her teeth!" He shook his head. "Thing is, he ain't gonna find us. He's gonna chase Billingsly's dead ass all the way to the New Britain Isles and he ain't gonna find us." He chuckled. "You know what he's gonna think? He's gonna think them Brits are either hidin' you girls . . . or they did somethin' to you."

Sandra and Rebecca were both silent for a moment, suspecting Silva was probably right.

"What do you suppose he'll do?" Rebecca asked at last.

Silva chuckled again. "I don't know, li'l sister, but I guarantee they're gonna hate it."